MAP

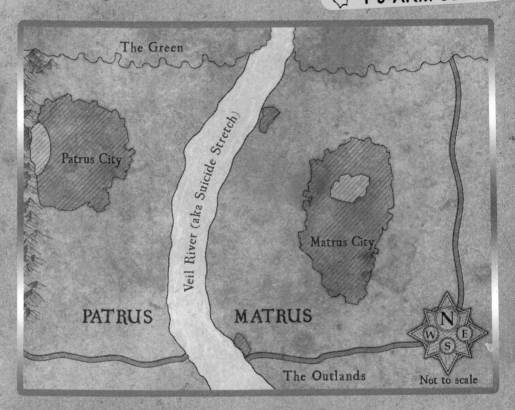

The Green

Patrus City

Veil River (aka Suicide Stretch)

Matrus City

PATRUS   MATRUS

N
W   E
S

The Outlands

Not to scale

THE GENDER FALL

BELLA FORREST

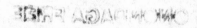

CHAPTER 1

Violet

Everything hurt. Every time I struggled to break through the thin web of sleep holding me, I was confronted by the pain. In my hand, in my arm, in my head. Was I dead? Was this the afterlife? Was I finally paying for all the horrible things I'd done?

No, something whispered, reassuring me. *This is reality.* I struggled as fragments of memories washed over me. A woman with the face of a bulldog, a vicious smile twisting her lips. A boot coming down on my wrist. The flashing silver of a knife as it came for me. A ball of fire that threatened to engulf me.

Sleep was a refuge, the sweet blackness beckoning me in, cradling and hiding me from the pain and confusion. I was tempted to just surrender to its embrace, but a part of me held back, turning toward the light. Something in me burned with an urgency denoting importance. Something was happening. Something worth facing the pain.

The thought created a buoyancy, forcing me to surface. Something was drilling into my consciousness: the sound of urgent voices. My eyes snapped open—and a weak groan slipped from my mouth as daggers of bright electric light stabbed deep through the two treacherous orbs, jabbing hard into my skull.

I clenched my eyes shut as pain and panic twisted my muscles. Someone whispered fiercely, "Hold her!" and hands like vices locked around my limbs—all except my right wrist. I tried to lift that hand to defend myself, only to find it was heavier, more painful than I remembered. Something touched my hand and guided it downward. The touch was agony, and I groaned again.

The menacing woman reappeared in my mind's eye, taunting me, and I fought harder as I recalled who she was. Her name was Tabitha, and she was going to hurt me. I needed to free myself, but belatedly remembered that she was so much stronger than me. Too strong. I couldn't let her win. I couldn't... And there was something else going on, something that needed my attention, *something*... I couldn't sleep yet.

Slowly, insistently, something warm and loving cut through my terror. A strong, steady voice, reaching through the hysteria, urging me to relax. I couldn't understand the words, but the tone itself felt like a warm blanket draping over my injuries. It told me I was safe. I was alive. That woman was gone, and I didn't have to fear her ever again. The voice was powerful, yet it was also gentle, reassuring.

A face flashed in my mind. A man—his green eyes haunted, a scar across his right cheek, wavy brown hair that gleamed black in the shadows and bright as chocolate when the sun hit it.

Viggo, my mind whispered, and I felt myself smile—then forced myself to stop as half my face erupted in tight, creaking agony. I took a deep breath, trying to soothe the aching area. It took a moment, but the pain receded. My mind felt clearer again.

I shouldn't hurt this much. Not if I was with Viggo. If I was with Viggo, I was safe. But something in me knew that wasn't right. Sometimes danger followed us. Was it danger that had woken me? My heart thudded hard against my aching ribcage. If nothing else, I needed to know what was reality and what was just delirium. I forced my eyes open, slowly this time.

Light, less stabbing than before, but still too bright, streamed down on me, and a brown pattern flew over me, unfamiliar, disorienting. It took me too long to realize what should have been simple. We were inside a building... I was staring at a ceiling.

My head bobbed up and down on something firm, but not hard. I could feel fabric under my fingers. There was a smell of sweat, but something underneath it. A scent that reassured me with its familiarity. I was in Viggo's arms. The thought was absurdly comforting, although everything still hurt, my environment still swinging dizzily before me.

His voice continued to murmur above me, and I turned my face toward the source, listening. He was saying something... something different now. I couldn't understand the tone anymore. It was... determined. But worried? Was that regret?

I wished I could understand what he was saying.

And then, abruptly, the voice turned to a different tone—sharper, harsher, more desperate. Then it hushed altogether.

The sensation was like sitting by a window, reading, only to become aware that the grasshoppers had stopped singing—a sign that a predator was among them, in the bushes, waiting to feast on the first brave soul who started to sing. The quiet convinced me, again, that something was horribly wrong. And yet the ceiling above me continued swaying before my eyes, moving past me, as though our flight was uninterrupted.

I tried to speak, just a word. A question. But my mouth felt like it was stuffed full of cotton, my jaw a taut spring, impossible to uncoil. I rounded my lips, forcing sound out anyway.

"Wha—?"

"Shhhh," someone replied, and our movements seemed to increase in tempo, vertigo swelling in my stomach with the motion. I briefly closed my eyes, trying to fight the nausea. Stabbing pain bloomed from my sides every time Viggo's body jostled. I swallowed, my mouth going dry. But when I opened my eyes again, I realized I had a sense of direction—we were moving downward.

I tilted my face away from Viggo's body, and suddenly I could hear the thump of feet hitting stairs. I burrowed my head back into Viggo's shoulder, and the sound faded. I slowly sucked in air, still trying to calm my stomach.

Someone was talking. His voice was familiar, but muffled, as if I were listening to it underwater. I tilted my head slightly, and suddenly his voice was loud again, so sudden after its absence that it felt as if the familiar voice were shouting from inside my skull. Owen. I sagged in relief as I recalled his name. The recollection was strong enough to cut through the pain, and I clung to it. It was hard not to. It helped keep me in the present. Something was happening. I needed to be a part of it. If I could just figure out what it was…

I tilted my head again, only a little, determined to be ready for the burst of noise this time. The sound got louder, and I *was* prepared—focusing on Owen's voice. Intensity and foreboding flooded his tone. He was conveying information, but his words were coming so fast I could barely understand them.

One word—a phrase—stood out. I hung on to it, repeating it like a mantra. *Matrian patrol.* I couldn't recall why I knew it was important. It was more of a feeling, like having someone's name on the tip of my tongue. The more I pressed, searching for the information, the more it eluded me, like trying to catch butterflies in a meadow.

I took a deep breath and then stilled myself. I let my mind relax, and the answer came to me. We were in serious danger. It *was* fear that had woken me.

Memories flooded me then—female guards bearing a crest. Explosions. Screams of terror and confusion. Gunshots. It was confusing and disjointed. *Is any of this real?* The thought frightened me, and I felt my hand tighten around something, a whimper escaping my throat.

Big hands on my shoulder and thigh squeezed back, reassuring me with their casual strength. We had stopped moving; I tried to look around, figure at least *something* out. My eyes slid around the room, overwhelmed by the jarring unfamiliarity of the things in it. Or rather, I recognized them, but my brain couldn't supply me with the words to identify them. Some of them seemed to move in ways they should not. More than that, everything about this room felt wrong. It wasn't where we were supposed to be.

A shadow passed before my eyes, and I blinked, trying to focus on the face near me. It was more a swirl of colors than a face, and it made me dizzier, my stomach turning again. I closed my eyes.

There was a muffled sound of thumping, of rasping, of voices—maybe a new one this time, but I couldn't be sure, with how the sound kept cutting in and out. I kept my head still, trying to quiet my beating heart, which was thundering under my ribcage. We moved forward, Viggo clutching me tighter to him as he walked, then relaxing his grip. We stopped moving abruptly. I heard another muffled thump, followed by the repeated sound of wood sliding on wood.

Then silence. I risked opening my eyes again. It was dark now. So dark it took my eyes a long time to adjust, but at least it seemed less painful to focus. When the picture finally came into some clarity I realized I was looking up at Viggo. In the dimness, his eyes were hard and distant, and there was tension around his mouth. He was worried.

I slowly looked around, and my gaze found Owen, just a few feet away. From the little I could see, his mouth was turned down in an uncharacteristic frown. His mouth was moving. I licked my lips, narrowing my eyes. I should be able to hear him now, I realized.

Curious, I tilted my head farther, exposing my sensitive ear again, and flinched, reeling as his voice came through. Even the low sound encouraged the dull, aching throb in my skull to dial up to a sharp, stabbing sensation, one that felt like it was ripping my skull in two.

I couldn't hear out of one ear. And at that moment, it was just too much. An icy rush of fear shot through me, causing my skin to feel too tight, sucking the oxygen from the room. All my thoughts of remaining as still as possible disappeared, and panic began to spread into my limbs. I jerked, trying to escape, trying to scramble away somehow.

Viggo grunted as I flailed, and I heard Owen murmur something, but I couldn't stop—something was terribly wrong. I needed to get up, needed a gun, needed to fight—

But my body resisted the very idea of motion, betraying me. I felt my strength leaving me like water down a drain, and suddenly the darkness was back, beckoning to me. I tried to escape from it, the desire to fight and overcome still burning like a fire inside me.

The darkness didn't care. It loomed over me like a terrible, ancient thing. My lips barely had the chance to form the word 'no' when it crashed down on me, dragging me back, deep into unconsciousness.

CHAPTER 2

Viggo

Violet went limp in my arms, and it took everything I had not to panic. I carefully adjusted her until my fingers could seek out her heartbeat against her chest. I felt the steady thud against my hand and let out a breath I hadn't even been aware I'd been holding, biting off a growl of irritation at having to move her again so soon. Too soon. But there was nothing that could be done about it.

We were in a dim, cramped space beneath a set of wooden stairs in the house of one Mr. Alton Kaplan. The dim space smelled like old sawdust, and I could feel the crunch of old spider webs disintegrating as I brushed against them. We'd stumbled across the man by chance a few hours after escaping from the palace. We'd been desperately driving around on the dark, dirty backroads of the farm country in search of not only a doctor, but fuel for our car, hoping some scared countryfolk would take some of our modern tech arsenal as payment for letting us siphon a tank from a tractor or unused vehicle.

We'd managed to find something even better: a huge, busy old ranch that kept a supply of gasoline in their own tanks for their farming equipment. We'd managed to trade one of Ashabee's guns—the rancher had been more than happy to let us fill up to get his hands on the state-of-the-art semiautomatic we'd had in the trunk. And then, as we'd been debating the safest way to get Violet some medical attention, the local veterinarian had come out of the barn, fresh from treating a cow with some kind of infection... Close enough.

Mr. Kaplan was a kind, older man with no family to speak of, and his skills were probably the reason Violet was still breathing now, why she was even somewhat conscious. Upon seeing her condition, he'd let us follow him home for the remainder of the night, shaking his head at our notion that we would immediately continue our journey. Owen had slept. I had not—I couldn't let this stranger operate on Violet throughout the long night, on his own. He had been able to set her arm, stitch up cuts, and provide strong medication that was helping to stabilize her. It was also effectively doping her up, keeping the pain at bay but doing who knew what to her logical reasoning. At this point, I didn't care what kind of animal the sedatives had been designed for. It would at least tide her over until we got back to Ms. Dale and the others and let our doctor look at her.

If we got out of here.

Even if we did, we would be scrambling to keep ahead of the other patrols flooding the area, in search of the terrorist who had bombed King Maxen's palace. These farms were out of the way enough that they hadn't been immediately searched, and I had hoped, last night, the patrols wouldn't get around to it until after we were gone… but no such luck.

I wasn't sure what news had filtered out into the area regarding the attack—the news tickers had gone out around the same time the palace had fallen, according to our host's news report—but I was certain that while the public was being told the official "terrorist" story, the Matrian wardens were well aware of whom they were looking for.

Violet was barely twenty years old, but she was Matrian enemy number one. She was being held responsible for the assassination of her home country's former monarch, Queen Rina. She had actually killed another one of their princesses, although that operation had been kept much quieter. Two princesses, if Tabitha had been killed in the blast in the palace, as I fervently hoped.

Now it was morning again—much too early in the morning after yesterday, barely past dawn—and we were hiding from an approaching Matrian patrol in a storage compartment under Mr. Kaplan's stairs. Our host was outside the door, casually adjusting the painting that hung over the already seamless spot of wall that marked the hidden door. He was a man who spoke softly and asked few questions, for which we already had cause to be grateful.

"It will be all right, Mr. Kaplan—just act natural," Owen coached our ally quietly through the wall, though I thought he might have been more nervous about this than Mr. Kaplan was. The blond man met my questioning gaze, but kept talking. "Be polite, calm, and answer their questions without giving it too much thought. Avoid lying when you can. Be vague."

I frowned at his growing list of suggestions. Everything he was saying was good advice, individually, but it was like taking months of spycraft training and trying to condense it down, then jam all the tips for being questioned into a thirty-second speech.

Mr. Kaplan's replies were soft, too soft for me to make out from my position beside Owen. I looked down at Violet and felt my heart clench.

She looked terrible. Her face was ashen, the violent red-and-purple bruising that covered one half of it standing out in stark contrast. Her eye was swollen and black on that side, her lip split. White bandages enveloped her neck and chest, covering the first- and second-degree burns she had received from being caught in the blast. Parts of her hair were singed off, and other parts were clumped together.

It was gut-churning to see her so damaged, and I felt rage at Tabitha swelling in my chest. That monster had hurt my girl. If Tabitha *had* survived the blast, I was going to tear her head off.

"That's perfect, Mr. K," Owen replied, interrupting my dark thoughts. "And please… if they try to take you somewhere, and you have a chance to run, then run. Please." I shook my head at him, half worried that the statement would upset the older man, half worried that Owen hadn't made his warning stringent enough. Elena's wardens were tasked with reducing the male population of Patrus by sixty percent—by systematically isolating them from their families and loved ones, and then executing them.

I turned to set Violet down, taking great pains not to jostle her too much. She shifted fitfully as I rested her against the wall, but her eyes didn't open again. I gently pushed hair out of her face, then turned back to Owen.

"How much time do we have?" I asked, studying his face.

Owen shrugged, then raised his arm to wipe away the sweat collecting on his forehead. "Hard to tell. I spotted them when they were close to the turnoff for the farm, but I hightailed it through the field. They had to go the long way around, but they were in a car, so…" Owen made a gesture with both his hands, as if weighing something, then let his hands drop down.

I grumbled a curse and grabbed my gun, sliding back the muzzle and chambering a round. Owen's look was wary, but he didn't hesitate in pulling out his own gun. I took a deep breath, trying to calm my frazzled nerves. To say I hadn't gotten a lot of sleep the last few days would be an understatement, what with the Matrian attack on Ashabee's manor, and then Violet running off to face Tabitha in order to rescue her family. Granted, she hadn't gone alone, but if I hadn't gone after her…

I shook away the grim image of myself shouting over her body as I tried to force her to breathe again, and exhaled slowly. After a moment, I looked at Owen. "Did you remember to hide the—"

"Of *course* I remembered to hide the bloody car," the younger man spat back, his spine stiffening. "I'm not a moron, Viggo."

I grinned at him in reply, and after a long, hard look at me, he relaxed slightly. I wasn't sure when this teasing had worked its way into our exchanges. Truth be told, I had been ready to hate Owen since day one. After hearing Violet talk about him… excessively.

But after she had convinced me there was nothing between them, and after all the things Owen had done for us, the man had earned my grudging respect. I had even started considering him a friend, which was rare for me. I tended to be a loner, even before all this insanity had started. Apart from Alejandro and his wife Jenny... No, I preferred to keep my list of loved ones small.

Owen had earned my friendship, however. He had been firm, fair, and honest, and had a depth of integrity I rarely saw in people. He may not have always done the right thing, but when he made a mistake, he took responsibility for it. The man had refused to abandon me and Violet in our hour of need—it had never even been a possibility to him. I was glad to have him with us.

"Y'know," Owen drawled, and I looked up to meet his gaze. "Getting into a fight in this position might only make things worse." He looked pointedly at our guns.

I understood what he was saying. I even agreed with it to a certain extent. Better to not have to start shooting, because that would only get us killed. Better to give in at first, then try to escape later. But then I looked back at Violet, at the damage to her face and body, and felt myself hardening as reason escaped me.

"They're going to have to kill me before they can lay a finger on her," I replied, my voice as sharp as steel.

Owen's eyes widened in alarm, and I looked down and realized my hands were shaking with barely repressed rage. All the humor from earlier had evaporated under the force of my fury. I forced myself to take a deep breath. And another. And a third. It was enough, for the moment, to quell the seething anger that had built up in my stomach and chest, tense and raw.

"Sorry," I grated out after a moment. "I'm just…"

"I get it," he whispered back, his face softening. "We'll get through this."

I glanced back at Violet and was surprised to see the twin silver slits of her eyes were open, glistening with awareness, catching a sliver of light that came in from the stairs. She feebly tried to push herself up into a better sitting position, and the cast on her right hand scraped loudly on the floor, making me wince. She didn't seem to notice, her breath coming in shudders and gasps as she struggled to move.

I squatted down, smoothing a hand over her hair. "Violet," I whispered softly. "You have a fractured skull. You need to stay down."

She ignored me, her left arm shaking with strain as she tried to shift her position on the floor but failed weakly. I sighed and reached out, taking her under the arms and moving her slightly, until she was braced in the corner. She grew paler, and I saw clearly that she was resisting the urge to vomit.

Her eyes glazed over, becoming unfocused and sliding left and right around the room. Then they fluttered closed, and a slight wheeze escaped her lungs. I hovered nearby, concerned she might still vomit in spite of her heroic attempt to hold it back, but she continued to fight it off. After a moment, her eyes snapped back open, awareness returning in them.

Her gaze drifted down to the gun I clutched in my hand, and then up to me. She swallowed, her mouth working as if she were trying to speak. I waited, and Violet sighed in apparent frustration. She glanced back to the gun, then up at me again, and this time I noticed the fingers of her left hand twitching as she looked at me, the expression on her face imploring underneath the marring of her injuries, visible even in the dimness.

I hesitated, questioning the wisdom of giving her a gun. She had a severe concussion, and she was slipping in and out of consciousness. Half in and half out of reality, in terrible pain... The last thing she needed was a weapon in her hand.

I decided to let her touch one just briefly, hoping it would provide her with a thread of comfort. I reached down to the waistband of my pants, freeing my second pistol. I set it on the ground next to her before gently lifting her left hand, taking great care to avoid the bandaged cuts on her fingers, and resting it on the butt of the gun. The relief in her eyes was palpable as she gave me a fraction of a nod.

Then her eyes closed. I waited for them to open again, but her world had gone dark once more. *Probably better this way.*

I replaced the second gun in my waistband, then straightened and turned toward Owen, who placed a finger over his lips. I held my breath, listening closely.

I couldn't hear much through the boards, but after a moment, my ears caught the distinct whine of brakes being applied and the sound of a car engine shutting off, followed by doors slamming closed. My hand tightened on my gun.

We listened in silence as several reedy, thin voices carried through the walls. The owners of the vehicle were definitely female. Which meant they were definitely Matrian. Patrian women weren't trained to drive.

Then the distinct sounds of heavy boots filed into the room on the other side of the wall, and I had second thoughts about taking the gun from Violet. The thought of her having to face the Matrians defenseless sent a current of fear through me, and I looked down to notice my hands shaking again.

Then the fiery rage was back, burning like a molten core in my gut. I resisted the urge to growl. Violet wouldn't have to use any gun. If I had anything to say about it, they wouldn't even get a good look at her. I'd be damned if anyone laid a hand on her.

I gripped my pistol harder and ground my teeth together. As the sounds of crashing and clattering resounded through the house, I stared at the wall panel like my life depended on it. I would fight if I had to.

Like hell they'd ever touch my girl again.

CHAPTER 3

Violet

I had closed my eyes, but I hadn't given up my tenuous hold on reality. My fingertips had been resting gently on the butt of a gun, but then it had been pulled away. The movement had left me swimming in anxiety, but I felt incapable of expressing it.

My stomach roiled suddenly, and I pressed my lips together, trying to quell the urge to vomit. It took a great deal of focus. Focus hurt—it made my head ache frightfully. An image floated across my mind, of a tomato growing inside a tin can. It grew and it grew, until the tin can became too small for it, and then grew some more, the red, fleshy fruit expanding, swelling... until it popped.

I giggled a tiny bit in the back of my throat. That was how it felt: my skull was the tin can, and the tomato was my... Oh. The realization sobered me. The image was not as funny as I had originally thought. I was confused by my own morbidity.

Confused and…

My thought process stuttered out as the urge to vomit returned.

I sucked air in through my nose. Sweat poured down my face and neck, making me shiver in the cool air. I focused on relaxing my body. It was hard—even breathing was its own form of agony. My ribs pinched with each inhalation, and I hoped to God they weren't broken.

The darkness was beckoning me again, trying to seduce me into its sweet release. I wanted to respond to it so badly.

Stay in the moment, I urged myself, repeating it over and over until my breathing returned to normal, although the pain in my skull did not lessen. It was important I stayed awake, because something important was going on. I remembered that. I remembered something bad was coming. The thought tethered me.

My eyes snapped open as I heard a faint squeak above me. Viggo and Owen were looking up overhead. I tilted my head back slightly, trying to find what they were looking for, and immediately the room started to spin, tumbling on its axis, becoming a blur.

Were those voices nearby?

I waited. Moving was distinctly uncomfortable in more ways than I could even begin to categorize. It was also dangerous, judging by the soft, desperate breathing of the two men near me. Movement carried the threat of giving away our position. Better to remain still.

I squeezed my eyes together as I tried to gasp for air quietly. I dove a little deeper into the beckoning darkness—not quite all the way in, but not quite all the way out either. It was a halfway point, one that left me floating in gray. The floating was nice. It would be so easy to settle in deeper, close my eyes, and just drift.

So I did. Only for a moment, I promised myself. Only a moment to settle my stomach and still the pulse of pain that seemed to be harassing my entire body. Only for a moment…

The next thing I felt, besides a spike of agony, was movement. Whispered words torn harshly from mouths. A steady rocking that caused my pain to return.

I slowly opened my eyes, taking care to open them a fraction at a time. Something had changed since the last time I'd woken. The light seemed dimmer this time, cooler, more natural. My vision was filled with warm brown stalks that were the tallest things I had ever seen. They were withered and dying, but I smiled when I looked at them, knowing they carried an important function, one I had enjoyed in the past. I was aware of the faint rustling sound of our passage, and turned my head to the right, slowly.

The dizziness that accompanied head movement flared up, but I was prepared for it, and took my time. By the time I had finished moving, we were pushing through the corn stalks—*That's what they are,* I thought victoriously—and into an open green area that led toward tall brown pillars crowned with green, looming out of the earth around us. Viggo hefted me higher against his chest, the movement causing the world to tumble. As soon as it evened out somewhat, those bigger brown-and-green objects had started flashing past my eyes, the whole scene shivering and rolling in many different ways at once, spinning me into even greater confusion. Still, I couldn't help but stare at them, a strange sense of awe coming over me as the swaying shapes passed over my head, the tangles of their branches making intricate, snarled knots of greenery.

Trees, my broken brain informed me. *A forest.* And we were moving through it. I tilted my eyes down and saw that I was close to Viggo's face again. He was carrying me. Again.

For some reason, that realization made me want to laugh. There was something… a joke… about us? Something we did together, with each other, *for* each other.

My head sent me a warning throb. I was thinking too hard. I tried to focus on the trees again, but now they were moving too fast. The greens and browns blurred together, faster and faster. My insides felt like they were winding up, tighter and tighter, until my breathing intensified and I felt my stomach clench.

It was too much at once. I couldn't keep control. I gagged, and then retched. My body erupted in agony as I was forced to move, and I couldn't stop myself. I vomited hard, and felt tears streaking down my cheeks as my stomach clenched again. A strange dizziness struck me, and I became aware of Viggo's hands and body shifting and moving on me. It brought only the tiniest reprieve, which disappeared almost instantly as I retched again.

When it was over, I sagged slightly, unbelievably relieved my body had given up. I didn't want to, but I opened my eyes, peeling them back like the skin of an onion and squinting up into the forest's cool light. It took a minute, but I realized we had stopped moving. My view of the light blue sky was obscured by green tufts that felt soft and slick under my fingers and were wrapped in damp black granules.

Grass. It was the opposite of sky. I wanted to smile at my own cleverness.

Instead, I frowned as I was suddenly moved, gently lifted back into Viggo's arms. I realized his hands had been on me the entire time I was vomiting. They had been holding me up, keeping me from falling face first into my own mess.

I sighed as my cheek once again came into contact with the familiar beveled curve that was Viggo's shoulder. His hands held me tight against him, and I melted into him. He was so warm, and I shivered as a chill caught me unaware, causing me to burrow closer to his warmth. I stared at his face. He was so beautiful.

Frowning, I squinted and took a closer look. He was sweating. His breathing was ragged. There was strain around his mouth and eyes. His eyes were hard and burning with something. Anger? Desire? Determination.

That was it. He was determined. I struggled mentally, grasping at associations, and another face slid across my mind. It was the face of a young man. His hair was a dark brown mop of wavy curls, and his eyes were a familiar shade of glistening silver. He wore the same look as Viggo, but on him, I found it adorable and irritating at the same time. Like I didn't know whether to hug him or shake him.

Tim. His name came to me with the force of a wrecking ball, bowling me over with a wave of love, guilt, responsibility, and… a keen sense of loss.

My brother, Tim.

I couldn't see him. Was he with us? Of course he was... wasn't he?

I hated interrupting Viggo when he looked this stressed, but I couldn't trust my mind right now. My memories were jumbled and confusing, the headache caused by focusing so hard conflicting with my desire to know. Knowing won out.

"Tim," I said, and frowned at the croaking noise that erupted from my throat. I shook it off and watched Viggo closely.

His mouth tightened into a thin line, but he didn't respond. His face confused me—was he angry? Angry at Tim? No... he loved Tim. I was certain of that. Then what was it? I searched my memory—had I even asked the question I had wanted to?

I couldn't remember. It would be best to repeat it, I decided. I had opened my mouth to ask Viggo about Tim again, when his lips moved. I zeroed in on them, studying them intently as he spoke.

"We don't know," he said.

That... That wasn't right. Tim was... He was with two others... Thomas and Jay, right? That felt right, so I decided to trust it.

But then... why wouldn't Viggo know? He must know. Or be mistaken. That was wrong—Viggo was never mistaken.

A wash of fear came over me as I tried to piece together the two concepts. I could only come up with two choices. Either Viggo was confused about where Tim was, or he didn't know where Tim was... which meant something was incredibly wrong.

The fear grew in my mind, tearing it apart with images of the bulldog woman, plunging her knife into Tim over and over, and laughing at me.

I fled into the darkness, trying to hide from the returning panic, destroying any last trace of who I was.

CHAPTER 4

Viggo

I bit off a curse as we ran through the forest that bordered Mr. Kaplan's fields, my mind whirling furiously, the front of my shirt still damp from Violet's vomit. The air was still cold, the sun struggling to chase away the chill of night as it rose overhead. Violet was heavy in my arms, but her limbs drooped again, slack. She had slipped back into unconsciousness, and I wasn't sure whether that was good or bad, given the circumstances. The fact she kept passing out like this was alarming, spurring in me the desperate need to move faster. Despite the impulse, I forced myself to maintain my even pace. Racing blindly ahead would only get both of us hurt, and Violet was already suffering enough. I hated the idea that I was hurting her by moving her. Hated that I had to run with her through the forest in a mad dash to try to get her out of the area. But we couldn't afford to get captured. Her least of all.

The circumstances filled me with an anger that was almost impossible to control. I felt feral and raw, more beast than man. And yet, I knew under that, deep down, I was afraid. My heart ached for the idea of life without the woman in my arms. It protested this possibility fiercely, rejecting any thought that she could die.

The world was a crueler place than the one my heart seemed to yearn for. If anyone needed evidence of that, they needed only to look at my past. At how I had failed as a husband. At how I had failed to keep my wife safe, which had culminated in her execution.

It was selfish and greedy, but I couldn't go through that desolation again. If I lost Violet… I didn't know what I would do. And I couldn't trust luck, couldn't trust the environment we now lived in to be safe for her. I couldn't trust anyone with her but my own damn self.

So I ran, racing around trees, kicking up dirt and leaves, spurred on by my fear of a future without her jokes, her smile, her killer instinct, her charm, her eyes…

Owen ran beside me, his face red from exertion, his eyes wide. We knew it was only a matter of time before the Matrian patrol returned and started sweeping the edges of the woods. If we were caught out in the open like this, they would have us. They would have her.

I knew it was true because the patrol had taken Mr. Kaplan with them after they had torn apart his home looking for us. We'd waited far too long—for the silence that had reigned after the crashing and shouts. But nothing had happened. We'd had to push the painting off the secret entrance to our hiding place, and it had seemed sad to see it fall to the floor—until we'd seen the destruction wreaked by the Matrian wardens. As terrible as it sounded, I was glad Violet had passed out before the women came into the house. And I was glad she had stayed that way as we'd picked our way out of the overturned dressers and broken furniture in the hall, sneaking out into the fields, then to these woods, unsure whether the Matrians had truly moved on from the area yet.

It was clear the wardens hadn't known for certain we were there—if they had, maybe they would've burned the house down, or worse. I'd seen enough to know the kind of violence the Matrian wardens were willing to stoop to. I could only guess what lies Elena was feeding to her people to maintain her control on them… or if the fractured stability, as false as it was, that had settled over the land could even withstand the bombing of the king's palace. A part of me wondered if Elena hadn't just told the truth about who bombed the palace. Tabitha was a princess, after all, and Violet had attacked and—hopefully—killed her. The populace could easily side with the queen on this if they believed the "facts" they'd already been given.

I felt bad for Mr. Kaplan, but a part of me knew the Matrians would've taken him regardless of whether we were there or not. That was another element of their plan—taking the men of Patrus—and Mr. Kaplan, with his solitary lifestyle, would have been an easy target. Still, my heart ached for him, and the ache translated into rage pulsing through my blood as I ran, just another grievance to fuel the fire of my anger. I hoped we could stop this crazy secret war Elena was waging, and soon, before Mr. Kaplan suffered at their hands along with so many others.

But right now, I had only one concern: getting Violet to our doctor and to safety.

I glanced over at Owen, looking for some sign we were drawing closer to where he had hidden the vehicle. I frowned as I realized we still weren't there. That realization was followed by sudden irrational annoyance.

He should've hidden the damn car closer! We could've already been in it by now if Owen hadn't been so thorough.

It took an effort to push the anger aside, my rational mind picking apart the flaws in the sentiment. It wasn't fair to Owen—we were in grave danger, and the car was our only form of transportation. Keeping it safe from discovery was a matter of life or death. Besides, it wasn't Owen's fault we were running through the forest. It wasn't really Violet's, either. It wasn't even mine, although I couldn't help but blame myself somewhat for not reaching Violet sooner.

No—the fault for all of this fell at Elena's feet. And Desmond's. They had pushed us all to our breaking points and beyond. They had used us, manipulated us, and then tried to get rid of us, all in their ambition to take control of our little world. All for power.

And then Tabitha had lured Violet into the palace, using her family as leverage. Violet had gone willingly, and she had even devised a plan… but I still wasn't sure if it had been worth it. Not with how badly she had been injured in the fight. She would have died if I hadn't come for her.

My grip tightened around her involuntarily, as if checking she was still real. Still alive in my arms. I paused to gently press her chest, and was reassured by the steady thump under my hand. She was still there. The relief I felt was small and fleet-ing—we weren't out of the woods yet. Literally.

Owen tapped my arm and pointed at something, and I saw a flash of gunmetal gray through the trees. I made for it, fol-lowing Owen, my breathing labored. Owen scampered ahead, leading us into a small clearing. He had dragged a few branches over the hood and roof of the car we'd taken from Ashabee's ar-mory and was now snatching them off and tossing them aside. He had hidden the car while I was convincing Mr. Kaplan to help us, and it must have taken him a lot of effort to drive it this far and disguise it. I was impressed.

He was almost done when I reached the car, and he turned to look at me. "Do you want me to take her so you can drive?" I shook my head, subconsciously pressing Violet tighter to my chest. Not that I didn't trust Owen—I just wouldn't let her out of my arms until we were safe. He nodded, understanding, and opened the passenger door for me.

He moved out of my way as I carefully climbed into the vehicle, trying not to jostle Violet more than necessary. Once I had arranged her in my lap and moved her legs clear of the door, I gave Owen a hurried nod, and he closed the door quickly.

The young man raced around the front of the vehicle and got into the driver's seat. I waited, summoning my dwindling patience, as his movements seemed to take forever. He buckled up and slid the key into the ignition, twisting it.

The car whined and then fell silent. Owen looked at me, concern heavy on his face, and tried again. The whine returned, followed by a few sharp shudders, and then the noise stilled again. The concern on Owen's face intensified as he tried the keys once more.

My patience evaporating, I leaned over and violently slammed my fist down on the dashboard. With a roar, the car came to life. Owen arched an eyebrow, a bemused expression on his face, but I ignored it, turning back to Violet. Her breathing was shallow and erratic, and she stirred fitfully, as if caught in a bad dream.

She murmured Tim's name, and I frowned, a fresh wave of guilt hitting me. Her brother was so important to her—I had no idea how to tell her what had happened to him.

Owen put the car in gear and slowly pressed the accelerator, picking his way carefully across the forest floor, dodging trees and stumps, the wheels dragging in deep drifts of leaves. I kept my eyes sharp, looking for any sign of the Matrian patrol.

"Where is the rendezvous?" I asked, clutching Violet tighter as the tire bumped over something protruding out of the ground.

"A few miles to the southeast," he replied, cutting the wheel to skirt around an impassible thicket of young trees. "It was the closest we could get. It's too risky to be flying the heloship for long distances right now—and we're running low on fuel. The area around the palace has been absolute pandemonium, according to Ms. Dale."

I nodded. In the pre-dawn dark, when we'd decided most of our enemies would be asleep, Owen had taken the risk of contacting our allies on the handheld we'd brought, something we'd feared to do directly after the attack, as the airwaves around the castle would certainly be more heavily monitored. Since then, he had been more involved with receiving updates on our handheld from Ms. Dale and Thomas, as I had refused to leave Violet's side any more than necessary. It may have already been fourteen hours since we'd left the palace, but it made sense that the immediate area was too risky for the heloship. I just itched with impatience, wishing there was a way we could get Amber to us sooner.

"Did anything come through on the ticker?" I asked after a moment.

Owen shook his head, keeping his eyes on the path ahead. "Thomas thinks they're still down. Possibly even permanently. With the damage to the palace…"

He trailed off, taking a quick look at Violet. I followed his gaze, understanding the look on his face. Violet had torn the place apart. According to Thomas, who had managed to get back to our base with Amber and Jay, he and Violet had crafted the plan together. Three bombs, three explosions, which had gutted the palace and even caused one of the inner structures to collapse. It was a true miracle she had even survived her own bombs, given how much destruction they had wrought.

The violence of it all hadn't been lost on me. Violet had gone to great lengths to secure her family's freedom. I couldn't fault her for taking action, and I admired that she hadn't gone in there without a plan. Others would have blindly accepted the deal with Tabitha, nobly exchanging themselves for their family members.

But not Violet. She knew Tabitha. She knew what Tabitha had been capable of—we both did. Violet had experienced it firsthand when Tabitha had driven a knife through her hand in Matrus.

It felt like a lifetime ago that I had found her in Elena's palace, strapped upright to a board, the knife jutting out of her hand and blood streaming down her palm. At the time, I hadn't thought it could get any worse than that. Seeing her in agony, amid all the chaos and violence infecting our lives. It had been intolerable. And now...

Something chirped, and I blinked, looking over at Owen. He let go of the steering wheel to slide his hand into his pants pocket and pull out the black handheld, passing it over to me. I grabbed it awkwardly, trying not to shift Violet too much, and clicked it on.

On my way with doctor, the line of text read.

"Amber just checked in," I informed Owen, and he nodded. I clicked off the handheld but kept it out in case we needed it. My eyes resumed their scan of the forest, keeping watch as we drove.

"Good—we're going to make it, Viggo. Don't worry."

I frowned at him. "You can't know that," I replied stonily, my throat constricting tightly, making my words harsh even to my own ears. I swallowed, pushing back the strong emotions causing me this pain.

Owen shook his head, favoring me with a quick glance. "Yes, I can," he replied, his voice quiet and sincere.

I bit back a curse, frustrated by the younger man's attempt to bolster me. He didn't know—couldn't know—as much as me about how awful the world could be. How unjust and cruel it was.

I paused, cutting the bitter thought off. That was grossly unfair to Owen—he *did* know as much as me. His brother had been taken from him long ago, and he'd been fighting for him ever since. I was being too harsh toward him, resenting his optimistic nature when at another time I might have been the one offering similar words.

I shook my irritation aside, and Owen kept talking. "We *are* going to make it," he emphasized, meeting my gaze for a long, unwavering second before turning back to the forest. "We did not just go through hell to get her out of there, only to have her die. Besides"—he grinned, as he turned the wheel slowly—"Violet is too stubborn to die."

The way he delivered the statement, rough with affection and humor, managed to get a short laugh out of me. I looked down at Violet again, feeling my own heart swell with love for her. Owen was right—Violet was too stubborn to do *anything* she didn't want to.

As I looked down, the woman cried out something indecipherable as she writhed in my arms. I smoothed my hands over her hair, whispering to her in low, soft tones. She settled down after a moment, turning her head slightly and exhaling in a soft sigh. I held her tightly, and then did something I hadn't done in a long time—not since the night before Miriam's sentence was to be carried out.

I prayed.

CHAPTER 5

Violet

I became aware slowly, by degrees. This time it was different. There was no hush of tension or hint of urgency—nothing that justified me waking—but I woke anyway. I kept my eyes closed, remembering the pain that had usually intensified each time I had opened my eyes, and instead slowly turned my head, listening with my good ear.

I heard the sound of birds chirping, their noise joyous. I wetted my lips and sucked in a deep breath, ignoring the tightness around my ribs. I slowly lifted my eyelids.

I was lying in a bed, a worn homemade quilt pulled over me. The colors were muted, soft, and I felt a deep appreciation for that. But the bed was different than I might have expected. It was made of metal, not wood, and the mattress sagged slightly in the middle. A little pulse of alarm jolted me out of my half-slumbering state, and I took a risk, opening my eyes wider.

I had never seen this room before. It was small, cozy, with coarse wooden walls made up of slats. Framed, faded pictures hung on the walls, but my eyes slid over them as if they were coated in oil. I took a deep breath and then tried to roll over onto my side—my left side, as I distinctly remembered that something was wrong with my right arm.

As I rolled, a wave of pain and sickness swelled up in my gut, and my ribs screamed in protest. I gave up halfway through the motion, flopping back down into the blankets. Sweating, I forced my breathing to even out, taking pains to keep the panic down, in spite of protests from what seemed like every muscle in my body. I settled back on the pillows and gave myself a few moments to calm down, concentrating on simply keeping my stomach and head from exploding. Eventually, the throbbing pain and nausea subsided.

I eased myself up a little higher, using my left hand as a brace, and slipped my legs off the bed until I was in a sitting position. My arm and shoulder ached from the exertion; as soon as I was upright, I rolled my shoulder around in its socket, trying to alleviate the discomfort. Without any support, I swayed slightly and almost fell over, my hand shooting out to grab the bedframe before I toppled over. Bile rose in my throat, but my stomach felt hollow, shaky. Maybe I had run out of things to vomit up. I ignored the trembling of my limbs, the huge swamp of pain that was my ribs.

Swallowing hard, I took a few more breaths and stood up, the blanket sliding off me. I wavered, keeping my hand locked on the bedframe as the room tilted to one side. I tried to focus on an area of the wall, blinking away black spots. It helped, but

I still felt woozy, my steps not landing where I wanted them to. I felt like giving up right then, but I had no idea what could happen next. If I had been kidnapped... *You can do this, Violet. You have to.*

I leaned heavily on the bedframe and took baby steps, examining the room more closely. It was definitely new. My heart-rate increasing, I forced my eyes to check every corner for anything I could use as a weapon—and I needed to be sure that *she* wasn't there. The muscled woman with the sadistic gleam in her eyes who haunted my dreams and nightmares. Panic bubbled up in my chest at the thought of being in her clutches again.

My eyes settled on a book. It wasn't much, but if I slipped it in my pillowcase, then I could...

A sharp voice, distorted by distance and my deaf ear, caught my attention, and I paused in my scheming. There was something familiar about it. I swallowed, and slowly turned my eyes to the spot I had been carefully avoiding—the window—and the bright, shining beams of sunlight pouring in. The light blazed into my head, making me squint, but I pushed the pain back, letting my eyes adjust bit by bit. I took a cautious step toward it, then another, and another, until I had gone as far as I could without letting go of the bedframe.

Wobbling slightly, I released the bedframe and propelled myself forward. I stumbled, my equilibrium off, but managed not to fall. I reached for a desk that sat just left of the window and used it to steady myself, clutching it with weak, shaky fingers. I took a moment to collect myself—sweating, panting hard, and bone-weary. Then, I moved a few steps more, leaning on the desk.

At first the light outside was too intense, but eventually, shapes and colors began to form, slowly, and then faster.

The first thing I noticed was the trees. They seemed to stretch on forever, until I lost sight of the individuals in the enormity of their spread. The forest seemed to run along both sides of the house, thick and dappled. A worn dirt road cut through it across from me, and a wide yard stretched out before the house, with a small barn nestled at the opposite end. The ground was dark and wet, as if it had rained recently, and I noticed several tents along the edge of the woods, forming neat and tidy lines. Someone had cleared away an area at the edge of the tents, and I could see a hodgepodge of benches and chairs encircling the smoldering remains of a fire pit. People my beleaguered mind vaguely recognized were moving around the camp, some in and out of the tents, performing various tasks and chores around the yard.

I pressed my forehead against the glass, letting the cool from the panes seep into my forehead. It helped to push back the throbbing pain, numbing it slightly, as I continued searching for the owner of the familiar voice I'd heard.

I saw her standing by some stairs that probably led to a porch. She was with a young man, her brown hair bobbing as she listened intently. She said something, her voice calm and even, but even from this distance I could pick up the authority in it. I smiled as a memory of her sharp, no-nonsense voice, ordering me to keep my back straight and adjust the heel of my foot slightly, came over me.

Ms. Dale. She looked over her shoulder, back at the tents, for a moment, and then back to the man. Nodding at him once more, she pointed a finger toward the tents, and then the two parted ways. I watched her go, allowing relief to wash over me. If she was here, then I was safe.

I took a deep breath and then turned left toward the door, a new compulsion pulling my aching body forward. I was safe. Now I needed to see Viggo.

It must have taken me ten minutes to hobble over to the door, and when I finally reached it, I sagged against it for a moment, breathing hard, my hand barely resting on the handle. I just had to see him—I had to know he was all right. The doorknob felt odd under my left hand, but I managed to lean on it enough to push it open. The cast on my right made it impossible to grab anything, and my body was so damn weak.

The hall was dim, lit only by a single lantern that hung from a hook in the ceiling. Using the doorframe as a brace, I stepped out, the floorboards creaking under my bare feet.

Voices came at me from an open space just beyond the two other doors opening from the hall, so I moved toward them, grateful they seemed close, keeping my hand on the wall as I walked. I focused on one motion at a time. Take a step. Viggo. Another step—closer to Viggo.

As I moved, I once again became acutely aware of the absence of sound in my left ear. It felt as if someone had shoved a wad of cotton into it, and it ached fiercely. I still couldn't remember how I had damaged it. I guessed I could ask Viggo… but as I thought that, I realized there was another host of worries pressing into the back of my skull, one more rising above the rest. There was something I had to ask first. The urgency spurred me to move my feet faster, but that only made me dizzier, and I was forced to maintain the slower pace.

It took too long, but I made my way down the hall. As I approached the open space beyond, I was surprised to see it was a dining room. The people in it seemed to spin before my eyes, and I blinked them into focus, searching single-mindedly.

Yes—there was Viggo, seated at the table, and something in my stomach settled to see him there safe. A redheaded girl was sitting next to him, peering at some maps in front of her. I took in the unique haircut—shaved on the sides with a riot of curls on top—and smiled. Her name was Amber, and she had helped me.

Next to her sat Owen, and across from him, a short man with a paunchy stomach and dark, beady eyes. His face was like a rat's, sly and cunning, and I felt an odd echo of both distaste and trust. It took me a minute as his face wobbled in my vision; his name was much harder to find, but I eventually recalled that he was Thomas, and he had helped me, too. In fact… he had been with my brother.

My brother. I pushed off the wall and moved into the room. At first, no one noticed me, but I cleared my throat loudly, and everyone turned. I looked around at all of them, noting the alarm and surprise on their faces with a detached sense of curiosity. The ache in my ear pulsed; my ribs creaked as I breathed; my hand twinged; the walls of the room revolved around me gently.

Amber stood up, her violet eyes wide. My eyes dropped to her lips, watching them move. I turned my good ear toward her, and her voice came through.

"—okay, Violet?"

I nodded, my hand searching for support and fumbling with a bookcase. "I'm fine," I insisted. Viggo was already out of his seat, his expression concerned. I focused my thoughts. "Where's Tim?"

Amber froze and I looked around, turning my head slowly so as not to upset it, noting the expressions on everyone's faces. They seemed... worried. Worried and sad. Well—most of them did. Thomas was wearing a strange expression, his eyes fixed pointedly on the table.

"What's going on?" I slurred.

Viggo broke the silence, moving over to me. "Violet, Tim is missing," he said, his voice level, his expression becoming carefully neutral. I cocked my head at him, confused. He paused, as if searching for words, and then continued. "He covered Jay and Thomas as they fled the palace after rescuing King Maxen and Quinn. Somehow, in the confusion, they lost him."

I turned my gaze back to Thomas, studying him closely. His expression hadn't changed much, but his head had sunk a fraction of an inch lower. That was... guilt in his eyes.

The expression was so absurd on Thomas that I felt a laugh bubbling up from my stomach and out of my throat. "Very funny, guys," I said, smiling broadly, then wincing as my bruised face throbbed.

No one laughed.

"Tim?" I called. Amber looked away, clearly uncomfortable.

I took a few swaying steps forward, knocking over Viggo's chair with my hip as I reached for the table, my balance threatening to give out. I couldn't hear it fall, but I noticed Owen flinch as it hit the floor. "Tim?" I called again, my voice pleading.

"Violet, please—" Viggo said behind me, but I ignored him.

"Tim, where are you?" I cried, moving toward the door, my heart pounding. "Tim, please! Answer me."

My breathing was coming in gasps, the pain in my ribs increasing, and I half heard Owen mumble something behind me. I tried to move closer to the door, tears streaking down my face and pattering onto my chest. I had to find my brother! He had to be here!

I was reaching for the doorknob when the world gave up trying to make sense. My legs gave out. I would've fallen, but Viggo was there, his strong hands grabbing me before I hit the ground. He hefted me up with a grunt, tucking me tight against his chest.

Still I stretched for the door, crying out for my brother. Viggo shushed me as he carried me back down the hallway and into my room. I protested, but he ignored me, gently setting me down onto the bed.

I looked up at him, my vision hazy, and I realized I was still crying. Viggo snarled under his breath, though I wasn't sure why, and then picked up the blanket and slid into bed with me, covering us both. Carefully, tenderly, his arms came around me, so lightly that my ribs didn't even twinge. My entire body warped with pain, I still angled myself toward his warmth, wanting his comfort and strength.

"I promise we will find him," Viggo whispered in my ear, his hand trailing through my hair. I nodded, but still the tears poured from me. I cried against him, my tears soaking through his shirt, but he didn't complain.

Eventually, unconsciousness crept up on me, and I slept.

CHAPTER 6

Viggo

Violet's deep, even breathing told me she had finally succumbed to sleep. I stroked her forehead, hoping that if she dreamt, the dreams would be calming, loving. I rested her back against the pillow and pulled the blanket over her shoulders, then stared at her for a minute, my eyes struggling between avoiding and seeking out the tear-stained, injured side of her face. My stomach twisted in knots as I took in the damage, searching her countenance over and over again.

I knew the bruises would fade, and the cuts and broken bones would heal. But the bruising belied the bigger problem—Tabitha had punched Violet square in the face with her superhuman strength. I hadn't seen all of it, but I had watched the video Violet had recorded using a button camera on her shirt. I had only seen Tabitha's fist moving, followed by the sickening sound of flesh on flesh and Violet's cry of pain. It was a miracle

Violet was even alive after that hit.

I sat for a minute, running my hand over my face. I was exhausted, my eyelids heavy. I needed to shave—nothing new there—and I was deeply worried about Violet. I had hoped that, unlike me, she would be able to sleep until we figured out some way to ease her suffering with more than just painkillers. Unfortunately, things hadn't gone according to my plan. Her panic in the dining room, no matter how justified, was uncharacteristic of her, confirming what the doctor had feared: her concussion was much worse than we'd thought. He had warned me about this. If we didn't get her to a hospital soon…

I pushed the grim thought aside. I couldn't dwell on that. It sent too much fear through me, which in turn made me frustrated and angry. I wanted to do something—anything—that would help her, but we were flying blind here. We barely had any information about what was going on; the tickers were still down, confirming Thomas' assertion that the damage in the palace had affected them, and even with Tabitha likely dead, I knew with certainty Elena was not going to take this lying down.

Not to mention, Tim was missing. That alone terrified me, not only for Violet's sake, but for Tim's as well. I had grown fond of Violet's little brother. He was an apt student who had borne the brunt of his isolation and the experimentation he'd suffered with a resolve worthy of my respect and admiration. The young man was resourceful and smart, just like his sister, so I had to believe he was all right. I just needed to know where to find him. I hated not knowing almost as much as I hated knowing someone I was responsible for was missing, possibly injured…

or worse.

Behind me, there was a soft rap on the door. I turned, the bedsprings squeaking under my shifting weight, and saw Amber standing there, concern stamped on her features. Behind her was Dr. Arlan, the middle-aged Patrian man we had… coerced into helping Henrik, who had been shot during the battle at Ashabee's with the Matrian wardens. Dr. Arlan was tall and lanky, with a thick brown beard and brown eyes. He kept his brown hair cut close to his head, so you could barely see the thick waves in it.

Amber's eyes flicked to Violet in a silent query.

"She's sleeping again," I said as I stood up.

"I guess that's good," Amber said, though her expression remained dark and weary. "People have been asking about her ever since you guys got back. Jay. Ms. Dale. What's-his-face… her cousin. At least now I have a good excuse to keep them out of here."

I nodded appreciatively. "Yes… It might not be safe to bring a whole bunch of people in here just yet. We still don't know… We don't know…"

I trailed off with the words *if she's going to make it* hovering at the tip of my tongue.

Dr. Arlen seemed to take that as his cue, and stepped into the room, moving over to the bed. He pulled out a penlight and shined it into her eyes, pulling them open one at a time. Violet groaned and twitched at the intrusion but, worryingly, didn't wake.

I crossed my arms and leaned against the desk, waiting and watching closely as the man took her pulse, then pressed his fingers against her skull, probing gently. After he finished his examination, he stood up and turned toward me, his expression stoic.

"She needs to go to a hospital," he said. He had been saying that since his first examination.

"We're working on it," I replied with a tight nod.

Dr. Arlan's expression shifted from neutral to disapproving. "Stop working on it and do it. Or else this young lady will die. She has a severe concussion—that's why her pupils are uneven, though it looks like there's no major damage to her eyes. Her ribs are probably bruised, but they don't look broken—that horse doctor you talked about wrapped up her wrist pretty good. The worst thing is, her skull is fractured, which means there's likely bleeding into the brain. Depending on how fast the bleed is, her condition could deteriorate very gradually— she may lose functions slowly—or it could be over in only a few days. She needs surgery, and I don't have the tools or the space to do it here."

I held back my frustrated reply, one full of colorful language, and nodded. "We're working on it," I repeated.

He huffed, but didn't say anything. His glare spoke volumes. I met his gaze, and eventually he looked away. "Whatever it is you plan to do, be sure to do it fast," he said, striding to the door.

I exhaled slowly, fighting for calm, and cracked my neck, releasing the tension there. I met Amber's gaze as I straightened and moved toward the door. She backed up into the hall, allowing me to step out and close the door. I left it open a crack, just in case Violet cried out in her sleep, and started to move past Amber.

Her arm shot out, her hand hitting the wall with a thump, blocking my path. I took a step back and arched an eyebrow.

"You need to let us go to the Liberators," she said, crossing her arms.

I sighed—mostly out of exhaustion—and shook my head. "We've been over this. It's too risky." Which was true. Amber had been bothering me about this since she'd picked us up from the rendezvous point, and I'd thought it was a bad idea the whole time. Not only did the Liberators believe Violet and I were spies for our respective governments, but Desmond had likely informed them that Amber, Owen, Henrik, Quinn, and Thomas were all defectors, betraying their cause for ours. Granted, the Liberators had no idea Desmond was a treacherous snake who had been recruiting them for years, playing off most of their desires to rescue their lost sons, or, in the case of those like Amber, their desire to see meaningful change in the prescribed gender roles that separated the two countries. I doubted the group would look kindly on an unexpected visit from us. And they would probably show their displeasure by trying to kill anyone we sent up there.

"Too risky?" Amber retorted, sarcasm dripping from her voice. "As opposed to trying to get Violet into the city and to a hospital, without her being seen?"

I swallowed hard, trying to calm myself. Amber meant well. She was just as worried as the rest of us. Not just for Violet, but also for Quinn and Henrik, her two injured team members. I glanced at the room next to Violet's, where the two men were sleeping on twin beds, and then back at her.

"What makes you think it will work?" I asked, leaning a

shoulder against the wall.

Amber's eyes lit up and she smiled eagerly. "Well, for one thing, we have the video." I cringed as she mentioned it, my stomach roiling in disgust at what I had seen there. Namely, Violet, running for her life, bravely talking to Tabitha, getting her to reveal herself for what she truly was and confirming aspects of Elena's plan.

Not that the Patrians needed *confirmation*. Before they could even get to the stage of confirmation, they needed to be *informed*. In the eyes of the Patrians, Queen Elena had ridden in on a white horse to save her neighbors in spite of their ideological differences. She had sent in soldiers to help put out fires, doctors with medicine, and aid workers with food, water, and blankets. No one knew she was behind the fires that had ravaged a third of the city. Or that she was quietly having sixty percent of the male population exterminated.

"There's no guarantee the video will sway them," I replied. "And, if Desmond is there, you'd be walking into a trap."

Amber waved her hand as if chasing away the thought. "Desmond's not there," she retorted. "I got new information from Thomas when we touched down. He's been listening in on as many Matrian communications as possible, and he got some news of the Liberators." Her gaze tightened angrily, but she continued her logical expression of the new information. "Can't be sure, but he thinks the Matrians raided their facility in The Green. Desmond must have set them up somehow—I think the Matrians have taken control of the facility. And… and the boys."

"How is that good news?" I asked, a hollowness swelling in

the pit of my stomach. The Matrians had full control of the boys again. It made me want to punch a hole in the wall.

Amber blew out a hard breath. "One," she said, "because it means Desmond is probably not with them. She wouldn't risk being caught between the two sides. Besides, she's probably too busy trying to help Elena clean up this mess.

"And two, if the Liberators had to evacuate, then I know exactly where they all are. And it'll be much safer to travel there than the Facility."

I stared at her and reluctantly took the bait. "Where would that be?"

"Home base," Amber said, a gleam in her eye. "It's the original base, also in The Green's region—the one where Desmond brought us all before she found... well, before she let us in on the Facility with the boys."

"Great," I said, weariness making me snappy. "That sounds safe *and* easy."

"They have a *doctor*, Viggo. A good one... one who is well trained in mobile surgical care."

She was referring to Dr. Elizabeth Tierney, the Liberator doctor who had performed surgery on me, helping to repair my heart after I had damaged it in a fight to the death with the twin princesses of Matrus. Dr. Tierney had always struck me as a reasonable woman, but I still doubted she would help us.

"What about the heloship? It—"

"Is more than capable of getting to our home base, even on limited fuel," Amber cut me off. "It's fast, and it's large enough to transport any troops we might take, or any equipment Dr. Tierney might need to help Violet."

"I was going to *say* it's our biggest advantage right now," I replied, "and it's a bad idea to risk it—not to mention, we have no idea how heavily protected the border is."

Amber gave me a droll look, her lips quirking up in a smile. "Viggo, the Liberator home base is on the *Patrian* side of the river. We don't even need to cross a border. Besides, the point of the heloship is that it can *fly*. I could fly due east, until we were over the mountains, and then head north, avoiding most of civilization altogether. Circle back around."

I considered this new information, but still found myself shaking my head, fighting back the weariness creeping up the corners of my eyes. "Just as easy to go to a hospital and steal the equipment we need."

"And lead anyone who might be following right back here? Trust me, the heloship is the way to go. It can't be tracked from the air, and anyone on the ground would lose sight of it pretty quickly. Someone would have to be standing right underneath to know where it landed. And believe me, nobody is going to be standing where we're going to land."

"Without the ticker, we are flying blind here! We have no updates on anything remotely helpful, and no idea what Elena is planning. Tabitha's death won't set her back. It might if she had a heart, but…"

"Even with a super brain, it still takes time to coordinate things. Messages have to be sent, people have to be accounted for, troops have to move… We have a window of time here, Viggo. Let's take the opportunity, the chance. We have to—the people we care about are going to die if we don't." Amber's eyes shone with sincerity and determination. I could almost hear what she meant: *Violet* was going to die if we didn't go.

I looked into her eyes and exhaled slowly. "Are you sure about this? Do you think the Liberators will actually hear you out?"

Amber nodded, her red locks bouncing atop her head. "Desmond told them we were traitors, but I *know* people in there. They're my *friends*. They'll hear me out. Me and Owen. We've just got to get them to watch the video."

"You're placing a lot of faith in that video," I replied, and she gave me a stern look.

"Violet almost sacrificed her life getting us that video," she said, her voice brittle. "Because of that, we have something tangible to show people. We have proof Elena is behind the attacks on Patrus. That counts for something."

I tilted my head up toward the ceiling. Amber was right. I was letting my own personal hatred for the contents of that video override my logic. Truth be told, I didn't want *anyone* to see that video. I hated to imagine what they might think of Violet. After all, it also provided clear evidence that she was behind the bombing of the palace, and I wasn't sure that would go over well with anyone from Patrus, no matter her rationale behind it.

Yet I knew pictures spoke more to people than words ever could. I could shout at the top of my lungs that Elena was behind everything, and nobody would listen. But if we could show them evidence... then they might come around.

Amber held her hands up, palms together, and gave me a big-eyed, pleading look. I rolled my eyes, but a smile crossed my face. "Okay," I said, and she gave an excited squeal, clapping her hands rapidly together. I waited for her excitement to die down, giving her a sardonic look. "For the record, it was your well-thought-out and carefully reasoned argument that won, not the puppy dog eyes."

Amber shrugged. "Don't care, still won," she practically sang as she turned, heading back into the dining room.

I rolled my eyes again, but I was still smiling. Amber had an infectious way about her, and I felt slightly revitalized as I headed back into the dining room, stifling a yawn behind my fist, ready to do damage control.

CHAPTER 7

Viggo

I bent over, picking up the chair Violet had knocked over in her panic, and then sat down in it. Ms. Dale looked up at me from across the table, and I gave her a small nod and a tight smile. Then I realized everyone else was also looking at me expectantly, waiting for news about Violet.

"She's fine," I assured everyone. "She's resting. However, I've decided to send Owen and Amber into The Green, hopefully to convince the Liberators to switch sides, but, more importantly, to bring back Dr. Tierney and medical supplies."

Owen gave me a grateful look, a smile curling at the corners of his lips, and I nodded in acknowledgement. Ms. Dale leaned forward, her face impassive.

"Are you sure that's a good idea?" she asked.

I shot a glance at Amber, who raised an eyebrow at me. "Amber made some good points earlier, and I think it might be our best chance. However, before you two go"—I fixed Amber and Owen with a look—"would you mind staying for this meeting? Your insight would be helpful, and I have something to talk about with both of you afterward."

"Of course," said Owen, nodding. "We don't want to leave you in the lurch." Amber raised one eyebrow, but nodded.

"Good," I replied.

"Not good," contradicted Ms. Dale. I gave her a questioning look, but her focus was on Owen and Amber. "Not that I doubt you made good points to Mr. Croft here, but I just want to be clear—you're going to the Facility?"

"Oh, no."

"Not even remotely."

Amber and Owen exchanged chagrined looks as they spoke over each other, and Amber waved a hand, indicating Owen should take the lead. Owen met Ms. Dale's gaze with an earnest smile, before explaining they'd be going to their home base, hidden on the Patrian side of The Green.

"Amber and I talked about this, and we figure Desmond will be paying closer attention to the Facility than our base—because it looks like she kicked the Liberators out of it and gave the Matrians full control—and all the research for the boys is based there."

Ms. Dale met his gaze, then leaned back in the chair. "In that case, I'm satisfied," she said with a nod, though her eyes were still cold, probably at the thought of the poor boys' plight.

I felt myself smile at Ms. Dale, shaking my head in amusement. That woman was like a bloodhound when it came to finding flaws in plans, and I was once again impressed she had thought to ask that question. I hadn't thought of it until Amber had brought it up herself—I'd had no idea the Liberators even *had* another base. Then again, most of my time with the Liberators had been spent either in convalescence or training the boys. It hadn't left a lot of room for talking.

"All right," I said, settling back into the chair with a slight stretch and letting its back serve as support for my head. I was eager to move on to the next topic. "Thomas—what do we know about Tim?"

Thomas' head jerked up, his mouth dropping open and then snapping shut. I had caught him off guard, it seemed. He smoothed the front of his shirt, collecting himself, and then leaned forward. "Well, it's been chaotic with the move and the palace, but I've finally had a chance to hack one of the handhelds we collected from the Matrian wardens after their attack on Ashabee's estate. I've gotten just a smattering of information— they're using a sophisticated data encryption key I haven't seen before, but I've been slowly deciphering the messages. A lot of it is fragmented, but even then… so far, there hasn't been any description of a captured male fitting Mr. Bates' description."

I felt disappointed but unsurprised. It hadn't seemed likely that answers would just fall in our laps, but still, it would've been… nice. "Keep monitoring it," I said, and Thomas nodded. "What else have you found?"

Thomas leaned forward, excitement shining in his dark eyes. "Well, I've got good news and bad news—which would you prefer?"

I gave him a look from beneath my heavy eyelids, but it was Amber who answered. "Bad news," she said sweetly. Everyone looked at her, and she gave a little shrug. "I like getting the bad stuff over and done with first—makes the good news all the more delectable."

I refrained from sighing. "You heard the lady," I muttered. "Give us the bad."

"Well, I have no idea where the Matrians are holing up. A general call was sent to retreat to a location after the bombing at the palace, but they're referring to the location by a code name, which is meaningless to us. Any chance we had of sabotaging their retreat or taking out a supply line is out, until I crack the code or they slip up."

"That might be for the best," replied Ms. Dale. "The people in this room are the best-trained operatives we have at the moment. I'm working with the recruits day and night, but they are nowhere near ready. Attempting a major offensive right now would be more than risky."

"I agree," added Owen. "We aren't strong enough to hit them directly. Better to look at indirect ways of bringing them down."

I leaned forward and looked at Thomas. "What's the good?"

"I've decrypted several messages regarding another location and put them together. I think I've found where they are taking the men after they separate them from their families."

"That's interesting," said Amber. "Where?"

Thomas sifted through several of the maps on the table, pulling out a big one. "This would be so much better with that hologram projector on the heloship," he grumbled as he picked up a red pencil and studied the features on the map. After a few moments, he circled an area northeast of our position, about forty miles away. "There."

I slid the map closer to me and studied it. It took me a few seconds to focus, as the map seemed an amorphous blob to my tired eyes. I blinked several times, trying to make everything come together through sheer force of will. "Why do you consider this good news?" I asked after I had taken a good look at it.

Thomas gave me an incredulous look and then sighed in irritation, pinching the bridge of his nose with his fingers. "Because they could mean recruits for us! More people to fill out our ranks and make us more formidable."

Considering his answer, I looked over to Ms. Dale and noticed she had a frown on her face. "What do you think, Melissa?"

She met my gaze and then shook her head. "I don't think it's a good idea," she replied. "We have no idea how accurate that information is—for all we know, this place is just a mass burial site for the people they've been killing."

"What?!" exclaimed Thomas, practically sputtering. "That's ridiculous—they wouldn't kill people and *then* transport them. Too much work, and it has the potential for alerting the remaining population to their true intentions. It's much more likely they are collecting the men, transporting them to the site, and then executing them. Less chance of witnesses that way."

"That's… actually a good point," Ms. Dale muttered. Thomas beamed, and Ms. Dale went on. "But that doesn't mean that they aren't just transporting them there to kill them. However, even if that's not the case, it's still not necessarily a good idea to charge in. The camp will be heavily fortified and defended. Besides, our top priority should be addressing what new information Elena is feeding the populace. The tickers are still down, which would cause mass chaos, but we have seen no evidence of chaos. Elena is probably disseminating the news to the population somehow. We need to send an agent into the city to find out how she's doing it. That way, we'll have a better idea how to proceed."

Thomas opened his mouth to launch a counterargument about how his idea was more important. I slowly stood up, keeping a careful ear on the conversation, but also desperate for a cup of coffee—I was on the brink of falling asleep, a sure sign I was overtaxing myself, and I knew getting up would force more life into my limbs, and coffee would help my mind. The debate continued as I rose, and I had to admit, both of them were making good points; both ideas were well reasoned and thought out.

I poured myself a cup of coffee from the metal coffeemaker and took a sip, grimacing at the stale taste, and then forced another sip, needing the caffeine. I moved back to the table, loudly setting my cup down as the argument began to grow heated.

Thomas and Ms. Dale paused, looking at me, and I held up my hand in a silent entreaty. They both shut their mouths and waited, and I was struck with appreciation for how well we all worked together.

"I think we should send two agents," I said, "one male, one female, into the city. Ms. Dale is right—we *do* need to know how Elena is keeping control. Knowing what lies she's telling is going to be essential to helping us know how best to move forward."

Ms. Dale gave me a smile and leaned back, smirking at

Thomas. I let her have her moment of victory before adding, "I *also* think we need to send scouts to the location Thomas pointed out. He's right—any chance we can spare lives, while also getting them to join up, is a possibility worth looking into. Besides, what if Tim was picked up and shipped there? That possibility makes it all the more important that we check it out."

Everyone nodded, and I took another sip of coffee.

"I think we should send Jeff into the city," Ms. Dale said. "He's got a clean record, and with Ashabee taken by Elena, he has a perfect cover. I also have some ideas for who else to send, so don't worry about that."

I gave her a grateful look. "All right. Is there anything else?"

"I should add that the move from Ashabee's manor to this location was mostly successful," Ms. Dale continued. "Thanks to the refugees, we were able to drive most of the vehicles in one big caravan, *and* fit all our people and supplies. We were able to move most of the items from the warehouse, as well as Solomon—but there were a few things left behind that we might want to go get."

"I don't think that's a good idea," Amber chimed in, looking at Ms. Dale. "By now, they will have figured out we were using the house for a while, and will likely be watching it, waiting to see if we come back."

"There's also the fact that they have Amber's father," added Owen. "If they've tortured him..."

"They might *not* be torturing him," Amber said, although by her tone of voice, I could tell she hoped they were.

"They are," Thomas cut in darkly. "Why wouldn't they? They would've already pieced together that something was wrong when their patrol never checked back in. It would be the first thing they'd do. It'd be the first thing *I'd* do. It's better to think about this in terms of worst possible outcomes, so that we can take every precaution foreseeable."

"That's why I've secured King Maxen at an alternate location," added Ms. Dale. "It's also where I'm holding Solomon. I'm the only one, besides the guards I placed with them, who knows where it is, and the guards check in with me regularly." She shot me an apologetic look as she continued. "The precaution is necessary to prevent anyone else from being leveraged like Violet was."

I nodded, carefully considering her words, repressing an irrational flare of anger. I knew she wasn't placing blame on Violet, but it was hard not to feel like she was. Violet had jeopardized a key part of our plan by bringing Maxen, but she had also taken pains to make sure he got out in the confusion—and had lost her brother in the process. Everyone in the room knew it.

"I agree," I said. "Better to be cautious than foolhardy. Melissa, if we assume Ashabee is compromised, is this location secure?"

"It is, reasonably. Ashabee pointed out a few places, including an abandoned farm, but I actually found this place on my own, on a lark. He didn't know about it, so that makes it safe. For now."

I accepted this with a nod and then looked around. "Anything else?"

Everyone shook their heads, and I nodded again. "All right. Let's get to it, then. Amber, Owen—discuss what you'll need for the mission before you get packed up. I want a list for Ms. Dale, so we can keep our inventory organized. Bring it back to me before you head out."

The effect of my declaration was immediate. Thomas slipped out of the room, muttering about plans and strategies, while Amber and Owen nodded and scooted closer together, quietly discussing what they needed as Amber scribbled on a piece of paper.

Ms. Dale got up and moved over to me, resting a hand on my shoulder, dragging my attention from the two of them. "How is she, really?" she asked, and I sighed, rubbing my eyes in a futile attempt to relieve the headache starting to form.

"She's going to get worse if we don't get her that help," I replied, and Ms. Dale squeezed my shoulder tightly.

"She's tough. And you made a good call tonight. Several, actually, but the one about the Liberators... I've thought it over, and it's a good idea. They have training, and they can help us. I'm just glad *you* came to the decision." I gave her a curious look, and she shot me a half-smile, her expression wistful. "I thought if I brought it up, it would seem too... self-interested."

Frowning, I reached up and covered her hand with mine, giving her a little squeeze back. "How is he?" Ms. Dale knew I was referring to Henrik. She didn't respond, but I could tell when her expression froze into that unreadable mask that his prognosis still wasn't good. "We'll get them to come," I told her, confident. "Dr. Tierney will be able to help him."

Ms. Dale gave me a hard look. "You and I are too old to believe in miracles, Mr. Croft."

"Whoa—I'm not that old," I retorted. "But please, tell me,

what was the earth like before the destruction of mankind?"

She withdrew her hand and smacked me smartly on the arm, but she was smiling, a twinkle in her eyes. I chuckled as I rubbed the spot, and then turned to Amber and Owen, who were in the process of rising from their chairs. Owen handed me the list, and I skimmed it, noting the subvocalizers on the equipment list.

"Looks good," I said with a nod. "Just make sure you grab enough for the three of us."

CHAPTER 8

Viggo

There was a long pause after my announcement, and I saw confusion flit over the faces of everyone in the room. Amber gave me an especially dubious look. "The three of us?" she repeated, her voice rising with the question.

"Yes," I replied, standing up. "You, Owen, and me. I'm going with you."

Owen gave me an alarmed look, shaking his head. "I don't think that's such a good idea, Viggo. You might want to sit this one out."

"Yeah," said Amber. "We might get a pass because the Liberators have known us for a long time, and that alone might make them willing to hear us out. If you're there... they won't be so inclined to talk to us."

"Well, that's too bad, because I'm going," I replied calmly. Owen and Amber exchanged looks, and I noticed Amber shift her gaze over to Ms. Dale, a pleading look in her eyes. I suppressed a sigh. I knew this was not going to be an easy sell—it was why I had waited until after the meeting to bring it up. Yet I was resolved to go with them, whether they liked it or not. I just needed to convince them.

Ms. Dale studied my face closely, crossing her arms. "Why do you want to go?" she asked.

"For one thing, Violet's life is on the line," I replied. "But honestly, it's more than that. We're trying to convince them not only to break from Desmond, but also to join with us. And that means with Violet and me. They need to come to terms with the fact we aren't traitors."

"I agree, but it still doesn't make sense, Viggo," replied Owen. "Why not let us go, show them the video, and then explain about you?"

"It's a point of integrity at this point, Owen," I replied patiently, my weariness thrumming underneath the argument like a sluggish current in my brain. But this was important, dammit. "I need to show them that, in spite of them supporting Desmond when she ran us out, we're still willing to be their allies," I continued. "It's the best way to put a positive foot forward."

Owen seemed to take a moment to consider. "That's a good point," he said. "I hadn't thought of it like that."

Amber gaped at Owen and then shook her head emphatically. "It's admirable, but still a really bad idea. They don't trust you, and they'll trust us less with you there."

"That might be true," I replied, "but we have no idea what you're walking into. For all we know, they'll throw you in a cell and call Desmond. I'd rather be there, just in case—because I know cells and how to get out of them. We'll work better as a team. Besides…" I let a little smile crawl onto my face. "I think it might actually bother me if something happened to you both."

A ghost of a smile crossed over Owen's face, but Amber rolled her eyes at my joke, clearly not amused. She opened her mouth to argue, but I held up my hand, cutting her off.

It was hard, but this time, I let the raw emotion I had been struggling with slip into my voice. "In all honesty, I am grasping for straws here. With Quinn, Henrik, and Violet injured, we're all infinitely more vulnerable. And we're each infinitely more valuable to the enemy. We can't all go—Ms. Dale needs to stay behind to make sure the mission will be carried on without us—but we also don't have to compartmentalize *this* much. I want to be there to help if I can, argue when I must, and help ensure our survival overall."

Owen picked up where I had left off, his face animated. "He's right, Amber. They might not like it, but if we're going to get them on our side, they need to face this reality sooner or later. Might as well get it out of the way sooner, rather than the later. Besides, by going in with Viggo, we show that we support him. We are allied with him. And we follow his leadership one hundred percent. They need to be on board with that, and all that it implies."

Amber fell silent, her gaze drifting down as she thought about it. Then she nodded. "All right," she conceded. "I don't like it, but you're right."

I let out the breath I had been holding and held up my finger. "Okay. I'll go grab my bag. Owen, would you and Amber mind packing up the equipment you listed, and I'll meet you on the porch?"

Owen raised his hand to his forehead in a mock salute, which was spoiled by his wide grin. Then he and Amber turned and headed back outside to the barn to gear up.

I turned to Ms. Dale, who frowned as she met my gaze. "It's good you're going," she said after a pause. "Just, please, be careful. I do not want to end up doing this alone."

I gave her what I hoped was a reassuring smile, then headed down the hallway. Carefully, I pushed open the door to our room. Violet was just as I had left her—eyes closed, breathing deep and even.

She, Quinn, and Henrik were all sleeping in these rooms because they were either sick or wounded. The rest of us were relegated to sleeping in tents, which was only fair. Those of us in charge had decided early on that we needed to show the refugees we were all in this together. However, I was exempt for the time being, as I wouldn't leave Violet's side for longer than I had to... and sleeping next to a sick girl didn't take up any more bed space in the house.

Grabbing my bag, which I'd left under Violet's makeshift sickbed, I did a quick check to make sure my gun was there, then left space for the equipment Owen would be bringing me for our mission. I took the egg out—a gleaming silver case, deceptively simple in its design, but heavy in my hands. The egg had been at the center of all this mess, and while in some ways I owed my relationship with Violet to its very existence, I hated the thing for what it represented. If I had my way, we would toss the abomination into the Veil River and be done with it.

But the egg was still our most effective bargaining chip, if we could use it correctly. It was the physical manifestation of research started by the previous Matrian queen, Rina, and Mr. Alistair Jenks to create artificially enhanced humans. Elena had been the first child to receive this boost; her mother had allowed Mr. Jenks to experiment on her daughter in the womb. However, like most cutting-edge research, the treatment had a barrage of side effects, ranging from emotional to physical, which seemed to have made the advancement more of a curse than a blessing. I knew this firsthand after seeing the boys they had experimented on to create this supposedly flawless version of the egg.

It was Elena's endgame—she was going to force humanity to advance, setting up a dynasty of super humans, but under her rule. It was ambitious, but horrifying.

But as long as we had this egg in our possession, we had something Elena wanted desperately. And now that everyone thought the real egg had been destroyed in the palace when Violet had detonated the false one and taken out Tabitha, it was even more crucial we kept this secret until we needed it the most. I tucked some spare pillowcases around the damn thing and rolled it under the bed for now, making a mental note to tell Ms. Dale where to find it and begin guarding it properly, as we probably should have from the beginning.

I shouldered my bag and made my way to Violet, kneeling by the bed. "Violet," I said softly. She didn't stir, which was for the best—with her head injury, her waking moments seemed to leave her in states of confusion, pain, or fear, and I didn't want her panicking over me leaving without her. Or, worse, trying to make me take her with me. I hated the idea of leaving her without a proper goodbye… but we didn't have time. The sooner I did this, the sooner I could come back with Dr. Tierney and the equipment to save Violet's life. That provided maybe the only motivation that could have forced me to leave her side.

All this running through my head, I leaned over and kissed her forehead. "It's my turn to go get you some help," I whispered into her hair. "Please… please still be here when I get back. Please… just keep on breathing for me, okay, baby?"

Then I stood and headed toward the door before my tired mind could urge me to forget about going with Amber and Owen and instead climb into bed and hold Violet close until I drifted off into sleep. The image was sweet, so tempting, and I promised myself I *would* get to have that moment with her. Just… *after* I had negotiated a peace with the rebel faction and secured a doctor and the equipment needed to save her life.

Amber and Owen were waiting on the porch as I exited the house, having taken next to no time to find the gear they needed. Amber quickly straightened, picking up her bag from where it was resting against her shin, and headed toward the forest, where we'd been keeping the heloship. It was a half a mile away, hidden in a clearing.

Night had fallen an hour ago, and the sky was clear, the light from the half-moon illuminating our path, even through the forest canopy. The air had a slight chill to it, a sign of the changing season, and my breath crystallized as soon as it escaped my lungs. I made a mental note to put someone on firewood duty, and another note to send out a search party for another place to house our small forces when it got too cold for the tents. Winter was coming, and there was no telling how long this conflict would last.

We reached the heloship quickly, and within minutes, we were in the air. I watched the small farmhouse disappear through the bubble window in the front, where Amber sat at the controls. I had only flown in helicopters a few times during my career as a warden—since flight was so restricted in general by both Matrus and Patrus—and only once in a heloship, when Amber had picked us up the day before, and I had remained in the cargo bay with Violet the entire time. So it was an interesting experience watching the dark mountains framing the rolling farmland beneath us. The lights of the city shone bright in contrast, but soon the glow faded as we moved steadily deeper into the mountains, away from humanity's prying eyes. The world where I'd grown up seemed so tiny and insignificant from up here.

"I'm taking us the way we discussed, Viggo," Amber said, her focus on the window, reading gauges and adjusting the controls under her hands. "It'll take about an hour... maybe two."

I nodded and took a step back, rotating my shoulder. "What's this base like?" I asked.

Amber gave me a rather mysterious look, her eyes twinkling. "Well, you're in for a treat."

"How so?"

"Let's just say... Well, it's better if you just see it. It's hard to explain."

I frowned, but let it go, too tired to dig deeper. Besides, no matter how unpredictable Amber might be, I trusted Owen. He wouldn't keep information from me if he thought it was worth mentioning. Which he clearly didn't, so...

I went over to one of the wall-mounted seats and pulled it down, taking a seat. The ride was surprisingly smooth. I wasn't sure what I had expected—roaring engines, rocking like a boat?—but this was not it. I leaned my head back against the wall and closed my eyes.

I must've slept, because the next thing I knew, Amber's voice was loud in my ears. I jolted forward and looked around blearily, stifling a groan. Ignoring the exhaustion, I stood up and moved over to where Owen was standing by the strange black table in the middle of the command area. It was glossy on top, but with a complicated, rolling, square-like pattern underneath it. On the surface, Owen had placed several items into three piles. He pushed one of them toward me, and I began sifting through the items. I slipped the aerosol canisters into a small black bag designed to attach to the back of my pants through the belt loops, followed by my gun in my waistband, and the subvocalizer around my throat. I kept the device off for now, looking at Owen.

"What's the plan?" I asked.

"Descending now," said Amber from the front, over my question. "It might get a bit bumpy, so hold on, gentlemen."

Owen slid his gun into the holster at his hip, grinned, and answered my question. "Why, we're in the neighborhood! It would be impolite to come all this way for a romp in The Green and not pay a visit to our dear friends!"

I smirked at his wide, beaming smile. "So we're going in the front."

He clapped me on the shoulder and nodded. "It's only polite."

I chuckled, slapping a magazine into my gun. It was a bold plan, and frankly, I wasn't sure I had the patience for anything more complicated than that. I couldn't deny the surge of adrenaline through my veins at the unknown waiting for us down below. The heloship shuddered, and I reached out to grab the table, using it to keep me steady as we descended toward the Liberator home base.

CHAPTER 9

Viggo

I peered out the bubble window as Amber lowered the ship down to a flat protrusion of rock that jutted out several hundred feet over The Green, dropping sharply on one side. It was flush with the mountainside, which was another sheer rise, almost like a series of steps for a giant. I couldn't see anything that remotely looked like a base, just stone and a light dusting of snow. I was suddenly glad I had remembered my jacket. The Green was mild and humid, but the mountains were not. As the heloship shuddered again, I was grateful for the nip in the air forcing more adrenaline into my overworked system, giving me clarity and a sense of renewed—albeit temporary—energy.

Amber stared at the controls, her entire body focused on our descent. She guided the ship smoothly down, despite the jolting wind, and we landed with barely a shake or a shudder. "Nice job," I said as the girl continued flipping switches and turning dials, powering the ship propellers down.

"Thanks," she replied absentmindedly, her eyes on the control panel. That was going to be the last audible word on this mission for a while; from here on out, it was toxin masks and subvocalizers. I geared up in silence, the tingle of my vocal cords freezing a weird counterpart to the air coming to my mouth in filtered bursts through the mask.

After donning the same gear, Owen slung a bag over his shoulder, and I double-checked that the video chip containing Tabitha and Violet's altercation—one of numerous copies Thomas had made, for strategic purposes—was in my pocket, protected by the plastic box he had put it in.

Amber moved past me, pushing open the narrow door that separated the command deck from the long, cavernous cargo bay. I followed her inside, past the small passenger door, toward the large rear door that dropped down to form a ramp—a useful feature designed for transporting vehicles.

She moved to a panel, sliding her own mask over her face, and then glanced back at us, clearly making sure we were both wearing ours. I gave her a thumbs-up, and she pulled a lever sticking out of the wall. There was a slight shake as the door cracked open, and then it lowered down smoothly as she worked the lever. I watched as the ramp dropped, frowning when all I could see was the night sky, followed by a never-ending black void.

I looked at Amber, wondering what she had planned, but she had her back to me. She squatted down, throwing open the lid of one of the benches that lined the walls of the cargo bay, and began pulling out a bundle of black nylon rope. As she shook it out, I realized it was a harness, not unlike ones used for rappelling or rock climbing.

She tossed one to Owen, who immediately put it on, sliding his foot through the leg holes and pulling them up over his pants. I watched for a moment, then turned back to Amber to find her standing in front of me, holding an identical harness out to me.

So… the base is below us? I asked via the subvocalizer, accepting the straps.

Amber arched an eyebrow and gave me an impish smirk, then reached out and hit a yellow button. There was a hum overhead, and I looked up to see the lines of rope running from the front to the rear of the heloship begin to move. Two lines descended from the winch, and Amber reached out to grab them.

Pretty much. We'll be going down the cliff face, she informed me as she bent over to hook up Owen's harness.

I cocked my head, looking at the harness in my hand. *Wouldn't it be easier to just land in The Green?*

Amber's fingers flew over Owen's harness as she tugged here and there to tighten it up, then ran the rope through several metal keys meant to tighten and prevent the climber from falling should part of the apparatus break.

The entrance to the base is actually in the cliff face, she replied as she worked. *It's faster to go down than to climb up the outside entrance.*

I took a step closer to the open space, looking down into the featureless darkness. I didn't share Violet's fear of heights, but I did have a healthy respect for them. Yet Amber's point was reasonable.

I began putting on the harness. Amber was there a moment later, helping me arrange the straps and tighten them. It was clear she had done this before, so I let her take over for me—this was something I definitely didn't want to screw up. In the span of several breaths, she had tightened the harness and laced the rope through the anchor points. She gave a few more experimental tugs on it, then nodded.

As she straightened, she gave us both a serious look. *All right, guys, here's the deal. I'm going to lower you down, because it'll just be simpler this way. Once you're in, I will rappel down behind you, and then we'll proceed into the base."*

Who will handle the winch on our ascent? I subvocalized.

Oh, I can do it remotely, Amber replied casually as she moved over toward the buttons controlling the winch. As she did so, Owen took a step forward and surrendered his weight to the harness, dropping a few inches out into space, his harness tightening and the rope jerking above him.

Then why not come with us? Maybe I was asking too many questions, but I wanted to make sure this mission plan was airtight.

Amber shook her head, pursing her lips through the mask. *As much as I love this heloship, I have no idea what weights these ropes were tested at, or how much they are able to hold. It's too much of a risk to go two on the rope. Especially with you strapping young men.* She smirked. *You've probably got a couple extra pounds of muscle.*

Try twenty-five pounds, I thought, careful not to project *that* one out loud. I walked to the ledge and peered down into the abyss. I tugged once at the rope, then eased out away from the heloship's floor, slipping my feet over the edge. I might as well get this over with quickly. My stomach gave a sickening lurch as the rope took my weight, and the harness jerked and tightened uncomfortably around my hips, but everything held.

Meanwhile, Owen grimaced, taking a new look at his rope. *So you're using us as guinea pigs?* he asked Amber.

Amber laughed, and then nodded. *If it makes you feel better, then* technically, *I used Violet's cousin and uncle first.*

It doesn't, but thanks for trying, Owen quipped, and I smiled. I looked down past my boots as I swung slightly back and forth, surprised by my lack of vertigo now that the initial drop was over. And, I noticed, the adrenaline spike in my muscles had left me feeling even more awake. I suddenly felt bad for Violet's fear of heights—she was obviously missing out on some fun.

Maybe we should change places, I said, looking at Amber with a wide smile.

She narrowed her eyes at me. *Why?*

Because I'm suddenly curious about what it's like to rappel down.

Amber laughed in response, and then waggled the fingers of one hand while her other one reached out and hit a yellow button. There was a sharp jerk in the rope, followed by the high-pitched sound of the winch activating again. I gave her a dirty look as we descended, but I was more amused than anything else by now.

The whine of the winch quickly faded as we were lowered. We dangled maybe fifteen or twenty feet from the cliff face. In spite of the moon being out, the rock face was bathed in shadow. I carefully pulled out my flashlight and clicked it on, my beam joined by Owen's.

My excitement at dangling over the edge and the adrenaline that it had initially created soon dissipated, and I quickly became bored as we dropped. The black and gray strata in the rock drifted slowly by, and I looked up, surprised to see the heloship wasn't that far ahead.

Any way we can speed this descent up? I transmitted through the subvocalizer.

I would rather not burn out the rotors in the winch, replied Amber. *But I'll ramp it up a little.*

Owen rolled his eyes at me. I shrugged.

The rope shuddered slightly under my hands, and the rock face began to move by more quickly. The sensation of falling increased, and I leaned into it, letting the fear and excitement drift over me and taking advantage of the adrenaline pumping through my veins. It was helping to focus my mind.

I felt myself starting to swing slowly around, turning away from the rock face. I stuck out a leg, trying to turn back toward the wall, but only managed to spin the other direction. I met Owen's gaze as my front turned toward him, and he gave me a sharp look. *What are you doing?* he subvocalized, clearly amused.

My reply was another shrug as I attempted to steady my spinning. *I'm not sure,* I replied dryly. *But you should try it— the view is spectacular.* I continued to spin around, picking up speed, as the more I tried to remain still, the faster I spun. After a moment, I sheepishly admitted defeat. *Can you... uh... help me out?*

He rolled his eyes and reached out to grab my shirt,

steadying me. *Thanks,* I transmitted in reply.

You gotta remain as still as possible, Owen replied, his focus on the darkness below. *When you start to shift your weight, that's when you start spinning.*

Ah. I paused, suddenly curious. *So, was this part of your Liberator training?*

Owen cast me a sidelong look. His transmission was cagier than I'd come to expect from him. *Not… really. Call it information learned through more questionable means. A product of a misspent youth.*

I absorbed that information in silence, keeping my flashlight pointed down. The sentence was ambiguous, but it seemed to say Owen's upbringing had been outside the legal system. Somehow, I couldn't picture it. Owen seemed too honest and genuine to really thrive in a criminal lifestyle. Then again, anything was possible. Maybe he had changed into the person he was now after the Matrians had taken his brother.

My flashlight cut across a break in the cliff face below us. *Is that it?* I asked Owen, pointing with the light.

He nodded and immediately relayed our discovery to Amber. *Great,* was all she said in reply. While our descent had seemed slow, with no context to judge our movement in the darkness, it was now clear we were approaching the gap quickly, and I began to move back and forth on the rope, swinging the way I'd just learned not to.

Almost too soon, the gap was there before me, and I planted a foot on the ledge, leaning forward to keep my balance. I got my other foot under me, and then turned to grab Owen, hauling him roughly onto the ledge with me. He unhooked my rope for me, and I helped him with his.

Owen relayed our success to Amber, and I turned, shining my light around. We were standing in the lightly humid air in the mouth of a cave. Not just any cave, but a wide one—my flashlight had a range of maybe thirty feet in the dark, and I couldn't detect any of the sides from where I stood.

Curious, I moved forward, keeping my flashlight pointed ahead. The rock was damp, but porous enough that it wasn't slippery. I moved forward maybe fifty feet, and then stopped when my light hit a wall. I swung it right, then left, pausing when the light cut across a massive airlock door.

My eyes widened, and I took a step forward, taking it in. It was similar in design to the one from the facility where the boys were kept. Still, the fact it had somehow been set up here was beyond odd. It was almost unbelievable. Suddenly, a lot of the hero worship the Liberators felt for Desmond started making sense. I could imagine how they must have felt—scared, alone, uncertain—only to be confronted with this mad feat of engineering and technology. How grand Desmond must have seemed. How connected she must have been to make this happen, miles and miles from anything resembling civilization.

But Desmond had an alliance with the Matrian elite. Maybe this base wasn't just made of sheer moving power on Desmond's part. How much help had she gotten from her benefactors? Did they know it was here? Could they guess we would come?

A glitter above the door caught my attention. I pointed the flashlight upward and encountered the metallic, predatory glare of a security camera. I'd known we would be watched, but it still unsettled me to see it. Unease prickling my back, I swept the beam of light elsewhere, trying to find more cameras, to see if there could be a blind spot… My light hit the edge of another one aimed near the door, cut down at a sharp angle, and I took a step back, just in case. I found another two cameras pointing right, their angles revealing a hard-to-spot path leading off onto a large piece of rock that seemed to stretch out slightly beyond the cliff, slanting into open space. I assumed it took a turn at some point, to make it navigable going down—this must have been the way people usually climbed up to the base.

Guys, I began, *we've got cameras. How long do you think—*

An excited shriek interrupted my report, and I turned back toward the ledge at the cave mouth. I could see the light from Owen's flashlight pointed out from the ledge, and caught the fine movements of the rope. Amber whooped again in excitement, the subvocalizers perfectly recreating her exuberance right in my ears as she rappelled down the cliff above us.

Really? I growled through the device, and her voice turned bashful—but not quite repentant.

Oops! Sorry!

I could see Owen smiling through his mask, and I moved over to him, ready to help him pull her onto the ledge. But it was apparent neither of our efforts were needed as Amber kicked off the rock a final time, swinging out and away in a graceful arc before doing something with the rope that arrested her fall. She glided into the mouth of the cave, landing five feet from the edge, both her feet planted firmly.

All right, I'm jealous, I said as I helped Owen slip the rope from her, and she grinned wildly through the mask. Owen grabbed the lines and held them out over the cliff face; Amber keyed something into a little blinking control pad that tucked neatly into a pocket of her jacket, and the lines jerked and began slowly winding back upward.

The cave remained silent but for the scuffling sounds made by the three of us, the regard of the cameras weighing heavily on me. It was almost worse knowing the Liberators had probably seen us—and still hadn't done anything. What could they be planning?

No welcoming committee? I commented, trying to keep my tone light, as we moved toward the airlock.

Owen and Amber looked at each other and shook their heads. *I'm sure they've seen us by now,* Owen said, *but we're not trying for stealth. We've gotta show them we have nothing to hide.*

Admirable, I said, swallowing. *As long as they don't choose to shoot first and ask questions later.*

We were at the airlock. This would be the moment of truth—from here on out, we were going to be completely surrendering ourselves into the hands of the still-hostile Liberators. In the airlock, they had full control over whether we lived or died. It was either a brilliant persuasive move, or suicide. I took a deep breath, ready to find out which, just to get it over with.

I pressed down the handle and pulled the massive door open wide enough for all of us to step into. Owen helped me pull it closed, while Amber moved over to the opposite side, heading for the glowing red button that would activate the chamber's detoxifying technology. She waited while we closed the door—when I heard it catch with a slight sucking sound, I gave her a thumbs-up. She hit the button.

Red lights started flashing on the doors, and I felt the

pressure in the room change as the toxic air was filtered out. I looked at a glowing green sign on the wall with a digital countdown on it, watching the time running down. The numbers dropped from forty-five to thirty. They were quickly approaching fifteen when a loud klaxon alarm sounded, and the numbers froze.

I looked sharply at Amber and Owen, who returned equally sharp looks from under their masks. Go time.

Subvocalizers off, Amber transmitted to us, her voice lacking its usual sauciness. *We'll be needing our voices to negotiate.* Owen and I clicked off the devices just as the alarm abruptly cut off.

A sharp rapping sound came through from the inner airlock door, and I turned toward it, peering at the small round pane of glass in the door. There was a puff of static, followed by a sharp whine, as audio piped through from a hidden communication device.

"Put down your weapons," a female voice demanded. "Or we'll let you rot in there."

CHAPTER 10

Viggo

My hand was already reaching for my gun when a face appeared behind the thick glass of the window—a woman with dark skin and deep brown eyes who looked vaguely familiar. I exhaled and stopped myself just short of pulling the gun. It wasn't Desmond. Still, I couldn't recall who the woman was.

I turned to Owen for information, and his voice was low enough to reach only my ears: "Meera." My brows drew down in confusion; there was an odd disconnect between my associations with the name and what confronted me now. When I had met Meera, she had been the cook at the facility. I hadn't really gotten to know her—in fact, I had only met her once. The rest of the time I had been either in the hospital area, training the boys, or holed up in my room, most of my meals brought to me by Violet while I worked on their lessons.

I turned back to the door, curious as to why *she* was the one who had answered, and saw that Meera was glaring at Amber, her eyes full of malice.

"You have a lot of nerve showing up here," her voice spat through the speakers, and I blinked at its vehemence.

Amber pressed her face close to the window. "Meera, please. You know us! You know we aren't traitors. Desmond is lying to you!"

"*You're* the liar," Meera retorted, her face becoming more livid, even through the wavy glass. "You betrayed us!"

"Never," Amber said more softly, her hand coming up to the window. "I would never betray you, Meera. You're my friend. I care about you. I've… I've *missed* you. It's why we're here—we have proof that Desmond has been lying to you. If you just give us a chance…"

Meera's drawn face did not lose any of its suspicion. But even in her voice, I could sense more than anger—a deep weariness, undercut by pain. "To what? Come in here and kill us all? Try to find Desmond so you can kill her? Go back, Amber, or I will shoot you. I will shoot all of you."

I turned to Owen, keeping my voice low so the woman behind the glass wouldn't hear. "What else do we know about Meera? What else can we use to get her to give us a chance?"

Owen's eyes moved back and forth. Then he gave me a strangely reticent look, and said, "Solomon is her son."

That was all I needed.

Like a gunshot, I was off, striding for the door. I gently pushed Amber out of the way and pressed my face to the window. "We have your son," I told her.

Meera's eyes grew wide, then narrowed. "You're lying," she hissed.

"No, I'm not. He was being kept with Thomas in Patrus, right? Let me ask you... did Desmond tell you Thomas defected?"

The woman opened her mouth and then hesitated, and I smiled. "It's not a hard question. I figure she had to, in order to justify changes in your security for your handhelds, right? What did she tell you, Meera, about Solomon?"

Meera's lips quivered slightly, and then she pressed them together in a thin line. It was enough to make me guess Desmond had told her that he was dead—no doubt that Thomas had killed Solomon as he was escaping, or something of the sort.

"He's alive," I told her. "Violet begged Thomas to get him out. She didn't forget your son and the sacrifice he made for her. He's still in the same condition, but he's alive, and as healthy as can be expected."

Meera took several deep breaths and then looked over my shoulder at Owen, apprehension battling the suspicion on her face. "Is it true?" she asked, her voice thick.

Owen gave her a gentle nod. Meera stepped away from the glass and disappeared from view. My heart pounded in my chest, and I wondered if I hadn't just made a mistake mentioning Solomon. What if Meera was like Desmond—willing to sacrifice her son for what she considered the greater good?

A few moments later, Meera was back. The area under her eyes was puffy and the sclera around her irises were bloodshot. I realized she had stepped away to cry. Thank God, Meera wasn't like Desmond. She was a mother who genuinely worried about

her son. Finding out he was alive after being told he had died…
I couldn't imagine what she was going through at this moment.

Still, she bore it well. Her face had returned to a hard mask,
but the viciousness had softened considerably. "What do you
want?" she asked.

"Before I can tell you, answer this question for me. Is
Desmond at this base right now?"

Meera hesitated, then shook her head. She looked guilty,
but seemed to push it aside.

"Good," I told her. "You asked what we wanted, and all
we're asking for is this: twenty minutes alone with you and your
leadership, with a promise that you'll watch this video first." I
held the case with the chip up to the window for her to see.

"What kind of video?" she asked, revealing nothing.

I paused, not entirely sure how to answer her question. I
turned to Owen for help, and he took a step forward, one hand
up. "It's better if you watch it first, and then ask questions," he
told her. "Just… please, trust me. The last thing I want to do is
hurt you, or anyone inside. We all feel that way."

Meera licked her lips and then nodded. "Fine. Here are
the terms: unload your weapons and put them on the ground.
You'll watch the video with us, and we will have guns trained on
you the entire time. If we're not satisfied…"

"We'll cross that bridge when we come to it," I cut in. I
pulled out my gun, taking a few steps away from the door, then
ejecting the clip and clearing the chamber. I set the gun and clip
on the floor. I could hear Amber and Owen doing the same, but
I didn't take my eyes off Meera. I also didn't relinquish the knife
tucked into my boot. She didn't need to know about that.

A few minutes later, we were inside the brightly lit, timeless rock-cut halls of the Liberator base. After the dimness outside, it felt like the time had changed abruptly, as though here it was always midday operational.

We were led to a room with a long table, filled with Liberators—almost all of them women. Several of them patted us down and quickly confiscated my knife, much to my chagrin, but Meera was willing to overlook my interpretation of her terms. Looking at her hard face, I suspected she knew she would have attempted the same in my position. I looked around the room, studying the people there. I knew some faces, but most I didn't recognize. They stared expectantly at a wall of massive screens stacked on top of each other. The air in the room was decidedly hostile. Amber, Owen, and I each had not one, but two guards pointing the promised guns at our backs. I kept my head up and stared straight ahead, not meeting any of their gazes, but feeling the sights trained on my vitals almost physically.

It was clear something had shifted in their power structure. Meera was clearly in charge, but the reason for the change was not yet apparent to me. Maybe it had something to do with the sudden move from the Facility Amber had mentioned— if they'd truly had to evacuate, that could've shaken the command chain up significantly—and I guessed it was also making them even more suspicious than usual. With the mention of Solomon, I'd found a crack in their defenses, but that had been lucky. It had bought us a temporary respite from uncompromising hostility, but there was no guarantee that would continue once they watched the video. I hoped Amber and Owen weren't putting *all* their faith in it. I hoped they, like me, were looping scenarios through their heads, planning what to do if this business went south.

Meera moved to the screens and briskly popped the video chip into the reader. A loading screen showed on the wall of monitors, and then the video started playing.

It was my second time watching the video, and that didn't make it any better. In fact, it was somehow worse now because I knew what was coming. I felt my hands clench into fists as Violet stepped from the garden and onto the stone platform with a fountain. Her voice carried through, loud and strong. Tabitha's voice was not as strong, due to the distance, but you could still make out her response.

I watched them exchange words, and nodded to myself, once again admiring Violet's bravery in manipulating the situation to get the women and children of her family out of there. But as the seconds ticked by, my unease returned. When the first explosion caused the view of the camera to shudder and shake, I felt my gut tense, knowing the camera had been on Violet's person at the time, that it was *her* bearing the brunt of being thrown to the ground.

The video continued, tracking Violet's path as she fought with Tabitha before the second explosion went off. When Tabitha started talking about cracking the code for enhancing humans, I noticed several of the Liberators lean forward, probably becoming aware of the implications in that statement—namely, that Elena and Tabitha had access to Mr. Jenks' complete research, something even Queen Rina hadn't been given full access to.

But the real kicker came later, on the staircase, when Violet mentioned the boys. There was no mistaking the deadly intent behind Tabitha's reply, and the room echoed with several audible gasps. I saw people raising their hands up to their mouths, as if covering up their shock would make the betrayal sting less.

We were getting close to the end of the video, and suddenly, the room felt incredibly small. I wasn't sure I had the strength to watch it again. In fact, I knew I didn't—I couldn't watch as Tabitha smashed Violet's face in, or as she propped her into a standing position so she could give her a so-called "honorable death". Or listen as Violet laughed manically as she clicked the button, detonating the bomb on the fake egg. I looked from side to side; the two young women guarding me both stared, riveted, at the images on the screen. I nodded mildly at each of them and slipped toward the door.

I didn't look back to see whether my guards were following me; the fact that there were no gunshots was enough. In the hall, I let out a shuddering breath, and then sucked air into my lungs. I moved over to the wall and pressed my hot forehead against the cool stone, trying to calm my boiling blood. Rage flowed thick and hot through my veins, but without a target, it was just burning me up.

I felt my hand curl into a fist again and closed my eyes, trying to resist the urge to use it on the wall. I knew it wouldn't help. And with so many of us injured, it was not a good time to risk breaking my knuckles just because watching Violet being hurt like that made me want to kill something.

I fought for calm, trying to slow my breathing and practicing mental exercises to distract me from the feeling. I was halfway through one involving the alphabet when I felt a hand on my shoulder. I jerked away abruptly, and saw Owen—and then became aware of the four women who stood in the corridor with us. Obviously both my guards and Owen's had followed us. They were watching our every move. But maybe that was a good thing. Maybe it would make them see us for the tired, scared human beings we were.

"What's up?" I asked Owen.

"Video's done," he reported. "Amber is giving her report about Tabitha and... and Quinn. She, uh... she took some pictures so they could see." His face looked younger than usual as his horror at his friend's treatment shone through. I wondered again if our guards thought us cowards—or friends.

I shuddered, thinking of the endless number of stitches Quinn had received in the past twenty-four hours. Tabitha had torn the poor young man apart in front of Amber's eyes. Amber had a lot of grit taking those pictures as evidence, but I was glad she had. Pictures spoke louder than words, and the story these told was just another reason for the Liberators to accept our testimony as fact.

Just then, Amber stuck her head out the door and gave us a look. Her face was uncharacteristically grim, but she didn't look defeated, just emotionally drained.

"They're ready for you," she told me.

I took another deep breath and steeled myself. As I entered the room, my guards following silently at my heels, I expected to still feel the burgeoning hostility that had characterized the room earlier. I expected there would be a lot of pushback.

I didn't expect the mingled expressions of curiosity,

grudging respect, and vulnerability on the faces of the people in the room. Whispers shuttled around between them, dozens of low-volume conferences with heads together and eyes darting to us, to the screen, and back again. The Liberators in the room had the grim look of people who had just realized the string of tragic events that had been occurring the past week was indirectly their fault, and that some of them had even been duped into aiding the Matrian takeover. I could also see a growing anger in them, one I guessed would smolder for a while before erupting in a white-hot rage.

I didn't know how this was going to go down. This was far scarier than some more dangerous missions I'd been on, but as I stood at the end of the table, I allowed myself a brief moment of hope. With a group of people like this, looking at me with those naked emotions, I could accomplish something. In fact, they looked like they were actually ready to hear me.

I let out a breath and started to talk.

"Look, I understand this is all coming as a shock to you. I'm certain, like Amber and Owen, you were all recruited personally by Desmond. She's been a source of hope, and empowerment, to you all. I'm guessing you don't know what to make of this, or what you can even do about it. But here's the thing… Just because Desmond has been lying to you, it doesn't change the fact that there are some pretty major fundamental flaws in our nations. Both of them. Our governments have either been indifferent, or robbed us all of something precious. They have used their agents to filter out any of you who would protest, and then used you to work to their own goals."

Several people nodded as I spoke, and I heard the murmured

conversations growing more animated.

"You can't change what has happened to you," I went on, "but you can choose how to handle it now. We"—I used my hand to indicate Owen, Amber, and myself—"have chosen to fight. Not for ourselves, and not for our survival, but rather for the people who are caught in the middle. People like your families, your sons, your brothers.

"But I have to tell you, the odds are against us. They have been from the start. Elena and Desmond have spent years putting this in motion, consolidating resources and personnel. But you and the rest of the Liberators have things we need. You have people who have been training to fight for years, but most of all, the spirit to make a difference. We need that—our soldiers are refugees who have barely held a gun, let alone thought of using one, before now. But they share the same feelings you have. They're also fed up with our governments. They also have taken it upon themselves to make a change in the world around them. You and they have a lot in common. There's a lot you could teach them, if you wanted."

Silence reigned for several heartbeats, and I looked around the table at each person here, trying to gain some evidence, some inkling of proof that I was getting through to them.

A woman with a short brown pixie cut leaned forward, resting her hands on the table, her green eyes studying me. "That's a very pretty speech, Mr. Croft, but frankly, why should we even bother to get involved? It seems more like a death wish than anything else."

"Erin!" Meera gasped, her brows drawing together. "How can you say that? Your son is out there."

Erin speared Meera with a reproachful look, shaking her head. "I will never give up on my son," she said. "Malcolm is my world. But if you think for one minute that means I'll blindly agree to consign the rest of our people to a war against Desmond, you are mistaken."

"Erin has a point," announced Lynne, one of the few Liberators I knew by name, from across the table. I glanced at her, and she gave me an apologetic shrug. I guessed her flirting days were done, though I didn't consider that a loss when she'd never stood a chance against Violet. I wondered if she'd gotten in trouble for the stunt we'd pulled borrowing the harness to spy on Desmond in the Facility, but pushed the thought aside.

"We would be going up against trained wardens, controlled by Desmond," Lynne continued. "She knows where our base is, and she'll notice if something is up."

"Exactly. Our position here, in The Green, was given to us by her. We would have to move everything to enter a battlefield that, frankly, we have little reason to be involved with in the first place." Erin shook her head, her lips a thin, flat line. "No, I'm sorry, but we need a better reason than that."

"So you're saying you'd rather stick with Desmond?" I asked, my heart sinking.

The look Erin gave me was shrewd. "Not even remotely. But going to war isn't a solution to our problem. Finding our boys is."

"We'd have a better chance finding them with Mr. Croft," said a woman I didn't recognize. Her hair was blond and braided around the top of her head in a long, thick rope. "My brother was taken twelve years ago, and, from what I've been able to piece together, Mr. Croft and his team have done more to try and help our boys in the past three months than I have been able to do for all that time. I remember his training program for the boys… back in the Facility… I finally thought we were going to get them back…" Her voice trailed off in emotion, and the woman next to her patted her on the shoulder, while around the room I could hear noises of acknowledgement. And anger.

Thomas had been right—these people had recently lost their boys again. Finally, the blond woman continued, "That was the first time I saw some progress with our boys. And I think that, while our goals aren't exactly identical to Mr. Croft's, they do run along similar lines. Mr. Croft's fight extends to all citizens, while we are only invested in our families. Perhaps we need to re-examine that."

Erin gave the other woman a considering look and then sighed, shaking her head.

I couldn't help but jump in at that point, circling back to what she'd first said. "So the Matrians… they really have control of the boys again?" I didn't bother to hide the frustration that coursed through me at the thought. It sounded like a nightmare. I knew everyone in the room was on the same page about that.

Grimacing, Erin looked at Lynne, who met my gaze and sighed, the expression on her face mirroring what I guessed my own must be. "Shortly after Desmond threw you and everyone out of the airlock, we had to exercise an emergency evacuation." She spat the words out distastefully. "Desmond radioed to tell us she'd just found out the Matrian wardens were closing in. There was no time to free all the boys, so… she ordered us to leave them behind, promising that if we had found them once, we would find them again."

"*I* argued against it," retorted Meera, folding her arms across her chest. "*I* wanted to stay and fight for them. We all did, but Desmond... she was just as reasonable and practical as ever, telling us we needed to maintain our Liberator anonymity. She told us we would get caught if we tried to move the boys and care for them in the evacuation—that even their absence would be noted." She met my gaze and shook her head. "It all makes so much sense now. We played right into her hands, didn't we?" Her voice was bitter, seething.

I wasn't going repeat a fact she already knew and hated. "Do you think they are still at the Facility?" I asked instead.

"Perhaps," responded Lynne, leaning back in her chair. "But to be honest, it's unlikely. If she had time to clear them out, she would've... And destroyed the facility for good measure, no doubt. Just in case any of us were tempted to go back in a desperate attempt to see our boys."

"That's Desmond for you," Amber chimed in, dropping into an unoccupied chair. "When she carries out a plan, she follows it through." She paused and squared her shoulders. "Look, when Violet and Viggo first told me about what was happening, I was honestly like 'so what?' To me, as a Patrian-born female, the only thing I could think of was that this war hadn't come soon enough. Most of you know my story... You know what my father did. I had every reason to hate him and any other Patrian male. But, after everything, after working with Viggo and Violet, I realized not everyone is like that. They genuinely care, and what's more, they taught me working together makes us stronger than being apart. I urge you to consider this proposal. They care about the boys too, and it's one of our highest priorities to get them free."

"Those goals are intertwined," Owen added, taking a step toward the conference table. "Getting them free will help us stop this war—and on the other hand, stopping this war will help us keep the boys from being used as human weapons. It helps, either way. So working with us might be the best way forward. We can help each other in more ways as well. Once we push the Matrians out of Patrus, we can focus our goals exclusively on Desmond, and by extension, Elena. She's the real monster here—she's the one who wants to use the boys, boys like my brother, like soldiers in her army. We are going to need all the help we can get in taking them down."

"You know, we *are* in a unique position to cause some harm," said Meera thoughtfully, giving Erin a cautious look. "We could spy on Desmond for them. Use the information we receive from her to help them coordinate plans of attack. Anyone who doesn't want to go out and actively join the war effort could still—" She paused, letting the venom of her words sink in. "—get some *payback*... Start up some lies of our own."

Erin squinted at Meera, considering her, and then gave a small, almost imperceptible nod. "That might be something," she said after a beat. "It would certainly make *me* feel better, after she took our boys away from us, right out from under our noses." She turned to me and arched an eyebrow. "What exactly do you want from us? What would you need, were we to consider doing this?"

"Dr. Tierney," I replied automatically. "For Quinn, Henrik,

and Violet… and anybody else who gets hurt out in the field, which seems more and more likely. She can also help us take care of Solomon," I said, directing the point at Meera. "Medical equipment, and a few operatives to help with training and general operations until we can get our own people trained up. Also, any information you can get on Desmond would be incredibly helpful."

"Well, to be honest, Desmond has been less than forthcoming with us recently," said Lynne. "But there are a few people she's set to tap at any time. If we can get them on board, we might be able to figure out what she's up to. But their safety comes first. If she wants them to plant a bomb somewhere, we have to let them plant the bomb. She can't have any hint that we are working against her. None."

I nodded. "I understand. But… is that a yes?"

The others at the table looked around at each other for a moment, and then Meera nodded. "You have our support, Mr. Croft. But let's be clear. We're getting something out of this deal, too. We want any and all information on the boys, as you encounter it. That is non-negotiable. They become top priority when you find them. Is that clear?"

"Yes, ma'am," I said solemnly, nodding my head.

"Then we have a deal."

CHAPTER 11

Viggo

The darkness that had served as our cloak was beginning to fade into early-morning shadow as Amber lowered the heloship into the clearing. I stared at the lightening sky, having spent the flight home in a kind of triumphant, half-awake daze. Beside me, Dr. Elizabeth Tierney clutched the harness securing her to her chair, her brow furrowed, sweat shimmering on her temples. I could understand somebody being nervous about flying, but it seemed Dr. Tierney was beyond nervous—she was practically allergic to it. We'd barely gotten off the ground when she had begun shaking her head, cinching down the safety harness nobody else had ever used.

As soon as we touched down in the clearing some way off from our base, I was moving. The faster I went, the longer I could avoid my exhaustion. I helped Dr. Tierney to her feet and led her to the cargo bay. She gave me a grateful look as I guided her, some of the color coming back into her cheeks and face. The six women and two men who had accompanied us back were getting to their feet and stretching as we entered. Immediately, as though she hadn't been shivering and taking deep, calming breaths in the heloship half an hour ago, Dr. Tierney was *on*.

"Adam, come over here and grab this box," she instructed. "I don't want any of this equipment broken, all right? And Lynne, can you *please* make sure you get all the bags in this round? I do not want to have to set foot on this infernal contraption ever again, if I can avoid it."

I suppressed a smile as she continued to bark orders to the Liberators, unflappable even in the face of her own nerves. My eyes focused on Lynne for a moment—the leggy brunette with moss-green eyes. She moved with an efficacy that made it seem like that moment was dead and gone, to my relief. My gaze returned to where Dr. Tierney was standing just in front of me, partially blocking my path to the bay doors. I moved to step around her, but she whirled around and placed a hand on my chest. I could feel her eyes examining me closely, taking me in as if she hadn't really seen me before, and sensed displeasure radiating from her.

"Mr. Croft, has anyone told you that you look like death warmed over?" she asked, her tone telling me she was informing me more than asking. I blinked, trying to decide whether I should be offended or not. She smiled, as if sensing my discomfort. "I only say this because, as one of my former patients, I feel a certain responsibility for you—if only to make sure my work is not tampered with."

I narrowed my eyes at her and frowned. "It's been a long

couple of days," I said, unsure what she was getting at, and exhausted enough that I didn't even want to have to deal with a nonessential conversation right now. "And there's still too much to do. What would you suggest?"

She raised an eyebrow and gave me a hard look. "Your bed, Mr. Croft. I suggest you find it before you keel over. Or before I slip a sleeping pill into your next beverage."

A startled chuckle dropped from my mouth. I couldn't help it. The woman barely came up to my chin, and looked about as dangerous as a newborn pup, but here she was trying to put me to bed like an unruly child. I appreciated her concern, though. Truthfully, climbing into bed with Violet was all I had been thinking about in every free moment since before we'd left tonight—or, rather, last night. As soon I saw that the doctor was examining Violet and got Ms. Dale up to speed, it was going to be lights out for me.

"I'll do that, Doc," I said earnestly to Dr. Tierney, and she gave me an approving nod before turning back to continue barking orders at her group. Stepping around her, I moved toward the rear of the cargo bay, where Owen was lowering the ramp. He looked almost as tired as I felt, and that was saying something.

"We did good," he said, and I held back a laugh. He *was* tired if all he could come up with was that generic platitude. Still, I couldn't fault him—I didn't feel like I was capable of much in the way of conversation either.

To be honest, I couldn't think of anything to say other than, "Yup. I'm glad Amber talked us into going."

He grunted in response. The ramp lowered and I was

immediately greeted with the visage of Ms. Dale, standing at the bottom with her arms crossed and an irritated expression on her face. I gave Owen a knowing look before heading down the ramp. I was certain he did not envy me the task of finding out what was wrong this time.

"Hey," I said, unable to muster more enthusiasm. "What's up?"

"What's up?" she replied archly, an edge in her voice. "Mr. Croft, maybe you could explain to me why your latest transmission was only 'coming home'? Frankly, it was a bit alarming in its vagueness."

I stifled a smile. "I'm sorry," I offered.

Her gaze narrowed in suspicion. "Why do I detect a 'but'?"

Rolling my eyes, I scrubbed my face with my hand, grimacing at the rough feel of stubble turned beard. "*But,* we couldn't risk the message being intercepted. I didn't want to reveal too much, just in case Desmond has scrounged up another computer whiz like Thomas to hack into our communication channels. Besides, allying with the Liberators gives us a unique advantage."

She gave me a considering look, and then nodded. "I'd figured as much," she said, her irritation dissolving. "Still, ambiguous messages are a risky business. I had no idea what had happened to you—for all I knew, you'd been taken and were leading them back here."

I looked over her head at two cars that had struggled through the underbrush to meet us at the heloship's location, both of which had armed refugees inside, and then back to her. That explained the welcome party; she must have been preparing for a fight. Ms. Dale shrugged in noncommittal fashion at my look, but her gaze soon turned speculative again. "So, why all the need for secrecy?" she asked.

I grinned at her, allowing pride to get the better of me for a moment. What we had been able to accomplish with the Liberators had been well above our expectations. I was still reeling from how quickly everything had shifted. Hours ago, I had been frustrated by so much, angered and worried for Violet, and exhausted. Now, I was still most of those things, but had managed to paint a much-needed silver lining onto those dark, overwhelming storm clouds.

Opening my mouth, I began to explain all the details of the plot—only to stop as Ms. Dale's eyes went wide in surprise. "You got them to agree to spy on Desmond, didn't you?" she exclaimed.

"Yes," I said with a smile. "It's why I kept the message short. I was going to tell you—but you just *had* to ruin the surprise."

She laughed and patted me on the shoulder. "Sorry, Viggo. I just started thinking about it, and it was the only thing that made sense."

"Well, don't get too excited." I grimaced, shifting my weight from one foot to another, explaining what the women had told me during our meeting. Desmond had been away on mysterious missions, as she often had been in the past, but she'd checked in often enough, dropping hints and plans, that it seemed pretty normal. And they'd been so worked up over their haphazard, last-minute transition from the Facility in The Green back to their base that they hadn't been paying too much attention to her comings and goings. She had always been a very independent leader.

"Well, that isn't surprising," Ms. Dale said thoughtful-ly. "She's got too many pokers in the fire at this point. The Liberators are isolated enough that it makes sense she would put them on the back burner."

I nodded, having come to the same conclusion during my meeting with their leaders. "Well, at least it's something. Meera is really fired up about going after Desmond, but we convinced her to stand down for the time being. Still, I don't know how long we can keep them from going after her themselves."

Ms. Dale frowned, her expression drifting away as she thought about it. Then she shook her head. "We'll have to wor-ry about that later."

"Yup."

One of the Liberator men came up to Ms. Dale and began talking to her about the amount of equipment and the room in the vehicles, and I took it as my cue to leave—I could walk back to the house and leave the cars to take the bulk of our equipment. After all, Dr. Tierney had practically ordered me to bed… I began moving toward the cars, ready to get back to the house and check on Violet. As I approached the lead vehicle, I started to slow, then came to a stop when I saw a man wearing handcuffs in the passenger seat. "Uh… Ms. Dale?"

I turned back and caught her eye. She murmured some quick orders to the man and then jogged over. "What?"

"Why?" I asked, pointing at the man in the car.

"Why the restraints?"

I nodded, and she gave an exasperated huff and crossed her arms. "That's something I needed to talk to you about. That's

Cad—Violet's cousin. One of the men caught him sneaking back onto base a few hours ago."

"*Onto* the base?"

She nodded, her ponytail bobbing. "Yup. I wasn't entirely sure what to do with him."

"Didn't Amber bring him and his family back in the helo-ship? After she picked up the women on the side of the road?" I wasn't completely familiar with this part of the story, having been frantically driving around in search of a safe place to treat Violet at the time—I'd just been filled in on the big parts.

"She did. Violet's uncle and aunt didn't want to be part of the war effort, so I sent them to the place I am holding King Maxen. They're not allowed to leave, but I don't think they will, since Cad and his wife decided to stay in our camp with their children."

I frowned. "Violet's aunt and uncle left without stopping by to see if their niece was okay?"

"Yup." Ms. Dale's voice had a sharp note to it, and I couldn't blame her. It was pretty rotten that they would up and leave like that, with no consideration for the woman who was family to them—and was right now half broken because she had risked her life to save theirs. We shared a moment of distaste, and then Ms. Dale continued, "Anyway, I had Cad cuffed and detained in that car so we could keep an eye on him before you got back. I wanted to see what you wanted to do."

"But why did he sneak off?"

"I don't know. He wouldn't say."

I growled in irritation and then marched toward the car. Cad's head was tilted toward his hands, and he didn't seem to notice my approach until I threw open the door. He jumped in surprise, his eyes bulging.

"Why did you sneak off base?" I demanded.

Cad shook his head a bit, blinking. Then he opened his mouth and slammed it shut with a click of his teeth, his expression mutinous. He'd probably been asleep in his cuffs.

Exhaustion made me impatient. "Now is not the time, Cad," I said, my voice low and guttural. "I've had a long couple of days, and if you don't talk, I'm going to have to assume you're a spy, working for the enemy."

That broke him out of his silence. "I'm not a spy!" Cad shot back, his face flushing red. "I was out there looking for someone."

That had *not* been one of the things I'd expected him to say. The surprise of the realization helped reduce my boiling temper to a simmer. "Who?"

He gave me a long, hard look before sighing. "I was looking for my cousin."

"Violet? She's in the—"

"*Not* Violet. Tim. I heard… I heard some people say he was missing after the stuff at the palace. I put some pieces together and realized he had stayed behind. And since Violet is down for the count right now, I had to do something. So, a little before sunset, I took one of the cars and went back to the palace to look for him." His reticence was gone, his expression raw, both defiant and guilty.

I absorbed this knowledge and turned to look at Ms. Dale, whose irritation had disappeared under the carefully crafted neutral expression she'd always worn when I'd first met her.

A part of me wanted to yell at Cad. He had put us all in jeopardy with that stunt. If he had been caught, he could've given away our location. On the other hand, he had done what I hadn't been able to yet, and I found myself respecting that. He had gone back to the palace to look for his cousin, in spite of the danger. I rocked back on my heels, idly wondering if suicidal bravery ran in the family, and then realized that it also ran in me, so…

I exhaled and nodded at Ms. Dale. "Let him out of the cuffs," I said softly. She nodded, and Cad offered up his hands as she moved toward him, searching in her pockets, presumably for the keys.

"Did you find him?" I asked Cad.

He shook his head, his face full of regret. "No. There was no one there at all."

"You must have seen something," I insisted. Maybe we could use this impromptu trip for intelligence. "Was there anything odd or out of place?"

Cad frowned, his gaze becoming unfocused. "When I said there was no one there at all, there was *actually* no one. I mean, there's got to be important documents or files there, right? Equipment? People cleaning up the… the mess? But there weren't any crews sifting through the rubble. There were no bodies, either, but… It's only been like… what… thirty-six hours since the palace was running just like normal? Maybe forty? Where is everyone?"

I considered his observations. Definitely odd. I wasn't sure yet whether it was worrisome, but it was something we could process after I got some sleep. The thing pressing down heavier on me was that he hadn't found Tim. As much as I wished Cad hadn't gone on an illicit raid, I wished more he had something to show for it, something that could make the wild light in Violet's eyes when she asked about her brother disappear forever.

"Listen," I told Cad. "I get that you want to help. I do. But next time, you need to clear it with Ms. Dale or myself. It was a big risk going out there, and if you had gotten caught, it would've put everyone at the camp in a lot of danger. Right now, this place and these people are all we have."

He flinched, but nodded. "All right," he conceded, but his eyes were still hard. "As long as you promise you aren't going to stop looking for him."

"I won't," I vowed solemnly. I had already made that promise to myself; this was just speaking it out loud.

Cad nodded. "Good. I also would like to see Violet. With all the moving and setting up camp, I haven't gotten a chance to see her. I tried before I left, but Dr. Arlan told me she was sleeping." His voice turned sharp, almost pleading. "I just want to make sure she's okay."

I grimaced and nodded. "She's not… but hopefully with the equipment and the doctor we just brought back, she will be."

"I still want to see her."

I ran a hand through my hair and nodded again. "All right. Let's go."

CHAPTER 12

Violet

Something bright burned into my eyes, and I groaned at the discomfort. I tried closing my eyes against it, but something was holding them open, forcing me to look into the blinding light. Searing pain exploded in my brain, throbbing along the inside of my skull until I felt the heat rushing into my face. I was on fire. I was going to burn to death.

I jerked violently away, and the movement was agony. I cried out in pain and my breath stalled. "Fire," I coughed, trying to catch air in my lungs. *It must be the smoke*, I thought. Red dots flashed across my vision, obscuring bits and pieces of the room I lay in. My peripheral vision showed things clearly, but anything I stared directly at was blurred and unrecognizable.

Fire? Who had started it? I gasped and tried desperately to figure out what was happening. A bomb—it was a bomb. Had I been thrown somewhere from the force of the blast? Where was Lee? I had to get the egg—after that I could see my brother.

Shakily, I pushed against the surface I lay on, trying to get up, my panic-stricken mind recognizing one thing: someone was trying to hurt me. But even that motion made me shake violently. I stopped in a sitting position, sweat breaking out on my forehead. I tilted my head up and became aware of heavy footsteps on the wood near me. I tried to swing my head toward the sound, but as soon as I did, the room blurred around me, my head throbbed, and my stomach swooped, almost enough to force me onto my back again. I breathed heavily, coughing, and the footsteps came closer. I couldn't go back to the bad people. I had to figure out a plan.

My heart thudded hard against my ribcage, too loud in my ears, and I shuddered when hands came down gently on my back, and a soft voice spoke behind me, fading in and out like a bad handheld connection. The tone of the words was soft and coaxing, but that was even more alarming. They must be trying to trick me. I tried again to turn my head to look at them, but it *already* felt like my head was turning… I stared at the image of my hands before me, swimming in fabric that covered my legs, as the hands continued trying to shush me. Sheets. I was in bed. Then the hands gripped my shoulders, pushing, and the mattress rushed back to meet my back as my muscles failed to move me, failed to do anything at all.

God. I was helpless.

I was on my back again, all my most vital parts completely vulnerable to attack, as an unrecognizable figure leaned down over me and made words. I blinked again and again, trying to clear my vision, straining to focus my eyes in the stabbing light.

But when the image in front of me finally managed to solidify, horror flooded my body. It wasn't just a stranger, a guard, a warden—it was Elena, her mouth lifted in a sweet smile while her eyes promised pain. Panic lent strength to my muscles, and I scrambled back as the Queen of Matrus looked down at me.

The pain that lanced through my body at the motion was nothing compared to what would happen if I didn't, if I couldn't get away… But I was moving horribly slowly, my body jerking and weak, like in a nightmare. Elena didn't move forward immediately, but stared down, her hands held out in front of her as if to help me. She murmured something, reaching out, and I screamed and knocked her hand away with the heavy cast on my right hand, causing her to back up slightly.

"I killed your sister," I taunted, my breath heaving.

Elena was on the right side of the bed, while I'd managed to move almost to the edge. I would fall off it if I had to. Maybe crawl underneath… I could hear her. She frowned, speaking in a gentle, even voice. "Let me help you," she said.

I shook my head and began to scoot backwards again, crying out for Viggo, but I couldn't move fast enough, couldn't push through the pain… I was as weak as a newborn kitten, and Elena knew it. Her hands came back, and, effortlessly, she began to pull me toward her. I tried to pull away, beating my fists feebly on her shoulder and arm, but she was relentless, pulling me away from the edge of the bed, some unknown punishment in store, no doubt.

In that moment, I knew I had been wrong. It wasn't Elena; it was Tabitha. I hadn't managed to kill her, and now she was here to finish me off before I could. Slowly. The image of her blade slamming into my palm flashed across my head, and I fought back with renewed strength. She was going to butcher me with her shiny silver knife, one cut at a time.

"Violet!" Tabitha shouted in my ear—my good one—her voice cracking sharply into my skull. "Violet, just let me—"

"No!" I shouted, jerking my right arm out of her grasp. The cast hung weighty on my arm, and I lashed out with it, driving my hand into the woman's core. I was rewarded with a loud 'oof' and a stab of pain from my own hand so intense I could barely focus to hear it.

But it had worked. Her hands slipped from me and she backed up, doubling over, resting her hands on her knees. My ribs screaming at the motion, my head reeling, my hand quested about as far as it could reach, searching for a weapon... anything to make sure she couldn't get near enough to touch me again.

The woman didn't say anything. I felt myself go still as she just looked at me, her eyes filled with tears of pain, fear tightening her face. The expression was so wrong, so unfamiliar, that my hands fell to my ears, my mind trying to understand. Tabitha didn't cry. She didn't acknowledge pain. If anything, it only made her angrier and more violent.

There was something here I could not grasp. Something in my brain seemed to be disconnected, something shaking loose or falling into place. I stared, disoriented and dizzy. Whoever it was I had been attacking, it was not Tabitha.

My breathing was coming in loud pants, and I was sweating and shivering again. I looked around. I was still in the same bedroom, the one at the camp where Ms. Dale and my companions had been. I looked back at the bed, and noticed Viggo wasn't there anymore. I remembered—he had been here when I'd fallen asleep. When had that been? Had something gone wrong at the camp? Why were they doing this to me? Was there anywhere I was safe?

A wave of frustration filled me, and I noticed the scalpel sitting on a tray next to the bed—something I hadn't been able to reach in my panicked grasping earlier. Reaching out with my left hand, I snatched it up and pointed it at not-Tabitha, trying to keep my hand from shaking. "Where's Viggo?" I shouted.

Not-Tabitha raised her hands slowly, her palms facing out. She was watching me warily, but there was something… something about her face. "He's coming soon," she said slowly, taking great pains to enunciate.

"You're lying," I retorted. Of course she was lying—everyone in my life had lied to me. Rina, Lee, Desmond, Elena, Tabitha… No, that was wrong. I swayed, the knife blurring before me, as the memory came to me of people who hadn't lied to me. Viggo. Tim. Owen, Quinn, Amber, Henrik, Solomon…

I repeated their names like a litany in my head, trying to find some way to reconcile my two different realities, unable to accept them both as truth. I became increasingly aware of my body trembling, shivering. A different kind of fear swept through me suddenly. Something was wrong with me. I was losing myself, and I didn't know how to stop it. I looked back at not-Tabitha, noting the fear in her face and the slight trembling of her hands, and then my eyes drifted down to where I was clutching the scalpel tightly, my fingers bloodless, almost bone-white from the force of my grip.

Violent Violet. Violent Violet. I dropped the scalpel and folded my hands over my ears, the cast bumping my temple with a flush of pain, as I tried to block out the voices as they sang, taunting me. The air in the room evaporated, and I couldn't seem to breathe. I gasped as the room spun around me, the voices in my head screaming.

What was real? I didn't know anymore. A sweep of cold nausea sucked the blood from my body down deep into my stomach. My head pounded, my body throbbed, and time evaporated, consciousness draining from me.

I was flat on my back. My left arm, my only good arm, had a needle stuck in it. I felt a groan bubbling up in my throat, but I bit it back, trying to compose myself, using my cast to fumble uselessly at the needle taped to my skin...

The door opposite me opened, and my eyes grew wide as I watched two men and a woman enter, their faces all fixated on me. Their voices cut back and forth, their faces blurry... Hands fell on my arms and legs, holding me down, and I wheezed in fear. I could barely feel the tears leaking out of my eyes onto my cheeks, the way my breath was coming shorter and shorter, the way my cries were subsiding into moans. My energy was waning fast, and my limbs began to feel leaden. It would be so easy to stop struggling—but who knew what would happen if I calmly let these strangers have their way with me? I couldn't stop, couldn't think, and the pain that shot through my side every time I wrenched my hips was getting to be too much.

The people who held me were talking, but too fast to make any sense and too loud to calm me down. Then I heard a voice, strong, commanding, powerful… I homed in on it, the warm cadence alone slowing my thrashing, making me stop and breathe.

"That's it, Violet. Just take deep breaths, and listen to my voice."

I went limp as Viggo's deep timbre rolled over me, and I sighed and turned toward it. It didn't stop the pain, but it was enough to make me stop squirming, to get my eyes to focus on what was around me. I looked around, searching for him, but couldn't see him. I couldn't see… anything.

"Am I going blind?" I asked.

"Are you having problems with your vision?" came a sharp female voice, and I flinched away from it, trying to hide my face without being able to move.

Viggo's hands were on my face. I started to lean into them, and then remembered I had been crying, screaming, drooling. Embarrassment flooded me—he shouldn't have to see me like this. I began to groan as embarrassment added to the stew of helplessness and fear curdling my stomach.

I heard somebody say something, but it was too far away for me to hear. Viggo was whispering in my good ear, trying to soothe me, his hands stroking my face. "It's going to be okay, Violet. You're sick, but we're going to help you. I promise." There was a pause. "Your cousin is here."

Panic skittered across my numb limbs, and I jerked. "He can't be here! He can't see me. If Lee finds out that he knows, he'll kill him! Please, Viggo! Please."

He shushed me, his hands on my hair, trying to soothe me. "You're safe, Violet. I promise."

His words didn't make any sense. How could we be safe? I was trapped in Patrus, trying to fulfill a mission I knew nothing about. "I'm not supposed to tell you," I gasped. "I tried to fight him. I tried to tell him no, we could find someone else to blame. I didn't want it to be you! I didn't want him to hurt you. You've been hurt so much, Viggo. And now I have to hurt you too."

Hot tears spilled over my cheeks, and I saw my brother's face as he fell into the river, his eyes wide and full of terror. He was only eight! Why did they have to take him away? I began to cry in earnest, harsh, violent sobs that seemed to scrape out of my lungs, making my throat raw.

"Do it," Viggo said.

Something bit into my arm, sharp and fast, and I turned toward it. I was so drained I couldn't even react as I looked at the black centipede wrapped around my forearm. Its pincer mouth was dripping blood, and I realized it had bitten me. I let out a shuddering breath and looked down at my feet, realizing I had never been held down. I was still in The Green, hallucinating. Soon I would die, and the eggs the centipede had just planted in me with its bite would feast on my corpse, until there was nothing left but bones.

"Violet?"

Viggo's beautiful voice shook me from the quiet calm that had fallen over me as I accepted the truth. "It doesn't matter," I said, my voice slurring. I licked my lips, noting that they were dry, that my tongue felt swollen and raw.

"What doesn't matter?" he asked.

"It bit me," I replied. "I'll be dead soon."

I couldn't say why, but then I laughed. I laughed wildly through the tears, choking on them, until my arms and legs began to feel heavy. Even then I chuckled. Then my eyelids began to droop, and suddenly I was so exhausted I couldn't even find the energy to speak to Viggo, to tell him not to worry about me, to forgive me. I closed my eyes and drifted into a black sleep, certain in the knowledge I would never wake up again.

CHAPTER 13

Viggo

I reeled back on my heels, staring at Violet as she continued to thrash and moan in her sleep despite the sedative Dr. Tierney had administered. Fear for her condition had cut through my exhaustion, sending me into a kind of surreal, hyper-alert state, my focus entirely on her. Dr. Arlan had said the bleeding in her brain would cause her to deteriorate, but I hadn't expected it to be this fast—or this emotional. This was not normal for her, even on her worst days. She'd been ranting about things already in the past, dead and buried. But somehow, in her mind, they had been happening right now, all over again.

I shuddered, knowing Violet's history was full of pain and betrayal. The fact she had survived it once was a testament to her inner strength and character. I wasn't so certain she could survive it all a second time. And in her delirious state, given her final statement before succumbing to the drugs, she had given up hope. As she had said those horrible words, fear had started to creep into my mind, reminding me fate had been cruel enough to rob me of one woman I loved—it wouldn't hesitate to do the same again. I'd saved her from a quick, brutal death by violence and explosions, but what would it be worth if she stopped breathing again, her beautiful mind and body deteriorating, this time while I watched helplessly?

Looking over at Dr. Tierney, I noticed she was still suffering the aftereffects of Violet's wild attack on her. She was pale, taking long, slow breaths, and she was rubbing her stomach absently with one hand; that must be where Violet had elbowed her.

Cad, Ms. Dale, and I had walked into the room toward the end of the exchange. When I'd seen Violet pawing her head, a scalpel loose on her bed, her face a mixture of confusion and anger… the scene had been difficult to comprehend. The worst part had been when she had looked at me. There had been no recognition, no acknowledgement in her gaze, just a glazed, blank look, as if she were seeing me for the first time. And then the horror that had filled her silver eyes as I'd approached to help Dr. Tierney.

Nervous, I ran a hand over Violet's hair and looked at the doctor. "Are you okay?"

Dr. Tierney gave a shuddering cough and forced herself to straighten from the hunch she was clearly sinking into. She nodded. "I'm fine," she replied, her voice hoarse. "It's not the first time I've had to deal with a troublesome or confused patient. She just caught me off guard."

I winced. "Solar plexus?" I asked, and she nodded, her

mouth turning down in distaste.

"Yeah. I've never felt torn between the decision to breathe or vomit before. So that was new and fun."

A laugh escaped my throat as her quip took me by surprise, but it was only a momentary distraction from the current of worry that seemed to be all that was fueling my body right now. "Is she all right?"

Dr. Tierney gave me a hard look, then shook her head slowly. "No. I'm sorry, Viggo, but she is not *all right*. If she's having hallucinations this severe... then it's definitely worse than I thought."

I looked over at Cad and Ms. Dale, who were hovering at the foot of the bed, silently listening to our conversation. Cad's face was white as he looked at his cousin, while Ms. Dale's had snapped shut in that familiar, neutral mask again, like someone had slammed the door closed on her face. I recognized it as a coping mechanism on her part—whenever she felt overly emotional, she would revert to that carefully crafted mask. But now, to me, that only made it clear she was worried as well.

"What's wrong with her?" I asked, turning back to Dr. Tierney.

She had moved over to the black case she had brought from the Liberator base and was in the process of opening it. She didn't stop at the question, pulling items out of it and lining them up on the desk right next to her.

"I think Dr. Arlan was correct in his findings," she said, her voice clinical. "Violet definitely has bleeding in her brain. It's what's causing her hallucinations and probably also part of the dizziness and difficulty with motor functions. If it's really affecting her eyesight, too, at least I have an idea what part of the brain might be affected. Now that she's really out, we can take a look at her with that portable scanner and see exactly what it is so I can operate as soon as possible." She looked me straight in the eyes—compassion and deep, serious worry measuring equally in her gaze. "Having a concussion and a burst eardrum on top of that… I can't imagine how Violet even sat up. She must have been completely panicked to even try to move. The only reason a person in this condition would do what she did is complete desperation."

Dr. Tierney's words settling in my gut like stones, I looked back at Violet. She had finally settled into her pillow, but that was somehow worse than her agitation. Under the bruising, her face was ashen, the blood completely drained from her lips, and dark shadows hid under her eyes. She looked gaunt, like she was wasting away. In fact, looking at her, it was hard not to see a woman who was about to die.

Letting out a curse, I turned my attention to Dr. Tierney. "What can I do for her?"

Dr. Tierney stood up and turned around, indecision on her face. Then she sucked in a breath and nodded. "Well, I'm going to need help, but anyone who can't hack the idea of gross medical procedures, just get the hell out. Ms. Dale, if you would be so kind as to fetch your other doctor, I'm going to need him as well. I don't care if he's awake yet. This needs to happen now."

Ms. Dale nodded and turned, heading out the door. Cad looked nervously at Dr. Tierney. "Can I do anything?"

She hesitated again, studying the younger man, her own lack of sleep becoming apparent for a moment as she blinked.

"Who are you?" she asked.

"This is Cad Thorne," I informed her, before Cad could introduce himself. "He's Violet's cousin."

Dr. Tierney's eyes widened in surprise. "You're the young man from the video," she said, realization coloring her tone. "I remember you—the image of you was a bit fuzzy, but…"

"What video?" Cad cut in, his face reflecting his confusion.

I sighed and shook my head. "I'll explain later. Right now we need to focus on Violet."

"Right," announced Dr. Tierney. "First things first. Cad, I need you to find rope or cloth to tie her down. The procedure I'm about to perform won't hurt her, and the sedatives should hold her for plenty of time, but I want to prepare for every possible scenario just in case. If she wakes up in the middle of it and is able to move, it could cause severe damage. Irreversible damage."

Cad nodded, his gaze going thoughtful. "My wife has been helping out with the washing for the camp," he said, "and she was telling me we have… an excess amount of sheets. Would that work?"

"That's perfect," Dr. Tierney replied. "We need to have enough to secure her limbs, torso, and head, so get as many as possible."

Cad was moving before she was finished talking, and I felt a surge of appreciation for the young man—he was clearly a man of action, which would be helpful in the days to come. As long, of course, as he didn't go rogue on us like he had done yesterday.

As he left, I turned back to Dr. Tierney. She was examining

her instruments, her mouth moving, reciting something to herself under her breath. I caught the words 'catheter' and 'antiseptic' and assumed she was going through her mental checklist for the procedure she was planning to perform on Violet. I was loath to interrupt her, but I wanted to help as well.

"Dr. Tierney, what do you want me to do?" The words felt odd as I spoke them. I rarely asked for advice on how to help people, trusting my gut instinct to see me through. However, I was certainly out of my depth when it came to medical training. Aside from the first-aid emergency response training I had received as a warden, I had no idea what to do. It was… more than frustrating.

Her blue eyes looked over at me, and she frowned, as if she had forgotten I was there. Her gaze flicked over to Violet, and she picked up a silver item from the desk and approached me. I held out my hand, curious, and she deposited a pair of clippers in my palm.

"I need you to shave off her hair," she said.

I felt as if I had been kicked in the stomach, and I eyed the clippers as if she had put a live venomous snake into the palm of my hand. "You want me to *what?*"

Dr. Tierney tsked and crossed her arms. "Her hair has to come off, Viggo. I need to be able to access her skull from all angles, especially since it's fractured. It's a good job for you—I know you'll be gentler with her than anybody else."

Numbly, I nodded, and then turned back to Violet. I sat down slowly and scooched a little higher up on the bed. Her hair was spread wildly all around her face, and though it was dirty and tangled, it was still beautiful. The brown tresses had grown since I had first known her, and the tips curled at the ends. The thought of shaving it felt… wrong, somehow. Like a violation. She had no way of consenting to this, and when she woke up, she would mourn its loss.

Just like I was mourning it right now. It was silly, but I loved Violet's hair. I loved how in the shadow it looked like the darkest night, and how in the day it was warm and inviting, like chocolate. Hints of brandished gold and amber threaded through its tips, and I loved them too. I especially loved how it felt in my hands when I kissed her. It was a part of her.

Dr. Tierney, sensing my reluctance, dropped a hand on my shoulder. "It'll grow back," she said softly. "I'm sure she'll forgive you for this one little thing. Besides, Violet is a practical girl. If it were a choice between her life and her hair… what do you think she'd choose?"

Grimacing, I turned on the clippers and, after taking a deep breath, I began to shave her head.

Even though it was practical, I still couldn't help but feel a twinge of pain as each lock fell to the pillow, revealing the pale skin of Violet's scalp below. I worked quickly, sometimes gently hoisting her up so I could have better access to the back of her head. In a few minutes, she was completely bald. I leaned back to examine my work, my heart pounding uncharacteristically. As if I'd had anything to worry about. She looked just as beautiful to me, even with her hair gone—with the exception of the large, swollen, angry bruise marring her scalp. I had winced when I'd uncovered that, but fought back my worry and finished the job.

I turned off the clippers and had begun to scoop up the hair when Ms. Dale bustled in, carrying a fresh set of linens for the bed. "These are clean," she announced. "And Dr. Arlan is on his way."

"Great," replied Dr. Tierney. "Viggo, would you mind holding Violet for a minute while Ms. Dale and I change the linens? It's not ideal, but any precaution we can take to avoid infection is better than none at all."

I slid my arm under Violet's knees and lifted her up, holding her tightly and taking a step back to give them space to work. Ms. Dale frowned at the loose hair, but refrained from commenting as she quickly pushed it to the center and gathered up the sheets. I waited in silence while they worked, pressing my cheek to Violet's newly shaven head. She sighed under me, nuzzling closer, and I smiled faintly. My girl was still in there somewhere.

Soon they had the sheets changed, and I set her down again. Cad returned with an armload of bedsheets, and, following Dr. Tierney's instructions, we quickly strapped Violet down to the bed. I tested the restraints one by one, making sure they were tight, but not tight enough to cut off circulation. By the time we were done, Dr. Arlan was there, and he and Dr. Tierney spoke in hushed whispers in the corner.

I stiffened, wondering if Dr. Arlan was going to resort to the behavior of a typical Patrian male and demand that he take over, but much to my relief, it didn't look like he was causing any problems. I cleared my throat and looked at them.

"We're done," I announced.

Dr. Tierney nodded. "Good. Now... get out."

I blinked. "What? You said you needed help. I'm staying."

Her face was hard, any sign of sympathy now buried. "I can't let you do that," she said. "It's admirable that you want to be here, but I can't trust you not to react to what I'm about to do."

"I shouldn't have to convince you that I'm more than capable of—"

"I'm going to be drilling into her skull, Viggo," Dr. Tierney announced, her voice calm and clinical. She picked the drill up off the table where she'd been organizing her equipment and held it up to me. "Possibly multiple times. The procedure is rudimentary and invasive, and I do not need you here to freak out when I do. Because I know that, while you are a practical person, this is the woman you love."

My jaw slackened as she spoke, the sickness I felt validating her words: instantly I felt a very strong urge to pick Violet up and run, in spite of the logical part of my brain trying to convince me that Dr. Tierney was a good doctor who knew her stuff. It took me a minute to calm my protective instinct, and the best response I could manifest was, "You're right… Good luck." Then I turned and walked out.

I made it as far as I dared to go—the farmhouse living room—and sat down heavily on the sofa, staring blearily out the window as birds fluttered around in the early-morning light. Cad gave me a curious look as he and Ms. Dale entered the room after me.

"I'll be outside," he said. "Um, let me know if you need anything or—"

"We will," replied Ms. Dale smoothly. "We won't leave you in the dark. I promise."

He nodded and left, which was fine by me; my overprotective nature was flaring up, and while I knew he was her family, the fact remained that I didn't *know* him. Besides, he had a wife to hold his hand. I didn't think I could handle his worry and mine at the same time. Ms. Dale turned her gaze back to me, her face pensive. After a pause, she went into the kitchen, and then returned five minutes later holding two large, steaming, slightly chipped mugs. "Try this," she said softly, holding one out to me. I felt warmth flow into my hand from the mug, and a distinct sweet, herbal aroma rose from it.

"Chamomile?" I asked, an incredulous look on my face. It seemed like forever since I had done something as simple as drink a cup of tea, especially herbal tea… A part of me went straight back to when Miriam and I had lived together, to an evening cup after a long and stressful day…

Ms. Dale smiled as she lifted her mug to her lips, perhaps taking my surprise for my normal sass. "I don't think you need any caffeine right now."

Unable to argue with that logic, I lifted the mug and took a sip. The hot liquid almost scalded my tongue, but it eased down into my stomach with a surge of warmth that seemed to lift the anxiety that lived there, if only for a moment. I rested it on my lap, staring at the little patterns on the battered mug.

"Thanks," I said, letting my gratitude pour out into my voice. Ms. Dale just nodded, and we drank our tea in silence.

After a while, Ms. Dale stood up and put down her empty mug. "I hate to say it, but I have business to attend to," she said. "I'm clearing your schedule for today, though—try to get some sleep, all right? I know things are tense, but we really need you fully functional. You're useless to us in this state."

I didn't even bother to protest, just nodded at her, watching her leave, and then settled back into the mushy seats of the couch, trying to get comfortable. My adrenaline rush had faded—I didn't remember when, but it felt like I'd been tired for my entire life—and, even with my stomach sick with worry, I drifted in and out of sleep.

Each noise of the house settling or sound from outside caused me to wake abruptly, instantly alert, searching for any news of Violet's condition. Several times, I caught myself starting to stand up to go check on them, only to try to convince myself to sit back down. There were a couple close calls, but for the most part, I managed to find a hidden reserve of patience.

By the time Dr. Tierney came out, I was holding on to my control by a thin thread. I felt raw, on edge, a feeling with which I was becoming hauntingly familiar. I stared at the walls, at the floor, at the ceiling, so out of it I didn't even notice Dr. Tierney until she somehow manifested right next to me. I felt dumb, sluggish, watching as she stared at the mostly empty, long-cold cup of tea before me, then picked it up and drained the rest of its contents in one gulp.

"It's done," she announced as she finished, setting the mug down on an end table with a decisive clink. I studied her as she wiped her mouth with the back of her hand. "We relieved the pressure in her skull and patched her eardrum with special paper—a trick of the trade, you know." Her exhaustion was apparent from the way her words came out of her mouth, a little slower, a little less coherent than normal.

"Will she recover?" I demanded, and Dr. Tierney met my

gaze, her eyes filled with sympathy.

"I wish I knew," she said honestly, and sighed. "She's strong, she's a fighter, but in cases like these, we won't know until she's awake. And even then, there still may be some side effects, like memory loss, problems speaking, vision impairment, balance issues... The list goes on."

I exhaled, the stone in the pit of my stomach growing. "So we did all this for nothing?"

Dr. Tierney shook her head sharply. "We drained the blood. We stopped her from *dying*. The bleeding in her brain was extensive. There's no way to know how long she would have lasted without this surgery. I think we caught it before there was critical and irreversible damage, but I don't believe in giving false hope. If it went well, then she'll be up in two days... three at the most."

I nodded, feeling numb. "Can I... Can I be with her?"

"Of course you can," she said, sounding offended that I'd thought there was a possibility I couldn't. "And while you're at it, get some sleep. Really."

As long as I could be near Violet, where I could check on her to make sure she was still there, then sleep sounded like the best plan I'd ever heard. I headed toward the door.

CHAPTER 14

Violet

I woke up slowly. It seemed that recently, all I had been doing was waking up and falling asleep again. I'd come to before—I remembered in various degrees of clarity—more than once, with weird tubes protruding from me, restraining my movement and adding minor discomforts to the fading pain in my head and body. Some of the times I'd been scared, fought... but mostly I'd been sleeping. I couldn't tell how many days it had been, but there had been darkness and light in various periods... Viggo was often with me when I woke, and his presence always convinced me that I was safe, that I wasn't being treated only to be tortured by my enemies.

This particular moment of waking was significant, though, for several reasons. There was no sense of urgency or panic. None at all. Even odder, I felt strangely calm and relaxed, even taking a moment to stretch out my limbs as I slowly peeled back my eyelids.

My memory of what had happened after the palace and before the surgery hadn't come back fully, just a vague sense of bad things happening, sometimes punctuated by flashes of memory that came to me in sharp, painful glimpses. But now I could remember waking several times before, as well as conversations—though all of them still had a fuzzy, surreal quality I couldn't place.

Dr. Tierney had taken me off the IV earlier—I wasn't sure how long ago, but I was sure it was hours, not days—and told me I would be getting some food in me, too, as soon as I rested a little longer. She'd even removed my catheter and helped me go to the bathroom, much to my embarrassment. She wasn't here now, probably having stepped out to do errands, tend to her other patients, or maybe sleep.

The absence of pain in my head was... exhilarating. It still ached slightly, like a bad headache, but I was no longer confronted with agony every time I moved, and in comparison, it almost felt like an absence of pain altogether.

No, the pain wasn't absent, but it was manageable. As my gaze started to come into focus, I panned it around the room, ridiculously happy as my eyes caressed objects while my mind provided me with their names—and they didn't even spin! I noted with clarity, for the first time, that I was in the same room as before, but my clothes had been changed.

Out of habit, I reached up to push my hair out of my face, and was surprised to encounter a gauze bandage wrapped tightly around my head. Almost more alarming was the unfamiliar stubble on the top of my head, causing me to snatch my hand back in alarm. I'd felt this sensation before… but every time, I had forgotten and had the same reaction. This time, though, I looked around the room for some sort of mirror or reflective surface, but got distracted when the doctor pushed through the door carrying a pitcher.

"Dr. Tierney?" I croaked, and then coughed, suddenly realizing how dry my mouth was.

"Oh good, you're awake." Dr. Tierney smiled warmly and moved over to the other side of the bed, pouring some water into a cup. I eagerly grabbed it from her hands, slipping the straw between my lips and sucking down the cool liquid. It had a slightly metallic taste to it, but it seemed like it was the most delicious thing I had drunk in days. Who knew—maybe it was.

As I drank, Dr. Tierney tilted my head up with her fingers and shone a penlight in my eye. I stared blankly, but apprehension churned through me as she did so, my mind vaguely recalling a time when this would've caused instant pain. Confused by the obscure memory, I stopped. "Something… something happened," I said.

Dr. Tierney withdrew the pen and gave me a thoughtful look. "What do you mean?"

I frowned and shook my head, unsure how to answer her question; and then I realized there were more pressing ones I needed answers to. "How are you here? Why are you here? Where's Viggo? Where's Tim? Does Desmond know? Oh my God, is she here? Are we all prisoners again?"

Questions were now spilling out of me so fast I could barely get them all out with my dry throat, and they would've continued had Dr. Tierney not raised her hand in a universal sign for *slow down.* I felt a twinge of impatience, but blinked, waiting.

"Oh my," she said with a little smile, sitting down on the bed. I took being silenced as an opportunity to drink a little more. "Looks like switching to the weaker pain medication really did the trick… Where do I start? Desmond is not here, and you are safe. Viggo is here, but I'm not sure where exactly—he comes and goes as he pleases. No one is a prisoner, but as your doctor, I will tie you to the bed if you overexert yourself, so I reserve the right to amend that answer whenever I please."

I put the water cup down. "No Desmond… Then how did you… come to be here?"

"Viggo, Amber, and Owen went to our—the Liberators'— home base," she explained. "They had the others… watch your video."

"Oh." I had forgotten about the video. I couldn't decide how I felt about them showing it to the Liberators, until I remembered that was exactly *why* I had made it. Still, the fact everyone had borne witness to me getting the stuffing beaten out of me by Tabitha? Talk about embarrassing. I put it aside and focused on the more important issue. Biting my lip, I looked up at her. "And my brother?"

She frowned and shook her head. "Sorry—I'm just your doctor. Viggo would have a better idea of… Hey, you sit back down right now!"

I ignored her, trying to get my limbs to obey me. Even though I was wide awake and *mostly* clearheaded, my arms and legs were stiff, so much so that moving had become quite troublesome. I grated my teeth together as I slid my legs out from under the covers and over the side of the mattress.

Then Dr. Tierney was there in front of me, her hands on her hips. At that moment, I despised the ease with which she moved, almost as much as it irritated me that she was in my way. I stared up at her, but she stood firm.

"Lie back down, Violet," she ordered, crossing her arms over her chest.

"Please," I said. "I have to know about my brother."

"Violet, I cut open your skull two days ago. You were bleeding internally, and I had to drill not one, but two holes in your head. Not to mention your fractured skull, which is only a small injury and will heal itself... But only if you take care of it. The good news is that you're awake, and you seem lucid. But I am not letting you out of this bed until I can at least check you out."

I frowned. "If I let you check me out, will you please let me go find Viggo?"

"Wouldn't it be better if I went and got him?" she asked, the hard edges of her face softening slightly.

"No!" I snapped suddenly, with vehemence that surprised me—a surge of fear hitting me hard. I looked up, noted the clinical look on Dr. Tierney's face, and immediately forced my fear aside. "No," I repeated, modulating my voice to be softer and more reasonable, but with no room for argument.

Dr. Tierney sighed and squatted down until we were at eye level. "Sometimes, some patients who receive this kind of surgery are prone to emotional reactions that are illogical, or not rooted in anything rational. It's perfectly normal, but before I agree to let you do anything, I need to know: why are you being so stubborn about this?"

I hesitated, trying to determine why I had been so upset by

the idea of staying in bed. It was difficult to put it into words.

I took a deep breath and then exhaled. "I don't know how long I've been in this bed, but I can tell it's been a while. I need to get out and move... even if it's just a little bit. Please? Please just... let me? For a few minutes?" *Also, I don't want Viggo to see me in this stupid bed again,* I thought, but didn't feel the need to add that part out loud. I knew it was a point of vanity, but I didn't care. I just wanted to show him I was well, so he could stop worrying and feel better.

Dr. Tierney's gaze was hard and searching, but I met it straight on, letting my resolve give me strength. Finally, she sighed and nodded. "After I check you out," she said, her voice full of warning.

I smiled and nodded, folding my hands obediently in my lap.

"What's your name?" she asked, standing up.

"Violet Bates," I replied without hesitation.

"When were you born?"

"September 7th, two hundred and eighty-one years after The Fall."

"How old is your brother?"

"Sixteen, but he'll turn seventeen at the end of the month." I felt a pang—the end of the month might have already passed, for all I knew. It had only been fifteen days off when I had gone to the palace for my showdown with Tabitha. Suddenly I was overwhelmed with worry for him. I pushed it aside for the moment, knowing I needed to prove I was all right before I could do anything.

"What day is it today?"

I screwed up my face, and gave a shrug. "I have no idea—how many days have I been unconscious?"

Dr. Tierney smiled softly as she scribbled things down on her notebook. "From what I understand? It's been four and a half days since your fight, two and half since the surgery."

I counted it off in my head. "August 20th? 21st?"

Her smile grew as she set the notebook down. "It's the twentieth," she supplied as she moved closer. I followed her orders as she checked my reflexes, pupillary responses, and the functionality of the patch in my eardrum. I asked her questions as she went, quizzing her on the injuries, how long it would take for them to heal, what she'd done to my skull... I couldn't quite bring myself to ask why my hair was gone, though. I didn't want to tell her how embarrassed I was.

Most of the checkup was painless, but I did hiss when she asked me to raise my arm over my head, and I quickly lowered my arm and placed my hand on my ribcage. "Well, they're healing up as fast as we can expect," she said. "You should be fine to walk. Just take it easy and slow, all right? Let's get you up and moving."

She bent down, and I gingerly put my arm over her shoulder, while she wrapped hers around my waist. I hadn't noticed before how much shorter than me Dr. Tierney was, but my bruised ribs were incredibly glad of it now. With both of us working together, she eased me into a standing position. I swayed into her, glad she was there, as a wave of dizziness assailed my senses, making everything lean hard to the left. Dr. Tierney held me through it, and after a few seconds, the world righted itself.

"You okay?" she asked, concern thick in her voice.

I wasn't exactly *okay*, but I would be damned if I was going to tell her that. She'd just send me back to bed.

"I'm good," I replied. The look she gave me was filled with doubt, but I ignored it. "Let's go."

We made it to the door, moving painfully slowly, but I didn't think I could move much faster than that. Together, we opened the door and stepped into the hall. I gazed around in wonder, as if I were seeing this place for the first time, even though I knew I had seen it before... and I wasn't even sure how many times. Ahead, I could hear the welcome sound of Viggo's voice.

The deep, comforting, authoritative sound bolstered my weakened strength, and I moved toward it, eager to see him. As I came out of the hall, Viggo continued talking, seeming not to notice me; but one by one, everyone sitting around the table looked up at me, their eyes widening. Viggo didn't notice it at first, but after a moment, he paused, then shifted in his seat to look at me.

Everything I had gone through was worth it, just to see his face in that moment. I watched, as if in slow motion, as a tumble of emotions passed across his normally carefully composed face: pure shock, surprise—was that rueful, fond irritation?—all of them eclipsed very soon by one of his rare, brilliant smiles.

I felt myself blushing, a smile rising to my face as well. I couldn't explain why, but in that moment, under the weight of the stares of everybody in the room, I felt an impish urge to raise my hand and waggle my fingers at them.

So I did.

CHAPTER 15

Violet

My wave only had half the desired effect: Owen and Amber smiled, but Thomas' face was pure apprehension, and Viggo was already out of his chair, moving toward me, concern etched on the strong lines of his face even through the smile he wore. He also looked tired, and I could imagine him sitting by my bed, unable to sleep. It wasn't hard to imagine at all—it was how I had spent my time during his coma, and Viggo might have been even more protective of me than I was of him.

Dr. Tierney still had her arm around me, and I felt the insistent press of her hand, politely reminding me that, yes, she was helping me—but I was also heavy. I reached out to take Viggo's hand, a tingle going through me as our fingers met, and allowed him to take some of my weight from her. Together, they helped me hobble toward the nearest empty seat. Amber sprang out of her chair and pulled it out for me, and I gave her a thankful look as they helped me sit down, taking care not to show exactly *how* relieved I was that I hadn't had to deal with that particular obstacle.

Sitting was awesome. So much better than standing.

As soon as I sat down, Dr. Tierney let me go. Viggo, however, knelt down by me, his hand sliding down my arm, threading his fingers through mine. "Are you okay?" he asked, his green eyes searching. I felt my face soften, and I gave him a small nod.

"As well as can be expected," I replied with a smile. Okay, I was exuding more optimism than I felt about my condition, but I was in no mood to admit it. I needed to get up, find out what had happened to Tim, and figure out what was going on.

He gave me a dubious look, but nodded. He pressed my hand against his cheek, his eyes drifting closed as he leaned into it. I curled my fingers slightly, feeling the rough beard forming on his jaw, and relief poured through me. We were alive, and together. That meant anything was possible. Dropping a kiss onto the palm of my hand, he stood up and slowly pulled away, heading back to his chair. A part of me wanted him to stay, longing for more of his touch—but I knew Viggo was too private a person to let our reunion linger in front of all of our companions. I'd seen enough in his eyes in that one moment to know he was intensely grateful I was up and walking.

I watched him a moment longer, before Amber's arms draped around me, dragging my attention away from him. She rested her head on my shoulder, squeezing gently. "I'm so glad you're awake," she said. "I was really worried about you."

I smiled and patted her arm. "C'mon… you know no stupid princess of Matrus could keep me down," I said, and Owen and

Amber smiled. Thomas' expression stayed locked in that same look of nervous expectation, while Viggo's lips turned downward in a brief shadow of a frown. Okay, so maybe it hadn't been a very tasteful joke, but I couldn't really help it.

I was particularly concerned about Thomas. There was something going on with his face, something triggering a memory, half remembered and almost dreamlike. I licked my lips, focusing on it, until I was able to piece together the last time I had been in this room. I pushed away the embarrassment and squared my shoulders, exhaling in order to calm the nervous flutter in my stomach.

Thomas was worried about how I was going to treat him. He knew that losing my brother, even temporarily, was a deep wound to me, and he was afraid I was going to blame him. Truth be told, the thought was rattling around in my skull. It would have been so easy to blame him. I had trusted him with my brother's life.

But that wasn't exactly true, either. Thomas didn't like confrontation, or battles he couldn't control, so sending Tim and Jay with him had been a way of making sure he got in and out okay. It had also allowed me a bit more control over what the boys were doing. They had snuck onto the heloship when Amber and I had left, and they had been insistent on helping. I hadn't liked it, so sending them with Thomas to help him plant the bombs on the fuel reserves for the palace generators had seemed like a better solution. And if Amber and I hadn't convinced Thomas to come with us to the palace… well, maybe he wouldn't have been there to lose Tim, but all of us might also have died.

I couldn't blame Thomas. It wasn't his fault. It wasn't Jay's fault, either, although I was sure the young man was experiencing his own feelings of guilt. Tim had stayed behind of his own volition. He must have wanted to help his friends escape. I couldn't fault him for that—it was the exact same thing I would have done.

"Thomas," I said softly, trying to catch his attention. He looked up at me, his eyes wide in alarm. "I just want you to know I don't blame you for what happened with Tim."

I looked him in the eyes, trying to convey my sincerity, and he gaped at me. Apparently the man had never factored in the possibility of me forgiving him, and I knew if a stiff wind had blown into the room at that moment, it would have knocked him over. After a moment, his shock wore off, and he shook his head, as if to clear it from a punch.

Viggo took advantage of his silence. "Violet, are you hungry?" He looked up at Dr. Tierney. "Can she eat?"

At the mention of food, my stomach growled, like an angry beast being woken from slumber, the promise of food bringing it to life again. I flushed at my noisy stomach, but was too hungry to deny it.

Turning in my seat was painstaking, but I did it, turning my eyes toward the doctor. "That would be amazing," I said. "Can I?"

Dr. Tierney smiled at me, nodding. "Actually, I've had a broth waiting for you—I was about to have someone bring you some when you woke up—so I'll go and heat it up, okay? And you need to drink a lot more fluids."

She moved over to the kitchen, and I turned back to the

table, shooting a grateful smile at Viggo. He met my gaze, the corners of his lips quirking slightly. Exhaling, I turned back to the table and returned my thoughts to the question burning a hole in me. I smoothed my hand over my nightgown. "So... H-Have you heard anything about Tim?"

Asking the question was hard, but not as hard as not asking it would have been. I already knew what their answer would be. After all, nobody had said anything when I had come in, and judging from Thomas' guilty face, it was clear there hadn't been news.

Or worse, there *had* been, and they didn't know how to tell me my brother was dead. My heart contracted painfully in my chest, hard enough for tears to well behind my eyes. I reined them in, reminding myself it was too soon to jump to conclusions.

"I'm sorry, Violet," Viggo said, breaking the silence and meeting my gaze. "We haven't heard anything, one way or the other."

That helped calm me, though not much. It was fuzzy, but I had the distinct impression that I'd completely lost it earlier. It wouldn't be productive to have a sob fest right there in front of everyone, no matter how worried I was. Besides... I knew I was going to find Tim. I had lived for it before, and I would be just as vigilant now. I just hoped it didn't take another eight years this time.

"Your cousin Cal went back to the palace," announced Amber from her new seat at the end of the table. "He snuck off base in broad daylight. Ms. Dale caught him coming back in, though. It was totally badass."

I chuckled—it was hard not to. "His name is *Cad*," I informed her with a bemused smile. Amber waved her hand in the air, as if dismissing an inconsequential bit of information.

"Whatever. He went, anyway. He didn't find any sign of Tim, though."

I felt a stab of disappointment, even though I had been prepared for it. I looked up as Dr. Tierney set a steaming bowl in front of me, filled with a clear broth that smelled faintly of potatoes and onions. I frowned at it, wishing there were more substance to it, and she reached out and squeezed my shoulder. "I know it isn't much to look at, but we should start with a simple broth. If you can keep it down, I'll give you a little rice so you feel a bit more sated. I want to take it slow, though. You haven't had anything substantial in your stomach for the last four days."

Nodding, I awkwardly picked my spoon up with my left hand, leaned over, and tasted the broth. It may have been simple, but at that moment, it was the most delicious thing I had ever tasted. The doctor squeezed my shoulder again encouragingly, before withdrawing her hand.

"All right. It seems like you have important things to discuss, which is good, because I have other patients to check up on. Violet, as soon as this meeting is over, you go right back to bed—no 'buts.' I'm sure someone will help you back to your room."

"Damn right I will," Viggo growled, and I cocked my head at him, surprised by the intensity in his voice. He seemed to notice me watching, and raised his eyebrows at me, seeming to brook no argument. Dr. Tierney gave me a knowing smile as she departed, leaving us all alone in an awkward silence.

I frowned, confused by this sudden surge of protectiveness. He had seemed concerned earlier, but there was no need for him to be so… animalistic. What was up with him?

Then I felt stupid. Of course Viggo was worried about me and the fact I was out of bed and trying to be included, in spite of my recent near-death experience. He was acting like an over-protective bear, his foremost desire to shelter and protect me from being hurt again. I probably should've been mildly annoyed, but instead, I felt a sort of strange delight in the realization. I was *definitely* going to have to talk to him about it, but still… it made me feel cherished and safe.

I decided to test my theory. I took another sip of my soup, and then looked at Owen. He'd been strangely quiet since I arrived. "So, Dr. Tierney's here. Does that mean…"

"That we heroically flew to The Green, managed to convince the Liberators that Desmond is pure evil, and then got them to lend us equipment, their doctor, and a few men? All while you were lazing about and taking a nap?" I smiled at Owen's joke, fighting back a laugh as he struck a heroic pose and then flipped imaginary hair over his shoulder. It was infectious, and even Amber and Thomas laughed. Viggo shot him an incredulous look, and I let out a soft chuckle at his obvious annoyance.

"That was a mouthful," I said, "but that's awesome. How did you manage to convince them?"

Amber's voice was soft and filled with reverence and a touch of awe as she answered, "We showed them your tape."

"Oh." *Right.* Dr. Tierney had told me that. Once again, I was struck with discomfort, which deepened as I saw the looks of appreciation that seemed to be radiating off of everyone as they looked at me. Even Thomas had a touch of it, which was saying something, because I didn't think the man was capable of hero worship—besides his admiration of Owen, of course.

I cleared my throat and took another sip of broth, my eyes darting to Viggo. His hands were balled into fists now, and I could see the disapproval in his face. It was evidence, but not very damning. I needed to push harder to confirm my suspicions.

"So," I asked, "what lies is Elena spinning to contain the mess at the palace? Do you have any ticker tapes I could read later?"

Thomas leaned forward, his chair squeaking slightly as he moved. "Well, the tickers went down after the explosion, and honestly, I don't think they are coming back."

I frowned and looked around. "So we're flying blind?"

"No, not exactly," replied Owen. "Ms. Dale sent Jeff to the city to try to figure out how Elena is spreading news. She figured if Elena wanted to maintain control over the people, she had to be getting the news out somehow. Otherwise there would've been chaos and rioting in the streets, and he said it was actually pretty orderly out there."

I nodded as I sipped at my soup, but paid careful attention to Viggo. His expression was downright thunderous, and I masked my smile, knowing he was close to detonating. It was what I was waiting for, honestly—if he didn't, well, then I would know my hypothesis was wrong, and he wasn't being overprotective of me.

I was confident I wasn't wrong, however. I continued, "So,

what did Jeff find? Was Ms. Dale right?"

Thomas nodded emphatically, his lips pulling back in a smile. "Yes, she was. Elena is getting her information out through public forums at sporting arenas and parks all over the city. In fact, one of them is the stadium where Mr. Croft once fought, which presents a unique opportunity to—"

He was cut off by Viggo's low growl. "I think this all might be a bit too much excitement for Violet to be handling right now," he said tersely.

Thomas came to a stuttering halt in his news report, and I watched as everyone looked at Viggo. Tension in the room formed suddenly, like a rubber band being stretched, and I felt it threatening to snap.

But I maintained an air of confidence, as though Viggo's outburst hadn't fazed me in the slightest. I took another sip of the soup and then put my spoon down, the broth finished. I picked up a napkin and took my time wiping my mouth with it, before turning to Viggo.

"That's very considerate of you, Viggo, but I'm feeling much better now, and I would like to be involved in whatever's going on. I may be injured, but I am not incapable of helping."

Then I leaned back and waited.

CHAPTER 16

Viggo

Everyone was stone quiet as Violet made her little declaration. I could tell they were waiting for my response, but, for the moment… I didn't have one.

Of course I was happy to see her up and moving again. It had filled my heart with joy to see her standing on her two own feet. Not to mention my relief to see her talking lucidly, without the persistent confusion followed by horrible panic. She was conscious, active, and appeared to be on the mend.

She was also being stubborn, and if she wasn't careful, she was going to wind up hurting herself more instead of healing. I drummed my fingers on the arm of my chair and realized the conversation was starting to pick up again, noting the soft whispers Owen and Violet were exchanging.

That exchange irritated me even more. Owen should have known better than to let her go on with this. He had been at the palace with me. He had seen her hurt and bleeding! She didn't need to be talking strategy—she needed to be in her bed, resting, even if I had to carry her there. I couldn't help but savor such a tempting thought. In fact...

I stood up abruptly and began moving before the logical part of my brain could talk me out of it. Everyone had fallen silent again, but I ignored them all, my focus solely on Violet. She looked up at me, her gray eyes regarding me calmly from behind her long eyelashes. I caught a flash of amusement there, which only made my resolution stronger.

I didn't say anything, just effortlessly picked her up. She didn't struggle or protest. As I turned to march her out of the room, Violet rested her chin on my shoulder and waved her left hand to the group. "Bye, guys! Apparently, it's time for me to go to bed." Her voice was cheerful.

I bit back a growl at the round of chuckles that erupted in our wake and resisted the urge to throw her over my shoulder, reminding myself she had *just* had surgery. She needed to be treated with care and not manhandled—yet, if there were ever a female in need of a spanking, it was Violet.

That wasn't the Patrian in me talking; that was the alpha in me talking. I knew I was capable of reasoning and logic, but not on this matter. Not when she had almost died four days ago. Violet was going to go rest and stay there, even if I had to tie her to the damn bed.

I stormed into the bedroom, using the heel of my foot to shove the door closed behind me. Then I crossed over to the bed and deposited her in it. Straightening, I expected to see her looking angry or frustrated, so I was a bit surprised when she stared up at me, a bemused grin playing on her lips.

My eyes narrowed into slits, and I regarded her warily. Why was she grinning? There was nothing funny about this! She needed to learn to stay in bed when she was unwell. Unless… I felt some of my anger diminish as I remembered what Dr. Tierney had said about one of the side effects being emotional imbalances. Had I hurt her when I moved her?

Before a surge of panic and concern could hit me, Violet leaned back into the pillow, the bemused expression deepening. "Your alpha male side is showing again," she said, a little song in her voice.

That was definitely Violet, I thought. Good—I wanted to be angry for this. Her lucidity made it easier for me to act, because I knew it wouldn't distress her too much. If I was honest, I knew it wouldn't sway her in the slightest, but I still had to try to convince her. "I don't care. You need to be in bed," I announced.

The look she gave me was one of amusement mingled with that knowing look, as if she realized I was being irrational somehow. I wasn't, of course—I was far too in control for that—but *still*.

"For how long? Dr. Tierney let me out. That means I am capable of leaving it."

"Violet, I know you—you're going to push yourself too hard. You don't need to worry about what's going on out there; you need to focus on getting better."

Violet frowned and shook her head. "Viggo, I'm not going to stay in this bed forever," she said softly.

"You will if I have anything to say about it," I retorted.

Violet cocked her head and narrowed her eyes. "My brother

is out there," she said flatly, and I frowned, recognizing that I had trodden into dangerous waters.

I cleared my throat and tried a different tactic. "I know that, and I promise, I will find him. But Violet, you need to understand that you almost died—no! When I found you, you weren't even breathing! You *died*. Do you understand what that was like for me? I thought I had lost you!"

My voice ended in a shout, and I blinked, taken aback by my own outburst. Looking down, I realized my hands were shaking, and I balled them into fists just to hide the tension. My heart thudded loudly in my chest, and I took a giant step back and turned away, trying to calm myself.

While I breathed heavily, I heard the bedsprings squeak under Violet's weight, followed by the sound of her bare feet hitting the floor. I exhaled sharply and closed my eyes, searching for strength, but finding none.

With a groan, I turned around and began to move around the bed toward her. Violet froze and dropped back onto the bed, halfway into trying to stand. "What are you doing?" she asked softly.

"Getting into bed," I said. "You're clearly going to try to come and comfort me, and I don't want you leaving the bed, so I'm coming to you."

Violet's smile bloomed, and I could see her fighting back a laugh. I realized how ridiculous I was being, but I didn't care. Her health was more precious to me than my pride—but that didn't mean I had to be happy about it. My motions were abrupt and tense as I pulled the blanket down to the foot of the bed before dropping into it, the bedsprings sagging under my weight.

I propped myself up with some pillows and then crossed my arms. Violet had already lowered herself into a lying position, and I felt her scoot over slightly next to me, her right shoulder bumping mine, her left hand folding over her body to rest lightly on my chest, over my heart. I sighed, trying to hold tightly to my anger, but it was hard. Lying next to her was its own special torment, but one I wouldn't trade for anything.

Silence lapsed between us. Then, Violet broke it. "I'm sorry," she said quietly, and I looked at her, raising an eyebrow. "Don't get your hopes up. I'm still going to be getting out of bed and helping out," she chuckled, noting my hopeful expression. I let out a frustrated sigh and turned back toward the ceiling. Her hand stroked over my chest, pressing against my heart. "But I am sorry for scaring you like that. Honestly, I wanted you to be with me the entire time I was at the palace—I was so scared. But you know… You know I had to go."

I did know that. It didn't make me feel any better. It was irrational, but it was how I felt. I remained silent, but turned toward her a little so I could look at her face. She bit her lip. "You know I'm going to want to help. I'm in this fight, Viggo. I just can't sit out for six weeks while my arm and head and ribs heal. But I also know I'm a liability right now. As far as missions go, I know I can't participate."

"*Thank* you," I said, relief pouring out of me. Finally, she was being reasonable. Now if I could just…

"Hold your horses," she said, and I halted. "I know you're sitting there planning just how to give me jobs to keep me 'busy' and make me feel 'useful,' but can I remind you that when you were in my shoes, I never did that to you?"

I opened my mouth, and then closed it sullenly. Curse her and her damnable logic. Maybe I *was* being unfair to her, but it was who I was. Couldn't she see that?

"I know being protective is just who you are. I don't blame you, but you need to lighten up," she said, and I wanted to groan at how well she knew me… and also knew just how to defuse me. "But on this, I can't compromise. I can't—I won't—stop. This is just as much my fight as it is yours. We're partners, remember?"

I sighed, more irritated by the fact she was right than anything else. My anger had already started to dissipate. "Why do I suddenly feel like women are getting too many rights in Patrus?" I grumbled.

Violet smacked me lightly on the chest, and I turned to take in her bemused smile, angling my body more fully into her, until we were face to face. I sucked in a deep breath and then exhaled, letting my anger and irritation go. But I needed to get out one more thing as well.

"I was so scared," I admitted, my voice hoarse with raw emotion. "It was terrifying to see you in that bed. It wasn't the same, but when Miriam was awaiting her sentence… every time I went to see her… it was the exact same feeling. I didn't know how to help you."

Violet's smile melted, and her face grew sad with empathy. She reached up and cupped my cheek with her good hand, and I leaned into it, needing her touch. I hated feeling vulnerable around anyone except her. She was the only person in the world who could comfort me, and it was easy to let her. I loved her.

"Oh, Viggo," she sighed. "If I could go back in time and

change how it went down, I would." She reached up and skimmed the bandage around her head with a rueful expression, and then snatched her hand back as soon as she stroked over the stubble. "Believe me, I would."

I chuckled. "To save your hair?"

She shook her head, a crooked smile on her face. "To spare you this pain, for one thing," she said softly. "And to figure out what happened to Tim… I know you won't give up looking for him. He's as much your little brother as my own. Just… Just don't leave me out of this. I couldn't bear it."

My heart broke for her as I took in the pain that brimmed in her eyes and turned her lips down, and I reached out and grabbed her chin. "I would never do that," I said softly. "I would never leave you out of this, and I promise to keep you in the loop. But you have to promise to take it easy, and tell me when things are getting to be too much for you, okay? You're not being a burden when you do, so promise me."

Violet gave a halfhearted smile and nodded. "I promise," she whispered. Her gray gaze flicked down. "Thank you," she said.

I smiled at her, caressing her cheek with my thumb. "Of course, baby. I love you. Not to mention… you're going to be my wife soon."

She smirked at me and raised her left hand, showing me her bare fingers. "I don't see a ring here, do you?" she teased.

I snorted and leaned in closer to her, loving the cheerful sound back in her voice, my focus entirely on her lips. "As soon as I have a chance, I'll go ring shopping," I whispered against them. "Or looting, or robbing, or…" Whatever else I was going to say was lost as she closed the tiny gap between us, pressing her lips to mine.

I hadn't gotten a chance to tell her how I felt when she'd come into the room upright and lucid; I had tried to tell her in words in our argument, but everything had kept coming out jumbled and wrong somehow, overprotective, angry. So I tried to tell her now, with my lips, something I was unable to put into words. Slowly, softly, we tasted each other for the first time in what felt like years. I was incredibly delicate, and I took my time, enjoying the soft little murmur of pleasure she let out against my lips, the way her mouth pressed harder into mine, trying to get a reaction out of me.

There was no way we were doing anything more than this gentle kiss when she was so injured, but parts of me that had been silent, crushed under the weight of sleeplessness and constant worry for our lives, came awake at even this soft touch. I groaned, and allowed my hand to gently brush up her left arm and over the sides of her neck, like she was a fragile thing instead of the tough, resourceful girl I knew her to be.

"HEY, VIOLET!" I froze at the excited shout that cut through the door. Violet's eyes shot open; she and I barely had a moment to exchange glances when the door was thrown open.

Jay bounded into the room, his youthful face a mask of pure excitement, completely unaware of the tender moment he'd interrupted. I'd managed to pry my lips from Violet's in the second we'd had before he saw, swinging myself up into a sitting position. Meanwhile, Violet carefully turned herself over onto her back, her face grimacing in pain again, and looked up at the young man as he gave a whoop and flung himself at her.

"Jay—" I winced and surged forward to hold him off if I needed to, but reason caught up with Jay, and he paused just short of tackling Violet with a hug. He hovered instead, his blue eyes filling with concern as he took in her bandaged head and bruised face. She looked self-conscious, though I couldn't see why, but seemed to push it aside, smiling at the younger man.

"Hi, Jay," she said, sitting up and holding her arms open to him. Relief lit his features, and he carefully slid in to hug her, obviously taking great pains to rein in his incredible strength. She held him close with a light grip. I'd seen him around the base various times during Violet's convalescence, but I realized she hadn't, and it was plain to see the relief on her face that he was all right, save for a few small cuts and bruises on the side of his face.

He let go of her and perched on the side of the bed. She reached out and lightly touched the side of his face, where the bruises and scrapes were already mending. "How'd this happen?" she asked. I felt no jealousy watching her tenderness with the young man; he felt as much her brother as Tim did, after all, and it was sweet to watch her dote on him.

Jay frowned and looked away, his cheeks coloring slightly. "I, uh… ran into a wall in the palace," he admitted. "We were being chased, and someone was firing, so I had to get low quickly. I wound up slipping."

"Not bad at all, considering what could have happened," I pointed out.

"Yeah," Jay said, some nervousness emerging in his tone.

Violet frowned and lowered her fingers. "I'm glad you're okay," she said. It had apparently been the wrong thing to say, however, as Jay shot her, then me, a guilty look.

She cocked her head. "What's wrong?"

His shoulders slumped and he stared up into her eyes, his eyes tearful. I had no time to worry what this was about, although I was beginning to guess…

"I'm so sorry, Violet," he said, his voice thick. "*I* should've been the one to stay behind. But I thought Tim was right behind us. By the time we noticed he was gone…"

Realization dawned, and I felt a jarring sense of empathy. From the look on Violet's face, she felt the same way. Of course Jay blamed himself. All of us felt horrible about Tim, and Jay had probably been the first person to know he was missing; why should he be any different?

I tried to find words to say, but Violet was ahead of me. Reaching out, she took Jay's hand in her own, patting it gently. "It's okay, Jay," she soothed him, taking a deep breath. "It's not your fault. Tim did what he thought was right, and I'm sure if your positions had been reversed, you would've done the same thing."

"But *I* should've done it," the young man practically shouted, his voice belligerent. "*I* should've been the one to stay!"

I sighed and shook my head as Violet continued to pat his hand. "Let me ask you a question," she said. "When you found Quinn, how did you decide who would carry him?"

Jay blinked in confusion. "What do you mean? Of course I had to carry him—I'm stronger, and Tim's skin makes it hard for him to… oh…"

Violet's voice was firm, and I continued to watch, admiring the way she had allowed the young man to come to the conclusion on his own, even as I felt deeply for him. "Exactly. You both played to your strengths. Tim is better with a gun because of his advancement, just like you're strong enough to carry a fully grown man for a long time. Jay, I'm sure you would've stayed if your positions had been reversed, but… they weren't."

Jay's face darkened, and he shook his head, as if shaking off the comfort. "But Tim is your *brother*," he exploded. "He should be here with you! *I* should be the one missing."

Violet paused for a longer moment at that one. Watching them, I wondered if maybe, just maybe, a part of her would want that. But then I saw concern blossom over her face—and tenderness. Even if she somehow felt that way, Violet would never let it conquer her.

"But then we would be just as worried about you, Jay," she said. He stared only at her, his eyes serious. "You're family too," she added.

That got her a ghost of a smile, and she pulled him back into another hug. After that he seemed to feel better, because he leaned forward eagerly and peppered Violet with questions, making me chuckle.

"How are you? I have to say, I really like your cousin, he's cool. Did you know he snuck out to go find Tim? I wish he had told me, I would've gone with him. Oh! And Viggo got the Liberators to join the cause! In less than twelve hours!" Violet shot me a glance at that, one that imparted not only her admiration but a bit of her exasperation at the barrage of thoughts and feelings. I shook my head, a smile tugging at my lips, and her own smile grew in response.

"Ms. Dale has been working with our new recruits, but

they are really, *really* awful, not to mention…" the young man continued, and I decided to rescue Violet. As soon as Jay drew in another breath to speak, I quickly interjected.

"Hey, Jay, can I ask you a favor?"

He blinked in surprise. "Of course! What?"

"Could you help us out and get Violet something to eat? Dr. Tierney said if she could keep down her soup, she could have a little bit of rice, so…"

Jay was already up, practically vibrating with excitement. "Of course! I'll be right back!" He left, closing the door behind him, and I turned back to my gray-eyed girl, who looked infinitely amused.

"Well, that was excellent timing," she said, raising her eyebrows at me.

"Impeccable," I agreed. "But it was probably best we stopped there anyway. You're still recovering." I knew better than to say 'fragile,' which was the word I had been thinking the whole time. "And I… Well, let's just say it's hard holding back sometimes."

Violet cocked her head at me, seeming mystified but amused. "Even when I'm all bald and… and gross?" she asked.

"You've never been gross to me," I said honestly, moving toward her and kneeling next to the bed, level with her face. "You were beautiful even when you were about to be operated on. Even when I picked you up off the ground in the king's palace and carried you to the car…" It was normally hard for me to say emotional things like this, but with Violet, somehow they came naturally and felt right.

She reached out her left hand to me, and I took it gently, threading our fingers together. She didn't respond for a while, just looked at me, her storm cloud eyes brimming with emotion that said more than words could.

"I love you," she said after a while. "Thank you."

"Thank you for not being dead," I murmured. "And I love you too."

Violet smiled at me, and then her grip slackened a little bit, and she yawned.

"Tired?" I asked.

She nodded. "Yeah."

I got up and leaned over her, pressing a kiss to her forehead. "Get some rest. See if you can eat something when Jay gets back. I'll be in later to check on you—and tomorrow, I promise I'll start getting you more up to speed."

She nodded again, sinking more heavily into her pillow. "Okay. Just… you're not going to sleep somewhere else, are you?"

I looked back down at her, smirking. "I'm a gentleman, Violet, not a saint. I'll be damned if I'm going to sleep anywhere but next to you if it's humanly possible."

CHAPTER 17

Viggo

I kept my arm around Violet's shoulder as we stepped off the sagging porch together. It was Violet's first day outside in the three days since she'd woken up properly after the surgery, and though it wasn't the first time she'd walked around, it would probably be the longest she'd been upright the whole time.

We'd both managed to get some rest and recovery during those days, and now Dr. Tierney had given us the go-ahead to get her up and moving this morning, but had cautioned she should only have short bursts of activity. Violet, who had been begging the doctor to let her go out for almost all of those three days, hadn't liked the news, but her desire to do *something* had forced her to agree.

"I'm still going to make you stop if you push yourself too hard," I warned her as we stepped onto the damp grass.

She shot me a mischievous smile. "At least I'm letting you

help me." She smirked, and I looked away, my face heating. I knew she was just kidding, but the fact I had chased her off during my recuperation after my own heart surgery still speared me with feelings of regret. It was not one of my prouder moments, and she'd already reminded me of it more than once.

"I'm just glad you aren't being as pigheaded as I was," I muttered. "I'm glad you're letting me help you."

She chuckled, leaning into me. "Well, that's just because I'm clearly better than you. You are so lucky to have a girl like me." Her eyes twinkled with humor.

"Well, that might be true," I agreed with a laugh, guiding her toward the barn.

The camp had been set up efficiently—Ms. Dale had taken care of that. The narrow yard had been sectioned off. Tents were erected in twin lines against the forest on either side, leaving plenty of room around the small dirt road for vehicles to pass through—and close enough to the woods that they would be harder to spot from the air. The barn was off to the right, built close to the tree line, and the vehicles we had procured, most of which wouldn't fit inside it, were parked beside it, opposite to the road.

As we walked, I explained that most of the equipment and weapons from Ashabee's estate had been placed in the barn. We were up to fifty-three recruits in our small army, but hadn't yet found any more refugees to recruit—if there *were* any more refugees. Ms. Dale had managed to raid one of the weapons storehouses that Ashabee and the king had identified for us, so we were set in that regard. Yet now we had more weapons than soldiers to carry them, which was problematic, as there was no way fifty men and women could stand up against the entire might of Elena's wardens.

I hid nothing from Violet, and she listened carefully as we walked, her head nodding here and there as I outlined all our problems one by one. When I got to the issue of food, she paused, cocking her head.

"There was a ton of food at Ashabee's," she said, her voice questioning.

I shook my head. "Yes, there was, but fifty people eat a lot. We're going to be out of food in a matter of days, not weeks. But we're brainstorming solutions. Somehow, we'll make it work."

She nodded thoughtfully, then sighed, shifting her weight. "I'm getting tired," she admitted.

Looking around, I spotted a small hill between the house and the barn with a tree growing atop it—well, it was more of a mound than a hill—and nodded toward it. "Let's go sit down."

Violet began hobbling toward it, her expression stiff with determination. I hesitated, then scooped her up in my arms. She gave me an exasperated look, but didn't protest as I carried her over to our destination. I sat her down gently, then dropped to the ground next to her.

She leaned against the tree, pulling her borrowed jacket tighter around her body. It was a beautiful day, with high clouds sailing in a blue late afternoon sky; the tree above us swayed in the breeze, and long, soft grass grew beneath it, making a wonderfully cushioned seat for us to take our breather. Still, there was a chill in the air, and I could see some of the green of the trees beginning to drain away, leaving leaves trained with red and gold. Fall was coming, with winter right around the corner.

As if reading my thoughts, Violet looked around the camp and asked, "What are we going to do if we can't stop Elena before winter?"

"Ms. Dale has been scouting around, but right now, we don't have a plan. We're looking into it."

She nodded. "I'm sure we'll figure something out. It might be a good idea, once we get our people trained, to start embedding them in the city instead of hiding out here."

I smiled. Ms. Dale and I had already discussed that, and had both argued for other ideas before reluctantly deciding it might be the best way forward. Violet may have had a broken skull, but her mind was as sharp as ever.

She sighed, tugging the rough woolen cap that covered her bandages down farther on her forehead. I cocked my head at her. "Feeling self-conscious?"

She shrugged. "It's stupid," she said. "It's just hair, and it'll grow back, but I can't help imagining that I look like a… a giant baby."

I laughed before I could stop myself, and she gave me a sharp look. "Sorry," I said. "But… seeing as I was the one who shaved your head, I can safely say you do not look like an infant without your hair."

Her features softened, a smile sneaking onto her lips. "I noticed you haven't caught me up on the actual news from the city and any of the plans you have going on."

"Well, that's just because you haven't asked. I've been waiting for you to tell me you're ready."

"I'm ready. So what's been going on?"

Reaching into my pocket, I met her gaze. "I'd much rather

you hear it from the horse's mouth, so to speak. Jeff's been waiting for me to contact him, and I figured you'd want to sit in."

"Should we get Owen and the others?"

I shook my head as I pulled out my handheld. "There's too much going on to stop and have a meeting every ten minutes. We'll meet in the morning to get everyone up to speed. Sometimes it's my job to talk to Jeff, sometimes someone else's. I asked for the job today."

Moving closer to her until we were pressed shoulder to shoulder, I keyed in the code for Jeff's handheld and waited for it to connect. A moment later, Jeff's face filled the screen. "Good morning, Viggo. And you as well, Violet. I'm glad to see you recovering."

"Thank you, Jeff," she said, a smile on her lips. "So they sent you into the city, huh? How's that going?"

"As well as can be expected. I have established myself at a boardinghouse, and have received a job helping to clean up the burnt-down sections of the city. For some reason or other, the Matrians don't see me as threatening, which I find quite useful, all things considered. The job itself is not exactly exciting at the moment, but it does put me in a position to notice things."

"Oh, really? Like what?"

"Well, nearly one hundred Matrian wardens have arrived by boat at the city."

My eyes widened. "Are you sure about that?" I asked.

Jeff nodded, his blue eyes grim. "Tiffany—one of the maids from Ashabee's—followed them for a bit, until it became too risky for her to go any farther. We're still not sure where their main base is, but we're working on it."

I exchanged looks with Violet. Her face was drawn; the severity of this information was not lost on her. More troops meant Elena was stepping up her plans. "What about the news?" I asked.

"Ah, yes, well—the announcers noted three things of interest. The first is they are implementing a national registry and the issuing of identification papers. Apparently, a lot of citizen information was lost due to the destruction of the palace, and in order to track rations, they are requiring all citizens to register."

I absorbed this and frowned. "Damn, that's going to be tricky. Do you know if they're going through with those security checkpoints you mentioned the other day?"

"Yes—that might be why they are bringing more wardens into the city. In order to combat terrorism, as they put it." Jeff's voice was prim as he announced it, but his face reflected his distaste. "On that note, they also announced that after a thorough investigation, they have discovered the culprits behind the bombing of the palace were the Porteque gang. Apparently, they disagreed with the interference of Matrians in their city."

"What?" exclaimed Violet. "That doesn't make any sense. Why wouldn't they stick with the Daughters of Patrus as a scapegoat? Or even point a finger at me?"

"That does seem like it would be easier…" I agreed.

"Well, perhaps identifying a single individual wouldn't help them maintain a state of fear, but other than that, I really don't know," Jeff responded, clearly also baffled by the news. "The only thing I can think of is they couldn't fabricate a good enough reason. The Daughters are touted as a pro-female-rule organization, and with the news that Princess Tabitha was to assume control with Chancellor Dobin by her side… Well, maybe they thought it likely that the Daughters would approve of a female ruler." He gave a shrug, but by the look on his face, he thought it was a bit of a stretch as well.

I thought about it. Maybe the bad cover story was good news—it showed Elena was grasping at straws to maintain control over the population. Then again, this new terror threat only added to the level of fear among the populace. They had been used to hearing about the Porteque gang in the past, and now, with two terrorist groups, public demand for the violence to end would be high. Any actions Elena took to eradicate them on behalf of the people of Patrus would be considered a great win, and at least the Porteque gang was a real target for her to show off her firepower.

"What's the last bit of information?" Violet asked, leaning forward.

Jeff smiled then, genuinely. "Matrus is having a day of mourning for the death of Princess Tabitha. It was revealed that she did die in the palace, along with several key advisors—both Matrian and Patrian—and Chancellor Dobin."

"So Dobin was in the palace?" Violet asked.

Jeff nodded. "Apparently, he was in a portion that collapsed. They recovered his body early on, but with all the dead… it took a while to identify him."

Violet's face fell, and I recognized immediately that the news wasn't as uplifting to her as maybe it should have been. But I couldn't blame her. A lot of people had died during her attack on the palace. I knew she hadn't wanted them to; I also knew that if Tabitha had accepted Violet's deal, nobody—not even Tabitha herself—would've died. I reached out and took her hand in mine, knowing she needed the reassurance.

"Thank you, Jeff," I said. "But how are the people taking this news? There's gotta be some concern that with no leaders readily available, the Matrians are trying to seize control, and I know the people of Patrus won't accept that lying down."

"I'm glad you asked. The follow-up to that announcement was that Elena is asking for there to be a general election of a leader to represent the country's interest during this time. The message remains the same—the Matrians are only here to help restore order, not to assume control."

I exhaled. "And in the meantime, while we're waiting for the election to take place, Elena's in charge."

"She's making a show of working within the Patrian legal system, but refuses to execute women in cases where they would traditionally be executed while men would not—the only exception being the women who have been accused of being part of the Daughters of Patrus. Nobody is making a fuss about her refusal, though, because at least looters and criminals are being caught and held accountable. It's gaining her a lot of support, to be honest."

I nodded. "Thanks, Jeff, I think that's all I have to ask. Someone will contact you tomorrow. How does six o'clock sound?"

"It sounds good. See you then."

I clicked off the handheld, ending the call, and turned to Violet. "Thoughts?"

"Will Jeff have a problem getting registered?"

I shook my head. "He shouldn't, but I might encourage him

to find an alternate identity, in case Ashabee has dropped his name."

"Have we heard anything about Ashabee?"

"No, nothing since he was taken to the palace. It could've been that he was in the palace when everything went down, but he also could've been anywhere. To be honest, I'm not sure we'll ever know what happened to him."

She nodded and swallowed. "Elena's certainly good at manipulating the people. She's trying to respect their laws and keeps encouraging them to take control over their own land. Maybe eventually they'll just vote to have her assume command, especially if their leaders keep getting murdered."

I didn't agree, but it wasn't a farfetched conclusion to draw, especially for someone who still only had a limited understanding of Patrus. I could see why she would think that: with Elena manufacturing or capitalizing on the disasters, assigning blame to a familiar enemy, and promising results, she was giving the people an idea to rally behind, the idea that they could trust and rely on her. Still, the inferiority of women wasn't just an idea to Patrians—it was a hard-held belief. I didn't think that was going to change soon enough for the people to ever vote Elena into power, definitely not in her lifetime.

Either way we looked at it, it wasn't looking good. But I had to admit I was still hopeful. With the video, we had a starting point to create our own propaganda, and hopefully turn the tide against Elena.

I looked up and smiled, drawn out of my thoughts, as I saw the familiar form of Ms. Dale heading toward us. I nudged Violet and raised a hand in greeting.

CHAPTER 18

Violet

Viggo and I watched Ms. Dale approach, her feet tearing through the soft grass, heading up the little hill toward the tree we sat beneath. I started to rise, but she motioned me to stop with an imperious wave of her hand. "Don't bother getting up on my account," she announced. "Right now it's much easier for me to come down to you."

Smiling in bemusement, I complied, remaining seated as Ms. Dale dropped down on one knee and gave me a quick, gentle hug. I hugged my former mentor back, relieved to see she was all right, in spite of the chaos of the last few days. "Hey, Ms. Dale," I said fondly, and she squeezed me slightly, still taking care not to upset my injuries.

Afterward, she leaned back, her hands in her lap, and studied my face closely, tsking under her breath as she took in the still livid bruising on the side of my face. The swelling around my eye had gone down, but other than that, the bruises remained, turning interesting shades of purple and green. Ms. Dale's hand stretched out, and she gently took my chin between her fingers and turned it slightly so she could get a better look.

"You brave, sweet girl," she murmured under her breath, and I resisted the urge to both beam with pride and flush with embarrassment.

"It's nothing," I insisted, gently removing her hand. "The worst is over."

She nodded, but her face reflected her doubt. "I'm sorry I didn't pop by sooner to check on you. I did while you were… um…"

"Unconscious?" I suggested, giving her a little smile, and she nodded.

"Yeah. But the past thirty-six hours have been a little hectic, what with the scouts returning from the refugee camp Thomas located, and coordinating with Viggo and Owen regarding the plans for tonight."

I cast a glance over at Viggo and raised an eyebrow. "The plans for tonight? Oh, really?"

Ms. Dale picked up on my tone and speared Viggo with a look of her own. "He didn't tell you."

Viggo idly picked at a blade of grass and gave a shrug. "I just haven't had a chance to yet." I studied him closely and then smiled.

"I'm sure he was *going to* tell me, he just hadn't gotten to it yet," I said dryly, winking when he shot me an indignant glance. I was rewarded by the sight of his face melting, and he shook his head and leaned back on the palms of his hands, clearly bemused. I turned back to Ms. Dale, confident I would get the plans for tonight out of Viggo at some point soon.

"How goes training of the new recruits?" I asked, curious.

Ms. Dale gave a huff and crossed her arms. "About as well as can be expected, I suppose. I can't speak too highly of them yet, but we'll get them there. Some of them—the women, of course—have taken to guns like birds to flight, so there's some hope." She gave Viggo a sly look, and he rolled his eyes at her.

"Well, not *all* birds can fly, so…" He trailed off, and I had to bite my cheek to keep from laughing as Ms. Dale's amusement soured. I always loved it when Ms. Dale and Viggo teased each other. At first it had been truly hostile, but now it was just quintessentially *them*. It was reassuring to see some things never changed.

I ran my left hand over the springy grass, turning back to Ms. Dale, who was staring at my face again, and frowned—was that a glimmer of guilt in her eyes? That was weird. Why would she feel guilty looking at my face? It must have been some sense of responsibility. Maybe, as my former martial arts teacher, she felt responsible for my having lost the fight with Tabitha so badly. Well, technically I'd won in the end…

The expression I was pondering was gone in an instant, as Ms. Dale's face returned to its normal impassive state.

"On that note, I have to get back to preparations," she said, standing up. "Viggo, I will see you tonight."

Viggo inclined his head in wordless acknowledgement, and I leaned back onto the trunk of the tree behind us as Ms. Dale moved off to other parts of the camp. My thoughts drifted to Tim, and I felt a deep ache in my heart. Still no word, no sign, no intercepted report… nothing. That was really why I would have agreed to anything to get out of bed. When I wasn't sleeping, my brother was always on my mind; even when I slept, my dreams were troubled, his voice and his face making appearances in places that had nothing to do with him. Doing something else—anything else—was the only way to keep the worry from becoming impatience and making me want to do something drastic.

Viggo's arm dropped over my shoulder, and I looked up at him, shaking off the dire thoughts. His mouth was pressed into a thin line. "Tim?" he asked. I nodded, and he tugged me closer, holding me tight.

"We'll find him," Viggo breathed against my forehead. I nodded again, but the doubt still lurked in my mind, racing over the dozens of possible outcomes, none of them good. "Actually, we have a bit of a lead…"

A grin formed on my lips as I put two and two together and cast a gaze up at him. "You mean… Does it have something to do with your mysterious mission tonight?"

Viggo nodded, and I straightened slightly, brushing invisible lint off the pants I was wearing. They were borrowed—probably outfits recovered from Ashabee's manor, or donated by some of the refugees—and a bit large, but serviceable. "Spill."

He chuckled and began explaining the camp Thomas had found, the one where the Matrians were shipping most, if not all, Patrian males. "They will have records," he said. "Possibly even computers we can hack into." He hesitated, meeting my gaze with a wary flick of his eyes. "I'm hoping we might find some sign of Tim… If he's been picked up, they might have taken him there."

I fidgeted as a sliver of hope threaded its way into my heart. I sternly reminded myself there were no guarantees. Viggo reached over and took my hand, squeezing it gently. We sat there for a few minutes, Viggo comforting me while I fretted, worried about what they might find at this camp—and, even worse, what they might not.

I was so deep into my musings that when Viggo spoke again, it took a moment to register. "Look who's over there…"

He pointed, and I followed the direction of his finger, my eyes finding a man standing a fair distance away, near a group of people standing in line by the shooting range set up some ways behind the barn. He was peering directly at us. Even at this distance, it took me less than a second to identify Cad, and I straightened, self-consciously tugging my cap down over my bald head. Cad seemed to realize it was me, and gave a little whoop, loping over toward us.

This time I did try to stand, using the tree and Viggo for help, and was on my feet by the time my cousin reached us. "Violet!" he exclaimed, throwing his arms open wide. I stepped gingerly into them, just relieved to see him, and he hugged me extra gently, his arms barely brushing my healing ribs. We held each other like that for a moment, and he pecked me on my forehead. "I'm so happy to see you up," he whispered.

"Me too," I whispered back, releasing him. He stepped away, and I saw his eyes were brimming with gratitude.

"Violet, seriously, words can't even express how grateful I am to you for what you did for my family," he gushed, and I looked away, embarrassed by the praise. "I mean, I don't know if I ever could've done what you did for us. What you sacrificed for us."

I frowned, thinking of my brother, and then shook my head. "That's not true," I reminded him softly. "You already did—you went back to the palace and went searching for Tim. I can't even tell you how much I appreciate that."

Cad rubbed the back of his head awkwardly and gave me a sad smile. "I just wish I had found him," he replied.

I wanted to say "me too" again, but I didn't. Cad already knew that—and, obviously, he didn't need to be reminded of his failure. The two of us stood awkwardly, uncertain what to say next. The sound of gunfire punctuated the moment, and I looked over at the range, watching Ms. Dale marching up and down the line of trainees, before looking back to Cad.

"So… how's training?" I asked, fumbling for a conversation topic.

"Eh. So-so. I'm not so good with a gun, but my wife…" He trailed off, his eyes going wide. He looked around for a second, and then held up a finger. "Hold that thought—I'll be right back."

I watched as he raced back toward the group on the range, and exchanged baffled looks with Viggo, who shrugged. Cad approached a woman in the firing line, and, when she put her gun down, tapped her shoulder and began speaking to her, his hands gesticulating wildly. After a moment, the woman smiled and nodded.

"Looks like you're about to meet the family," announced Viggo from beside me, and I felt my eyes growing wide.

"Right now?"

Viggo chuckled and nodded. "Right now," he agreed.

I fidgeted, smoothing my hands over my clothes, suddenly stupidly self-conscious. I felt Viggo's eyes on me. "They're going to love you," he said. "Especially after what you did for them."

My expression soured. "Just because I saved their lives doesn't mean they're obligated to love me," I muttered.

"Why not? It worked for me."

I squinted at him. "Didn't you save *my* life first?"

"Case in point," he teased, nodding his head toward the unfolding scene. It took a few minutes for Cad and his wife to trudge around behind the house, out of our view. Then they reappeared and headed toward our little hill, now followed by two children and a shaggy brown dog.

"Is that Samuel?" I asked incredulously, glad that in all the chaos, the dog hadn't been left behind.

"Yeah," Viggo said, smiling a little at my astonishment. "It's funny, actually. There's kind of a little refugee daycare going on—especially with the parents training all the time at the firing range—and the kids all love Samuel, so now they're looking after him, too."

Come to think of it, it was odd seeing Cad's children here; it was strange they were only a few minutes away while their parents trained for war. Knowing they were playing in the house's backyard, being monitored by one of the refugees, comforted me.

"Violet," Cad said when they reached us, while Samuel ran up to Viggo and attempted to jump on his knees, "I want you to meet my wife, Margot, and our children, Alice and Henry. Everyone, this is Violet, our cousin."

I felt myself smiling naturally as I took in the taller woman. She was almost Cad's exact height, statuesque, with warm brown skin and deep brown, almost black, eyes. The corners of her full mouth held smile lines. Her round face was framed by black, curly hair tied under a blue kerchief. I had seen her picture before, but it had barely been able to capture her radiant beauty.

"Hello," I said softly. "It's nice to meet you."

Henry, the little boy hiding in Margot's skirts, smiled shyly, then hid his face, while Alice peered at me from behind the small fist she held up against her mouth, sucking her thumb. I waved, and she blushed, looking away, absently putting a hand on Samuel as he pushed his nose into her shoulder.

"Violet!" Margot exclaimed, taking my left hand in hers and squeezing. "I'm so happy to see you doing well, all things considered. By the look of your face, you really went through the wringer for us, and I can't even begin to tell you how grateful we are. That Princess Tabitha was a real piece of work, right? Can't say I'm sorry to hear she died—served her right. What kind of a monster kidnaps an entire family—even two innocent children?" She paused only for a moment before continuing with the answer to her own question. "The evil kind, if you don't mind me speaking out of turn. Ugh, if she were here, I'd claw out her bloody eyes for scaring my babies—God, and for hurting you."

I smiled as Margot spoke, barely taking a moment to draw in a breath. Cad gazed at her while she talked, his eyes warm with affection, and I could feel the love radiating from him. He caught my gaze and winked. "Isn't she wonderful?" he said.

"Absolutely," I agreed with a smile, and Margot's cheeks grew dark with a blush. I realized she had been nervous too, and that comforted me. "Don't take this the wrong way, but… are you sure you were raised in Patrus?" I asked.

Margot laughed heartily. "You mean 'cause I talk so much? Well, my father was convinced I'd never get married because of it, but I can't help it. I seem to lack that filter between thought and mouth sometimes. I was pretty certain he was right, but then *this one* came along, and for some reason, he couldn't get enough. At first I figured he was just another jerk with ideas about 'taming' me or some other kind of nonsense they like to go on about, but he persisted."

"Couldn't your father have just married you to him without your approval anyway?"

Margot gave me a knowing smile. "Yeah, he would have, too, 'cept Cad wouldn't tell him he was interested until I agreed. That's when I started realizing he was sincere."

Cad blushed and beamed at the same time. "What could I say? I was into women's rights before it was popular."

Margot snorted and put her hand on her hip. "Oh, really? Does that mean you'll do the dishes after dinner tonight?"

"I'd be happy to do the dishes," Cad replied without missing a beat. "You have only to ask."

Margot glowed, and I was struck by how well they blended together, complementing each other almost effortlessly. Both gave as good as they got, a mixture of teasing and solemnity that seemed breathtakingly sweet. It made me wonder whether this was how Viggo and I appeared to the world. I kind of hoped so.

"Cad, Margot, Henry, and Alice, I'd like you to meet Viggo Croft," I said, taking advantage of the momentary pause in Margot's chatter. "He's my fiancé."

Cad cocked his head in surprise, looking Viggo over, while Margot beamed at me. "Well, he's certainly a looker," she said, boldly eyeing him.

Viggo coughed, his cheeks reddening at her brazen comment, and I bit the inside of my cheek to keep from laughing.

"We've met," Cad announced blithely, impervious to his wife's forward behavior. "Although I didn't know you two were engaged…"

Shaking his hand, Viggo shrugged. "It didn't seem like the best time to formally introduce myself," he replied, and Cad chuckled, nodding his head in agreement.

"Yeah, probably not."

The three of them continued to chat, which was good—I was less apprehensive than earlier, but I still wasn't feeling at my best, conversationally speaking. I kept one ear on the conversation between the adults, but focused on Henry and Alice. Dropping down into a squat took a little bit of effort, but I managed, grateful my legs hadn't been damaged along with the rest of me. Margot, aware of what I was doing, immediately sat Henry down next to his sister, and I shot her a smile before giving the two children my full attention.

The little ones stared at me, and I could sense their nervousness. After a moment, I slowly puckered my lips like a fish, then stuck out my tongue. I waited for some response—then Samuel, noticing that I was at his level, came snuffling over and tried to kiss my face. "Oop," I said, pushing away the wet, sloppy dog; by the time I managed to calm him down, I saw that Alice was smiling shyly.

"Ew," she said to the dog. "Bad Sammy!" I laughed a little. Meanwhile, Henry had come closer and reached out his hand to touch my face.

I let his fingers stroke lightly over the bruises, tracing them. "Are you a Valkyrie?" he whispered after a second.

"What an interesting question," I replied, stifling my embarrassment. "Why do you ask?"

"Mama says Valkyries are women who save people," Alice replied, her voice whisper-thin. "Mama says you saved us."

"Well, do you think I'm a Valkyrie?"

"No," replied Henry, almost belligerently. "Mama says Valkyries ride horses and hold fiery swords. But you don't have any."

"That's very true. You're really smart, aren't you?"

Henry nodded and puffed his chest out proudly. "I got the best scores in letters and spelling," he proclaimed.

I smiled. "My brother is good at math. Are you?"

Henry shook his head, but Alice perked up. "I am! Do you want to hear me do multiplication?"

"You can multiply?" I asked, filling my voice with awe.

She nodded, her eyes glowing. "Dad taught me. I can do nines! I know a trick!"

"Really? Can you teach me?"

Biting her lip, she nodded, and began to show me the trick using her fingers, peeking slyly up at me every so often as though to check whether I was baffled. I figured out the trick by nine times two, but let her continue anyway, looking properly excited. Henry, seemingly bothered by being ignored, stepped closer and opened his arms. I immediately settled back down into a seated position, glad for the opportunity to relax from my crouch, and he climbed into my lap while we watched his sister.

We were at nine times six when Cad squatted down. "All right, kiddos—it's time to go. Tell Violet goodbye."

A surge of pleasure washed over me at their plaintive protests. "It's all right, guys. I have to go anyway. But we'll see each other again soon—I promise."

The two children immediately held up their pinkies, and I grinned, recognizing the gesture. It was awkward with my left hand, but I held it out, pinky extended. Alice wrapped her pinky around mine, and Henry followed.

"Okay, ankle-biters," Cad said. "Let's go. C'mon, Samuel, I guess we'd better get you back too."

I watched as he took his children's small hands and began heading down the hill. Margot and Viggo helped me up, and Margot gave me a soft yet warm hug. "Thank you," she said against my shoulder. "Thank you so much for coming for us. We will never forget it, and you are always welcome with us, whenever you need anything."

"Thank you," I whispered back, holding her close for a moment longer before releasing her.

She nodded, raising a hand to Viggo before following Cad and their children down the hill. I watched them go, and then turned to Viggo, prepared to let him know I was ready to go back in, when the contemplative look on his face made me pause.

"What?" I asked, looking down at my arms and legs as though they were somehow accountable for the warmth in his expression.

"Nothing," he said nonchalantly. "It's just... you seem really good with kids."

Slightly dazed by his words, I immediately deflected. "Yeah, well, at the rate we're going, this will be a kid-free zone until you put a ring on my finger."

"Hmmm..." Viggo said, his green eyes growing even more thoughtful. "Noted."

I chuckled and slipped my arm through his as we got up and made our way down the gently sloping hill. As we walked, I couldn't help imagining holding a small boy with Viggo's eyes in my arms, nestling him close to my chest. Blinking at the un-accustomed thoughts of a future I wasn't sure would ever happen, I decided I didn't quite hate the idea. In fact, it filled me with a thrill of excitement.

Smiling, I rested my head against Viggo's arm and allowed him to lead me.

CHAPTER 19

Viggo

Violet and I were halfway to the house when the sound of my name being shouted loudly from the other side of the yard made me pause. I turned slightly, craning my neck toward the sound, and saw Thomas rushing over, his cheeks flushed and his eyes bright with excitement.

"Viggo!" he repeated, closing the distance rapidly.

"Hey, Thomas," I greeted. "What's up?"

He came to a stop before us, his breathing coming in short pants. I exchanged looks with Violet, who shrugged, and turned back to him, curious. He gave a few racking coughs, a definite sign he was not comfortable with running, and then seemed to catch his breath.

"Do you remember those cases we hauled from Ashabee's? The ones we didn't recognize?"

I racked my mind for the memory of a previous conversation

about it, but came up short. If we had, it had slipped my notice, either due to exhaustion, my preoccupation with Violet, or just too much going on to retain everything. "Not really. But I take it you figured it out."

Thomas nodded, his breathing still labored. "I did! They're *drones*," he proclaimed with a broad smile. I frowned at the unfamiliar word and looked over at Violet, who was wearing a similar confused expression. Thomas looked back and forth between us, his smile slowly slipping away, to be replaced by an incredulous quirk of his head. "*Drones,*" he repeated.

I shook my head. "I'm sorry—last I heard that term, it was for mindless worker bees in a hive. So unless you're saying the boxes contain beehives, I have no idea."

"Don't be obtuse," Thomas grumbled, and then flinched when I gave him a stern look. "Sorry," he amended. "Was there a better way to say that? Social protocols sometimes elude me. Maybe… don't be stupid?"

I didn't reply, torn between rolling my eyes and laughing, but Violet grinned at Thomas. "Don't worry about it," she said. "However, the word you're using is actually unfamiliar to us, so can you please explain what a drone is?"

Thomas nodded in excitement. "A drone is a machine capable of flight that can be piloted remotely. It has cameras on it with night vision and thermal scan settings! Do you understand what that means?!"

I considered what he was saying, and then smiled. "It means you have a way of checking out the camp before Owen and I even enter."

"Exactly!" he exclaimed. "It is the perfect spy tool! And

there are three of them!"

Opening my mouth to respond, I paused when I heard the loud sound of Violet's stomach growling obnoxiously. She had the good grace to blush. "Hold that thought, Thomas," I said. "We should get Violet fed."

She grinned up at me, leaning on my arm as we made our way into the house, Thomas hot on our heels. I got her settled in a chair at the dining room table, and then moved to the kitchen, where the ever-present pot of soup—this one containing rice—was sitting just short of the hearth, hung from a hook that could be pushed closer to the fire to cook. I ladled her a bowl, noticing Thomas was waiting impatiently, shifting his weight from one side to the other. Once I had set Violet up to my satisfaction (and her dutiful amusement), I sat down, motioning for Thomas to join us.

Violet sipped at her soup while I turned to Thomas. "So, this drone thing—you're saying we can use it tonight?"

"Of course! In fact, it'll be perfect for helping you sneak around. Using it, I can monitor guard movement and guide you remotely on the subvocalizers."

"Will it work from that distance, or will you have to be close?"

"I checked the radio transmitter that controls it—it will work at that range. Its configuration is quite interesting. It seems Ashabee based the transmitter design off the ones used for the subvocalizers, but it's far more sophisticated. I looked at the code, and it is amazing. I've never seen anything quite like it. You see, it operates at a—"

"Thomas," Violet interrupted gently, her spoon halfway

between the bowl and her mouth. "Can *anyone* fly the drone, or do they need piloting experience?"

That was a good question. I turned to the small man and waited for him to respond.

"Oh, no, the controls are quite simple. Anyone could pilot it."

"I see. And does it require two hands, or one?"

Understanding struck me, and I turned to Violet, watching as she delicately sipped her soup, the corners of her lips turning upward in a hopeful smile. Bemused by her cleverness, I sat back, watching the scene play out.

"Oh, just the one, really. It's very user-friendly."

Violet set her spoon down with a clink. "Excellent," she replied, leaning forward and catching my eye. "So *I* can pilot it."

Her words confirmed my supposition, and I hid my smile, waiting to see how Thomas would react.

"What?! But I wanted to… I mean… I realized what it was, so *I* should be able to fly it!" His voice was petulant with a bit of whining thrown in, and I realized I would need to step in before things got anywhere remotely near heated. Not that I was worried about Violet—she was watching Thomas with a bemused expression. No, Thomas was more prone to missing social cues, so better to help convince him than let him feel like he was being left out.

"Actually, that might be a good idea," I interjected. Thomas gave me an appalled look, his eyes wide. "Thomas, we're going to need your tactical mind focused on the bigger picture," I added before his ego could get *too* crushed. "Besides, you can't pilot *and* hack their computers—if they have any—at once.

Not to mention, you're one of our best strategists. We need you overseeing the entire operation with Ms. Dale."

Thomas considered my words and then nodded, mollified. "You're right, and I'm sure Violet is feeling useless, so that will be helpful for her. I'll go get one ready for her to practice on."

He stood up and walked out, and I looked over at Violet. She blinked, as if clearing her head from a strong left hook. "He's not wrong," she said dryly. "I would like to not feel useless."

I smiled at her, shaking my head. "You're not useless, baby. Besides, even if you weren't injured, having a remote operative without the risk is really a good idea. I think I might go a bit crazy with just Thomas and Ms. Dale in my ears."

She chuckled, her gray eyes sparkling. "You're just saying that to make me feel better," she chided. "And this time... I am totally okay with that."

"Well, maybe a little bit," I admitted. "But honestly, it *is* a good idea for many reasons, the main one being that I trust you and your judgment. I like Thomas, but he's often a little too clinical for my comfort. Ms. Dale is mission-oriented, which is a bonus, but sometimes she overlooks the emotional aspect of things in the name of the mission. I trust you to be their counterpoint."

She gave me a doubtful look. "I think you might be building me up a bit there, but since you're not arguing with me, I'm going to take it."

"Look, I think this is a perfect solution—you won't be in the field, but you also won't be sitting around worrying about me. You'll be involved. I *want* you to be involved."

As I spoke, her doubtful look melted. "Now, that *was* better, but seriously, you don't have to keep convincing me you're okay with it. I believe you."

I blew out a breath. "Sorry, am I going overboard? I just… I can't fully imagine what you're going through."

She frowned and stirred her spoon through her soup a few times. Then she set it down on the table with a click and pushed the bowl away. "I'm worried half the time, frustrated the other half, and so much of my body is still sore all the time. If I'm being honest, our walk took more out of me than I care to admit, and I just… I don't like feeling helpless." She met my gaze with a small smile. "I guess what I'm saying is, thanks for not fighting me on this. Even when you don't fully understand what I'm going through, you're still able to give me exactly what I need."

I reached out and took her left hand, rubbing the tips of her fingers with my own, then kissing them. We stared at each other, and I felt a surge of love for her that seemed to flood out of my chest and into every part of me, making me feel stronger, calmer, more whole. Even after everything that had happened, we were still standing, still together, and—best of all—still partners. It was reassuring that even when we were at our weakest, we each had the other to back us up.

"I love you," I told her, a surge of male pride running through me as her eyes lit up and her lips curled into a full-bodied smile.

"I love you, too," she said back, running her thumb over my own. I stared at her, a smile on my own lips, and for a moment, the world and all our problems dropped away, leaving only us, together, in that moment, rooted to each other like two trees in a forest.

Sighing at the knowledge there wasn't enough time to just *be* with each other, I released Violet's hand and stood up, moving to a small table by the couch that was stacked with papers and notes. I pushed through the various files, picking up the one with the photos of the worker camp the scouts had come back with. I held them up as I walked back, and dropped into my seat.

"Here," I said, placing the file in front of her. "These are the pictures we got from the scouts. They did the best they could under the circumstances, but it doesn't show much other than the structures and some of the configuration."

She nodded, flipping open the folder and looking at the grainy, faraway pictures. I had already studied them this morning. The camp was set in a large meadow, bordered on one side by forest, leading to another empty meadow on the other. A mountain range loomed in the background, near enough to block out almost all the sky. To all appearances, it was out in the middle of nowhere; the rutted tracks that led to it seemed to have been made specifically for coming to this camp, since there was still brush and weeds growing in between the tire tracks. The structure itself was a tall barbed-wire fence with rows and rows of tents inside surrounding four rectangular structures that resembled the massive trailers I'd often seen used to haul food. They had windows, but the scouts hadn't been able to risk getting closer, and at the distance from which the photos were taken, they only appeared as opaque squares.

Violet grimaced at the graininess. "What's the exact goal for the mission?" she asked as she slid the glossy photos around, lining them up on the table in various positions.

"Well, information gathering, to be honest. We know for sure they are sending the men they've been collecting from the city there, under the guise of training them with new skillsets, but most likely for execution. Of course, we want to be able to find out what the true purpose of the camp is. But beyond that, we're gambling that they have a computer there. If Thomas can hack into it remotely…"

"Then we can figure out where Elena's forces are, what orders they're being given, and maybe…" She met my eyes, and I saw the small spark of hope there. "Maybe find out where Tim is."

I nodded. "Exactly."

She swallowed hard. "All right," she said. "Take me though your plan."

Hours later, Owen and I had finished loading the crate that held the drone into the back of our vehicle. Violet stood at the foot of the porch, her left hand on her hip. The crate was heavy, but not impossible for two men to lift.

The sun had set, and even the light of dusk was fading. It was time. I shut the door and turned to Violet. She quirked up the corners of her lips encouragingly, but I could see the longing in her eyes. "You okay with this?" I asked.

Her smile became a bit less strained. "I have to be," she admitted ruefully. "I just… I wish I was going with you."

I rested my hands on her shoulders. "I know how frustrating it is. I had to watch you and Owen run off to defuse bombs while I was flat on my back in my hospital bed."

"That's true," she admitted, blowing out a breath. "Well, it might be a good thing I'm not going anyway, given my track record lately."

"What do you mean?"

She grinned impishly, her eyes sparkling. "If I go, things might explode."

I fought back a laugh and dropped a chaste kiss onto her forehead. Her eyes fluttered closed, and her hands went to my sides. "Be careful," she breathed.

"I promise. Besides, if things go wrong, I can always use Owen as a human shield."

"That's only if I don't use you as one first," Owen replied as he threw a duffle bag in the back.

"If either of you does that, I'll skin the other alive," growled Violet.

I let her go and stared down at her. The joking had helped chase most of the shadows out of her eyes, but some still lingered. I was torn between wanting to comfort her further and the need to get going and focus on the mission. Violet lightly pushed me toward the car. "Go," she urged. "I've got your back."

Placing one more kiss on her forehead, I nodded and left, climbing into the driver's side. I threw the vehicle into gear, took one last look at Violet—standing wearily, but on her own, in front of the farmhouse, her cap pulled down over her forehead—and then took off. I turned my mind to the mission ahead, confident in her and my ability as a team, even with distance separating us.

CHAPTER 20

Violet

The fingers of my left hand, save for my thumb, all rested inside four identical hollow metal tubes, which tapered at the bottom until they connected to wires that jutted out of the remote control. The device itself was about as wide as my forearm, as thick as the palm of my hand, and as long as my foot—probably about eight inches or so. Hard black plastic encased the device, and several buttons and dials were within reach of my thumb. The rest of the surface was filled with a screen, and I peered at it intently as I carefully manipulated my fingers.

In response, the camera angle shifted until it was pointed at a small window. A smile grew on my face as I raised my right hand, cast and all, and waved at the drone I could just see, a flicker in the dark, through the thin glass. Caught by the drone's front-mounted camera, my actions were mirrored on the screen in real time. The drone's design was sleek, not entirely unlike a heloship on a much smaller scale—about three feet in length and two feet in width. It stood a foot and a half when set on the ground, and was painted a matte black. The conical nose sloped back wider into the first set of wings, branches with propellers set in them at an eight-inch distance. The wings drew back in at a right angle, ending as they connected to the rectangular body. Another set of wings with inset propellers sat behind the first, probably eight to twelve inches away. It looked like an "H", but with the connecting line in the middle jutting out farther on either side.

I lowered my hand and used my left thumb to click one of the dials, changing the camera to the one mounted on the drone's belly. I then flipped a switch, activating night vision. Immediately the screen glowed a neon green, and I could see the ground just below where the drone was hovering.

I used my index and middle finger to pull the craft up and away from the window, while my ring finger and pinky controlled the turn. Once it had spun in a tidy circle, I relaxed my smallest digits and used my index to press it forward, while my middle finger controlled the height. I flew a slow loop around our camp beside the road to the farmhouse, over the tents, noting the placement of our guards and facilities.

The drone was remarkable. Its engines were whisper-soft, and the controls were sensitive to miniscule movements, yet somehow fairly intuitive. Piloting required a certain amount of dexterity, but remained mostly user-friendly, especially since the sensitivity of the controls could be adjusted. I smiled as I thought of Thomas' demonstration earlier that evening, which had resulted in the drone getting lodged in a tree, clicking angrily.

It had been two hours since Viggo and Owen had departed, and while I knew I should have been resting, I had instead taken the time to practice my flying with one of the spare drones from the barn. I wanted to make sure I had a complete understanding of all the controls and features. It was as compulsive a need to me as checking a gun for ammunition or cracking my neck before a fistfight.

Besides, there were too many unknowns on this mission to risk Viggo and Owen's lives with my inexperience with the equipment. Not that *anyone* was an expert on drones right now, of course, but that didn't give me license to relax. I was too edgy to rest anyway. Watching Viggo leave today had been difficult, and even though I was definitely part of the mission, it wasn't the same as being physically there with them. On the other hand, the moment wasn't always what it was cracked up to be—the tension seemed to exist no matter which end I was on. This tension was actually almost worse, because if anything went wrong, I was literally too far away to do anything about it. I was certain Thomas felt the opposite, while Ms. Dale just rolled with the punches one way or the other.

A sharp rap on the door jolted my attention from the screen, and I flicked another switch, putting the craft in a locked holding pattern, before looking up. The woman herself stood in the doorway, her brown eyes on me. "They've arrived at the destination," Ms. Dale announced with a nod. "They're unboxing the drone now."

"Give me one second," I said, and she nodded and left. I quickly adjusted the controls and flew the drone toward the barn, landing it right outside one of the doors. Powering off the remote, I slid it from my lap—it was too heavy and awkward for me to lift with my cast—and then stood up.

I moved down the hallway, through the dining room and kitchen area, stepping into a room on the opposite side. The strange room took up the width of the house on this side and was clearly a trophy room of sorts. Animal heads were mounted on the wall, while furs stretched over the mismatched chairs sitting near the fireplace opposite the door. A sofa running along the inner wall also had a few dark brown furs draped over it. I wasn't sure what kind of animal the skins were from, but if I'd had to guess, I would have said bear.

In this room, Ms. Dale and Thomas had set up a long, collapsible table along the rear wall of the house, and they'd carried in several screens and computers while I was tinkering with the drone. I had offered to help, but Ms. Dale had waved me off, insisting my time would be better spent resting or practicing. As I entered, Ms. Dale was leaning over Thomas, going over a few of the pictures once more, and neither seemed to notice me at first.

We were using some of our camp's precious electricity for this mission. Since I'd been awake, I'd learned the farmhouse had been off the grid when Ms. Dale had found it, but she'd picked it partially for the old generator in the basement. Thomas and some of the refugees had managed to patch it up, and while they'd also brought several smaller, state-of-the-art generators from Ashabee's stash, it would be easy to max them out for non-emergency situations.

Besides, Ms. Dale and Thomas had both insisted keeping the lights off made us much less of a target at night in case another heloship came by. Thus, the camp had fire-cooked soup and tea heated on the wood stove in the kitchen, hand-washed laundry with hand-pumped water; the makeshift sickbay, the handhelds that needed charging, and Thomas's spying equipment were the only things we were allowed to use power for. It was vital for this mission, especially for staying connected to our crew—and since the drones charged electrically as well, I was insanely grateful we had it.

I moved over to a ladder-back chair pulled out in front of the table, the familiar remote control set up in front of it. Sitting down, I looked over to where Thomas and Ms. Dale were still softly speaking and cleared my throat. Almost as one, they turned toward me.

"Good," Ms. Dale said, straightening up, as though I had announced myself. "Viggo just let me know the drone is out of the box. Here." She handed me a gray case, and I opened it up, pulling out the headset and earbud that would allow me to communicate with Viggo and Owen. Unlike the previous missions we had used subvocalizers on, there weren't any separate channels set up, which meant everything would be heard by everyone. Ms. Dale and Thomas were already geared up in simple headsets with microphones; since the three of us were in a secure location, we wouldn't need to use the subvocalizers, and would be patching our regular voices into Owen and Viggo's ears through these while they communicated to us via subvocalizers, the devices scanning their vocal cords and reconstructing the sounds they would make in exacting detail.

I pushed the earbud into my ear and pressed the small button on the base. Immediately I heard Viggo's voice coming through the line, probably speaking to Ms. Dale.

—set up the drone about fifty yards from the base, beyond the tree line. Getting ready to activate, advise when Violet is ready.

"I'm here," I said into the headset's mic, smiling despite myself as I heard his voice.

Good, came Viggo's reply. *We'll power up the drone now.*

"Go ahead." I clicked on the remote and looked up at the drone's view screen, which Thomas had wired to also display on the television across from me. The screen flickered, filled with darkness; I turned on the camera on the drone's belly and flipped the switch to night vision. Immediately, green and black filled the screen, and I found myself looking at tree trunks and grass. "Back away from the drone," I ordered as I slid my fingers into the metal tubes.

We're clear, announced Owen, and I immediately moved my middle finger up, causing the drone to rise up into the air. I kept the speed slow, remembering the drone's engines would be stiff until they warmed up. A small red proximity alarm flashed on the screen, and I used my thumb to quickly switch the view to the nose camera, adjusting the drone until it was pointed upward. A large branch cut across my path, so I adjusted the course, weaving slowly in and out of the forest canopy until I cleared the tops of the trees.

Reading the compass on the display, I manipulated the tubes again, angling the drone toward the labor camp. A series of bright white lights began to appear, set on tall, thin poles barely visible in their own light—I blinked, momentarily turning away from the screen and switching to the drone's low-level light setting as the camera flared with green, the night vision setting taking in far too much light. Recovered, I moved toward the bright balls, knowing those were the lights that illuminated the camp.

I kept the drone fifty feet off the ground, and as I approached the chain link fence, away from low-hanging trees, I switched over to the belly camera, knowing the proximity sensors would pick anything up before I hit it, provided I wasn't moving too fast. At this height, the airspace above the camp would be clear enough, anyway. We had almost the whole night before daylight made the mission infeasible, so I was confident we could get through our recon.

Angling for the closest corner of the fence, I positioned the drone, hovered it, and looked over at Thomas. Sitting next to him in the farmhouse felt surreal; my eyes already strayed back to the screen, as though what was happening out there was more real than this room. "Ready for recon," I informed the small man, and everybody in my company. He nodded, his fingers flying over the computer.

"Ready," he replied.

The plan was simple. I would fly the drone in concentric circles, first around the fence and then moving inward, noting guard positions, movements, and weapons if possible. Thomas would input the data as I moved in, hopefully mapping out likely movement patterns so we could make it easier for Viggo and Owen to get in and out undetected. It was frustrating that we couldn't send them the map directly, but the handhelds continued to have their limitations, one of which being that we couldn't give them a live feed. We all knew it was a painstakingly slow process, but were also confident we could get the whole thing done in under an hour, two tops. If the drone was spotted, I would fly it out of there, and we would abort.

I began my circuit, announcing guards as I came across them. So far there were only four wardens walking the perimeter, but as I drew inward, I could see several more in what seemed to be stationary positions around the camp—all around the tents, all standing. The tents were tall enough to obscure some angles of approach from view of the stationary guards on the inside, but the initial approach would definitely be tight.

Rows and rows of tents filled the camera as I circled around them, so many it was difficult to count how many I had passed after a while. After some time flying in mind-numbing circles, with only my display readings to guide me, and Thomas to notify me of course corrections, I finally spotted the break that constituted the open space around the trailers in the center.

"Thomas, how many rows of tents are we up to?" I asked as I flew the drone around another line of them.

Thomas clicked something on, and I heard his chair squeak as he nodded. "Ten deep and ten wide. Each tent can hold two to four people, so… it's possible there's over three hundred men in the camp, and we could give or take a hundred or so."

"There are no mass burial sites," commented Ms. Dale, who was prowling the room behind us, closely watching the screens Thomas and I were working on. "Definitely no sign this is a death camp."

What do you think it might be? Viggo articulated through the line. I had to admire his patience—he and Owen had been sitting on standby the entire time, still on the eroded car track in the forest, probably itching to move, but unable to start their stage of the mission until we had finished ours.

Ms. Dale pursed her lips and shook her head. "I'm not sure," she admitted after a pause. "It's a mystery—but I'm honestly considering letting go of it for the time being and sending you guys home. We presumed this was some sort of execution camp, and without any evidence of it, it's making me reconsider what might be going on here. I'm questioning what kind of evidence we'll find."

I wanted to argue with her. There could be some sign of Tim in the camp! I bit the impulse back, recognizing my motivations were purely selfish. I had to trust Ms. Dale had our best interests in mind and not let my personal feelings get in the way of the mission. That would definitely give my team members justifiable cause to exclude me from future missions. I also knew acting recklessly now could put Owen and Viggo's lives in danger, and I could not risk their lives, no matter how much I wanted to know about my brother.

Why don't you let Violet use thermal scanning on the trailers first? Owen suggested. *That way we'll have a better idea how many guards there are, and whether it's worth taking the risk.* I smiled, silently cheering him on.

Let's also not forget that any information they have on the computers there is worth the risk, added Viggo. *I would find it hard to believe if they had three hundred men in the camp and no filing system.*

Ms. Dale released a heavy sigh and nodded at me. I didn't need to be told twice. I flew the drone over to the trailers using the low-light vision, then clicked over to the thermal scanner. Immediately, the picture changed to a complex, mottled image of black, blues, and purples, a few yellows and greens in between.

On the screen, the trailer beneath the drone showed a very dark blue, indicating a low level of heat next to the cold, black outside around it. I carefully piloted the drone over the top, noting the hotter, brighter bodies inside. This trailer had four individuals inside, their bodies glowing a complex, almost beautiful mosaic of blue, green, and yellow that phased to orange, just a bit of red, at the centers. Unlike the other trailer, I could make out individual limbs that indicated they were lying down, but beyond that, they weren't moving.

"Southwest trailer has four bodies inside, not moving. Possible sleeping quarters," I informed everyone. I piloted to the next one and repeated the procedure—this one had only two people inside. On the third trailer, I paused as I took in the three people in the box, painstakingly pushing my mic's off button with my right hand so I could conference with Ms. Dale and Thomas without bothering Owen and Viggo.

"Before I tell them anything is wrong—Thomas, why would two of the three people in this room be showing up as way redder than the other one?" I asked.

Ms. Dale and Thomas both turned off their mics. Thomas glanced over at my screen and frowned, perusing the screen, then gave a little shrug. "It could be an area set up for first aid," he announced. "Those two might be running a fever."

"Should I count them as guards? Do you think they are some of the Patrian males?"

Ms. Dale answered for him. "Until we know better, they are guards. If they're running fevers, that might be to our advantage, but I would prefer not to test that theory. Let's report three hostiles to Viggo, but warn him that two could be sick."

Decided, we patched back into Viggo and Owen's line, and I informed Viggo, who acknowledged me tersely. Then I piloted the drone to the last trailer, relieved when I saw it was empty. "Northeast trailer is empty—I recommend it as a first stop."

Only if we get the go-ahead from Ms. Dale, Viggo replied.

Ms. Dale moved over to Thomas, studying his map closely. "Do you see a point of ingress?" she asked the pudgy man.

Thomas shook his head, his fingers flying. "If they approach from the same direction as the trailer, fifteen feet from the corner, they'll have a minute-and-a-half window to get through the gate and into the tents. It'll be tight, but it's doable."

Ms. Dale nodded. "All right," she transmitted. "You get that, boys?"

Started moving five seconds ago, came Viggo's dry response.

I suppressed a smile and transitioned the camera back to low-light vision, using it and Thomas's directions to help pilot the drone over to the point Thomas had indicated on the screen. Then I waited for Viggo and Owen to come into sight, that one spark of humor bleeding away into tension as the seconds slowly clicked by.

CHAPTER 21

Viggo

O wen eased the car to a stop as we slowly pulled up through the forest nearest the northeast corner of the camp, killing the engine. I got out, taking care to close the door quietly. I almost felt naked with no backpack on my shoulder, but the small bags at my belt contained everything I was likely to need, packed tight so nothing bounced around.

The night air was cold, and my breath crystallized as it encountered the frigid environment, but my black cargo pants and heavy wool sweater kept me warm enough. I also wore a black hat pulled down over my ears, and gloves covering my hands. There was no moon tonight, the night dark under a haze of obscuring clouds, but Owen had brought a small flashlight that shone dimly through a filter lens, radiating only enough light to make our way slowly through the forest.

We moved quickly to the tree line, stopping just short of the open grassy field that separated us from the fence surrounding the camp.

We're in position, I announced through the subvocalizer.

"Hold on," came Thomas' reply. "You have an opening in forty-five seconds."

I checked my watch. *Waiting for your order*, I replied.

My breathing felt abnormally loud in that moment, but I knew from experience it wasn't. As the seconds ticked by, I ran through a mental checklist, making sure I had remembered everything we needed. The gear was split between Owen and me, but we had gone over it together as Violet and Thomas mapped the camp. We were ready for this.

"Go in five, four, three, two, one… Go."

Owen and I leapt into motion, loping across the field, keeping ourselves low to the ground. Light generated by the high, bright spotlights within the camp helped us see, but it also meant a stray eye might spot us. Luckily, the ground was flat and mostly even, so we made short work of it.

At the fence, we crouched down low, hugging the earth, and moved a few feet down.

"There," came Violet's voice. "That's the spot."

Owen slipped a hand into one of his bags and pulled out a small white tube. I palmed my gun and kept an eye on the inside of the fence, watching for the guards, just in case something in the situation changed. There was a thirty-foot gap between the fence line and the first row of tents, and the tents obscured my vision of the other side. Still, I could make out dark forms standing at attention just on this side of the tents—two on either corner. If I could see their shadows, they might be able to notice us if we made a mistake.

There was the snap of the tube's plastic cap being opened, and then Owen pressed its mouth to the chain link, squeezing small dollops of the cream on the insides of the joints. He moved quickly and with confidence, applying the cream from top to bottom in a long, even line, and was two-thirds of the way done when the first fence links he'd marked began to sizzle and smoke, the metal melting and dripping down with soft plops. Careful not to let the stuff touch his fingers, he screwed the cap back on and slipped it into his belt, and by the time his hands were free again, the last spot was beginning to hiss and sputter.

"Forty-five more seconds," announced Thomas.

My stomach was a tight knot, but I ignored it as I grasped my half of the fence, sliding my finger through the holes. Owen mirrored my movement, and we lifted and pulled, taking painstaking care not to rattle the fence. The two halves split apart as easily as butter sliced with a knife, and I held mine open as Owen slipped through.

"Thirty seconds. You need to move now." Ms. Dale's voice was brusque, but I detected the hard edge of her concern as I worked my body through the hole, Owen holding it open for me. As soon as I was on the other side, we were running.

Sweat beaded on my forehead as I kept low to the ground, the threat of being discovered sending an icy chill through me. I kept a careful eye on Owen, not wanting to get separated as we raced ahead.

We made it to the tents, moving in three deep and one over, where Thomas had indicated it was safe, before taking a moment to catch our breath and await the next set of instructions. I looked up and noted the shadow of Violet's drone overhead, suppressing a curse.

Violet, the drone needs to be higher—if it's under the lamps, its shadow might be noticed, I commanded.

"Oh, shoot," her voice came back. After a moment, she asked, "Is that better?"

Yes, I replied. *Awaiting advice for the next move.*

"Head straight down the row you entered, and then turn left after three tents," came Thomas' reply.

I looked at Owen, who nodded and took lead, walking quietly and keeping low. I was still out of shape after my surgery, I noticed, my thighs and back already burning slightly from holding my body so low. I was riding a wave of adrenaline on top of tension, which meant I could probably keep this up all night if I had to—but I kept moving, knowing if I stopped for too long, the overtaxed muscles would grow stiff and cumbersome.

The bright white lights gave off a kind of low-pitched buzz that seemed to drill itself into my ears; other than that, it was eerily silent in the camp, and our footsteps sounded too loud, as though they would wake the sleeping prisoners at any moment. Owen and I hooked left, and then took an immediate right at Thomas' instructions, the two of us sliding through the tents in a pattern that seemed random, but I knew was based on our team's careful observations. We quickly threaded our way through, stopping one row short of the end, with the group of trailers visible.

Eyeing the thirty feet between us and the door to the nearest one, I hesitated. *Violet, can you do a quick sweep of the area around the trailers?* I asked, prudence taking control.

"Roger that," she replied. Owen and I waited in tense silence as she swept the drone around the area. "No guards outside," she informed us after several minutes had gone by. "The trailer is still empty."

I released a pent-up breath, trying to ease my body's tension, and then nodded. Tapping Owen on the shoulder, I took point, heading for the door, leaping out into empty space and rushing headlong at the building. At any moment, I expected an alarm to go off, to hear a woman's angry shout... but nothing came. Breathing heavily, I planted my back to the metal structure and watched as Owen twisted the knob with his hand.

He frowned and shook his head. *Locked,* his lips moved soundlessly, but I could hear his voice in my earbud. In response, I reached into a bag at my belt, pulling out our lock-picking device and handing it to him. He slid the thin rods into the lock and pressed the button on the side.

The machine made the slightest of whines as it turned on, followed by a click. I winced at how loud the noise sounded, looking around. There was nobody there to hear it, but the sooner we were inside, the better. Normally there would have been background noises to mask the little device's operation, but in a place this quiet... Owen unhooked the machine, handing it back to me, and I slid it into my bag as he opened the door and stepped in. I was right behind him, pushing it closed behind us.

The narrow building was devoid of any internal structure save small windows at either end, which let in little slices of cold light from the camp's lamps. I swung up the flashlight that hung from my jacket pocket, clicking it on to survey the room as Owen did the same. Filing cabinets were stacked along the walls, taking up every inch of space around the edges of the trailer. There was a desk sitting to the left, a computer atop it.

We're inside, I transmitted. *Good call on this trailer—we've got a computer and walls of file cabinets. Are we clear to proceed?*

"Good to go," replied Ms. Dale. "Our scope is clear of any guards, but be careful—you are only a few feet away from the other trailers."

I turned to Owen. *Computers or file cabinets?*

He eyed me and then shrugged. *Dealer's choice,* he replied with a smile.

Smirking, I moved toward the computer, leaving the cabinets to Owen. I took pains to move quietly on the off chance that my footsteps would thud on the aluminum floor. I was just sitting down at the chair when Owen slid open the first drawer, the rattling, clunking sound grating loudly in my ears. Gritting my teeth, I ignored it, knowing he was making sure to do it as quietly as possible.

I focused on my task, sliding a small black plastic stick into one of the open ports on the computer before turning the whole thing on. *Device in,* I communicated over the line. *Computer on. Do your thing, Thomas.*

"Already on it," came the man's reply. I turned my attention to the desk, slowly sliding the top drawer open. I heard Owen slide open another drawer, this one squeaking slightly, and frowned as I stared at the clean, empty gray space inside.

I closed it and slid open another desk compartment, finding it empty as well.

Viggo, there are no files in these drawers, said Owen, his voice in my ears accompanied by a light, vacant-sounding scraping as he slid another one open. I felt a chill rush down my spine as I opened a third drawer and found the same result.

"Are you sure you hooked the uplink up correctly?" asked Thomas. "I'm not getting anything here."

I looked down at the blinking device and then the computer screen and realized nothing had come up on it after I'd hit the power. The screen was black, the only sign of life a single blinking cursor flashing white on the bottom left corner. I was halfway to my feet, my mouth opening to announce my suspicions, when Violet's voice cut through the silence, sharp with tension.

"Guys, I don't know how, but this must be a trap—there are guards closing in on your position now."

CHAPTER 22

Viggo

Violet's words were still ringing in my ears when I staggered back, a curse slipping from my lips. I looked over to where Owen stood frozen, and then past him, toward the window at the end of the trailer. A light was bobbing against the wall of the adjacent building.

How had they known we were here?

I snatched the transmitter from the computer, throwing it into the bag it had come from and whirling for the window just as Violet said in my ear, "Two guards are approaching from the west and two more are exiting the trailer directly in front of the door. You've got a moment to get out of there if you take the east window, but do it *now*."

There was a crash beside me, and I jumped, whirling, only to see that Owen had pushed one of the stacks of empty filing cabinets over in front of the door, helping to block it, and was in the process of toppling another, a pained look on his face. It crashed to the floor with a noise that seemed about to bring the roof down. *The whole camp will hear!* I shouted at him, and he snapped back, *They know we're here already!*

Just get over here! I darted toward the window on the east side of the trailer, Owen leaping over the overturned cabinets to keep pace with me. Through the transmitter, I could hear Violet speaking, giving us more information, her voice sharp and focused.

Go—I'll cover you. I stepped aside and let Owen get to the window first, pulling my gun and training it on the door. Behind the scattered, piled-up filing cabinets, the doorknob rattled, and I clicked off the safety, sweat trickling down my forehead. I heard Owen grunt and threw him a look, alarmed when I saw him struggling with the window.

Shining my flashlight on it with my left hand, I exhaled another expletive as I saw that long metal spikes had been driven through the window frame, securing it closed. The doorknob rattled again, the door opening a crack, but getting stuck on the piles of cabinets, and the sound of low, urgent voices outside came to my ears.

Owen, I vocalized, *throw another one of those cabinets.*

Owen didn't argue, just found the nearest stack and began to topple them, the sound exploding into my ears again. As soon as the first crash sounded, I drew my hand across my chest and slammed the butt of my gun into the glass, shattering it loudly—but not, I hoped, loudly enough to be heard over the racket Owen was making. I used the muzzle of my gun to sweep away the shards that jutted out of the remains of the frame, telling him, *Enough!*

Just then something heavy slammed into the door, and it scraped open another foot. I leveled my gun at the door and fired three shots at it, the silenced gun making little sound, but the guards outside yanked the door closed as the bullets struck the frame. *Go,* I ordered Owen, and he ran back to me, diving headfirst through the window. I kept my gun trained on the rattling door, but used my free hand to grab the top of the window frame, lifting my legs up and out of the window, then dropping down into the dirt outside.

My landing wasn't hard, but it wasn't graceful, either, and I dropped to a knee as I tumbled out. I could hear the sounds of muffled voices and movement just around the corner; Owen was at the edge of the building, his own gun drawn.

They're still trying to get inside, he transmitted, his eyes wide as he looked back at me.

Good. If they hadn't heard the window breaking, they would be expecting us to still be inside. That gave us a few precious seconds.

I stood up and fired two more shots through the window, hoping it would confuse them further and buy us some time. I kept careful count of my bullets—already I was running lower than I would have liked. Five down, six more to go in this clip, with another twelve in my backup.

Violet, which way?

"Go to your left, straight down that path—you've got fifteen seconds!"

I was already moving, patting Owen on the shoulder as I passed him and headed down the long path, flanked by two more trailers that ran perpendicular to the one we had just left. I kept low to the ground, stopping as soon as I reached shelter on the other side, covering the gap for Owen as he ran across it. All the time, my ears were trained for the sound of running feet; I thought I could hear shouting, but from where? Had they discovered yet that we weren't in the trailer?

As soon as he was across, we ran again, making a straight line for the rows of tents just past the trailers. We were three rows deep when Ms. Dale's voice was in our ears, shouting at us. "VIGGO, GET IN A TENT, NOW!"

Her order was delivered with such urgency that I grabbed Owen out of instinct, jerking him with me as I dove for a tent, yanking aside the dangling flaps that separated the interior from the outside air. We came to a stumbling stop just inside the tent, and I turned and grabbed the tent flap, trying to hold it still from our rapid entry. Just as my fingers touched the fabric, something dark whizzed past, moving at impossible speed.

I froze, glancing over at Owen, finding his face drawn and his eyes wide, as though trying to stare through the gap in between the tent flaps. Good—that meant I hadn't been hallucinating. He had seen it too.

Taking a slow step back, I heaved in a deep breath of air as calmly and silently as I could, my stomach turning at a slight but deeply unpleasant stench in the air. My skin crawling, I subvocalized to our team, *What the hell was that?*

There was a pause before I got any response, and the wait felt longer than it was, the silence chafing on my raw nerves.

Finally, Violet announced, "Viggo, there are two enhanced humans there." I could hear an angry bite in her voice, but I wasn't sure whom her anger was directed at. "Their bodies are way hotter than the average human's. We thought they were running a fever when they appeared on the infrared, but it seems we were wrong."

I felt the air escape my lungs as I took in her words. That meant we were either dealing with two new princesses from Matrus… or we were dealing with the boys. As much as I hoped it was the princesses, I sincerely doubted Elena would risk any more of her sisters after losing three to us. Not that she was sentimental. To her, the boys were just more expendable.

Owen waved a hand, catching my attention. I frowned as he pointed to the ground, and then my eyes followed his fingers. I froze.

Visible in the dim light that filtered in through the tent material from the bright overhead lights, on the floor beneath us, men were stacked up like cordwood, one atop of the other. They had been stacked on either side of the tent, three on each side, all with bullet holes in their foreheads. Now that I knew they were there, I recognized something I had tasted in the air the moment I had stepped into the tent: the smell of death. These bodies had clearly not decomposed enough yet to smell too bad, but it was there all the same.

I exchanged looks with Owen, who had gone pale as he took in the… the bodies.

Violet, he transmitted, turning away from the gruesome sight, his voice shaking even over the subvocalizer. *You should know that these tents… well, they are filled with dead people.*

"What?" replied Ms. Dale. "All of them?"

I'm not sure about all of them, I mouthed into the

subvocalizer. *But in* this *tent, there are six bodies. Did you run a thermal scan of the tents?*

Another pause filled the line, and I pulled Owen down into a crouch on the floor as the sound of running feet drew close, loath to move my face closer to the dead men, but knowing they were still our best cover. I held my breath as the quick footsteps passed, expecting them to slow—but they didn't.

I was in the process of exhaling, trying not to breathe in if humanly possible, when Violet came back on the line. "It was my fault," she admitted. "I didn't scan them. I figured any threat would come from the trailers. I'm sorry."

"We can worry about that later," interjected Ms. Dale's hard voice. "We're working on getting you a clear path out of there. Just hold for one second."

Believe me, we're holding, replied Owen.

Agonizing seconds ticked by while we sat in the tent surrounded by murdered Patrian males. My brain was submerged in mission mode; I couldn't think about it, couldn't feel it, or else it would be too much for me to go on. My blood was thrumming in my veins, but I knew my team would warn us if they thought we were in immediate danger. A group of guards came by, distinguishable from the enhanced humans by the low murmuring of their voices and their slower pace; we held our breaths, but they didn't check the tent. Maybe they thought nobody would hide in such a grisly place.

After what felt like time enough for the entire camp's guards to converge on us, Violet's voice came over the line again, terse and harsh.

"Head out of the tent and continue left," she ordered.

Owen was in motion ahead of me, pushing the tent flap aside and moving out soundlessly, his eyes wild. We jogged down the pathway between the tents, keeping our heads down and our footsteps as quiet as possible.

"Turn right," Violet's voice ordered.

As one, the two of us slipped off the beaten path and between two adjacent tents, moving down the narrow gap between them. We had to move slower here. Stakes and ropes jutted out of the ground, and we had to step over them carefully so as not to trip—or shake the tents and give away our position. Owen made sure to check each row for guards as we darted across, and I covered the rear, glancing over my shoulder, looking for any sign of pursuit.

"Left again, for five tents, then right down another path like this one."

We moved around the tents into the wider path, and were halfway down when suddenly Violet shouted, "DUCK!"

Without thinking, I grabbed Owen's shoulder and pushed him roughly down as something whizzed by overhead, moving so fast my hair shifted from the breeze it stirred. Looking up toward where it had landed, I saw a shadowed blur skid to a stop and whirl. The figure was small—it had to be one of the boys. He was dressed head to toe in black, with a black mask obscuring his features. Except for his eyes, which stared blankly at me.

I was keyed in for the mission, my emotions compacted into a tiny place somewhere in the back of my mind, cut off from my actions. Still, I knew what I had to do.

I stood up slowly, raising my hands and letting my gun dangle from my fingers, one hand moving cautiously to my throat to turn off my subvocalizer. "Hey," I said softly, trying to get the boy's attention, my voice cracking as my vocal cords unfroze. "We're not going to hurt you, buddy. I'm Viggo."

The boy's eyes stared at me. No, they stared through me, still vacant, devoid of anything resembling emotion. After a pause, he cocked his head, as if listening to something.

"Affirmative," he replied, confirming my suspicions. He was receiving orders from somewhere.

So sudden was his movement that I had no time to react. One second he was staring at me, his eyes empty of anything resembling a personality—the next he was in motion. I had a moment to brace myself, preparing for impact, when suddenly the blur before me became an uncontrolled tumble. Owen's hands pushed me hard, and I slid right as the boy flew between the two of us, hitting the ground and sliding into a tent. I heard the thump as he hit the ground inside, taking a set of stakes and poles with him, and as he whirled with a grunt, the tent collapsed around him.

"What just happened?" I growled at Owen, so shocked that I let my words slip out loud.

He gave me a chagrined look as I switched my subvocalizer back on. *I threw my gun at him,* he replied, glancing at the tent. *I didn't even have time to think—I think it tripped him.*

I blinked once. I could explore how much luck we had expended with that one later. For now, we needed to get moving.

"Viggo, another one is drawing close," Violet gasped through the earbud.

Owen was already a few steps ahead of me, a knife glinting in his hand, and I started to follow… then turned back, staring at the collapsed tent, the fabric billowing where the boy thrashed and rolled silently around. I wondered if he was upsetting bodies in that tent, too. I heard Owen hissing my name through the subvocalizer, but I ignored it, taking a tentative step back toward the tent.

"Viggo," Violet's voice said tightly.

I couldn't leave the boy behind. Not only was it possible we might get important information from him... but more than that, I couldn't let Desmond and Elena continue to use him like this.

"What are you doing, Viggo? You guys need to get out of there!"

Trust me, I replied to Violet's anxious voice, working as fast as I could.

I reached forward and yanked at the tent, pulling at the collapsed material until I uncovered the boy tangled in a lumpy pile of canvas and bodies, grunting as he tried to shift the objects off him, his mask askew. Hesitating for only a heartbeat, I reached out with my left hand and snatched at his mask, keeping my gun trained on him just in case. The boy's hands reached up from among the wreckage, and he grabbed my hand in a grip that felt too weak to be that of an enhanced human, but he was too late. The mask was off.

I froze, my heart stopping for a moment as I recognized Cody, one of the boys who had been in the first group I had trained. Once he had taken a swing at me, but I had taken him down to prove a point. As I looked at him, I felt deep anger rising up in my chest. Cody wasn't some dead-eyed drone; he had been precocious and challenging. And he was only eleven.

Elena was not only using genetically modified teenagers, but *children* in her disgusting war.

Cody didn't even seem to register that I'd removed the mask. His eyes still vacant, he let go of my arm, panting with exertion as he pushed at a dead man who had flopped out over his legs. I took a chance and holstered my gun, then quickly plucked the earbud from his ear and slipped it into my pocket, wondering if it might be useful.

Immediately Cody's movements stilled, and he gazed at me, his face blank, his mouth hanging slightly open. As gently as I could, I grabbed his shirt and then carefully leveled a blow at his jaw, wincing as it impacted. He immediately went limp. Feeling sick, I carefully dragged the unconscious boy out of the tent and into my arms, taking a few more of our precious moments to check his pulse. I hated having to hit him, but even little Cody was too dangerous to take with us while he was conscious—I had no idea what he would do awake, how deep his loyalty to Desmond truly ran.

I heard fidgeting behind me and was suddenly grateful he hadn't made a fuss over the detour. *Viggo,* Owen said, his voice low. *There are guards coming back. I can hear them. Let's go.*

Take my gun, I replied. *Try not to throw this one.*

At the same time, Violet's voice rang through my ears. "Viggo, I'm not sure what you're doing down there, but they are closing in on you. Go straight through the tents ahead. Cut your way out if you have to." From the hard edge in her voice, I could sense our luck was running out.

Got it. I nodded to Owen, who immediately went for the tent in front of us. I stepped up behind him, waiting, breathing through my teeth as he cut a hole in the fabric and then stepped aside for me. I raced for the next tent, and Owen followed, repeating the action. We were at the fourth one when Violet spoke again.

"The other boy is close. You need to move."

Owen's response was to rip another hole, his hand jerking on the knife, and motion me through. I stepped through, and, outside the door of the last tent. I finally saw the trodden-down empty space between the fence and the rows of death tents. There was still that thirty feet of open land between us and the hole we had made in the chain link. I felt a sinking in my stomach, despite all my preparations. We weren't going to make it.

I had opened my mouth to tell Violet as much when her voice crackled in my ear, so loud it was practically a shout. "I'm going to create a diversion for you. Go NOW!"

I had no time to ask what that diversion would be before my ears picked up something whizzing lightly by overhead. I caught a glance of Violet's drone as it headed toward the trailers. The humming of the motors died away as it moved out of earshot, and then an explosion rocked through the night.

All the lights that had illuminated the camp fell dark at once, and shouts erupted behind us, the guards' voices farther than I would have expected, and—thank God—getting farther away still. Owen and I took that as our cue, breaking into a run as a fireball rose up from the spot where Violet had crashed the drone.

Owen reached our escape hole before me and yanked the fence aside, letting me go first. I turned sideways and slipped through it, taking care not to catch Cody's dragging limbs on one of the jagged ends of the wire. After a few seconds, we were both through, racing toward where we had parked the car.

Our footsteps thudding through the darkness, we made it through the tree line and to the car without alarms ringing out or bullets flying after us. Owen opened the back door first, and I deposited Cody's limp body into the backseat; then, as Owen climbed in shotgun, I raced around the car and practically dove into the driver's seat. Jamming the key into the ignition, I slammed the car into gear and took off, not even bothering to check what direction we were going. In the review mirror, I saw Owen peering back at the darkened camp behind us, clearly checking whether we were being followed.

I clenched the wheel tighter and pressed the accelerator, too tense to feel any form of relief.

CHAPTER 23

Violet

We *made it to the car,* Viggo announced over the radio, breaking the tense silence that had stretched out between us. I exhaled sharply, leaning back against my chair as a wave of relief hit me hard, making my muscles sag on my bones. Around the room, the rest of the group was visibly relieved as well. Ms. Dale had one hand on her hip, the other braced on the table, which looked to be the only thing holding her up, and even Thomas seemed shaken.

"What was that?" I asked Viggo. "What took you so long?" I'd been monitoring the area around Viggo and Owen, watching the guards and the person—it must have been the boy—who was racing around the camp at impossible speeds, his body fiery colors. As desperately as I'd wanted to hover over Viggo and Owen, watching their every move, I hadn't had time to stop my surveillance and really see what was going on where they were located.

We took one of the boys, Viggo told me solemnly. *It doesn't look like we're being pursued, but we need advice on how to proceed.*

I turned back to my controls, prepared to use the drone to give them some information about the area, only to remember, as I saw the black screen buzzing with static in front of me, that I had crashed the drone into the generators. I slid my hand out of the metal tubes, almost sadly. Beside me, Thomas' fingers were flying over his keyboard as he spoke.

"Do not come back here," he said into his mic. "We don't know who's tracking those boys, or how. I'm researching an area remote enough to direct you to. What direction are you heading now?"

I frowned and cocked my head, shooting a glance at Ms. Dale, who was bobbing her head in agreement with Thomas. I stood and moved over to her, shakily stretching my limbs. Seeming to catch the question in my eyes, the old spy told me in a soft voice, "Thomas is right. We could lead them right back here, and we can't compromise the integrity of this base. Especially since we don't have a fallback location ready yet."

I bit my lip and nodded, feeling slow for not recognizing that earlier. "Of course," I said. "That's smart."

Ms. Dale gave me a conciliatory smile and placed a hand on my shoulder. "I'm sure you would've puzzled that out for yourself soon enough. You did really well tonight."

I ran a hand down my face. "I appreciate you saying that, but I'm not so sure. I mean, I should've used the thermal scanning on the tents. Then we would've known it was a trap, and none of this would be happening."

"No." Ms. Dale's grip on my shoulder tightened, and she shook her head emphatically, her hair, in a tight braid, jerking over her shoulder. "There were three people in this room, and we *all* missed that. Yes, it was a dumb oversight, but you aren't to blame. If anything, *I* am—I should've asked you to do it, but to be honest, I was more concerned about those trailers than the tents as well."

Her words made me feel a little better, but still… "We need to be better next time," I said stiffly.

Ms. Dale grinned at me. "We're *always* going to need to do better," she replied. "It's just part of being in charge. Don't be too hard on yourself."

I nodded and then turned to see Thomas looking at us expectantly.

"What's the plan?" I asked, bringing my mind back to the task at hand: getting Viggo, Owen, and the captured—hopefully, now rescued—boy safely back here.

"Not a lot of good options in the area. That death camp was practically at the foot of one of the mountains. I have them heading south now, trying to buy a little time, but there aren't a lot of roads for them to use."

"Roads would be a bad call anyway," replied Ms. Dale, toying with her braid with one hand. Her gaze was thoughtful as she considered the problem. "The guards at that camp will have already notified their higher-ups, and, seeing as the camp was bait, I would be surprised if they didn't have troops nearby, ready to do a sweep. No—we need to do something a bit more unexpected to buy us some time."

I frowned and crossed my arms. "Thomas, do you think you could look at the map and theorize where they might've hidden their troops, if they have any? Best guess is better than nothing."

Thomas' fingers flew over his computer, and I looked at the screen connected to it, watching as a 3D topographical map appeared. Thomas began clicking on areas, placing a few red hexagonal markers. I watched closely, noting the location of the base and the direction Thomas had advised Viggo and Owen to go.

"Where should Viggo and Owen be now?" I asked him, and he nodded. A few more clicks on the keyboard, and a blue triangle appeared on the map.

Ms. Dale came up beside me and watched intently as well. "That's good, Violet. Thomas, eliminate all but four or five of the proposed troop locations. I can't imagine they would commit any more than that, and even that might be a bit excessive."

I watched as several of the red hexagons disappeared from the map, only a handful remaining. "Of course, this is only conjecture," said Thomas. "But if I were them, that's where I would be."

Ms. Dale took a step back, nodding. "You were right to send them south," she said. "We can find a spot to cover the heloship while we check the boy for trackers so we can airlift them out of the area. Can you show me what the area is like forty to fifty miles away?"

The map on the screen shifted left, revealing more of the geography beyond the camp, the lines moving in wavy ovals and circles that grew wider or closer together, depending on the elevation. Thomas continued to scroll until Ms. Dale's hand shot out, pointing at a spot.

"There," she said, tapping the screen. It was a low valley, surrounded by four hills. "We can bring the heloship in here." Her gaze was steady on the map, and she pointed to a spot less than a mile away. "Have them meet us there."

Thomas frowned, his eyes studying the screen from behind his spectacles. "It's bad terrain," he announced. "It'll take them at least two hours to get there."

Ms. Dale turned and nodded solemnly. "It is *really* bad terrain," she agreed, sounding almost pleased. "But it's equally bad for the enemy. They're going to be tracking them using the boy. But it's the best shot we have at getting them out before anybody catches up with them."

"Dr. Arlan will need to go," I said. Ms. Dale and Thomas looked at me as I worked the plan out in my head. "Someone has to cut the tracker out, assuming the boy has one, and Dr. Tierney is busy caring for Quinn and Henrik, so…"

"You're right," said Ms. Dale. "And good idea—the rest of us won't have to dig around in him blindly looking for it."

A thought occurred to me, and I frowned. "Thomas, do you know anything about trackers that are put into gels or liquids?"

He cocked his head at me, frowning. "Uh, no. Why do you ask?"

"When I was working with Lee, Desmond's son, he had trackers you could put into someone's drink. It would stay in their system for two weeks, and then get flushed out. I was just wondering, just in case—"

"In case the boy doesn't have one surgically implanted,"

Thomas concluded for me. "No, I don't have any experience with them. They may be new and rare Matrian technology, or maybe it was something Lee developed on his own."

I glanced at Ms. Dale, noting her look of dismay. "So even if the boy doesn't have anything implanted under the skin, he still might be tagged?" she said. "That's disconcerting."

Looking down at the table, I sighed. "I agree. We might have to consider leaving him behind." I hated the way those words sounded in the air, but I couldn't leave a single option unexamined, not with our entire camp in the balance. My cousin's children flashed before my eyes, reminding me what was at stake. As much as I hated it, I knew in my heart that just because we couldn't find a tracker under his skin didn't mean we could bring the boy back with us.

"I might be able to whip up a scanner of sorts," Thomas announced abruptly. His head was tilted up toward the ceiling, exposing the folds of his neck. He spun slightly in his chair, his legs kicking a little. "Even trackers use some sort of power source. I can scan the boy to see if he is emitting any sort of abnormal frequency."

"Do you think it'll work?" I asked, taking a step forward, relief surging through me.

He looked at me, and straightened. "Yes. Barring equipment complications, if he has them, I can find them. If he comes up clear, then we can bring him back. If not…"

Hey, guys? I'm still waiting on a plan here. Viggo's voice buzzed in my earpiece. We had been so absorbed in how to proceed, I realized we hadn't been communicating to him.

"Viggo," I said, "we're going to meet you in sector

thirty-seven C, two miles from sector D, and four miles from sector thirty-six C. We can direct you as needed. Be careful of potential Matrian troops in the area. Keep heading south until you hit a ravine, and then turn east. We'll be waiting for you in the heloship."

Copy that, came his reply.

I turned again, tugging my headset off, trying not to upset the soft cap I still wore. "I'll go get Amber," I said. "Since we'll be flying."

Taking a step forward, I felt a strange sensation, not unlike falling, and the room started to tilt to the left. No—I *was* falling. My hand shot out to grab at the table, and I felt my knuckles rap sharply against the wood as I half tumbled into it, breaking my own fall.

Stabilized on the flat surface, I closed my eyes and tried to fight the dizziness that had assaulted me. Then I felt a hand fall on the middle of my back, between my shoulder blades, another one gently supporting my elbow as I breathed, willing the world back into clarity.

"Are you okay, Violet?" Ms. Dale's voice overflowed with concern as she carefully helped me move away from the table. I kept my eyes shut, trusting she wouldn't walk me into anything, and then felt something brush up against my knees. "Chair here," she murmured, helping me to turn, and then allowing me to lean on her as I slowly sat down.

Settled in the chair, I took a few more deep breaths, and then, slowly, opened my eyes. The world trembled slightly, threatening to spin off the rails again, but I pushed the sensation back, focusing on my hands in front of me, steadying myself. "I'm fine," I breathed. "Just got hit with a dizzy spell. Give me a minute and I'll be good to go."

Ms. Dale gave me a doubtful look as she dragged a chair over, sitting down in front of me. My skin felt clammy, a cold sweat dotting my forehead, upper lip, and shoulders. My breath was still coming sharply. "Violet," Ms. Dale began hesitantly. "You have done enough for today. I think we'll be fine if you stay here."

I felt the urge to protest, which must have shown on my face, because Ms. Dale leaned forward, her expression soft. "It's not just because you're unwell, although that is a good enough reason in and of itself. However, Viggo and Owen are gone. Thomas, Amber, and I—we all have to go to the pickup, for various reasons. That's *all* our leadership, Violet. If anything were to happen to us…" She met my gaze, her brown eyes glittering with intensity. "We need you here to carry on, should anything happen to us. Someone has to remain behind."

She was right, of course. I had known that even before she'd started speaking. At least, I had known that, physically, I was still in no condition for fieldwork. Viggo and I had talked about it just yesterday. But the other stuff… Well, that was something I had not considered right at this moment. Even though I'd definitely used that argument on other people in my care before, I'd never really thought to apply it to myself.

"I know," I told Ms. Dale, risking a nod. "And we have a good plan. I just… I'm having a hard time accepting my new, uh, limitations." I gave her a small smile, just a flash of humor, and Ms. Dale smiled in response. "I trust you and Viggo to get in and out of there. Thomas, I trust you, too," I added, noting the reproachful look Thomas had shot me over Ms. Dale's head. I hoped that affirmation would tell him I knew fieldwork wasn't his forte, but he was doing his best. If he needed the support, I was happy to give it.

"We'll be back before you know it," Ms. Dale assured me, and I watched them exit the room, presumably heading off to find Dr. Arlan and Amber.

CHAPTER 24

Viggo

Even as I drove through low grasses and around bushes, the uneven terrain jerking the wheel under my hands, I couldn't help checking over my shoulder at the backseat. It was almost habitual at this point. I needed to make sure Cody was still unconscious, and not about to leap into action and kill us both.

"He's fine," Owen assured me for what felt like the fiftieth time. "He's still out." We'd turned our subvocalizers off for the time being, relying on the regular microphones included in the little black collars; there seemed to be no point to subvocalizing, with the two of us in the airtight car.

I turned my gaze back to the landscape ahead of me, slowing us to a crawl in order to roll over some very pointy rocks, and nodded. "Last thing we need is for him to wake up right now."

"I've got my gun trained on him," Owen informed me, his

voice brittle. "I'll do what I have to, if it comes to that."

I held back my retort, partially because I knew it would be counterproductive and partially because I knew those words coming from Owen's mouth were forced through his teeth. He didn't like the idea of hurting Cody any more than I did.

Downshifting, I pushed hard on the throttle and began heading up a hill, my eyes drifting over to the topographical map Thomas had downloaded to my handheld before the mission. The area Violet had given us had to be close; there weren't a lot of other hills. The car's engine growled and roared under us in protest, but it held firm.

"Viggo, you should be coming up to the area soon," Violet announced in my earpiece, almost on cue. "Ms. Dale and the team are waiting."

The terrain before me began to level off, and I exhaled in relief as we crested the hill and began slowly, carefully, heading down the other side. I could see the silhouettes of Ms. Dale, Thomas, and Dr. Arlan standing next to a car at the bottom, the headlights cutting through the darkness like a beacon. They had told us they would bring a car in the heloship and land the latter nearby, but not where.

"Viggo, please confirm that's you I'm seeing," Ms. Dale's voice came crackling over my headset. Peering toward the figures I was nearing, I saw she was waving to me.

"Yes, ma'am," I said, and flashed the lights in response.

When I finally made it down the hill, I stopped our car a few feet away from theirs. Leaping out, I raced around to pull open the passenger door. Owen had already gathered Cody's small form in his arms, and he passed him over to me. I gathered the boy up and raced as quickly as I dared over to where Dr. Arlan was waiting, setting him on an old camp blanket they'd spread over the drying grasses as we descended the hill.

By the time I had arranged Cody as comfortably as I could, Dr. Arlan held a syringe in his hand. He stabbed the tip into a bottle filled with amber liquid, then pulled the plunger back and removed the needle from the bottle, slipping the liquid back into his pocket. Turning, he looked at the form on the blanket and paused, his eyebrows furrowing in confusion.

"This is just a boy," he said, his eyes moving up to meet my gaze.

Before I had a chance to reply, Ms. Dale tsked, snatching the syringe out of Dr. Arlan's fingers. Without hesitating, she dropped to one knee and slammed the syringe into Cody's thigh, depressing the plunger.

"Think of him as a weapon," she informed Dr. Arlan as she pulled the needle out. "Or rather, a victim of experimentation who has become a weapon in the wrong hands." She met Dr. Arlan's appalled gaze as she held the syringe out to him, her eyes flashing. "He's dangerous right now, and he has superhuman powers. We cannot afford to relax our guard just because of his age or his size." She stood up, brushing dirt off her knees.

"We need to find that tracker," I told the doctor gently.

He blinked, turning his gaze from Ms. Dale to me, and then nodded. "Of course," he replied.

Thomas moved around him, holding out a long, skinny rod connected to a small box by what looked like a good deal of electrical tape. He hovered the rod over Cody's body, running it up and down and staring at the box. As he worked, Dr.

Arlan slipped a small, pale metal box—which I recognized as Ashabee's portable medical scanner—out of his own pocket and began following Thomas' motions, performing his own scan. I took a step back, giving them space to work.

Owen came up beside me, watching closely. The box Thomas held beeped as he drew it over Cody's thigh. "There," he announced.

Dr. Arlan moved his box over it, and frowned. "It's there," he confirmed, looking up. "But they put it in deep—it's danger-ously close to the femoral artery. If I try to perform surgery on him out here and slip, he'll bleed out in moments."

"We have to remove it here and now," I said, sensing the doctor was going to insist on moving the boy to another place. "It's too dangerous for us to keep it in."

Dr. Arlan bristled and stood. "You people are too much," he said, placing his hands on his hips. "I'm a doctor, and I swore an oath to help my patients, and not to put them in any unnec-essary danger."

I felt my breath come out in a deep huff. I could respect Dr. Arlan's position, but at the moment, we needed him to get the job done—we had no time. "This boy was being used as a slave," I informed him. "He's on medication that makes him suscepti-ble to control by our enemies. He has a tracker in his leg they are certainly monitoring, and when they find him, and us, they will kill us all, and he will go back to being a slave. I understand the risks, and I wish we had a better way, but we don't. So please just do it."

I sighed and ran a hand through my hair, the adrenaline still surging through my veins making my muscles twitch and jump under my skin. But my impassioned rant about the boy had done something other than motivate Dr. Arlan—it had jarred my memory of how they'd been controlling Cody earlier.

I fished the earbud out of my pocket and held it out to the group. "By the way, he was wearing this."

At the sight of the thing, Thomas cursed. Marching over, he plucked the earbud from my hand with two fingers and rushed over to the car he'd come in. Curious, I followed, watching as he opened the back and pulled out a black box, about the size of a jewelry box, but considerably heavier, from the way he was handling it. He grunted as he pulled the lid open, and then dropped the earbud in and slammed it shut with a thunk, flipping down the top and locking it.

Silence followed, and I felt a keen sense that something was wrong. Everyone else seemed to feel it as well, because, almost as one, we turned to look behind us, as if something had managed to sneak up on us. The headlights from both cars illuminated the small clearing, but shadows pressed in relentlessly beyond their reach. I searched them, finding nothing, and after a moment, released a tightly held breath.

I turned back to look at the others, and then felt a chuckle slip from me. "Well, that was anticlimactic," I quipped, and I saw Ms. Dale roll her eyes, while Owen grinned nervously.

While Dr. Arlan efficiently set out his tools and began preparing to make an incision in Cody's thigh, sanitizing and marking the skin while wearing a deep frown of concentration, Thomas stepped toward us, away from his heavy box, dusting his hands. "The box is lead-lined. They won't be able to track that earpiece through the frequency they were utilizing anymore."

"I'm glad you brought that," I said. "I had completely forgotten to mention that earbud earlier, but I figured it might be
something you could use."

"Maybe," Thomas hedged. "But it'll be useless taking the
tracker out of that kid if they can track us through their earbud.
I don't know if it was worth the risk. Won't know until I get it
back—and even then, I recommend taking it far away from the
camp before we try."

Ms. Dale cleared her throat, and we turned, looking at her.
"The boy," she said. "Tell us more about how he acted when you
were fighting him."

"Right," I said, shaking my head. "His eyes were… blank.
Like there was nothing behind them. He wouldn't talk except to
whomever was on the other side of the earbud. It was like he'd
been programmed or something."

As I spoke, even I noticed the emotions beginning to vacate
my voice as I tried to distance myself from the anger still surging hot and deep in the pit of my belly. I needed to focus right
now, and that anger would only make the situation worse. But
God—he was just a boy.

There was a rustling sound, and I craned my neck over the
top of Ms. Dale's head in time to see Dr. Arlan gesturing with
a free hand, the other holding a set of small, intricate tools. "I
need a little help," he announced.

"I got it," Thomas replied, heading over to Dr. Arlan. I
watched him go, and then turned back to Ms. Dale and Owen.

"How could they do that to those kids?" I asked after a moment. "How could they train them to be *so* obedient?"

Ms. Dale licked her lips. "There are methods, but to be

honest, it takes longer than a few weeks. The process could take months, even years."

"It must be the Benuxupane?" Owen asked, crossing his arms. "Violet mentioned that when she took it, she felt more compliant?"

"She said she was able to resist a bit," I replied. "It didn't seem to have a very strong effect on her. But to make those kids into emotionless drones… They must have really made some changes to the formula."

"Desmond has access to the whole Matrian government's top scientists and funding," Ms. Dale said. "If anyone could isolate the component that had that effect, I would imagine she'd have the resources to do it. And once they isolated it…"

"They would have enhanced it," I spat.

Ms. Dale nodded, her jaw clenched. "I really hate that woman," she said under her breath.

"You and me both," I muttered.

"Guys, you better not leave me off the list—plus Amber, Henrik, all the Liberators, Jay…"

I chuckled as Owen began ticking off the names on his fingers, waving a hand in front of him.

"All right," I said. "We all agree that Desmond is a vile witch. But that doesn't get us anywhere."

We fell into silence, mulling over the seriousness of the problem. Finally, Owen sighed. "We really need to find a way to destroy the Benuxupane. Something that does this to people… it shouldn't even be allowed to exist."

Heads nodded all around the group. I agreed too—once again, we'd been so caught up in responding to one crisis after another that we'd lost sight of the bigger picture. We had to find a way to strike back.

"Destroying it is only addressing one part of the problem," Ms. Dale said. "We have no idea how the boys' bodies will react without the Benuxupane. Desmond might have found a way to, I don't know, make them dependent on it. If we destroy it without testing that, we might be killing them."

"Good point," Owen replied. "What if they react violently? Right now, the drug might be helping them cope with the side effects of their isolation and emotional maladjustment. It might be like kicking the crutch out from under a man with a broken leg."

I raised my eyebrows at the metaphor, but couldn't help but agree. "I guess that's a bridge we'll cross when we get to it. Right now, the fact that the Matrians are using them at all is a bigger concern, so anything we can do to…"

I trailed off, noticing Ms. Dale and Owen's eyes had jumped to a place just over my shoulder, their faces blanking, draining of casual emotion. A tense silence had once again descended upon the clearing, and I felt a prickling at the back of my neck as the hair there rose in anticipation of danger. As slowly as possible, I turned.

Another boy wearing a black mask and black clothes stood only twenty feet away from me. My fingers twitched as I stared at his small form. He was breathing heavily, his shoulders and chest heaving, and I could see, even in the sparse light, that his black outfit was soaked with sweat.

I watched as the boy pointed at his ear, and then looked at me expectantly. I stared, baffled, and the boy slowly lowered his arm and then waited. After several long heartbeats, he repeated the gesture.

"Maybe he wants us to put the earpiece in," Owen whispered behind me.

Seeing no better option before me, I cautiously moved toward the trunk of Ms. Dale's car, keeping a careful eye on the boy. He didn't move, making no sound but that of his labored breathing, even as I opened up the trunk and pulled out the box, grabbed the earpiece, and slid it into my ear.

"Hello, Mr. Croft," a feminine voice crooned from the other side.

I balled my hand into a fist, my response scraping out through gritted teeth. "Hello, Desmond."

CHAPTER 25

Viggo

"There's no need for that tone, my dear boy. After all, I'm just here to congratulate you on revealing which of our frequencies you had that dear, sweet moron Thomas monitoring."

My eyes flicked over to Thomas, and I pointed at the earbud, shooting him a pointed, questioning glance. "What do you want, Desmond?" I asked.

Nodding sharply, Thomas moved over to the car, and I stepped aside to give him access to the trunk. I heard him moving items around behind me, but I didn't look, turning my full attention to the boy standing in the clearing. He hadn't moved, but I knew he was listening in. I could only hope nothing Desmond said now could be interpreted as a command on his part.

Desmond chuckled through the line. "You know, I really *do* have to congratulate you," she said. "You were clever not to return to your secret base. I'm surprised to see you had that much common sense. Is my failed protégé with you?"

"Which one?" I retorted. "I seem to be collecting a set of them."

"I see you still have that clever mouth… and zero insight about when best to use it," the woman chided. She clucked her tongue in disapproval, and I resisted the urge to add something else incendiary. "The failed protégé I was referring to is the industrious Melissa Dale. Tell me, is she there with you?"

I cast a look at Ms. Dale, who was watching me closely, her mouth pressed into a thin line. "She's here. She says you should go take a dive into Veil River."

"I'm sure she did. Ah, well, she never really was up to my standards. I won't miss her after I kill her."

I clenched my teeth together, refusing to rise to the bait. "What do you want, Desmond?" I repeated.

"Patience, patience, Mr. Croft. You're ruining all my fun… Now, where was I? Ah yes. It is a shame you haven't led me straight to your base, but no matter. I'll find it soon. Are you sure you don't want to help me out a little bit? Give me a direction?"

"How about down? Just stop when you see flames."

"Hmmm, color me unsurprised. You always were a stubborn little thing."

"Well, that's just part of my charm," I said.

Behind me, I heard Thomas muttering to himself. I looked back just in time to catch his eye: the small man motioned to his wrist as though he was tapping a watch, then flapped his hand in a circular motion as though to say, 'Come on!' *More time,* I realized. *He wants more time.*

Meanwhile, Desmond's predatory voice continued in the earbud, "I see Ms. Bates has encouraged your overinflated opinion of yourself. No matter. Even though you haven't led me back to your camp, there is still a reason I have approached you today. There's still a lesson you need to learn."

I took a few cautious steps away, not wanting Desmond to hear Thomas tinkering around. I also avoided Ms. Dale and Owen. We needed to be more spread out in case the boy flew into action. And I needed to keep her talking.

It wasn't hard, because I already had more questions than I could hold in. "A lesson? Was that what all this was about? The empty file cabinets? The rows of murdered corpses in tents? Did you just… *put* all this out here so you could teach us 'a lesson'? Is that what all these deaths were for?"

Desmond's voice grew, if possible, even more gleeful. "Why, Viggo, of course not. The Matrians already had an accumulation of bodies that had very little to do with you, all things considered. And the camp was here before. Since the Matrians don't care particularly how these men are disposed of, I just used the resources available to me. Then it was simply a matter of waiting for your merry band to sniff out injustice and come swooping in to save the day… I'm actually kind of glad that you ended up there, of all places. It's by far the best of the surprises I've left for you."

"There are more places like this?" I felt my mouth actually hanging open. The sheer scale of Desmond's plan was devastating. "There are more… traps?"

"Telling you would spoil all the fun, wouldn't it?"

I took that as a yes to my question. Had Thomas figured

out how to listen in on this yet? This conversation was growing more and more infuriating.

"All right," I said through my teeth. "Since it's clear you're not going to stop on this train of thought, what was that about a lesson?"

"A lesson. One of endurance. You see, you and your little Violet have merely been a nuisance up until this point. A fly in the proverbial ointment—disgusting, buzzing pathetically around, but ultimately ignorable."

I shook my head—was that an echo?—only to realize I was hearing Desmond's voice piping through something behind me. I shot a glance at Thomas, who grinned. He'd managed to hack the frequency, like I'd hoped he would. I noticed Ms. Dale and Owen moving closer, eager to hear the other half of the conversation they had been missing out on.

"And then the palace happened," I said, following Desmond's train of thought. "Tell me, did Elena shed a tear over the loss of her little sister? How was her speech? I bet it was suitably heart-felt and filled with overused clichés."

The woman's voice in my ear soured the slightest bit. "You'd better watch your tone, Mr. Croft. Otherwise this conversation will end before I have a chance to explain its purpose, and you will learn, in terrible and frightening ways, how much I can hurt you."

"What do you want, Desmond?" I asked, struggling to keep my tone neutral. I hated this feeling—the feeling I was a mouse with a cat crouching directly behind me, set to attack.

She sighed, a heavy, disapproving sound coming through the speakers. "You really do have poor conversation skills."

"I'll work on that."

"I very much doubt you'll have time, Mr. Croft. Not that you don't have a future, mind you. It's just already filled with unimaginable torment. You haven't even begun to scratch the surface of what the queen and I are capable of doing."

"Like with the boys?" My eyes were trained on the subject in question. He was still breathing heavily.

"Clever man. And, yes, the boys. Did you know what amazing specimens they are? They really are impressive. Their strength and stamina are off the charts. Take the boy who followed you, for example: he ran forty-eight point six miles without stopping. I could order him to keep running, too, and he would do it. He would do it until he dropped dead, his tiny little heart unable to cope with the strain."

I had no immediate answer to that. I took in a sharp, biting breath, red flashing across my vision, realizing my fists had clenched so hard my nails dug into my palms. I ground my teeth together and risked a glance over to Owen and Ms. Dale. Ms. Dale was already moving toward Dr. Arlan—I could almost see her plan forming. I turned back to the boy standing before us, his eyes empty, his chest heaving, as Desmond continued.

"I could make him fight you, you know. Have him take you all on. I'm not sure how he'd fare against you and Ms. Dale in his condition, but I'm betting it wouldn't matter. The strain alone would probably end him. Should I do that, Viggo? The young man's heart-rate is well above the norm, even after standing idly for a few minutes. Should I make him fight you until his heart explodes?"

Sick to my stomach, I closed my eyes, knowing I still had

not said a word in response to this new, mind-numbingly cruel threat. When I opened them, I wasn't any less angry. I spat the words through my teeth, vehement and raw:

"For the last damn time, Desmond, what do you want?!"

Desmond chuckled, low and husky. "I see I've struck a nerve. Good, because I want you to pay close attention to this next part. You asked me what I want, and it is this. The queen and I are willing to make a deal with you, Mr. Croft. You and your merry band of disillusioned rebels."

"What sort of deal?"

"Simply this: King Maxen and Violet. If you deliver those two to us, we are prepared to hand over the boys, a small plot of farmable land, and a promise you and those who have joined you will be spared. You will be free to raise the boys as you see fit with no interference from us... Well, barring a few minor exceptions."

It was hard to speak the next words over the snarl of rage fighting to escape my throat, but I knew I had to keep her talking. "What exceptions?"

"The boys will need to be used for breeding purposes, Mr. Croft. Their gifts need to be passed on to the populace in order to achieve Elena's goal of creating an enhanced people. Now, unfortunately, I know you well enough to know you will never agree. Not with Violet's life on the line. It's too personal for you. But would Violet? Or your friends? Two lives in exchange for a thousand... Such a small price to pay. I'll let you mull it over. In the meantime... Subject 984... Kill them all!"

The boy's head snapped up. I snatched the earpiece out of my ear and tossed it aside, spreading my arms and dropping into a fighting stance. He moved right toward me—I was closest to him, after all. "Please tell me you have a sedative," I shouted over my shoulder to somebody, anybody.

There was no time to listen for a response, as the boy blurred into motion. I barely had a chance to brace for impact when he collided into me. I fell on my back, only my reflexes sparing me from hitting my head hard. The breath escaped my lungs and my vision blipped black for a moment, but I managed to wrap my hand around his arm.

I remained calm, knowing that, while my body was panicking, sure it was dying from lack of oxygen, I would actually be fine. Still, it didn't stop my lungs from contracting as I wheezed, trying to force air in and out. The boy pulled back a fist, moving faster than I could track, and struck me in the face.

My teeth clacked together, and my ears rang—but I had sustained worse punches in the fighting ring. I twisted my neck back toward him just in time to see the blur that meant he'd drawn his fist back again. Grunting, I rolled over, dragging him with me by the arm, partially pinning him with my body. He was fast, I realized deliriously, but he was still only as strong as a preteen boy.

"That sedative would be real nice right now!" I yelled, trying to pin the boy down as he struggled against me. I clutched one of his wrists, but the other was free, and the boy's fist hit me in the chest multiple times as I tried to capture it. "Calm down," I grunted.

He gave a weird wrenching gasp as my weight pinned his lower half. I felt his fist smacking my back, using the same technique of rapid low-power blows, my shirt getting worked over in the commotion. Suddenly he stilled, and I took a closer look at his masked face in alarm, worried that his heart was giving out. Then I felt him lean toward me, tugging at my pants. When he leaned back, he held my pistol in his hand, pointed over my back, toward where Ms. Dale and Dr. Arlan had been putting together the sedative.

I grabbed the pistol with my free hand, slamming the flesh of my thumb in between the hammer and the pin just as he pulled the trigger. I felt the bite of metal there, and knew it had drawn blood, but didn't dare risk pulling it away. Instead, I closed my grip around the rest of the pistol, trying to jerk it out of his hands. He released it only to slam a knee into my gut, jerking forward at the same time, head-butting me.

My head snapped back from the impact, but I kept my weight on him. "HURRY UP!" I bellowed, tossing the gun over my shoulder.

The boy grunted again, his little legs beating against me, and I took a chance. Lifting my weight up slightly, I flipped him over and dropped back down. I wrapped my arm around his neck and began squeezing slowly, relentlessly cutting off the blood flow as I would an opponent in the ring. I heard footsteps rushing over as the boy gasped, then made a strangled squeak, his body jerking and twisting wildly—and then his struggles began to still beneath me.

"Here," said Ms. Dale from behind me. I looked back in time to see her jamming the sedative into his thigh. I immediately released the boy and scrambled back, keeping my eyes on him, waiting to see whether we had saved him.

CHAPTER 26

Violet

I checked my watch again for what felt like the millionth time. It had been thirty minutes since our last transmission, and I was edgy with anticipation. Even now, a million imaginary scenarios were flitting through my head, running from bad to worse to positively gruesome. And without word, some sign everyone was all right, I was powerless to stop those vicious thoughts.

I could, however, ignore them for brief moments, if I put my mind to it. Frowning at the dirty dishes one of the refugees had brought in, I quickly added a few of the large pots to the big metal tub in the kitchen, the hot water I had poured into it still steaming. The water was still too hot to plunge my single working hand into—which was probably for the best, as a lot of the pots had caked-over remains in the bottom. Sighing, I checked my watch again.

I gave up any pretense of doing a chore and clicked my headset back on. "Any update, Amber?"

"No, not since you asked me three minutes ago," came her dry reply.

"Well, I was waiting for dirty dishes," I replied almost defensively.

"I seriously cannot believe you are doing the dishes right now," she retorted.

"Okay, first of all, if you've been avoiding this chore since we got here, then I'm so bringing it up at the next meeting. And secondly, I need something to keep me busy. I'm freaking out a little over here."

Amber laughed, a loud, sharp bark, and I scowled at her—not that she could see. "I'm sorry, Vi," she said. "I actually know how you feel. Remember when I was shot?"

I did remember, although it felt like a lifetime ago. "How did you cope with it?" I asked, picking up a rag and wiping down the kitchen table.

"Well, I think it *is* a different situation than what you're going through," she replied. "Frankly, we had way less stress during those days, and not every single mission felt like our lives were on the line."

My hand froze mid-motion; I felt a physical jolt pass through my body at what she was saying. Not that she was wrong. Everything we had been through the last couple of weeks—months—had constantly felt like it was a matter of life or death. It was just something we never talked about. And now that I was on the outside, perfectly safe and sound, everything felt... off. It was like there was something held in suspense, waiting to fall, but I had no idea when or even where it would be.

"Violet?"

"I'm here," I said, shaking my head to clear it. Now was not the time for an existential crisis. "Sorry. Just let me know when you've got something, okay?"

"Will do. Unless you radio back first."

I rolled my eyes and resumed wiping down the table. Once it was done, I wandered back over to my bucket in the sink and checked the water. It was still too hot to actually wash anything, so I tossed the rag over one of the drying lines near the fireplace and grabbed the broom, needing to channel my nervous energy into *something*.

Despite how slowly I had to sweep to keep my ribs from twinging, my cleaning task was actually helping a bit, so when Amber's voice filled my ear a few minutes later, I nearly dropped the broom, staggering back in surprise.

"Violet! They're back. I—" She stopped talking so suddenly I tapped my earbud a few times, thinking the equipment had failed.

But then her voice came back, this time with a steely tone that made the hair on the back of my neck prickle in alarm. "Violet, we need to cut transmission. Turn off everything that sends a signal. Viggo's orders."

"Wait, what? Why?" I waited, clutching the broom handle tightly in my hand. "Amber? Viggo?" There was no answer, just the slight crackle of static in my headphones.

I tried again to contact them, but no one responded. The seconds ticked by, becoming minutes, but there was nothing in my ears, nothing except this rising feeling that I had to do something… I was in charge now.

I slipped the headset off my head. First, I had to decide whether Amber's request for silence was a problem or not. On the one hand, I trusted my team—if they needed radio silence, then there was a good reason. On the other hand, I had to consider the possibility they were under duress. Maybe they had been ambushed?

If there weren't any problems, then they'd be back in half an hour. But if there were…

Viggo, Owen, and Ms. Dale wouldn't break easily under torture. I knew this with certainty. Thomas would resist for a while, but not as long. He wasn't a loyalist, and if they figured out they could use Owen against him…

Dr. Arlan was a wild card. I didn't know him that well, and I couldn't bank on him not giving up our location. There were dozens of people in the camp, including my cousin, his wife, and their children.

Standing up, I made a snap decision and checked my watch. It had been about three minutes since Amber's transmission. Twenty-seven minutes until they returned, if the heloship flight went smoothly. I set the timer on my watch, and then headed down the hall. I pushed open the closest door and stepped inside. The room reeked of the plastic, antiseptic, medical smell that seemed prevalent in all hospital rooms.

The room was dimly lit, with only two battery-powered lanterns on the lowest setting illuminating the two twin beds on either side of the room. They were flanked by IV stands, which dangled clear plastic bags connected to the beds' occupants by long plastic tubes. Henrik lay on the left, Quinn on the right. I moved slowly over to Henrik, taking in the older male's sallow skin and the dark shadows under his eyes. Something stirred behind me, and I turned, seeing Dr. Tierney sit up from her makeshift pallet on the floor against the wall separating the hall from the room, her eyes squinting at me in confusion.

"It's all right, Dr. T," came a voice from Quinn's side of the room. "It's Violet."

Turning, I noticed Jay sitting on a chair at the foot of Quinn's bed, his legs drawn up on the seat with his arms wrapped around himself. Samuel sat underneath his perch, and the dog looked up at me with big brown eyes and thumped his tail against the floor a couple times, looking almost as careworn as Jay did.

"Hey, Jay," I said softly, and he smiled at me, but it was lined with tired edges. The young man didn't look like he'd been sleeping much.

"Violet?" Dr. Tierney's voice was thick with sleep, her brown hair mussed and tangled. "What's wrong? Did anyone get hurt?"

She was already beginning to push herself up off the ground, and I hesitated, then moved closer and offered her my hand. She squinted at it for a moment, and then batted it aside with a grimace. "No helping anyone up," she griped as she got her legs under her. "Let's call that doctor's order number seventeen."

I waited until she had stood and placed her spectacles on her face, then asked, "Dr. Tierney, what would you need to move Henrik and Quinn?"

She turned abruptly, her brows drawing together. "Why?" she asked. Jay leaned forward, the chair squeaking slightly under his weight, attracting my eyes. Nervousness fluttered unexpectedly in my stomach at this first moment of having to explain my plan, and I realized I was worried they might think I was overreacting. I steeled myself, explaining my worst-case scenario to the doctor with Jay listening in.

Surprisingly, she nodded. "That's prudent thinking," she said. She looked at Henrik, then at Quinn, her gaze thoughtful and considerate. "We'd need a vehicle large enough to transfer them and all this equipment. Theoretically, Henrik can be taken off most of these, but Quinn…"

She shook her head, and I moved closer to the young man, my heart heavy as I took in Tabitha's handiwork. It seemed like every bit of him was being held together by stitches—and I couldn't see much under the bandages. There was no telling where the cuts stopped or started. His face alone was crisscrossed with them. A set of stitches started over his left eye, just under his hairline, slashing horizontally before cutting straight down the side of his nose, down his cheek, and through his lips, stopping just under his chin. Tabitha had spared that eye, it seemed, but his other eye was covered with a bandage, stitches running from his eyebrow down his other cheek. His right ear was missing the uppermost part, while bandages covered the spot where his left should have been—but they looked suspiciously flat.

Quinn's arms were lined with stitches, running up and down his arm with no real pattern, and I could see, on his right hand, the bandaged pinky finger that stopped an inch short of where it should have.

"Can we move him?" I asked, my voice a whisper, my

mouth dry.

Doctor Tierney nodded. "As long as we can get a vehicle with a big enough open area in the back."

I nodded and checked my watch. Twenty-two minutes. "Jay, feel up to helping me?"

The young man was off his chair and standing in front of me in moments, his face intensely serious. "What do you need?"

"Well, I need you to find who's on guard duty tonight and send them to me in the den. I also need you to find Lynne and Morgan, and bring them to me. Do you know who they are?"

Jay nodded. "I know Lynne. She worked with us at the facility. Morgan I don't know, but I can find him."

"Her," I corrected. "She's another one of the Liberators. Lynne will know where she is. Ask them to meet me in the dining room. You come back too—I'll need your help."

Jay nodded and hurried off, and I turned to Dr. Tierney. "Do what you can to get these two prepped for transport. I am really hoping it won't come to it."

"I'm on it," she replied, already turning away from me, focusing completely on Quinn. I turned and left, leaving the door partially open. I moved back through the dining room and into the den with the creepy animal heads, grabbing a black plastic crate off the floor. I proceeded to shove all the loose papers and files we had somehow accumulated into it, not bothering with any sort of filing system. It could be sorted later.

I was halfway through when a dark-haired, tanned man— his name was Gregory—knocked on the door. He had a rifle slung on his shoulder, and his eyes watched me, alert.

"You're in charge of the guards tonight?" I asked him.

He nodded. "Yes. Jay said you needed to see me?"

"I need you to pull everyone scheduled for the second shift to join you in the watch. Have them patrol the area, and send a scout out to the heloship landing area in one of the larger vehicles."

"Problem?"

"I hope not," I muttered. Gregory gave me a wary look. "I'm not sure yet," I told him honestly. "But I'm taking precautions. Report back to me in…" I checked my watch and did a quick count. "Seven minutes. Make sure the scout takes a subvocalizer, and tell them to report back if the heloship doesn't show up in nineteen."

He nodded and left, and I was glad of the fact that he hadn't asked any questions. Time was a luxury at this point.

Almost as soon as he moved out of it, Lynne and Morgan pushed through the door of the den, followed by Jay. "Hey, Violet, what's up?" asked Lynne.

"I need you both to start pulling the vehicles around to the front of the barn and loading them up. Food and weapons, guns and ammunition are the priority. If you find you need more people, then wake them, but do it quietly."

Lynne arched an eyebrow. "Expecting trouble?"

"Like I just told Gregory, I hope not… but right now, until I know otherwise, I need to make sure we're ready to go with all we can carry. I'll know for sure if we need to start waking the rest of the camp soon. Jay, would you help them load?"

"Absolutely," he said with a nod.

"Let me know if you have any problems, and try not to cause a panic. If anyone wakes up and asks what you're doing, tell them to come see me, and I'll explain."

Lynne frowned and exchanged dubious looks with Morgan, who was managing to look sleepy and skeptical at the same time, her short black hair sticking up in all directions. "To be fair, you haven't really explained it to *us*," Lynne said, her green eyes narrowing.

I opened my mouth, realizing she was right. "Viggo and Owen went on a mission tonight, and it went sideways. They got bogged down, and we had to send Amber, Ms. Dale, Thomas, and one of our doctors to sort it out. No one's hurt that I know of, but their last transmission didn't have enough information, and, well… If they get back in—" I checked my watch again and blew out a breath. "Sixteen minutes, then we'll call it an evacuation drill. If not… then it'll be for real."

"You mean you'd leave them all to die?" gasped Morgan, her hand going to her mouth. I looked calmly at her and nodded, taking a deep breath.

"My first priority has to be you and all the people here," I said, my throat tight. "If Viggo and Owen have been captured, I will be the first one to mount the rescue mission, but I can't neglect my responsibility to everyone else. It's not what they would want."

"She's right, Morgan," said Lynne, giving me an approving nod. "Let's go move those vehicles and stop wasting time."

As Morgan followed Lynne out, I finished sweeping papers into the box, then turned my attention to the computers, slightly less haphazardly pulling wires and setting the long boxes in a line on the table. They would need to be packed, but only if there was enough space to take them. If not, they were going to have to be burned.

Eighteen minutes later, I was still packing, Gregory silently helping me, my eyes focused entirely on the task ahead. I'd passed my deadline, but I was giving them an extra five minutes until I woke everybody up—I just couldn't bring myself to really give the order until I was dead certain something had gone horribly wrong.

I had just looked down at my watch again when Gregory paused, his hand drifting up to his ear. I stilled, my heartbeat swelling like acid in the back of my throat. He mouthed something into the earbud, then reached up to turn his subvocalizer off.

"The heloship just landed," he announced. "There were no signs of hostile forces. The vehicles should be back shortly."

I somehow managed not to exhale loudly or choke in relief, and channeled it all into a nod. "Good," I said. "But we're not out of the woods yet. We still might have to proceed with the evacuation, depending on what they report. Have your men on standby—if the news is bad, I want first shift to head to the barn to help pack the vehicles, while second shift maintains the guard duties."

Gregory nodded and placed his hand to his throat, a switch clicking and his lips moving. I grabbed the box I had filled with wires and slid it to the end of the table, my ribs stinging at the effort. Picking up full boxes was still impossible for me, but I could at least push them if they weren't too heavy.

A few minutes later, Gregory gave me a look and then headed outside, and I dropped what I was doing, immediately heading for the door to the porch. I watched the lights of the guard's car approach and then pull around to the front of the house. The night air was cool, causing my skin to pebble.

The car's engine shut off, and I heard the doors slamming as the returning patrol got out. I nearly went weak in the knees as Viggo came around the vehicle, and my first urge was to go to him and make sure he was all right. But as he stepped into the dim light of the lanterns, I froze. His handsome face was bruised down the side, and he was favoring one leg. Worst of all, though, I could see even from this distance that his eyes were flat and hard, but it wasn't the hardness of anger. No, this was a look I knew all too well... from Ashabee's manor.

I looked around at the rest of the crew, watching as Amber, Ms. Dale, and Dr. Arlan came into view. Dr. Arlan was carrying a small boy, a red-stained bandage wrapped tightly around his thigh, in his arms. Thomas plodded into view, and my heartbeat quickened as I saw the same forlorn look all the others wore even on *his* face.

"Where's Owen?" I asked.

Viggo's brows drew together, and he opened his mouth, only to slam it shut so hard I swore I could hear his teeth clack together.

I heard another door slam and took a step off the porch as Owen came into view. He was holding another boy, probably around nine or ten, with blond hair. His eyes were closed, his cheek pressed to Owen's shoulder.

In the gray, wan pre-dawn light, Owen's eyes were swollen and red. He held the boy tightly in his arms, as if he would never let go. It would've been sweet if there weren't an air of deep sorrow radiating off him like a winter storm.

My eyes flicked again over the boy Owen was carrying, this time noting the similarities between the two. My heart plunged into my stomach as I met Owen's bloodshot gaze. Tears were swimming there.

"Ian," I gasped, and Owen swallowed, his face breaking as he sagged to the ground, clutching his little brother's lifeless body tightly to his chest.

CHAPTER 27

Violet

I moved over to Owen, kneeling next to him. He was sobbing, each breath heaving as though torn from him, as though his heart had been ripped out and cut in two before his eyes. In a way, it had.

I threw my arm around him, holding him close as his body shook under the force of his cries. Each one was like a knife to my own heart, and I tasted his pain—it was so close, too close, to my own. But this was… this was agony. It was cruel and un-just and *wrong*. I didn't have any words to make it right, because there were none. Nothing would ever make this right.

So I didn't say anything. I let Owen cry for a few min-utes, then gently coaxed him up. I didn't ask him if he wanted someone to help him with his brother. I knew if it were me in his shoes… I stopped that train of thought before it could even reach its conclusion. Owen needed me right now, and I couldn't, *wouldn't* let my worry over Tim affect me. Later, when I was alone, I would cry for Owen, Ian, and Tim. But right now, I had to focus.

"C'mon, Owen," I said softly, urging him forward. "Let's get him inside."

He took a shuddering breath as he plodded forward, and I stayed beside him, pressing him onward. Amber held open the front door for us, her eyes shimmering with tears, and I reached out and pressed my left hand into hers, squeezing it.

As we passed Gregory, I nodded at him. "Tell Ms. Dale what we've been doing and why, and she'll tell you how to proceed." He nodded and disappeared through the front door.

I coaxed Owen down the hall toward the room I had been sleeping in. I opened the door and let him in first, then closed it behind us. Owen moved over to the bed, his movements wooden and robotic as he laid Ian down on the blanket, resting his head on the pillow. Then he sank down to his knees and rested his arms on the mattress, taking Ian's small hand into his own.

Blinking away the tears already starting to drop from my eyes, I quietly moved around to Owen's side of the bed and lowered myself to the floor, sitting next to him. Owen's eyes gazed at me, but they were vacant, as if he didn't even recognize me. Tears had cut tracks over his cheeks, and his nose was swollen and red. He sniffed a few times, his nose clearly stuffed.

I reached into my pocket, searching for something that just might be in there… yes. Paper napkins. I passed them to Owen, and he reached out, taking them with the hand he wasn't using to hold his brother's hand. He stared blankly at them for a moment, and then dropped them to the bed, pushing the wadded edges apart with one hand until he had singled one out. He picked it up and dabbed it across his eyes, trying to sop up the tears.

I waited. There weren't words in the history of all languages to make him feel better. I knew that beyond a shadow of a doubt. Anything I attempted would only come off... wrong. Owen didn't need words, didn't even want them. He wanted his brother back, and that was a void in his heart words would never touch.

I remembered all the things everyone had said to me after my mother had died. All their words and attempts at kindness had only made me angrier. I didn't want Owen to suffer through that. So I let him keep his own pace.

The minutes dragged by, periodically punctuated by his sniffles and the few times he blew his nose. I sat through it all, certain this was where I needed to be. After a while, he met my gaze, his expression lost.

"I don't know what I'm supposed to do," he admitted hoarsely.

I nodded, tears pricking my eyes. "I know."

Owen leaned forward, brushing his fingers over Ian's blond hair, adjusting a few of the locks against his forehead. In death, Ian's eyes were closed, his face relaxed. He would have almost looked like he was sleeping, were it not for the fact that his chest remained perfectly still... and the tiniest amount of blood, or spittle, or a mixture, still trailing at the side of his mouth, even though it looked like Owen had tried to wipe it away.

"Our parents just accepted it. When they took him. They just... let it happen. Said it was for the best. But I knew. I knew it wasn't. I mean… how could they take him and leave me? *I* was the bad one. Somehow I passed their test, but I knew what I was. But Ian… he was so sweet, y'know? As beta as they came."

He met my gaze, more tears falling from his lashes onto his cheek. "He saved animals," he whispered, a ghost of a smile on his lips. "He would bring them home in a box if they were small enough to fix. A turtle, a bird, a kitten. There was this dog he found once—he must have escaped when he was younger, or maybe his owners abandoned him. I don't know. But he had grown up wearing this collar, and it was killing him. It was too tight, and it was…" He stopped, the words lodging in his throat as a racking sob shuddered through his body. I felt my own heart twist at his words' visceral reactions, wishing there were some way to comfort him.

He cleared his throat and scrubbed his eyes with his arm. "Anyway, he needed me to cut the collar off. He knew I had knives. Ian wouldn't touch them, you know…" He met my gaze, a forlorn look in his eyes. "That's when I knew the test was crap. When they took him… I knew. *I* kept knives, *I* used to secretly watch martial arts practice and try to replicate the moves, *I* used to break into houses to steal things… *I* was the bad son. The bad Matrian son. But they took him. And now he's…"

Shoulders shaking, he looked away, unable to say the words.

I swallowed hard. "I know there's nothing I can say to ever make this better," I whispered. "Even right now, every word coming out of my mouth feels inadequate. But you're my friend, Owen. You're my friend and I love you. Please, whatever you need, whenever you need it. I'm here for you."

Owen looked up at me, raw and vulnerable. His chin

trembled and he wiped away another tear, almost angrily. "I want to bury him."

I nodded. "Of course. I'll make the arrangements."

"Can I… Can I stay here with him? I don't want him to be alone tonight."

Fighting back tears, I nodded again. "Of course. You didn't even need to ask."

He shot me a grateful look, and then turned his gaze back to his brother. I sensed it was time to leave, but there was still one thing I wanted to know. It felt wrong to ask, somehow, but there was something more going on—I had seen it in Viggo's face.

"Owen, what happened tonight? I mean, how did this happen?"

Owen shot me a vicious look, his face growing mottled with rage, as if someone had flipped a switch inside his brain. "Ask your boyfriend," he hissed, his voice coming out like the angry leaking of a tire. I jerked back without thinking, as though he would launch himself at me.

A pregnant silence stretched between us, and after several long seconds, Owen leaned back and angrily wiped his eyes. "You should go."

I agreed. Wordlessly, I stood up and moved over to the door. As my hand touched the doorknob, I stopped, the urge to apologize thick and hot on my tongue. It was the part I had hated the most after my mother had died—all the apologies. I could never understand them. Now, I couldn't help but feel the same desire. It was a bandage of sorts. A way of making myself feel better for not being able to help him. I had always

misunderstood them; I had thought all those people were saying they were sorry my mother had died. Now I realized they
had been sorry they couldn't help me and Tim more.

I wasn't going to let Owen go through this alone, though.
He wouldn't get a "sorry" from me, because I would be there to
help him. I left.

I found Amber in the living room, sifting through the boxes I had slung together. She turned as I came out, studying me.
"I'm sorry about the transmission," she offered softly, crossing
her arms over her chest. "Viggo said they might have hacked
the frequency. We needed to kill the link in case somebody was
tracing it, trying to find you."

"It's okay," I replied, my voice still thick. "I think Owen
could do with your company. Can you go to him?"

She nodded and moved past me, heading toward the back
room. I scanned the room. Still no Viggo. I moved down the
hall and outside. The mood in the house was somber; as people
moved around, unpacking from the evacuation drill, I could
almost feel the news of the tragedy moving through our ranks,
making the conversations softer and the darkness outside feel
wearier and more dangerous.

Ms. Dale stood on the porch, talking in a low voice with Dr.
Arlan and Lynne.

"Yes, of course," she was saying to the young woman, "we
removed the tracker from Ian's body. As for the other boy"—
she turned to the doctor—"we could keep him in the barn loft
or the basement, but that's not the best area."

"I would hope to give him at least a little light… a place that
feels safe," Dr. Arlan said. "He's just a child. He'll probably be so

confused when he wakes up. Is there someone here he trusts?"
I realized, listening in, that they must have been talking about
the other boy who had survived the raid.

"That depends," Ms. Dale said, "on many things. The only
person here who really knows him is Viggo, but I have reason
to believe he's probably been conditioned to think of Viggo as
a traitor. It might be best if we have someone impartial first
attempt to speak to him… and a doctor there to find out how
he's responding to being off the Benuxupane. If that's what is
actually in him. We have a good opportunity here; we should
probably do a blood sample before he wakes up again, just to
find out what chemicals they're pumping into them."

Dr. Arlan's voice grew wary. "I can do that, yes. But our
'opportunity' is also a child. We can't forget that."

Ms. Dale nodded. "You're very right. That's why it's a difficult decision." She tossed a glance back at me, and I realized she
knew I'd been standing there listening. "Violet, can you think
of anything to do with Cody?"

Cody. The name was familiar. Through my worry, a memory surfaced of a surly kid who had once challenged Viggo's
authority as a teacher when we'd brought the boys out of their
cages in The Green. Shock passed through me as I realized this
made two children we knew, at least somewhat. It was all too
real right now.

I looked at Ms. Dale, trying to figure out something to say
beyond the buzzing in my mind. "I…"

"I know you're looking for Viggo," Ms. Dale said, nodding
her head toward the barn. "He's in there. He's hurting. You
should probably go to him. Dr. Arlan and I will take care of

Cody for now, although we'd like everyone's input later on."

Her suggestion was completely unnecessary, as I was already moving quickly across the dew-slicked grass. I had to force myself to slow down when my head started to throb and feel woozy. I had already pushed myself too far—skipping my nap earlier had been a mistake—but I couldn't wait to comfort Viggo until I felt better. Gritting my teeth, I pushed through the feeling and continued my journey to the barn.

The massive ten-foot-high door was cracked open wide enough for me to slip inside. Several battery-operated lanterns lit up the tables placed in there to organize the boxes of equipment, guns, ammunition, and other electronic devices. Far behind them, several rows of vehicles from Ashabee's manor gleamed in the lantern light. I weaved my way through them, searching for Viggo, and encountered Thomas instead.

He was sitting at the end of one of the tables in the second-to-last row, fiddling with something. Looking up as I approached, he met my gaze and then dropped his head back down, turning the object over in his hands. I slowed, then stopped, seeing how Thomas was also affected by Owen's tragedy.

I didn't want to wait, but I needed to reach out to him, too. "Are you okay?" I asked.

He blinked and met my gaze again. After a second, he shook his head. "I was making this for Owen," he announced, his voice whisper soft. "For Ian, actually. For when he…"

Trailing off, he set the object down on the table. I looked at it: it was a crude piece of electronics, with wires jutting out of it, but I could see it had been made in the semblance of a human.

Although, its head and limbs were more square-shaped instead of round.

"It's a robot. A machine that looks like a man," he admitted hoarsely. "It's just a toy, and it's not finished yet… I still needed some parts, but I—"

I touched his shoulder. "I know," I whispered, giving him a squeeze.

He looked up at me, his dark eyes teary, and sniffled loudly. "Is Owen… Is he all right?"

I shook my head. "No," I said simply. "Maybe one day… but not today."

Thomas nodded, picking up the toy again. "Viggo is in the back of the barn," he said. "He's not all right either."

Swallowing hard, I removed my hand from Thomas and headed to the back, moving behind the silent rows of vehicles. The barn was large, bigger than the house, and smelled thickly of mold. My boots slipped over the damp boards underneath me as I walked. I wasn't quite through the rows of cars when I began to hear the rhythmic sound of something hitting something else.

I headed toward it, and in the back, inside one of the defunct animal stalls, I found Viggo. He was shirtless, his muscled torso glistening with sweat. As I approached him, I saw his arm whip out again and again, his bare knuckles striking a freshly cut log the length of my leg, which was swinging from a rope off a beam overhead. I didn't need to see his fists clearly to know they were bleeding. If he kept this up, he'd have broken bones— if he didn't have any already.

Underneath the fury coming off him in waves, I could

sense his desolate mood, and my heart broke for him. I came
up behind him, not bothering to hide my approach, and laid a
hand on his shoulder. He stopped striking the board, but his
back heaved under my hand as he sucked in air.

"I'm going to need some time," he said after a long moment.
"Please, just leave me alone." He squared his shoulders and began hitting the log again, his fists slapping wetly on the wood.
Even under the dim light of the lantern, I could see dark blood
spattered and smeared across the bark.

My need to accept his words at face value was strong, but
not stronger than my need to find out the truth. I took a deep
breath, then stepped in between him and the board.

Viggo's eyes narrowed, and he pulled up short. He reluctantly lowered his fists, his green eyes meeting mine.

"I'm sorry," I said. "But I need to know what happened.
Owen blames you for some reason, but I know you, and I know
you would never—"

"Owen is right," Viggo breathed harshly. "It's my fault."

I shook my head. "I don't believe you. You would never do
anything to hurt those boys. To hurt *any* child."

Viggo stared at me, then looked away, shaking his head. "I
did this time." He made no effort to hide the deep disgust in his
voice, and I ached, knowing this was tearing him apart.

"Viggo, please. Talk to me. Tell me what happened."

He reached up to wipe his nose, stopping as he realized
that would just smear his bloody knuckles. With a grimace, he
moved over to where his shirt hung over the stall wall and tore
a long strip from the bottom. I watched as he fiddled with it
a moment, and then moved over to him, pushing it aside and

taking it in my left hand. "Let me do it," I said, placing the fabric in between the fingers of my right hand, which I could now squeeze together a little, if I tried. It was awkward with the cast, but I managed to pinch it between two fingers, holding the cloth secure as I wrapped him up with my left.

Viggo stood as still as a statue during a long span of silence. Then he began to speak, recounting the entire incident. I listened as he told me about his conversation with Desmond, and then Ian's attack, and felt my heart fracture further.

"He stopped moving," Viggo said, his eyes flicking to mine, his voice hoarse. "I had my arm wrapped around his neck, cutting off his air, and he just went… still. I moved away, got off him, but…" He released a shuddering breath and ran a hand through his hair in agitation. "God, he was so still. We didn't even know until… until Dr. Arlan told us. By then he had pulled off Ian's mask. Owen had just realized who he was when… Arlan said it was impossible to know what exactly had caused his heart to stop. He said it could've been the sedative, it could have been the wrong dose or something, but I know it was me. It had to have been me. I was on top of him. It was my arm around his throat. If I could've just…" He trailed off.

"It was my fault," he explained, finally meeting my gaze. His hand was still in mine, loosely, but he gently pulled it away. "If I had been faster… made a better decision… I could've saved him. I *should've* saved him."

I wiped my eyes, more tears coming, and shook my head. "It's not your fault," I said, trying to reassure him but knowing how hollow it must have sounded. "You did everything you could."

"It wasn't enough," he snapped back. "I should've done better."

He pulled away, jerking his torn shirt off the wall and throwing it over his head. I watched as he stalked out, arranging the shirt over his midsection, feeling utterly incapable of helping anyone.

CHAPTER 28

Viggo

The night had faded away into a gray, overcast dawn, the threat of rain bearing down in the form of ionized air. Everyone else had gone inside at one point or another and gotten some rest.

I hadn't slept—I couldn't even bring myself to try. Instead, I worked. I helped Lynne, Morgan, and Jay unload the vehicles they had packed up as a precaution. The work suited me just fine. I was in no mood to deal with human interaction, and our ceaseless labor didn't really make talking practical.

Once that task was finished, I moved on to another job, then another. I took the jobs nobody wanted: splitting firewood, digging out areas for people to relieve themselves and marking them with strips of yellow cloth, building more targets for the firing range… I did anything and everything I could to remain alone. The latest chore was laundry duty, which was probably the most annoying task in the camp, as it required me to fetch water from the rusted-over pump on the side of the house, heat it over a fire, and then dump it into a trough and scrub at the dirty clothes and bedlinens for grueling minutes. Even with the heavy plastic gloves I wore over my bandages to keep my raw knuckles from bleeding on the clean clothes, the heat of the water felt as though it was scalding me every time I put my hands into it.

It was perfect.

News of Owen's loss had hit the camp hard, muting the normal sounds of a waking, bustling camp of over fifty people. A somberness seemed to hang over us, just as heavy and thick as the clouds overhead. I kept my head down as I worked, making it known that I was not in a mood for conversation, and, for the most part, people left me alone.

Physical activity was a distraction, one I sorely needed to keep myself from going off the rails. I didn't think I could ever explain my turmoil to anyone, not even Violet. It was like a poisonous sack of bile writhing under my torso. It wouldn't do me the courtesy of letting me vomit, nor would it become less corrosive with time. It just sat there, periodically twitching, reminding me a boy had died, and I was more than likely responsible for it.

I knew Violet and Ms. Dale and… well… everyone except Owen didn't feel like I should blame myself. But I couldn't help it. I was the one who had fought him. I was the one who had wrapped my arm around his tiny neck and squeezed. If I had just been able to…

My gloved hand convulsively closed into a fist, and I had to swallow the urge to start hitting something again—a feeling

BELLA FORREST

I was growing more and more familiar with. I winced as my knuckles throbbed, almost able to feel the broken skin splitting further, and then relaxed into it, letting the pain roll over me, recognizing on some dark level that I deserved it. On an even darker level, I knew it wasn't enough to make up for my failings.

I released my clenched fist and exhaled before plunging my hand back into the soapy water, just shy of scalding, and beginning to rub the clothes against the washboard in the tub. I was engrossed in my work, but even so, time moved at a snail's pace.

There was a subtle clearing of a throat behind me, and my hands stopped in their vigorous scrubbing. Looking over my shoulder, I saw Violet there, her face somber. Her bruises had faded quite a bit over the past few days, but they lingered in yellow and green, almost fluorescent spots on the side of her face. I hadn't stopped to look in a mirror, but I assumed I now had a set to match.

"It's time?" I asked, and she nodded.

Swallowing the excess saliva that had built up in my mouth, I pulled the sheet I had been working on out of the water and dropped it into the next tub, which held cooler, clean water for rinsing. "I'll be there in a minute," I announced. "Just want to finish this."

I heard her sigh softly, but her shoes began to move, crunching over the soil and fading as she headed away. Exhaling in relief, I quickly rinsed out the sheet, wrung it out, and then threw it over one of the lines strung between two trees to dry. It took a few minutes, but when it was done, I felt just a fraction more mentally prepared for what was to come.

I gave a dark, strained chuckle as the thought went through

my mind. Who was I kidding? I was nowhere near prepared for this.

Steeling myself, I turned back toward the house, where I could see Ms. Dale, Amber, Lynne, Morgan, Jay, Thomas, and, of course, Owen, standing on the porch. Owen held Ian's small body in his arms, cradling the young boy, and even from this distance, I could see the sad draw in his mouth and eyes. The gray day, with low rainclouds drifting slowly across the sky, seemed designed to reflect our sorrow.

Violet placed a hand on Owen's shoulder, and together, they all started to move to the place where Violet had tasked a few of the refugees to help her in constructing a grave. She had picked a good spot for it: near the woods, just off the side of the barn, in the shade of the trees and out of the way of the daily routines of the camp. I watched as they moved, my throat tight.

The entire short day, I had been riddled with indecision on what I should do about this funeral. On the one hand, I needed to go—honor demanded it. On the other, without a doubt, I knew Owen didn't want me there. With how he felt right now, it would just be an affront to him if I were at the ceremony. It was a conundrum. I still felt strongly that I needed to be there.

So I had come up with the next best thing. Or maybe it was the next worst, depending on one's point of view. I waited for the funeral procession to make its way closer to the gravesite, and then moved around the opposite side of the tents, heading for the gap in between the tents and the barn. I moved quickly, businesslike but unassuming, not wanting to arrive late and draw attention to myself.

I headed directly for the tree line, pushing a few yards into the wooded area, then hooked back around so that I could come from the opposite direction, the light lower canopy of saplings shrouding me somewhat from view. As I neared the site, I heard the soft sound of voices and slowed down, picking my path as quietly as possible through the dead leaves and twigs littering the forest floor.

An old oak tree with gnarled branches was my destination. It sat far enough back that it blended in with the forest, but was close enough for me to watch the funeral without having to peer past dozens of trees. I approached the grizzled tree, coming to a stop next to it. From my vantage point, I was mostly out of view of the others, but I still had a clear view of the grave.

I watched as Owen placed Ian inside a small wooden box, resting the young boy inside the bright, freshly cut lumber and taking one last look at him. After a minute, he and Amber closed the lid, and Owen began hammering the nails into it one by one. It was hard to watch. With each nail he drove home, Owen's face grew more and more bleak.

Somehow, he managed to finish the task, pounding in the last nail with a decisive strike from the hammer. He stood up and tossed the hammer to the side in one fluid motion, taking a moment to scrub at his cheeks. Amber and Thomas moved toward him, but he held up a hand and shook his head.

"I'm all right," he announced hoarsely, his voice carrying to me. I could hear in his words the tears he was fighting back. I reached out and rested my hand on the tree to steady myself, feeling the churning twist of guilt in my gut.

Owen didn't break down completely. He managed to pull himself together, and, at his nod, Ms. Dale, Thomas, and Amber helped him lower the coffin into the ground, using the two ropes draped across the grave. The box hit the earth, the ropes were pulled up and placed to one side, and then Owen moved to the head of the grave. I could hear his voice clearly from my spot, and though it was faint, none of the emotion was lost.

"My brother was one of the gentlest humans I've ever known," he said. "He cared deeply for every living thing. I was ten when he was born, and even as a baby, he was full of smiles. I promised to be the best big brother I could, but I failed more often than I care to recall. It was only after he was taken that I realized how much I really cared about him, and when our parents didn't want to help him, I knew what I had to do. I became a better person for him. I started to care about the people around me, forced myself to, really, and after a while, I realized I liked it. And I have him to thank for that."

He stopped, his voice cracking. Looking away, he gave a shuddering breath, his body trembling. My grip tightened on the bark of the tree, the gnarled texture digging beneath my fingernails. There was a pause as Owen composed himself. When he looked back at the group, determination was stamped across his features.

"My brother didn't deserve what happened to him. He didn't. He was too good for it, too pure. It wasn't just, and it wasn't fair. All I can hope is those responsible will be made to suffer for the injustice they brought him. And I hope that I'm there to witness it. I tried to save him, and now I will avenge him. This is the vow I make to him, in the hopes that someday, he will find peace."

I blinked as his words hit me, the cold, angry bite of

bitterness in them setting my teeth on edge. I knew Owen was hurting, but I hadn't realized that hurt inside of him was a seed of anger and violence. I thought of the past he'd mentioned to me while we were dangling from the heloship in the dark, the past he'd mentioned again now. Maybe the old Owen, whoever that was, was reemerging. My heart was racing in my chest. *I* had played a part in creating this anger eating away at my friend.

Sadness and anger mixed up in my blood, strangling my tongue. Vengeance was a dark path. I vowed, right then and there, that I would be there for Owen, in whatever capacity he needed me. I might not be able to join him on that path, not if it called for cold-blooded murder, but I would try to help him back from that, if he let me.

Thomas picked something up off the ground and moved over to Owen, holding it out to him. As Owen reached out to take it, I saw it was a flat bit of metal with words burnt into the side. It took me a moment, and then I realized it was a make-shift gravestone. Thomas had probably put it together during the night.

As one, the rest of the group began pushing dirt back into the grave, first with their hands, then with shovels. Violet stood by one side with Owen, holding his hand in a comforting way as he watched the dirt fall into the grave. Thomas brought over a wheelbarrow full of small stones. I watched as he began lining them up atop the newly turned earth of the grave, piling them into a mound.

Owen let go of Violet's hand and moved to stand above it, placing the grave marker against the small half-hill Thomas had created. He held it up while Thomas stacked more stones around it, bracing it from both sides. Once it was done, he stood up, placing a hand on Owen's shoulder. He had to have said something too low for me to hear, because Owen nodded and offered him another attempted smile.

Eventually, the task was finished, and everyone began to move back to the house, Owen between them. Violet remained behind, her head turning as she looked around the area, clearly searching for me. I took a moment to collect myself, and then emerged from my hiding place as her eyes moved across the tree line.

Her eyes met mine, and she gave me a soft look, full of understanding that only twisted my guts up further. I knew I didn't deserve that mercy, and I came to a halt before I reached her and looked away, ashamed. I hated that she was giving me that look. I hated that she was so blinded by her love for me she couldn't see my limitations. Yet I loved her all the same for finding a strength that seemed to have deserted me, for having faith in me despite all evidence to the contrary.

That twisting hatred didn't stop me from letting her cross over to me. Nor did I stop her as she slid her arms around my waist, stepping in close and resting her head against my chest. My arms came around her shoulders softly, needing to hold her, craving the comfort of her warmth and acceptance.

"Owen will forgive you eventually," she murmured softly. I didn't say anything, but she knew I didn't believe her. "He will," she insisted, her arm tightening around me. "He's mad right now, but it will pass. He'll realize it wasn't your fault—it was Desmond and Elena's. They are the ones who deserve his anger for what happened, not you. And he'll remember that soon enough."

I didn't object, but I knew he wouldn't. Losses like Owen's were wounds that ran deep, cutting to the bone. They festered, and many never fully healed. He would carry the emotional scars for the rest of his life. Maybe he would get somewhat better, but the pain would linger. I knew, because the memory of Miriam still haunted me to this day, whispering that I had failed her.

There was no way to know how long we stood there, but eventually the sound of approaching feet forced me to put my growing melancholy aside. Letting go of Violet, I took a step back and saw Ms. Dale approaching, her hair, loose for once, getting caught up in the slight breeze and blowing wildly around her face.

"I'm sorry to interrupt," she said. "But I just came from the house, and Jeff is on the handheld from the city, with information he thinks we all need to hear. We're to call him back in ten minutes. This will give us a chance to talk about Cody."

I nodded and ran a hand over my head, lamenting the fact that even in moments like this, when we desperately needed silence and time to process, the news never seemed to stop rolling in. Hopefully, however, these developments would mean we were growing closer to achieving something, possibly even striking a blow to Desmond and Elena. One that would make them bleed. It wouldn't make up for Ian... but it might be a start on keeping other boys from the same fate.

"Is everybody already in there?" I asked.

Ms. Dale nodded, brushing some hair away from her face.

"Yes. We're waiting on you."

"Okay. Let's go."

I started to move, but Violet reached out her left hand and grabbed mine, the grip awkward, yet strong. Turning, I noted the concern in her eyes and the questioning tilt of her eyebrows.

"I'm fine," I tried to assure her, but the words were a lie. I could tell by her face she didn't believe me, but she nodded and then moved forward, wrapping her arm around mine and leaning into me.

Together, we headed back toward the house.

CHAPTER 29

Violet

The group of us had gathered in the den, the animal heads on the walls watching with glassy stares as Thomas jacked the handheld into one of the giant screens we had taken from Ashabee's manor.

I checked my watch, noting we had just under eight minutes to discuss what to do with the boy we had taken from Desmond.

"How is he?" Viggo asked, breaking the still air.

"Dr. Arlan says he's still unconscious," replied Ms. Dale, dropping a folder on the table we stood around. "A possible side effect to either the energy he expended last night, or withdrawal from the Benuxupane. The question is what to do with him when he wakes up."

"What do you mean, what to do with him?" demanded Owen, his tone biting.

Ms. Dale blinked, her brows drawing down slightly as she regarded Owen, concern etched into the fine lines of her face. "What I mean, Mr. Barns, is do we keep him here, or move him to our other hideout, where we are holding Maxen?"

Owen looked away, his jaw tightening slightly at her stiff rebuff.

"He's in the barn now?" I asked in the awkward silence, earning a small nod from Ms. Dale.

"Indeed. We've managed to cobble together a bed and secured him in the loft. It's mostly dry up there, but it won't do for much longer, now that the weather is changing."

Scratching a spot on her neck, Amber frowned. "Well, obviously we should move him away from the camp. Who knows what effects the withdrawal might have? He may only have enhanced speed, but he is still capable of hurting people, especially when moving fast enough. We can't risk the safety of the fifty or so people here."

I frowned. Logically, I agreed with her, but emotionally? I found the idea distasteful. Cody was already a victim of a despot who was indifferent to his very survival. He'd been cruelly treated, filled with drugs, and made to commit atrocities. He was just a child—what he needed right now was a little compassion.

"I think he should stay," I said abruptly, earning me the attention of everyone in the room. I met their gazes levelly, my head high. "He needs to know we are all on his side, rooting for him, believing in him. That we... we don't want to give him drugs to control him; we don't even want to control him. We just want him to be safe and healthy. We want to take care of him. We have the best people here who can help him. Dr.

Tierney knows more about enhanced humans than anyone. She can monitor his progress, noting how the withdrawals are, if any, and just keeping an eye on his health."

"You mentioned more than one person," Viggo said softly, next to me.

Licking my lips, I nodded. "Jay," I announced. "Think about it—he's the best one to help him, and he can certainly handle his outbursts physically. But best of all, he and Cody share the same trauma. They both come from the same place. If Jay can just show Cody there is another way, maybe even a better one… then maybe it'll go a long way in undoing what they have done to him."

The hush in the room seemed loud in my ears, and I suddenly realized how passionate I had gotten in my speech. I shot a furtive glance at Viggo, who was staring at me, one eyebrow raised. He looked impressed.

Ms. Dale coughed politely, drawing my attention. "Well said, Violet," she said. "I think with an argument like that, there's no need for rebuttal."

The room was silent, nobody objecting, and Ms. Dale burst out in a smile. "Great! Now, it's about time we were checking in with Jeff. Thomas?"

"One second," Thomas said, moving over to the handheld he had attached to one of the larger screens. He pressed a few buttons and then moved back.

Jeff's face filled the screen, looking down on our weary command group.

"Ah, good!" he exclaimed. "Well, not good, considering the circumstances. Owen, please, I hope you'll accept my deepest condolences regarding your loss. Words cannot even begin to express how much sorrow I feel on your behalf."

Owen was standing slightly behind the rest of the group, his eyes still red-rimmed and bloodshot. He looked up at Jeff and nodded robotically. "Thank you, Jeff," he said hoarsely. "It means a lot to me."

"Sir, I'm sure it's lost in the grand scope of your suffering and loss. To that end, I thank you for your politeness. If there is anything you should need, please feel free to reach out to me."

For some reason, Jeff's graceful handling of the situation, and the acknowledgement that he knew Owen was merely being polite in accepting, seemed to make the corner of Owen's mouth tip up slightly. Not much—only a fraction of an inch—but I couldn't help but feel a spark of hope that our Owen was still in there, somewhere. He just needed time.

Slipping my left hand into Viggo's, I squeezed.

"Jeff," said Ms. Dale. "What do you have for us? You mentioned an idea for how to get Violet's video out in the public eye?"

Jeff nodded, his hand coming up to stroke across his mustache, which he had grown out into a much bushier and less groomed version of its earlier cut. "Ah, yes, ma'am. Of course. Well, as you know, information has been broadcasted to the public at several stadiums across the city, but none are as popular as Starkrum Stadium. I believe Mr. Croft may even have fought there, at one time?"

"Almost fought there once," replied Viggo after a moment. "But I worked there as a warden on patrol many times."

Almost fought there. It was because of me that he hadn't.

Viggo had sacrificed his first-ever big league fight to chase after me, after the Porteque gang had swiped me from his changing room. That truly seemed like a lifetime ago now, even though it'd only been months.

"Well, fighting and all sports events have been cancelled for the foreseeable future," Jeff said. "Many of the fighters have disappeared, but there is one who has taken on a position of prominence at the arena. His name is Anello Cruz. Have you heard of him?"

Of course we had. Cruz was one of the top fighters in Patrus—the very fighter Viggo had been matched up against on that fateful evening. I also recalled a night before that, when Viggo had taken me to the stadium to watch Cruz square off against another major competitor named Rosen. And had quickly taken him down.

I could tell by the way Viggo was looking at me, his eyes still faraway but somewhere more familiar now, he too was remembering those early days of our relationship. I gave him a smile, and a ghost of one flew across his lips, then vanished. "I've heard of him," he replied to Jeff's question.

"Wonderful! Because I have become, well, 'friends' may be too loose a word to describe it, but we have become… acquaintances. Regardless, I think he likes me well enough."

"That's, uh, nice," said Viggo, looking somewhat taken aback. "But what does that mean for us?"

"Ah, right. My apologies—I ought to curb my rambling. I think Mr. Cruz and myself are on good enough terms that I might be able to impose upon him for a favor. Namely, I think we can use him to get to the control box in the stadium."

I frowned in confusion. Looking around, I noted similar expressions on the rest of the group's faces. "I'm sorry, Jeff... the control box?" I asked. "I thought Elena was having people announce the news in the stadium on a microphone. Did that change?"

Jeff tipped his head to one side, his eyes widening, and then his confused look changed to one of mild chagrin. "I'm terribly sorry, ma'am. You're right, of course. I forgot to mention Elena has gotten the massive screens working, and has now been sending out pre-recorded messages to all the public places they've been using to broadcast—mostly other stadiums." The man's mustached face grew almost animated, an expression I'd rarely seen from him. "Here's the most important part. In an attempt, I think, to show me how important his position is, Cruz let slip to me that Matrians have turned Starkrum Stadium into their broadcast center for all of Patrus, since the palace has fallen. Most, if not all of the other broadcasts are streamed directly from this stadium. They send a guarded technician there once or twice a day to upload the video to their feed. According to Cruz, it's all very specifically tailored to keep unauthorized access out—to broadcast, they need both the technician's gear and the computer in the broadcasting room."

I absorbed this, looking around the room, the magnitude of that thought just beginning to build up in my mind. "And Cruz has access to this room?"

"Well, not directly. But he can get into the staff area of the building, which means we can probably find a way to get him to take us close enough."

Ms. Dale jumped in over me. "What sort of man is Cruz?

What would prompt him to aid us? Money, power? Or does he oppose the recent power shift?"

Jeff's eyes grew shrewd. "Well, to be honest, he is a man who misses his former glory. He's managed to avoid recruitment into the labor camps by actively assisting the Matrians, but if you catch him late enough at night and lend a friendly ear, it is clear that he's *less than satisfied* with the status quo." Jeff looked around and leaned a little closer to the camera. "I believe he would respond well to some attention."

"What do we know about the stadium's current security?" Viggo asked.

"Not much, sir, but given some of the stories Mr. Cruz has told me over supper, security is tight, but not impregnable. He's talked about several different checkpoints in the stadium, four thus far, but I get the impression there are more." Jeff took a deep breath and frowned. "I'm sorry I don't have better information for you. It seems the more I speak, the more hopeless the idea becomes. I just figured you would want to know."

"No, no. It's definitely worth thinking about," said Amber. "I mean, our biggest concern is getting into the city." She looked around the room, her brows furrowed. "Those checkpoints are the biggest holdup, but if we can get in there and get a hold of that technician, I'm certain we can do something with this."

"That's a lot of 'ifs,'" Viggo muttered, crossing his arms. "We need to decide whether the payoff is worth the risk."

"Quite right, sir," said Jeff. "I do not envy your decision at all. Do you have… any further questions for me?"

I looked around the room as people shook their heads one by one. "No, it doesn't seem like it, Jeff," I informed him. "Thank you for this. It's a good start. Please stay safe."

"I will do that, ma'am, as long as you and everyone there promise to do the same. I'll call back in, um, twenty-eight hours. If you have need of me before then, send me a message signed by my cousin Tula." He smiled, pleased at his imaginary cousin's name, and I couldn't help but smile back.

"We will do that."

The screen went dark, indicating he had cut the connection, and Thomas moved back to the equipment, unplugging the wires. I turned to the group and exhaled, running my left hand over my stubbled head.

"All right, so what are we thinking?"

"It's risky," Ms. Dale replied. "And there are a lot of obstacles—like Amber said, getting in and out of the city is a pretty big hurdle in and of itself."

"That is mostly because we have no idea what kind of identification papers are being utilized," said Thomas as he dropped into the chair behind the computer. "If I could get my hands on one, I might be able to duplicate it."

"Is there anyone we can send to the city who already has a plausible reason for being there?" I asked, looking at Ms. Dale.

"Actually, any of the wives or Patrian women would be suitable. But it would be better if we sent one from a homestead out here. It would explain why she hadn't reported in yet—make up some story about the harvest or a vehicle breaking down."

"Wouldn't they ask about her husband?" asked Amber. She looked around the room, frowning, as if hearing something silly in her own question, but then she squared her shoulders and continued. "No, I mean, the wardens controlling the city are

Matrian, but they aren't stupid. They will doubt her story a bit if her husband isn't with her to get his ID."

Ms. Dale pshawed, waving her hand away. "Please, give me a girl who can cry on command and I can give you a believable story."

I nodded, a smirk on my lips. "I'm sure you could," I said. "Well, that just leaves the inside."

"Jeff seemed confident we could use this Cruz guy to get inside and bypass security," said Amber.

"Anello Cruz was an underdog," said Viggo, almost absent-mindedly. "No one thought he could take out Rosen, but he did. He was probably just settling into the fame and glory of his position when all this happened. I'm guessing that means he's still craving fans, in a place where everyone's biggest concern is for their personal safety."

"We can work with that," said Ms. Dale. "We can appear as fans, or even use Mr. Croft in some way—connecting a former fighter to another former fighter. Possibly looking for work?"

Viggo shook his head. "I think it might be risky to use my real name. They've probably dragged it through the mud and back. If I go, I'll have to wear a disguise of some kind."

Ms. Dale waved her hand again dismissively. "We can figure that out once we have a better way to proceed, but honestly, I do think this holds the seeds of something. If we could just get public opinion to turn against Elena…"

"It could weaken, if not destroy, her hold on Patrus," announced Owen. I turned, surprised to hear him speaking, and found him standing behind everyone, his arms crossed, his expression turned inward, contemplative and dark. "But is that really going to make a big difference for us? For the boys? All we do is take wild shots and chances, and all they do is recover and hit back—and when they do, they hit us where it hurts. How does this… plan… help us achieve any of our goals?"

I frowned and took a step toward him. "Our goal is to help people," I reminded him. "Patrians, Matrians—it doesn't matter at the end of the day, as long as we try."

Owen lowered his arms and shook his head slowly, as though thinking out loud. "Wouldn't it help more people, ultimately, if we went straight to the top? Maybe we should stop focusing on symptoms of the problem and go straight for the cause. Elena or Desmond, it doesn't matter which one, but that's who we should be going after. Finish things once and for all."

Behind me, I sensed Viggo straightening up, but it was Amber who spoke. "What are you proposing?" she asked.

Owen met my gaze, and then looked away, shifting slightly. "What if we give Desmond what she asked for?" he said hoarsely. "We do like Violet did: tell her about the real egg, offer her Maxen… or maybe even Violet, as bait. We just need something to tell Desmond. Something to draw her in close enough to put a bullet in her head." His eyes were suddenly glued to my face, as though pleading with me. "Then we could make sure she never hurts any of them again. Then we could… we could *protect* them."

I gaped at Owen, understanding the dark place in his mind this was coming from. Sometimes I had wanted just such an outcome so badly I could taste it. But we'd already chosen not to do things that brutally unless we were forced. Even if it was only one possible option, the thought of offering myself up again was almost nauseating. A wave of dizziness assaulted me as I thought about the last time I had done that, the twisted images of losing my fight with Tabitha—badly—coursing through me, taking me back to the worst moments.

"We are *not* doing that," said Ms. Dale, a note of finality in her voice. "*Nobody* is being used as bait again. It's too unpredictable, and it's certainly not humane." I almost sagged in relief as I heard her say it; then I felt a surge of guilt, as though cowardice had a flavor and I suddenly tasted it on my tongue. *Could I save the boys by sacrificing myself?* But at the same time, a more rational part of my mind protested as well. While Tabitha had been evil, she had also been exploitable. Her temper and arrogance had often gotten the better of her, and that had been her weak point. I'd known that going in.

Desmond had plans and fallbacks and a calm, rational mind that could cut through any gamble we took almost before we could conceive it. Even *if* I was willing to make that sacrifice—something I couldn't consider until I was fully functional again, at least—I wouldn't do it unless we had a foolproof plan.

I felt Viggo place his hand on my shoulder, and without thinking, I reached up and took it, appreciating the support. After a heartbeat or two, I looked up and met Owen's gaze. His expression morphed into one of regret when he met my eyes.

"I'm sorry," he said, his voice coming out a whisper. "You're right, of course. I just…" His hands curled into fists as he trailed off, and then he shook his head. "I don't think I should be here right now. I'm… I'm going to go get some air."

We watched as he left, walking out of the room with sharp, agitated steps, as if he had just lit a match and set the whole place on fire. As I watched him go, I couldn't help but feel that, in a way, he *had*. But instead of being angry, now it just made me feel worse for the choices before him. As much as it made my heart ache, there was nothing I could do for him right now. I knew, better than most, that this was a fight he had to face himself.

Sighing, I turned back to the others. "We have some pieces of a good plan here," I said. "I think we should move forward with seeing if we can duplicate the identification papers. Ms. Dale, are you okay with finding a woman to send out to get her papers?"

Ms. Dale nodded her assent. Everyone else seemed to agree wordlessly, and I noticed Amber and Thomas' eyes were still trained on the door. The plan wasn't optimal, and neither were any of our states of mind… but I had hopes for this mission. To me, this conflict was like a series of walls. If we broke enough of them down, we would eventually get to Desmond and Elena. By then, I hoped we would have the weight of the people behind us. And hopefully, my dearly bought video would be the catalyst.

CHAPTER 30

Viggo

Ian was struggling beneath me, his eye bulging as I tightened my hands around his throat. He kicked furiously, his little arms fruitlessly trying to push my weight off him, and I smiled and pressed my hands deeper into his neck, tightening them as he gagged for air. I felt his heart beating against my chest, light and fast, like a bird's wings flapping, harder, faster, until…

I jerked awake, my heart pounding and my breath coming in sharp, agonized pants. Sweat dotted my forehead, and in the cool of night, it chilled my skin. I looked over to where Violet lay sleeping on her side, her back to me, the fuzz of newly growing hair on her head just visible in the pale light from the window. She let out a soft snore and tossed fitfully, turning toward me, and I sighed, trying to calm my pulse.

Slipping the blanket off my body, I moved out of her way just as her arm flopped over where my chest would've been had

I remained in bed. I felt a pang of regret, but it did nothing to stop me from standing up. Moving over to the window, I grabbed my shirt from the back of a chair, using it to wipe the sweat off my forehead. Tossing it back over the chair, I pulled open the dresser in the corner of the room, grabbed another shirt I had pilfered from my cabin, and threw it over my head.

Looking out the window, I saw that the sun was finally coming up over the mountains. The yard was still gray in the pre-dawn light. My eyes immediately flicked over to where the guards were supposed to be standing post, checking to make sure none of them had drifted off or were out of position for any reason. They weren't, and I leaned my hip against the desk near the window, accepting that my pitiful efforts at distracting myself from the nightmare haunting me for the last couple of hours had failed.

I looked around the room, feeling trapped by its bare, medical confines. My muscles itched, looking for something to do, and I had to leave. It wasn't a desire, but a necessity.

As quietly as I could, I slipped out the door, pulling it closed behind me. I grabbed my jacket from the sofa in the main living area and slipped it onto my shoulders, thinking of heading to the barn. Maybe practicing some martial arts would help me…

I didn't even know if I *wanted* anything to help. I just knew I felt the press of anxiety in my chest, and needed to do something productive—or else risk something worse happening. Training would help with that. If I kept training, maybe I could prevent something like this from happening in the future. It was a feeble thought, but it was the only thing I could cling to at the moment.

I pushed open the front door, my eyes focused on the barn. A light mist coated the ground, its vague curls already dissipating under the softly forming rays of the sun, but still thick enough to swirl around my ankles as I strode through it. As I walked, hands in my pockets to ward off the chill, I reminded myself to wrap my knuckles before striking anything. They were scabbed over from the night before last, and even forming a fist stung, but if I wrapped them today and took extra care, then they would be…

I did a double take, pausing in my inner monologue and looking back at the tree line my gaze had brushed in passing. My tired eyes hadn't deceived me; Owen was sitting near the edge of the woods, right next to his brother's grave. His gaze was unfocused and lost, and he sat hunched over, his arms wrapped around his legs, perhaps for warmth.

I came to a full stop, indecision tearing through me. I knew I was the last person Owen wanted to see, and I couldn't blame him for that. But seeing him like this was too much. He needed someone right now, and I was the only one available.

Turning, I headed toward him, moving slowly. I paused about ten feet away as his eyes flicked over to me, registering my presence. They held my gaze for several seconds, and then flicked back over to whatever he had been staring at before. My guess was nothing and everything all at the same time. He didn't say anything, didn't tell me to go, and I knew that was as close to permission as I was going to get from him.

I closed the gap between us and sat down next to him. I didn't have a plan beyond that, but in truth, there was no room for any plan I could have made. I was there completely at Owen's discretion; I would follow his will here. If he wanted to talk, I would talk. If he wanted to yell and scream, I would take it. If he wanted to cry, I would do my best to comfort him. And if he just wanted to sit there in silence, well, I would sit there with him, if only so he didn't have to do it alone.

The silence stretched out, and I resigned myself that it was what Owen wanted. As much as I wanted to talk to him, to apologize even, I knew it wouldn't do any good. His grief was too deep, and my words wouldn't absolve either one of us.

We sat there long enough for the sun to fully come up over the mountains, for the camp to begin to stir.

"Everyone says I shouldn't blame you." His voice came so suddenly it took me a second to register that he was actually speaking to me. I turned toward him, and was surprised to see him looking at me. "They keep telling me it wasn't your fault. You were just trying to help."

I disagreed. Not about trying to help—I *had* been doing that—but that it wasn't my fault. No, maybe I wasn't solely responsible, but there was no way of telling what had finally caused Ian's heart to give out. The result was still the same. He had died in my arms.

I bit my tongue to refrain from saying anything to the contrary. Owen didn't need my validation or an affirmation of guilt. He didn't want to hear any of it. He just wanted to talk.

"I know they are right. Logically, I mean. I can see it as being a messed-up situation where you just happened to be in the wrong place at the wrong time. I mean, we both were, I guess." He drew his hands into fists and looked at them, shaking his head. "I can see the logic," he repeated, his voice thick with emotion. "But so help me, I can't *feel* it."

He looked away then, his hand going up to brush across his eyes, almost mechanically. He took a deep breath and turned his eyes to the sky. "I hate everyone so much for trying to, I don't know, *defuse* me with their logic. I hate them for trying to spare you my anger." He turned, meeting my gaze. "I hate you too," he whispered, his eyes glistening wetly. "I hate that they are right, and I hate you for it. Because I can't… I can't blame you like I want to."

I met his gaze head on, accepting everything he was saying. He clenched his teeth and then looked away. "I can't even look at you," he said hoarsely, his voice breaking. "I can't. Not without wanting you dead. Not without wanting to… to… *hurt* you. I know it's not right. I know it's not fair. But nothing about this is right. Nothing about this is *fair.*"

I just nodded. I felt a deep anger and a simmering hurt on behalf of my friend, and I wished, once again, there was something I could do to help him. Something *anyone* could do to help him—I wasn't selfish. I didn't care how he started to feel better, as long as he started. One day, at least.

"I hate feeling like this," Owen admitted after a moment. "I hate hating you. You are one of my best friends, in spite of everything. But… I can't stay here. I won't. I need time and… and… space. Away from you. From this. I mean… I actually suggested using Violet as bait, dammit! That isn't me, but at the same time, in that moment… it *was* me. I *wanted* that. So… I can't be here."

I let out a breath, a fresh wave of guilt moving through me. Not only had his brother died, but now he was running away from everyone here who cared about him. I hated it, but I could understand it. He had to do this. Or at least, he thought he did, and that was all that really mattered.

Owen slowly picked himself off the ground, as if every muscle and bone in his body bore the brunt of his sorrow. Casting me one last look, he simply moved away from me, heading toward the tents. I watched him go, a desperate, concerned part of me wanting to catch up with him and try to convince him to stay, but unable to figure out what combination of words would dissuade him.

But maybe it was better to let him go. After all, if he needed time and space, then he should get it. He'd given enough—too much—in this fight. He'd earned a reprieve. I just hoped it would also lead to peace.

CHAPTER 31

Violet

"Owen's gone," Ms. Dale announced, and I gaped at her, shock rolling through my body.

"Gone?" I repeated back to her, certain I had misheard. It didn't make sense. I had sat with him for a while again last night, the day after his brother's funeral, after the camp work had been done and the reports from the scouts had come in, and he hadn't told me anything about intending to leave.

Ms. Dale nodded, dropping into a chair next to mine, her lips pursed. "He came to me early this morning."

I checked my watch—it was barely after eleven in the morning—and then looked back down at the papers I had been perusing before she came in. The words on them seemed to blur together; I couldn't remember what they had meant.

"I don't understand," I said, looking back up at her. "Why would he just leave us? I mean… he didn't even say goodbye."

Ms. Dale gave me a sympathetic look and reached over, patting my hand. "I think saying goodbye would have been a bit too much for him, Violet. He's hurting. Badly."

"Is this because of Viggo?"

Ms. Dale sighed and leaned back into her chair. "Probably," she admitted with a small shake of her head. My face must've reflected the sudden stab of irritation I felt, because she leaned forward again, catching my gaze in hers. "You have to give them a little latitude, Violet. They're *both* blaming Viggo."

"It wasn't his fault," I replied hoarsely. "How many ways have we tried to convince them of that?"

"Violet, we all know that. I think even Owen knows that. But… logic doesn't hold a candle to what they are both feeling. Honestly, I think this might be for the best. Owen needs some distance from all this, and I think getting him out of the center of action will give him some time to heal."

I exhaled and considered her words. "Where would he even go?"

Ms. Dale's smile was genuine. "Don't worry. I didn't let him stray too far. I put him in charge of guarding King Maxen and watching over Solomon."

I shook my head, feeling a rueful smile playing on my lips. "I mean, Solomon is one thing. I wouldn't mind being able to check in on him myself. But King Maxen?" I made a face. "Yech."

Ms. Dale chuckled, her eyes dancing. "Tell me about it. The guards I have assigned to him hate the detail. He's more than a little bit of a handful."

"No kidding," I replied. "I do not envy their job." I picked up the sheaf of papers I had been holding before Ms. Dale had come in, and then set them down again with a sigh, realizing I still couldn't focus. "I just hate the idea of Owen trying to go through this alone," I admitted quietly.

"It's his choice," she said. "But, for the record, I don't like it either. I hope he'll come back to us soon."

"I mean, I just don't understand men! Why are they so damn stubborn?"

Ms. Dale's laughter filled the room, and she shook her head, combing her fingers back through her hair. "Honestly, I have no idea. If I did, I might hold the secret to winning this war."

I grinned, meeting her eyes as I leaned forward on the table. "Does that mean Henrik is getting better, and you're having… problems?"

Ms. Dale regarded me with a flat stare. "I believe that is none of your business, Ms. Bates," she said, arching an eyebrow.

"Interesting you should say that," I replied, smirking. "Because I get the feeling your days of teasing Viggo and me are numbered."

Snorting, Ms. Dale stood up, tugging at the hem of her shirt. "Absurd," she said tartly. "You and Mr. Croft simply flirt too much, especially in the most impractical and dangerous of situations."

I laughed, our little mock fight helping to distract me from the ache of Owen's departure. It was a silly thing, but if I had learned anything over the last few months, it was that humor was one of the only effective coping mechanisms.

Ms. Dale smiled warmly, and then nodded toward the

papers under my hand. "What's the verdict on the identification papers?"

"Oh." I looked down at the papers, smoothing my hand over them. The woman we'd sent to get her city identification had come back yesterday and given us her full report, as well as the papers themselves. She hadn't really seemed like the type to cry on command, but I guessed she must have been—whatever act she'd pulled off was what had gotten her back here safely. "Well, when Stacey brought them back and described the part of the process she'd seen, we were certain we could duplicate them, but now we're not sure."

"Really? Why? What's the holdup?"

"It's the ink," said Thomas from where he was sitting at the end of the table. I blinked, mortified that I had completely forgotten he was in the room. He had been so quiet since Ms. Dale's entrance. I hadn't even checked to see how he was doing with the news of Owen leaving us. "At first it appeared to be simple, natural ink, but actually, there's coding printed almost microscopically in each line, especially in the crest and the borders."

"Can't you replicate it?" Ms. Dale asked, leaning on the table.

Thomas frowned. "No. Well, at least not without another set of identification papers to compare for patterns… but honestly, I'm guessing each bit of code is unique in its own way, meant to bring up a corresponding file on whoever owns them. I wouldn't be able to do it without finding the server where they are keeping the registry, fabricating our own identification sets, and then writing the code that corresponded to the file. Without direct access to their mainframe, it would be impossible, and even then, I'd need…" He paused, his eyes becoming unfocused while his mouth moved silently, clearly doing the math. "About ninety minutes per identification set."

Ms. Dale whistled and shook her head. "Even if we could get you that time, we wouldn't be able to get you into the city to access their mainframes. Not without the papers in the first place."

Thomas nodded. "Yes. It would be oxymoronic, to say the least. I am looking at other options, however."

"Like?" I perked up. Thomas and I had been sitting there for an hour looking at the papers, but this was the first I was hearing about an alternative plan.

"Well, there is a chance some of the tunnels are unguarded, for one. We might be able to access some of them using one of the outer hatches, but seeing as Desmond knew about the tunnels…"

"We can't count on her leaving them unguarded," I finished for him with a frustrated sigh.

Ms. Dale leaned back on the table, deep in thought. "There has to be a way in," she murmured.

"Well, there are a few things to consider," said Thomas. "We could just have several individuals go in and get identification papers, but that poses a high risk of someone being discovered. Not to mention, if they have scanners at the border, our disguises would have to be flawless."

"It's too risky," Ms. Dale replied. "But… I have a thought. I'll need to talk to Jeff about it."

"What is it?" I asked.

Her lips quirked up and she met my gaze, her brown eyes

sparkling. "They have to be letting emergency services in and out of the city," she said. "It might be easier to call in an emergency, and then hijack their transport."

I leaned to rest my shoulders against the back of the chair, considering the idea. On one hand, it was bold. Chances were good the emergency services hadn't been dismantled yet, which meant most of their workers would still be male. That would get Viggo, Thomas, and Owen into the heart of enemy-controlled territory… I paused, suddenly remembering Owen wouldn't be there for this mission. I took a minute to allow myself the pang that accompanied the thought, and then turned back to the idea. If it worked, and if they weren't scrutinized too much at the border…

"I don't know," I said, doubt creeping into my mind. "I'm not comfortable with the idea of holding up an emergency response team, especially if someone else calls needing aid. We could be condemning innocent people to death or serious harm by holding them up."

"We have our two doctors," Ms. Dale replied practically. "And we wouldn't harm the emergency team. We could even leave a team with them to get them where they needed to go."

I bit my lip. "I guess. Check it out with Jeff and then run it by Viggo? It's workable, but not ideal."

"Agreed," said Ms. Dale, straightening up. "Well, I'll leave you all to it. If you come up with a breakthrough on the papers, let me know. If not, we'll see if we can't brainstorm a few more options before settling on a plan. Don't worry—this will not be where we get stalled." She winked at us, and I smiled.

"I'm sure it won't," I said, with more confidence than I felt.

I watched her as she left, and then sighed, doubtful. It seemed like every option we explored was coming up short, and without a viable plan to get into the city, we might be forced to rely on our refugee volunteers to carry this vital mission through for us. That was risky, as they had never worked as a unit before—or even been on an operation. It was a lot for them to accomplish with little to no experience.

Still, I had faith we would figure something out. This had to work. We couldn't keep chipping away at the edges of what Elena and Desmond were planning. We needed a big win, one that would hurt them deeply. Turning Patrus against them would be just such a blow, and would hopefully rock them both back on their heels.

I turned over to Thomas to ask what he thought, and then paused when I saw the middle-aged man staring at his hands, a sad look in his eyes.

"Are you okay?" I asked softly. "I mean, with Owen leaving?"

Thomas blinked behind his glasses and fidgeted slightly. "No," he mumbled. He took off his spectacles and began cleaning them on his shirt.

I hesitated, and then leaned forward. "Do you want to talk about it?"

He met my gaze again, squinting at me slightly before replacing his glasses on his nose. "What would I say?"

Shrugging, I settled back in my chair. "I'm not sure," I replied honestly. "It's more out of a… social obligation that we ask. I don't think it's required that you take me up on the offer."

"Would it be wrong of me to do so?"

"Not at all," I said with a smile.

Thomas nodded, his gaze drifting away for a moment. "Have I ever told you how Owen and I met?"

I shook my head. "No, you haven't. Would you like to?"

"I would." He paused for a second, collecting his thoughts, and then sighed. "A couple of years ago, Desmond had recruited Owen and two Patrian males to join the Liberators. She put Owen in charge, but the other males were… aggressive and short-tempered. Owen was having a hard time keeping them in line.

"Owen brought them into the sewers after a supply raid had gone off the rails. It was a last-ditch effort to avoid the Patrian patrols. Anyway, after they met me, they started to…" He trailed off, looking away.

"Bully you?" I offered, and he nodded, meeting my gaze, his dark eyes glistening and his mouth curling in distaste.

"That would be one word for it. Owen, well, he tried to get them to stop, but they knew what I was, and they were relentless. At one point, they broke my wrist with their 'teasing.' I guess that's when Owen had had enough." He met my gaze then, his eyes hard and flat.

"What did he do?" I asked.

"He crushed some sedatives from one of our first-aid packs into their food, and then tied them up. Then he brought me in to… exact some revenge."

"I see," I whispered, surprised by the bloodthirsty look on Thomas' face. No wonder Thomas had given Owen his allegiance so completely. The move was ruthless but had a kind of street justice to it, and under the circumstances, I wasn't sure I could blame Owen or Thomas. "What did you do to them?"

"Nothing that would be permanent," Thomas said softly. "Owen wouldn't allow it. He was hard but fair, so they were in relatively one piece when I finished with them, and they made sure to steer clear of me afterward." His face tightened almost imperceptibly. "They died on a mission a few months later, and I don't miss them."

"I'm sure you don't," I agreed, trying not to let my shock at the callous statement show. This was Thomas—I expected such statements from him now. "Still, I'm sorry Owen didn't say goodbye to you when he left. It seems like he was one of the few people you were really comfortable with here."

Thomas shrugged. "He's the only one who seems to care. He always makes sure I'm okay, and he… he wasn't put off by my… social ineptitude. He treated me like a person, not a tool. I mean, while I don't believe in emotional decision making, it doesn't mean I don't have feelings."

I frowned, realizing that I, too, had probably been a little cruel to Thomas when I had first met him. At the very least, I still didn't check in on him as often as I could, and I never told him how much I appreciated him and what he had done for us. I opened my mouth, but Thomas waved me off. "I wasn't asking for you to do that, Violet," he announced with some aplomb. "I just… I wanted to share what Owen did for me. That's all."

Licking my lips, I nodded. "Well, I appreciate it."

"Besides, there is an eighty-four point three six percent chance Owen will return soon. If I were a gambling man, I would say before the end of the week."

"Eighty-four point three six percent?" I blinked, a smile tugging at my lips. "I would not wager against those odds."

"Smart move, Ms. Bates." He met my gaze, a shadow of a smile on his lips. "I so dislike taking from those who have nothing in the first place."

I laughed then, my earlier disappointment and sadness evaporating under my delight at Thomas actually making a joke. It was so out of character I couldn't help but appreciate it even more. Besides, if Thomas said Owen would be back, I knew he would be. Thomas was rarely wrong about these sorts of things.

Fueled by that burst of optimism, I turned to the computer at my station and cued up the blueprints of Starkrum Stadium, seeing what possibilities it had to offer for our upcoming mission.

CHAPTER 32

Violet

Eight hours later, I was in my room, packing my bag, amazed at how quickly everything seemed to have come together. Ms. Dale had her conversation with Jeff, and, after only an hour and a half of what must have been carefully placed questions on Jeff's part, he had reported back that, almost always, emergency vehicles that left the city were given blanket clearance upon re-entry. Apparently, Elena's desire to appear merciful had helped play into our hands.

After that, Jeff had reached out to Anello Cruz, asking if the former fighter turned security advisor would be so kind as to give his family, who were coming into the city to undergo their registration process, a tour of the stadium. He had played to Cruz's ego, promising that his family were all huge fans, and the man had fallen for it hook, line, and sinker. I smiled at the very thought. I didn't know how good a valet Jeff had been, but as a spy and manipulator of assets… he excelled.

And now everyone was getting ready, packing their own equipment, just as I was. There was no way I was going to sit this one out. Not again, not after what had happened the last time. The worry alone had made me sick to my stomach, and this time around there would be little to no communication with our base, as Ms. Dale, Thomas, and Amber had insisted it would be too much of a risk. Using our handhelds that close to Elena's forces meant a higher chance of them tracing our calls and intercepting us—or finding their way back to our allies.

I was busy folding up a set of slightly-too-big black pants when the door swung open with a creak and Viggo walked in. He leaned against the doorframe, crossing his arms as I finished folding and set the pants in my bag. I tried to make the motion look as effortless as possible, but the cast around my arm made it almost laughable.

"What are you doing?" Viggo asked roughly.

I picked up a flashlight, shoving it into the bag as well, and didn't look at him. "I think it's pretty obvious."

I cringed at the tone of my voice. I had already dropped into defensiveness in anticipation of the fight brewing. I knew Viggo was going to fight me on my decision to go, and I was already snapping at him. It wasn't right, and it wasn't how I'd planned to do this.

I looked up to see him glowering at me. "I'm sorry," I said, fidgeting slightly. "I didn't mean to sound snappy."

Viggo took a step into the room, turning to close the door behind him. I heard him take a deep breath, in and out, before he came about to face me.

"We had an agreement," he said quietly, his eyes dropping to my cast and then rising back up to take in my bare scalp. I reached up to run my fingers over it, feeling the coarse, short hairs prickling me.

"I know, but I'm fine," I insisted. "I haven't had a dizzy spell since—"

"Yesterday," Viggo said sternly.

"How did you know that?" I asked.

"People in the camp are keeping an eye on you," he supplied. A flash of irritation made my skull heat up, but he held up his hands, palms out in a calming gesture. "I didn't request it. Everyone is just worried about you. They want to make sure you aren't pushing yourself too hard. They keep coming up to me and asking me how you're doing, telling me all these reasons they're concerned you're working too much."

I ran my hands over my head again, the emotions that flooded through me at that statement too complicated to parse right now. "Look," I began, "I'm not saying I need to be with you guys every step of the way. I just… I can't stay here. Not after last mission. It was… it was torment! I had no idea whether you were okay or not, and my mind kept taking me to dark places."

Viggo frowned, his dark brows furrowing over deep green eyes. I took a deep breath, then moved to him, taking one of his hands into my own. "This is who we are, Viggo," I reasoned. "We… we will never be the 'stay behind' type—we are both best in the moment. We both need to be there so that we can help each other, rescue each other… face these trials together."

As I spoke, Viggo's other hand came up and over my left hand, holding it tightly between his two larger ones. "Violet, you know I don't want you to feel left out. And yes, I agree, as far as teams go, there is no one I would rather have by my side. There is no one I trust more with a mission—and with my life—than you."

I smiled up at him, beaming with his praise, but the smile died when I saw the hesitation on his face. "But?" I asked.

"But you are not in fighting form right now. I say this with all the love in my heart I can possibly offer up... I know this will hurt you, but you are a liability right now." He bent his knees a little, bringing his face down to my level, his eyes searching my features for a reaction.

I sighed, turning my face away from him and sliding my hand out from between his. I moved away, each step making me more certain what he was saying was true, even if the truth caused my stomach to churn in frustration. Rubbing my opposite shoulder with my good hand, I turned my eyes upward and exhaled.

I heard the hard sound of his shoes on the floorboards behind me, and felt his hands come over my shoulders. "I'm sorry," he said. "I never want to hurt you."

"You're not," I said, my voice coming out a whisper. "I just don't think I can do this." I paused, my throat constricting. I was completely unable to help, and that was what was going to break me down—not the pain, not the unbeatable odds, but the knowledge I was useless.

"Hey," Viggo breathed, his voice gentle. I let him turn me around, and he reached out and placed a finger under my chin, lifting my head to meet my gaze. "What's this really about?"

I tsked, letting my eyes drift away in embarrassment. "It's

stupid," I admitted.

A crooked smile spread on his lips. "Try me."

I pulled away from him. "I guess I don't think I'm leadership material," I replied honestly, feeling inexplicably vulnerable at my admission. He gave a surprised huff, his smile growing until I got a flash of his white teeth. "You're laughing at me," I said sulkily, and he shook his head, his green eyes sparkling.

"Never," he said. "The idea that you don't think you're leadership material is just a little surprising to me."

I moved away, sitting down on the edge of the bed, my face going serious. "When everyone was gone the other night, and then I got that message from Amber about killing the transmission… my mind went to horrible places. I did my best to try to plan for the worst-case scenario, but it wasn't enough. And then I couldn't help thinking about how I had to lead everyone, maybe even evacuate them all, when I had no idea where I could even take them. I have no idea how to lead them now… or what to do if *this* plan doesn't work."

Viggo frowned. "Violet, you did everything you could've done, and frankly, I wouldn't have done anything differently. If you ask Ms. Dale, I bet she'll agree with me."

I doubted his words, even though I knew he wouldn't lie to me. To be honest, the doubt was directed at myself. It had been growing ever since I had woken up with a shaved head and a lot more limitations than I was used to.

Viggo, sensing my turmoil, reached over and took my hand. "You are more than capable of this. I trust you implicitly to take care of the people here—and to make decisions on their behalf. Not to mention… if I get captured, I'm going to need you to come rescue me. Just like old times."

A laugh escaped my lungs, taking with it some of my mounting apprehension. I shook my head, and then leaned into him, resting on his shoulder. His arm came around my waist, holding me firmly in his embrace.

"I still don't like it," I admitted.

"I know," he replied, his breath tickling my exposed scalp. "But this is what happens in war. Sometimes we have to do what we must, instead of what we want."

I went silent for a moment, and then asked with a wry smile, "So, if our positions were reversed, you'd be okay with me going and you having to stay behind?"

Viggo chuckled, pulling me tighter against his side. "I've already been there, back in The Green. You and Owen..." He trailed off, and I shot a glance up at him.

"Are you doing okay with all that? I mean, you seem less robotic now."

Viggo's mouth drew tight, and he shrugged. "Okay? No, definitely not. But I'm, uh, processing. This mission will help, I think. It'll keep my mind off everything for a while."

I looked at his face, noting its tired lines, and reached up to touch his cheek, stroking the rough edges of his beard. "I love you," I told him. "I don't care if it takes me a thousand years to convince you it wasn't your fault—I will never stop trying. And eventually, I will succeed."

Viggo paused, regarding me gravely. "Sometimes I wonder why you love me so much," he said after a moment. "But honestly, I don't care. You're my whole world, Violet. The last couple of weeks have been hell for us, but I promise you, there is an end in sight. Trust me to get the job done."

I stroked my thumb over his cheek, nodding. "I do trust you," I whispered. "I'm going to worry, a lot, but I trust you. Just promise me you won't take any unnecessary risks."

He nodded, his face solemn. "I promise. As long as you promise to do the same."

Laughing, I leaned back, raising my hand up to wave it around the room. "I think the most unnecessary risk I could take back here would be to try to argue medicine with Dr. Tierney."

Viggo smirked and nodded. "Yeah. Maybe don't do that one."

I smiled, and then, on impulse, wrapped my arms around him, pulling him close. It helped, but not enough to ease the sense of foreboding that seemed to be clinging to everything, making my stomach flutter with uncertainty. I clung to Viggo, breathing in his familiar, masculine scent. As I did so, I realized my ribs barely twinged when his arms came around me, holding me tightly at the waist.

Something inside me cautiously uncurled. Slowly, his presence was easing the anxiety out of my stomach. I knew it would be back, but right now, I wanted another feeling to cling to. I didn't want him to go, not yet, and he didn't seem to want to move either.

His nose nudged mine, and we stared at each other for a while, eye to eye. Then, feeling daring and just a little bit needy, I pressed forward and caught his lips in a kiss.

Viggo's kiss in response was unexpectedly intense. It left me breathless, dizzy, and I clung to him, reeling from the feel of his lips on mine. Sometimes when we kissed, he was demanding and rough, while other times, he was sweet and slow. This kiss was like the latter, but there was something more to it. A soft, gentle urgency that seemed to grow as our kiss continued.

My breath caught in my throat as he pressed the tip of his tongue to my upper lip, taking a slow, languid taste. My lips parted, but instead of sweeping into my mouth, his tongue continued to taste my lips, savoring them. He gently sucked my lower lip, and I moaned, overwhelmed with pleasure.

The kiss was teasing as well, a flitting series of tastes that were like fire across the sensitive nerve endings of my lips. I moaned in wordless demand, wanting more, but he denied me. Instead, his mouth moved over my cheek and chin, then down the soft skin of my throat. I shuddered as the rough whiskers of his face scraped against me, and decided I liked the roughness.

Trying to get closer, I rotated on the bed next to him, throwing my leg across his, so that I was facing him while straddling his lap, a desperate hunger awakening inside me. One of Viggo's arms curled around my backside, securing me, but he pulled his torso back from me, his eyes concerned.

"Violet, maybe we better—"

"Shut up and kiss me," I demanded huskily. I wasn't sure where this compulsion was coming from, but I needed this to continue. I knew that even though I was feeling better, my strength and stamina would fade quickly, but I wanted to take advantage of them while I still had them.

Yet it was also more than that. I needed confirmation that I was alive, and his mouth was reminding me that not only was I alive, I was loved. After being so afraid, so confused, so lost in everything that had happened, been happening, for so long, I hadn't realized how much I craved physical contact, if only to re-assure me this wasn't the end for us. He'd be back and safe and...

As if in response to my intensity, Viggo growled possessively as he kissed me again, this kiss growing deeper and harder. I moaned, shifting my hips, needing more somehow, and Viggo seemed to know exactly what was wrong. Carefully, he encircled my waist with both hands, then flopped back onto the bed, ef-fortlessly pulling me with him, so that I ended up on top of him, our hips pressed together. There was a twinge of pain from my ribs, but I didn't care.

As long as Viggo kept touching me, I would never care. I rested my left hand next to his head and kissed him back, us-ing my tongue to tease his mouth as he had mine. He gave an approving grunt, his hand finding my hip and holding it firm.

Without letting my lips leave his, I began fumbling with the buttons of the white long-sleeved shirt he was wearing, but it was hard with my left hand. It took me over a minute to get the first one undone, and after that, my patience was gone. I grabbed the fabric in my hand and pulled, rewarded by the sound of but-tons striking the floor. Viggo's eyes darkened as he watched me rip his shirt open, and I felt a thrill of excitement at the hungry look in them.

I stroked my hand over his chest, tracing the lines of his fit body. My fingers felt him lightly, caressing each little line and divot that made up his well-muscled physique.

Viggo broke our next kiss with a shuddering gasp as I touched him, but I wasn't done yet. So I lowered myself down on him, tasting the skin of his neck. His hand tightened on my hips, but I didn't stop, my lips meandering down to his collarbone. I heard the breath catch in his throat, and it encouraged me to press lower, moving over his pectoral muscles, then farther down. Stopping momentarily to glance up at him, I was amazed at the look in his eyes as he watched me.

He was gazing at me with a primal hunger, his green eyes vibrant and bright. As my lips skimmed the topmost ripple of his abs, he whispered a curse, his stomach jerking away from me. I hid my smile with another press of my lips.

To be honest, I had no idea what I was doing. I was driven more by instinct than anything else. I understood the rudimentary concept of sex, or at least what some of the staff at the correctional institute had felt compelled to teach us so we wouldn't be completely ignorant of that aspect of life. To be honest, when they had explained it to us, I had completely understood why many women chose to have Matrian doctors artificially impregnate them. Gross.

But none of those lessons had ever explained that it could be like this—this rush of need, the promise of pleasure compelling me to press my lips to Viggo's naked chest. It was running slipshod over my every rational thought, even any threat of pain from moving too much. I suppressed the urge to tease Viggo about harassing a sick girl, knowing that if I did, his reason would take over and he would make us stop—and I was not ready for that to happen.

I moved down to another row of his abdominal muscles, this time taking a chance and flicking my tongue out to lick him here and there. Another growl trickled from Viggo's lips, and I looked up at him to see the hunger in his eyes had grown, his pupils fixed and dilated. He gazed at me in pure intensity, and as I looked at him, he raised himself up slightly, leaned forward, and slid his hand down my thigh.

I shivered at the sensation. His hand was like fire, burning so hot I could feel it through the thickness of the pants I wore. I gasped as his fingers pressed into my skin, letting me feel the strength in them. He dragged his fingers up my thigh and hip, settling them almost gently against the bare flesh of my side, just under my shirt. Where the press of his hand over my pants had made me shiver, the light touch of his fingers on my bare skin was electrifying—infinitely more pleasurable. His fingers slipped just under the loose band of my pants and…

It was a curious sensation—after all, he had touched my naked skin before, when he'd had to patch me up our first time in The Green, when he'd still been on his mission from King Maxen to retrieve me. This was different, obviously, but it was still strange. I would dwell on it later—reason had deserted us. I had no comparisons, no complaints. All I could think to myself was *yes* and *more*. This was finally happening, and I didn't want it to stop.

I felt myself stretch my back like a cat, trying to press back into Viggo's hand. He rewarded me by sliding his hand up a fraction of an inch, tracing invisible lines into my skin, lightly pressing the blunt edge of his nails into my flesh. A moan escaped me, and I blushed in surprise, risking a glance up at him without my lips leaving his body.

His face had become feral and possessive. As I watched, his abs tightened under my mouth, and he leaned closer, hooking me under my arms and dragging me up the front of his body with a growl. I shivered from the intensity of it, my body quivering in anticipation as he tilted his chin toward mine in a silent demand for a kiss.

Powerful and sexy—that was how he made me feel. I had never felt that way before. I probably should've taken more time to explore it, but I was trapped in the moment. I slowly lowered my mouth to his, knowing this was it… it was going to happen.

Then, suddenly, it all stopped.

Viggo pulled back, letting out a harsh breath and ran a hand through his hair. At my confused and frustrated moan, he said, "We'd better stop."

"Really?" I asked, just a little bit hurt.

"Really," he said ruefully, plucking at the sides of his shirt. "We were getting a little… out of control there."

I reluctantly rolled off him and stretched out on the bed, chuckling. "Would that have been the worst thing?" I asked.

His eyes traced over my body as I stretched, and I bit my lip as I saw the sparkle in them. He met my gaze, and I noticed a dull red accentuating his cheeks.

"It's probably for the best," he bit out again, and I suppressed a laugh. I had seen Viggo caught in a myriad of emotions, but flustered had never been one of them. "Besides… I sort of promised myself we would wait until marriage."

I gaped in mock outrage. "Without consulting me?" I gasped. "That's a bit presumptuous of you!"

His eyes narrowed in disapproval, but the smile on his lips grew. "Damn straight," he replied. "You're going to have to wait. I'm not that kind of guy."

I laughed, but in truth, his words sent a thrill through me. I knew, without a shadow of a doubt, that he loved me. Ultimately, it didn't bother me to wait, but it did make me eager for us to get married. Extremely eager.

"I never knew you were such a romantic," I teased.

His eyes narrowed, but there was a smile tugging on his lips. "Yes… a 'romantic.' 'Cause that is totally what I am."

"Hmmm… a traditionalist?"

"Also that," he said, crossing over to the drawer and pulling out a new shirt. "You demolished another shirt."

"Well, give me time, and I'll be able to fix it," I retorted.

A knock on the door interrupted our banter, and without waiting for a response, Amber swung open the door with a lot more exuberance than necessary.

"Ms. Dale said you two should knock it off with the hanky-panky in here and get out there, so we can go over the plan one. More. Time."

She rolled her eyes dramatically and then gave me a lecherous waggle of her eyebrows before flouncing out. Viggo had his eyes tilted toward the heavens, and it was all I could do to keep myself from dissolving into a never-ending giggling fit.

"You are a terrible influence on me, Violet Bates," he said in mock anger, jerking his shirt over his lean torso.

"Yes, but you love it," I replied with a wide grin. He squinted at me, but I just smiled as he diligently helped me out of bed and onto my feet.

"Indeed," he drawled in my ear as he escorted me out into the hall. And I couldn't help but notice that as we walked, he kept his hand glued to my hip, where his clever fingers had been stroking earlier.

CHAPTER 33

Viggo

I had been doing this long enough to know nothing beat being lucky. Ms. Dale's idea to lure an ambulance from the city had gone like clockwork. In truth, I'd expected it to be a bigger event than it actually was. But we had traveled back to Mr. Kaplan's empty, torn-though farmhouse (despite the guilt that nudged me at the thought), called for emergency medical care, and then waited. Once one of our guards had spotted the incoming vehicle, we had set fire to the house, while Ms. Dale and Amber had lain down on the ground, smudged up with grime and soot.

The medics had fallen for it easily, rushing to their aid, allowing Cad, Thomas, Lynne, Morgan, and me to close in around them, pistols drawn. We took their uniforms, but left them with most of the medical equipment they might need in case a real medical emergency occurred. Lynne and Morgan stayed behind to act as their guards while we drove away. While no plan usually survived first contact with the enemy, this one had defied the odds.

From there, I'd expected crossing into the city to be difficult—but the tense silence of the ride, the glances at the road behind us, had all been worth it. Jeff had been right about the authorities not wasting any time waylaying medical units. With Ms. Dale and Amber hooked up convincingly in the back, oxygen masks set over their faces, we had been waved through the line of vehicles waiting at the checkpoint. As we drove on past, I had been confronted with the paranoid thought that it was too easy, the sneaking suspicion that we were, once again, being lured into a trap. It wouldn't have been the first time, and no matter how well things went, my skin crawled every time we passed a Matrian vehicle.

Yet, as we pulled up in the parking lot at the back of the hospital, there was no one waiting to stop us with flashing lights and weapons drawn. No sign that anyone even registered us as out of place.

As I wheeled Ms. Dale toward the double sliding doors leading into the hospital, I looked down at the older woman and noticed that, under the oxygen mask, her mouth was pressed into a tense, tight-lipped line.

"Relax," I whispered, though I wasn't sure if it was more to reassure her or me. "You look like you're choking on something sour."

She let out a soft snort, and I hid my grin, feeling a little better. Ms. Dale's demeanor had relaxed too—as much as could be expected for someone pretending to be in dire need of medical attention. I wheeled her gurney onward, the doors drawing open as I approached. We entered the emergency room, the crisp white beds lining the walls separated by curtains that were mostly drawn closed. Doctors and nurses were moving to and fro, checking on patients. We kept our heads down, allowing our uniforms to blend us in.

I angled the gurney toward the elevator in the back, just beyond the patient beds. I checked over my shoulder again, making sure Thomas was right behind me, and Cad was still pushing Amber on her gurney just behind him. They were, but the reassurance did little to unravel the tension twisting my gut into knots. Sweat was forming at the back of my neck by now. One wrong glance from a doctor could be the end of our expedition. Yet, as I drew nearer to the elevator bank, no one moved to stop us.

Thomas huffed as he moved around me, making a beeline for the buttons on the wall. I pulled Ms. Dale up short as the small man hit the button, and then watched the numbers on the digital readout count down from five. I hid my impatience by checking my watch for the time. It was just after four, which meant we had a little over fifty minutes before the final broadcast of the day.

Finally, the bell over the elevator dinged, and I looked up as the silver doors, shining bright as mirrors, spread open before us. A doctor was already inside, and he gave me a politely bland look as he stepped out, like he was suppressing curiosity. He held his hand against the door for us to keep it from closing.

"Much obliged," I said, trying to stop my teeth from clenching while positioning Ms. Dale to one side of the elevator to make room for Amber's gurney. Cad slipped in beside me, followed by Thomas. The doctor withdrew his hand, turning his face away, and then, thankfully, headed out into the emergency area. I exhaled and hit the button for sub-basement three, the lowest level of the facility.

"What was he staring at me like that for?" I snapped as we went down. "Is part of my uniform on backwards or something?"

The rest of the crew gave murmured versions of I don't know, but Thomas spoke up thoughtfully. "It is possible the man was surprised by the bruising on your face," he suggested. "I doubt most EMTs work sporting such injuries."

I huffed, thinking out loud. "We'll have to say it was a domestic dispute, and things got violent."

"Those things happen," Cad said eagerly. "I knew a guy who was an EMT once. Some crazy stuff happens to them sometimes. Once he told me that—"

The door dinged, and Cad stopped halfway through his sentence, joining the rest of us in staring at the door as it opened. If there were people on the other side, they might very well question the plausibility of us descending to a level far, far from triage. It seemed the door couldn't open fast enough—but finally, the metal wall drew back, and we saw an empty hallway.

As soon I nodded, Cad was moving. Turning the gurney, he pushed left down the hallway. Then I pushed Ms. Dale through, following Cad through the doors.

Violet's cousin remembered the layout we'd studied in blueprints perfectly, navigating us confidently through the gray concrete hallways filled with pipes sprouting from the ceiling and humming electrical boxes scattered on the walls. This was the maintenance level, where the backup generators, oxygen controls, and water mains for the hospital were all located. Despite Thomas' assurances these rooms did not have any security cameras, I carefully scanned the walls and ceilings as we moved.

This time he was right, and we made excellent time locating service room three. Cad flung open its door and wheeled Amber in. I followed quickly, with Thomas bringing up the rear and closing the door.

Once we were inside, Amber and Ms. Dale hopped off the gurneys, and from the storage space underneath them, we began pulling out the duffel bags we'd stowed our gear in. Within minutes, we'd all changed into respectable street clothes. The suit I was wearing was a bit too snug in the shoulders and crotch area, and the shoes pinched a bit, but it would have to do. I took a few painstaking moments to gather my hair into a ponytail, and then placed a pair of spectacles over my nose. The final touch was a round bowler hat atop my head.

I couldn't be sure how I looked; I just hoped it was enough to make me unrecognizable to Cruz. I'd had my fair share of fame in the fighting world, so it was a risk. One I was prepared to deal with if things went south.

Tucking the gun I'd brought into the special holster at the base of my back, I added four extra clips into the holster's built-in pockets, then took out the plastic box holding our video chip and slipped it into my back pocket. This one contained an edited version of Violet's video that Thomas had cut together, hopefully making it more comprehensible to the public.

By the time I had finished, Ms. Dale and Amber had lined

up their guns on a gurney and were in the only slightly ridiculous process of tucking them into various hidden pockets in their long, modest dresses. I tried not to stare, but not for the obvious reason—I'd had no idea how ingenious Patrian women's clothing could be. How could a single dress fit so many weapons inside? I was never going to look at a conservatively dressed woman on the streets of Patrus the same way again.

"How do I look?" I asked them all, adjusting my spectacles.

Cad looked up first and gave a low wolf whistle. I gave him an incredulous look, and he shrugged and smiled. "It's what my wife would've done." I rolled my eyes, and turned to Ms. Dale and Amber.

Amber gave me the onceover, her eyes roaming up and down my body. "I mean… you're not my type, but damn, do you make glasses work for you. Does Violet know this look exists? Because if she doesn't, I'm going to have to tell her immediately."

"I am not going to play dress-up for my fiancée," I muttered.

"Yes, you are, once she hears about Nerdy Viggo." Amber turned back to the weapons on the table with a smirk, sliding a thin knife into a thigh sheath before lowering her skirts.

Annoyed, I looked to Ms. Dale for an actual answer to my question. She gave me an approving nod, but I could tell she was biting her cheek to suppress some comment, and to be honest, by this point I was glad for her restraint.

"All right, it'll have to do," I grated out. "Let's go over our identities one more time."

Ms. Dale picked up a gun, chambering a round, and then slid it into one of the deep pockets of her gown, tugging at her skirts. "I'm Abigail Marks, beloved auntie to my two favorite nephews, Jeff and Jacob." She gave me a little nod as she used the name I had chosen as my alias. "I am also a distant cousin, several times removed, to young Vivian here."

"Don't forget you raised me, Auntie Abigail," Amber said as she pushed back her hair, sliding an auburn wig over her head, disguising her undercut beneath the thick mass of curls. "Why, I would've been lost without you."

I snorted at the sugary voice she used, turning to Cad. "And you?"

"Why, I'm Kurtis, Kurtis MacDougal," he replied. He met Amber's gaze as she leaned forward slightly, arching her eyebrow in question, and I bit back a laugh as a dull blush began to form on his cheeks. "I'm—uh—engaged to Vivian here."

"Don't worry, Kurt," Amber said, giving him a salacious wink. "Your wife doesn't have to know about us."

Cad's blush darkened, his cheeks becoming mottled, and I gave Amber a little nudge. "Be nice to the happily married man," I chided, but I was unable to keep the smile completely off my lips.

Amber pouted playfully, and then dramatically swept her long hair over her shoulder. "Oh, all right," she said. "But only as long as I get to tell his wife this story later."

"Let's *get* to a later first, and then we'll discuss who you're telling what to," I suggested, knowing it was time to rein in the playfulness. I could see Thomas in the corner, glaring at us as he threw aside his ill-fitting EMT disguise, clearly trying to let us know that he was tired of joking when there was work to do.

I checked my watch. "We've got to meet Jeff in seven

minutes. Is everybody ready?"

"Wait!" said Amber, reaching into her bag and pulling out a few little plastic tubes and containers. "I'm going to cover up your scar real quick. And I'll get rid of some of those bruises while we're at it."

I stood still as she quickly applied a cream, then a powder to my right cheek, masking the scar from view. I'd actually almost forgotten about it, but I supposed it was one of my more distinguishing features, and she was right to cover it up. I also had a sneaking suspicion Amber would be pretty keen to tell Violet about how she got to put makeup on Nerdy Viggo Croft. I was going to have to think up a fun form of retaliation. *Later*, I reminded myself.

Amber shut the compact with a click and nodded. "All right. Now we can go."

"Are we good?" I asked Thomas.

We grouped close together as the small man made his final inspection. "It's flimsy," he finally announced, his eyes beady, but then he nodded. "But most humans aren't as observant as I am, so it should work."

I smiled at him. "Are *you* good to go?"

In response, Thomas dropped down to a knee and pulled at a ring that had been pressed flat in a circular groove on the plain concrete floor. There was a heavy groan as the section of floor lifted grudgingly, and I resisted the urge to gag at the stench that wafted up from the dark opening. Thomas pulled a flashlight from his pocket and clicked it on, angling it down into the sewer below. He had chosen this room in the hospital as our dressing room for a reason. "It would appear so," he said after a moment. "I should be at the stadium in four minutes, and in their system within eight. I'll keep you all updated."

I nodded, suddenly apprehensive, and extended my hand. "Be careful," I said.

Thomas looked at my hand, and then took it, shaking. His grip was surprisingly strong. "You too," he replied, meeting my gaze. Then, turning, he grabbed a satchel full of his computer tools off the floor and swung it over his shoulder, quickly heading to the sewer access ladder and climbing down. As soon as he was clear, Cad shut the floor panel behind him.

I let out a breath, checking my watch again. Four minutes 'til our rendezvous. "All right. Let's go take a leisurely stroll to the stadium next door for a super fun family outing! Isn't it just lovely that it's only a few minutes away?"

Holding out my arm to Ms. Dale, I smiled as she rolled her eyes at me before slipping her arm through mine. "Whatever you say, Jacob."

CHAPTER 34

Viggo

Anello Cruz stared at me, his dark eyes studying the planes of my face, a half-asked question floating in them. It was taking everything I had to keep from adjusting my hat or my spectacles again.

Jeff stood by Cruz's side in the lobby of the stadium, which we'd reached one minute late, after having to explain to a curious but gullible doctor that our entire family had gotten lost during a visit to a relative in the hospital. The former valet's suit was well tailored, colored navy blue instead of the standard black. He stood with a straight back, a smile playing on his face as he introduced each one of us to the fighter. Cruz's suit was a bit more ostentatious—a deep purple in color, a black shirt slightly visible underneath—but he wore it well. Nothing else about the man had changed from what I remembered. He was still muscular and tall, close to my height, although he probably had several pounds of muscle on me.

"It really is a pleasure to meet you, madam," Cruz said, his eyes withdrawing from mine as he leaned stiffly over to press his lips against Ms. Dale's hand.

Ms. Dale tittered—a sound so unfamiliar I had to hide my cringe—and then affected a truly horrible pout as she reluctantly drew back her hand. "No, really, the honor is all mine! I was—am—such a fan. It really is unfortunate about all this."

Cruz straightened, nodding in agreement, but his smile seemed to grow despite the sad tidings they were supposedly discussing. "I wholeheartedly agree, of course. It *is* a shame about all this. But we survive, eh? Learn to carry on. And who is this lovely gem behind you?"

Amber, somehow—I couldn't imagine how—managed to blush as Anello's eyes fell on her, and she released Cad's arm to come over to him, her hand outstretched and trembling as she slid it into his for a light shake. Cruz leaned over to kiss it, and Amber gave a little catchy gasp, her flush deepening.

"Mr. Cruz, it is so… I mean… words cannot describe how much of an honor… oh dear." She reached down and tugged her skirts, looking completely flustered.

Cruz laughed, a warm, throaty sound, as he released Amber's hand. "Please relax, my dear. It is quite all right. I promise I won't bite."

Amber burst out into a giggle, and suddenly, I was disappointed Violet wasn't there to see this display. It didn't seem like it was going to be difficult to get dirt on Amber after all… I was going to have plenty to tell Violet.

"I'm sorry," the redheaded girl gushed, smoothing her

skirts out. "I'm just so nervous. I am such a big fan. My name is Vivian. I'm Auntie Marks' cousin, although I just call her Auntie Abigail. She practically raised me since I was nine."

"I *did* raise you since you were nine," Ms. Dale said smoothly. "And let me tell you," she added to Cruz, "this one was a handful."

Amber flushed prettily while simultaneously pouting. Turning around, she reached out for Cad and drew him forth. "This is my fiancé," she gushed. "Kurtis. Kurtis MacDougall. He's not quite as handsome as you, Mr. Cruz, but he's the love of my life."

Cad gave her a mortified look, and then turned to Cruz, shaking his head, almost ruefully. I wondered if Cad was having any doubts about this act now, but it was too late to back out.

"Hello, Mr. Cruz." Cad's voice was stiff as he accepted Cruz's hand, gripping it tightly. I could hear Violet's cousin grunt as Cruz squeezed back, but he didn't back down, instead firmly meeting the taller man's gaze. Then Cruz slowly withdrew his hand, giving Cad a brilliant smile.

"Pleasure to meet you, Mr. MacDougall." His eyes returned to me, and I stepped forward.

"Jacob. I'm Jeff's younger brother. Much younger, I know." I held my breath as he accepted my hand, squeezing it tightly. I didn't bother to play the male posturing game Cad had played with him, just squeezed a polite amount and relaxed my grip, indicating the handshake should be over.

Cruz didn't let go, his fingers tightening slightly. Then the light of recognition flared in his eyes. "Your name isn't Jacob," he said softly. "You're Viggo Croft. You're that punk who was supposed to fight me but didn't have the stones to show up."

I met his gaze head on and scowled, though my heartrate had shot up at the sound of my real name. Now wasn't the time to panic… it was just the other shoe. Dropping. A part of me had expected this.

"Jacob is my middle name," I replied, now tightening my own grip. "You'll excuse me for wanting to be out of the spotlight down here. And there were… extenuating circumstances that came into play that night." It was better to hold back the truth—avoid linking myself to Violet in any way.

"Extenuating circumstances?" he drawled, his voice turned toxic.

"It was me," Amber cut in smoothly, fidgeting with embarrassment. Cruz's mouth made an 'o' of surprise as his gaze was diverted from our staring contest over to her. "Kurtis and I were out walking, and… well…" A sob caught in her throat, and she turned away slightly. Cad came forward to take her shoulders.

"Actually, it was *my* fault my nephew lost his chance to best you," announced Ms. Dale. "Jeff here was busy at his job, and I couldn't find Vivian anywhere. I panicked, you see, and I called Viggo. It turned out to be a bit of a misunderstanding—apparently she had written me a note, you see, alerting me that she was going to be out with Kurtis, but it somehow slipped off the counter and under the refrigerator. I was so embarrassed, and by the time Viggo showed up, they were just returning. I feel terrible he missed out."

"If something had happened to Vivian and I'd still gone on with the match… well, I wouldn't be able to live with myself,"

I said, my voice heated as I realized how close that lie was to truth.

Cruz gazed at me, our hands still locked in a private grappling match. "Why didn't you ask for a rematch?" he asked, curiosity lining the nooks and crannies of his face. "I was so excited to beat down the upstart from the amateur leagues."

I jerked my hand from Cruz's and took a step back, tugging on the edges of my coat. "Because it's none of your damn business," I growled.

"Mr. Cruz!" Jeff cut in, rounding on the man with his hands crossed over his chest. "Now, I'm sorry I didn't tell you my brother was *the* Viggo Jacob Croft—to be honest, I have never approved of his love for fighting. Not that I don't enjoy a good fight." He held up his hands in badly formed fists, his shoes slapping loudly on the floor as he did his best to dance and weave. Cruz watched him, a sort of bemused wince coming across his features. Thankfully, after a second, Jeff stilled and resumed his position. "But Viggo had responsibilities that took priority, and he had shirked them for too long. After that night, we asked him to stop fighting. We couldn't keep worrying like that. With myself gone, and young MacDougall courting Vivian here, well… we wanted to make her safety a priority. Since my work took me out of the city, it fell to Viggo to pick up the reins of our familial obligation."

Cruz gave me a hard look, and I shrugged, grimacing noncommittally. After a pause that seemed to stretch out forever, he nodded. "I understand. Life is constantly complicated by our need to protect our women, eh? Well, it really is a shame, if you don't mind me saying so, Jeff. Jacob was quite the fighter, from what I heard. And I do honestly believe he had a chance. Probably not a good one, but hey—we underdogs have to stick together, right?"

"I guess so," I said with another shrug. "I hope you understand the need for my disguise, though. Since my brother asked me to give up the career and focus on family, my fans haven't really taken well to the decision. I just want them to get a nice private tour of the stadium without people interrupting."

Cruz clapped me on the back—harder than was necessary, but I held back my natural response to shrug him off—and laughed. "Well, it's no matter, and hey! You're here! It would be my pleasure to escort you around the stadium you almost got to fight in."

It was meant as a jab, but I had no regrets about missing that night. Violet's life had been on the line, and my fight with Cruz…. it had only been a fight. One I hadn't even been keen to sign up for in the first place. But I had a part to play now, and so I winced appropriately. The gesture seemed to appease him, because he immediately turned to Ms. Dale and Amber, extending his arms.

"Now, ladies, let us get on with the show. We only have a short amount of time to see everything."

Ms. Dale and Amber beamed up at him, manifesting the sense of joyous awe only really seen on the faces of fans, and slipped their arms through his.

"You know, Jacob is really underplaying the love of his fans," said Amber. "Auntie Abigail, do you remember when that one girl, Samantha something or another, followed him home from a fight? She tried to sneak into his window!"

"It was positively disgraceful," Ms. Dale gaped. "And you shouldn't bring that up in Mr. Cruz's company. It's not polite for a young woman to talk about."

"Oh, no, madam, I would love to hear more," said Cruz with a chuckle. "I too have had a few more... zealous fans put me in compromising positions. It's nice to know I'm not alone."

Ms. Dale studied him, then leaned over conspiratorially. "A woman tried to force her way into the shower room after one of Viggo's fights. I was so mortified when I heard! And grateful to stadium security for catching her! Can you imagine? Oh, it is a shame, a real shame, that more women don't seem to understand how to be a proper young lady."

I resisted the urge to roll my eyes as Cruz laughed again, and I tuned out of the conversation. He led us toward the stairs, ones I knew well. An odd feeling was coming over me—the sensation of my current life meeting my former one in strange ways.

The stadium was seven stories in total, with the ground floor entrances leading directly into the stands, and the middle stories of the building widening out from the fight ring. Concentric hallways around the outer sides of the building contained the many things needed to run the show behind the scenes: the changing rooms, bathrooms, concessions stands... and, somewhere, a projector room. I'd never been there in my many times in this building.

Jeff, Cad, and I followed Cruz, as the two women and former fighter turned manager continued to chat about me. I tried to focus on the conversation again, to be present and leave the strange feeling behind me. And promptly felt my face turning into a permanent grimace when the women's stories grew even more risqué than the previous two. All the same, I couldn't help but admire the way Ms. Dale and Amber seemed to play off each other, inventing tales and adding details with ease. No matter that it was at my own personal expense—as long as it kept us moving, it was all good.

The stadium was dimly lit, but that was normal. We headed up the handful of steps leading up to the wide hall that encircled the outside of the stadium. I could see the posters from past fights had been torn off the walls, which were now covered with announcements of when the news could be viewed, and instructions on how to proceed. My gaze narrowed in on signs announcing the restrictions on where one could go—namely the second floor and above.

"Is that going to be a problem?" I asked, cutting through Ms. Dale and Amber's banal chatter and pointing at the sign.

Cruz gave it a smug glance, and then smiled. "Not at all. I'm sure your brother has told you I am the facilitator of the stadium now."

"Does that mean you tell the guards what to do?"

His eyes considered me thoughtfully, but he shook his head. "Not exactly. But I was a popular figure, which helped attract crowds, initially. Because of that, I am afforded certain… luxuries."

"Pardon me, Mr. Cruz," said Cad. "But you said initially? Forgive us, we live out in the country. We have no idea how things have been happening in the city."

"Ah, well, when they were first trying to get the news out, it was most difficult for them to attract anyone to the stadiums.

People were scared, you see. So they hired celebrities to coax in crowds and spread the news, even made us responsible for it. But now that they've devised a method of displaying it on the screens, I'm mostly here in case the equipment fails."

There was no more time to interrogate him after that, as we rounded the corner and saw our first glimpse of a checkpoint, past which the stairs to the second floor could be reached. Sandbags were stacked up, making a barrier across the wide hallway tall enough to come up to the top of my thigh, while guards held their positions at various areas inside. I felt tension straighten my spine as one woman leaned on the sandbags, her gaze calculating as she took us in.

Cruz smiled as he drew closer. "Good evening, Ms. Capote," he greeted warmly, but I could see the tension in his jaw as he flashed his teeth at the woman. Her insignia marked her as a lieutenant.

"Mr. Cruz," she said, her voice clipped as she took in our group. I could see her frowning at the dresses Ms. Dale and Amber were wearing, but the expression quickly disappeared. I wondered if she was concerned about hidden weapons, or if she was just assuming the typical Matronising disdain for Patrian women's garb. "What's all this?"

"Ah, yes. These are my guests. I'm taking them on a tour of the stadium. They're allowing me to relive my glory days."

Ms. Capote's eyes took us in, a slow graceful arch developing in one eyebrow. "I see." She checked her watch and frowned. "It's only twenty minutes until we transmit. Will that be enough time…"

"It will, it will," Cruz smoothly cut in, flashing her a

brilliant smile.

She gave us all a considering look, and then nodded. "I can't see what the harm is. I'll need you to log them in here. I'll radio the checkpoints to alert them of your coming. You'll need to be fast, though—I don't want them near the control box when the presentation is about to begin."

Cruz laid a hand against his heart and bowed slightly, a smile on his face. "Thank you, madam."

She gave him a droll look, seemingly immune to his considerable charm, and accepted a clipboard from another guard, holding it out to him. One by one we wrote names down. Looking at it, she gave a satisfied nod, and then pointed us onward.

My heart was still thudding hard against my ribs, even after we had passed through the checkpoint. I couldn't believe this was all it had taken—she hadn't even asked for any identification papers. If she had, we might have been toast. Thomas had recreated forgeries, but the coding had all been identical. If they had taken the time to actually scan them, it would have been game over. Still, maybe Elena's arrogance was to blame for this oversight. After all, she did control the borders of the city; maybe she felt that was enough? Or, maybe she had too many things going on at once? It was either that, or we were walking into a trap. It wouldn't have been the first time Elena and Desmond had outmaneuvered us.

I kept my eyes peeled, searching for any indication that would spell our impending doom. But as we walked down the silent halls, empty and hollow without the bustle of fighters, managers, and press I had been used to when I'd patrolled here,

I saw nothing to indicate any form of a trap. No cameras, no posted guards between checkpoints, no nothing.

"Now, because of the Matrian queen's new way of showing the news, I no longer get to make the announcements like I used to," Cruz droned as we came around the landing to the next series of steps. "But I still know this stadium better than anyone else. Or at least, anyone still alive. A great number of the fighters in the PFL were caught in the fires that decimated the docks, valiantly trying to quench the hungry flames that threatened to consume the city."

"Were you there, Mr. Cruz?" Amber asked, her eyes wide.

"Of course I was! I was lucky enough to survive, but many of those fighters were my friends. I…" He trailed off, his voice becoming soft. "Well, I do miss them."

Ms. Dale patted his hand sympathetically as we came to the second checkpoint, this one guarding the main stairs to the third story. It had the same basic setup as before, but this time, there were half a dozen women in the checkpoint area. I felt my breath catch in my throat as they looked at us—there were a lot of them to take on at once! —but after a cursory glance, we were waved on. Cruz continued to drone on as we moved, heading to the steps.

It was all I could do to pretend I was even remotely interested in what he was saying. I was just glad Amber and Ms. Dale were there. They kept him distracted, asking questions here and there about the stadium and its history. All I could do was think about every shadowed nook and cranny and calculate how quickly I could get to the gun pressed against the small of my back.

We came up the final landing of stairs and headed right, moving toward the next checkpoint. This one separated us from the control room. My eyes noted the sign for emergency exit 3C, which had an arrow pointed down the hallway, and I exhaled. We were on the opposite side of the stadium now, as far away as we could get from the hospital. Deep into hostile territory with what felt like an army between us and our borrowed getaway car. I prayed we had made the right choice with this mission, because if we hadn't, we would all be dead soon.

At the checkpoint, one warden—a captain, according to her insignia—came over to exchange a few softly spoken words with Cruz. I could see the curiosity in her eyes as she took in the rest of us, but she gave a tight nod, pointing at her watch and holding up ten fingers. Cruz flashed her a suave smile and nodded, and then began pushing us forward.

"I'm sorry about that," he said as we moved through the wide hall, passing the wooden double doors every fifteen to twenty feet that led to private balconies for wealthier patrons to view the fights, our footsteps echoing loudly. "They are very concerned about the equipment, so we'll only have ten minutes in this area. Please hurry."

We walked in tense silence, moving around the stadium to the opposite side of the stairs. The hall continued on, curving around as we approached a final, sandbagged area right in front of what had to be the control room. I noted only two women guarding the light blue door to the projecting room, much to my relief. I exchanged looks with Ms. Dale, giving her an imperceptible nod, and we began to slow as one, drawing our steps out.

If Cruz had even begun to notice, it wouldn't have mattered, because Amber was already creating a distraction. "Mr. Cruz, can I ask you about that loss you suffered early on in your career? Not with the PFL, I know... This was a few years back. With Scarpelli?"

It did the trick. Cruz groaned theatrically and began to launch into the inconsistencies of a ruling that had not been in his favor, citing ridiculous facts and statistics, as well as the referee's loose familial ties with Scarpelli. I ignored it all, my heartbeat speeding up as we drew closer to the guards. I kept my body relaxed, my focus on the two wardens before me.

As we came around the sandbags, Ms. Dale reached into her pocket, withdrawing a handkerchief, dabbing her forehead, and then replacing the white cloth. I watched as Amber leaned into Cruz, practically resting her chest against his arms, distracting the man further.

There was no script for this next part, especially for Amber, Ms. Dale, and me—it was more of a gut feeling of when to go. Maybe to Jeff or Cad it seemed they'd missed a message, but in truth, there was none. One minute we were a group on a tour with a famous PFL fighter. The next, our guns were out and pointed.

It took a second for it to register with our targets, which was good, because that gave Cad and Jeff a chance to catch up.

Amber had her gun pressed against Cruz's temple, and Ms. Dale and I had surged forward toward the guards, our sights trained on them.

I saw one of them reach for her gun and gave her a warning look, tightening my grip on my gun. "Don't."

The guard's hand froze as she took us all in, and then her hand slowly withdrew, rising to the level of her shoulders. The second guard followed suit, her blue eyes growing wide with fear.

"Good," I said with a tight nod. "Now, each of you reach into your friend's holster, pull out her gun, and set it slowly on the floor."

The two women exchanged glances, and then awkwardly reached over each other for their partner's gun, most likely with their off hands. Good. Awkward meant they wouldn't try anything.

A few seconds later, the guns were on the floor, and the two women stood before us unarmed. I nodded to Jeff, who moved over and quickly patted them down.

"Clean," he said after several tense heartbeats.

I nodded and holstered my gun. "Ladies, I am terribly sorry for the inconvenience, but can you please open the door? My associates here are ever so eager to see the control box."

There was another exchange of glances, and then, reluctantly, one of them pulled out a security badge that dangled from her belt, holding it up to a black sensor box on the wall behind her. There was a beep, followed by a metallic clunk, and Ms. Dale hurried over to the door, pulling it open.

I took in the small room before us as a rush of adrenaline flooded my system. The room seemed strongly utilitarian, with an efficient and orchestrated feel. A line of windows into the stadium below stretched out across the opposite wall. Just in front of them sat a long black control panel, slightly longer than a desk, covered in rows of switches glittering with complicated little lights, sitting just in front of them. The walls were the same gray, but with pipes jutting out, presumably containing cables connecting to corresponding boxes on the control panel. And, currently its most useful feature, the room was empty.

"Inside now, ladies," I said. The wardens' eyes were wary, but they followed my orders. One of them—the younger one—was shivering slightly as she slowly went into the room, her head turning back over her shoulder several times to eye the five guns trained on them.

Once they were inside, I moved in, heading right for the control panel. I pulled a long black subvocalizer strip out of one of my pockets and buckled it against my neck, shaking my head against the tingle.

We're in, I transmitted on our channel to Thomas. *But I'm going to need some help with these controls.*

A lot of help. I drew a deep breath, taking in the long black box, maybe five feet wide and three feet deep. It was filled with all sorts of blinking lights, gauges, digital readouts, and too many buttons to count. Thomas had better figure this one out, because the rest of us sure couldn't.

CHAPTER 35

Viggo

"**O**ne second, one second," came Thomas' welcome voice through the earpiece, and I was relieved that he had, in fact, been able to go through with his part of the mission. "Okay. No alarm has been raised that I can see, so you're good there. Now, what's your problem?"

This panel is really complicated, I vocalized through the collar. A small sound of discontent, a jingling, turned my head. I nodded, satisfied, when I saw Amber and Ms. Dale were currently on phase two of our plan: stripping the guards of their uniforms. Behind them, Cad and Jeff pushed Cruz, who had a stunned expression plastered on his face, into the room as well, the door swinging shut behind them.

"Ah, yes," Thomas' voice came into my ear. "Is there a terminal in the booth?"

My eyes scanned the console, stopping at the built-in

monitor display with green lighting all around it.

Yes.

"Good. Go to it and type in what I tell you. I can't crack this beast if I don't know what it is."

I immediately headed over to the attached keyboard.

I'm ready.

In a rapid-fire stream, Thomas began listing out a series of letters, characters, and numbers—too many to count or remember—but I dutifully punched them in while Ms. Dale and Amber changed into the stolen guards' uniforms behind me, Jeff and Cad redistributing the rest of our hijacked weapons.

"You're insane."

The announcement was soft, but carried a heavy load of tension, and I hit enter before turning to face Cruz, who was watching me. His brows were drawn tightly together, a zip tie cinched tightly around his wrists, securing him to one of the pipes running from the walls. The two female wardens sat next to him, looking somewhat less belligerent. I regarded him coolly, shrugged once more, then gave him a little wave before turning back to the computer.

Is that all? I transmitted to Thomas.

There was a long pause. "Huh. That's interesting."

What's interesting? Thomas?

"Oh. Um. Well, it's not really pertinent, but I think I may have found Tim."

My heart skipped a beat as I interpreted his words.

Not pertin—? I choked. *Wait, really? Where? Is he alive?*

"I think he's alive, and yes, really. But, Viggo, the 'where' isn't relevant to us."

Ms. Dale stepped over, tugging the stiff edges of her uniform down, and reached out to place a hand on my forearm. She and the rest of the team now wore their earbuds, so they could hear the exchange. But since they needed their voices for this mission, I was the only one with a subvocalizer.

"Unless he's in danger, then…" She hesitated, her gaze drifting suspiciously to our prisoners, and then continued. "Our tech guy is right—it is not a priority," she said softly, meeting my gaze with an unwavering one of her own. I applauded her commitment to not using anyone's real names, realizing we had overlooked giving Thomas an alias.

I nodded, swallowing through the swoop of hope tugging at my heart. This wasn't the time or the place.

Thomas—is he in danger?

"No, not that I can tell."

Can you… Would you be able to transmit the information back to our base? Not to Violet, though, if you can help it—she might go off half-cocked to find him.

"I can do that. Should I attach a message?"

Whatever you think is best, I replied, after struggling and failing to think of something to say that wouldn't eventually make Violet angry I was covering this up. Ms. Dale gave me a nod, then hurriedly moved through the door and out into the hallway, Amber hot on her heels. The two of them, now dressed as the Matrian wardens who guarded the checkpoints, down to the electronic key fob and the identification papers—not that those would hold up under scrutiny—were going to do their job and guard the door.

This was probably my least favorite part of the plan.

Through the door to the room, Ms. Dale and Amber had no way of communicating problems to us beyond a simple tapping system we'd worked out. The two of them were on their own now, and while they were both more than capable, I knew anything could happen out there.

Thomas, wait one second. Ms. Dale, test the signal for me, I communicated to her. After a moment, I heard a very small tap, followed by a long scratch, signaling that she had heard me. *I read you clearly,* I informed her. *Go ahead, Thomas.*

"Okay. By the way, I now have some control over your console, although it's just about understanding the coding. I can guide you from here, but I need a test of buttons, left to right, top to bottom."

I waved Cad over and pointed at the console, and he nodded, approaching it closely. *Cad is waiting for your instructions,* I transmitted. *Jeff will be communicating with you while I deal with the hostages.*

"Okay."

I ripped off my subvocalizer and handed it over to Jeff, who fastened it around his neck. His eyes went wide as it activated, and I heard his voice coming over the speakers as I saw him mouth, *Is this normal?*

It hadn't occurred to me that Jeff hadn't worn one before, but I nodded at his discomfort and gave him a thumbs-up, certain he could handle the adjustment. Moving over to the hostages, I noted that Ms. Dale and Amber had been kind enough to dress the women in their Patrian clothes, although the fit was poor at best. The three of them sat with their backs to the wall, their hands all secured by zip ties, their feet tied with their own shoelaces.

Cruz was glaring at me, his eyes glistening with malice. "I get it. You're working for *them*," he spat. "The Daughters of Patrus or whatever those terrorist brats call themselves."

I checked my watch, my skin tingling. The tech hadn't been up to the room yet, but according to Jeff's information, there were only a few minutes before she was supposed to be here to load up the next news installment. It was very likely we needed the special case she carried with her, as it was coded specifically to connect to this terminal—without it, we couldn't play our video. We were lucky to have figured that one out beforehand, thanks to Jeff's information-gathering skills and Thomas' strategic thinking.

"Hey, I'm talking to you, you coward," Cruz continued.

"Jacob, people are starting to arrive," announced Cad, turning back from where he sat at the control panel.

I stepped closer, peering out the large panel of security glass. People were beginning to stream into the stadium, their paces sedate, picking their seats around the ring.

"Tell everyone to get ready," I told Jeff, and he nodded, his mouth moving. Already, I could see the strain of this amount of tension was getting to Jeff. Sweat was pouring off the older man's forehead and dripping down his cheeks. I gave him a reassuring nod when I heard his voice come through the earbud.

I turned to Cruz and squatted down. "I'm not part of a terrorist organization," I told him calmly as I grabbed the roll of duct tape I'd seen in the beaten-up red toolkit sitting on the floor near the console. "I'm just a man trying to do the right thing."

"You're betraying your own gender," he hissed, his hands jerking against his bonds.

I shook my head at him. "Well, maybe I am, but for the right reasons." I yanked a strip of tape out, tearing it off, and proceeded to place a piece over Cruz's mouth, ignoring his attempt to bite me. Then I moved on to tape the other prisoners' mouths. I checked my watch again. Only two minutes left before show time—where the hell was this tech? Just waiting like this was alarming in its own right, and if Elena or Desmond had somehow caught on to our plan, this little room could become a trap very quickly. I imagined, for a moment, trying to escape by breaking the security glass and leaping… first I'd have to find a way to break the reinforced glass; then, of course, would there even be something to hold on to—?

A sudden tapping followed by two long scratches sounded at the door, and I whirled, my gun leaping out of the holster under my jacket, the sights trained on the door.

"Get ready," I whispered softly.

I heard the muffled sound of voices, but it was difficult to make out what they were saying. Jeff and Cad stepped next to me, aiming for the door as well. A familiar beep sounded, followed by the metallic thunk I recognized from earlier. And then the door swung open, toward us.

The tech strode in, flanked by two guards, and then paused, her eyes widening, as she saw us. The guards behind her nearly slammed into her, the whole group a tumble of chaos as they reached for their weapons.

"I wouldn't, if I were you," said Ms. Dale from behind them. Her announcement was punctuated by a click as she pulled back the hammer of her own gun.

The women froze, and, in a moment of déjà vu for me, raised their hands up. The technician regarded us. She was short, and pretty, with a round face and hair so blond it was almost white, cut artfully around her face in a short bob. She licked her lips, clutching the black case in her hands.

"Who are you?" she demanded, her blue eyes watching us warily.

Ms. Dale and Amber reached into the guards' holsters, disarming them, and exhaled slightly.

"My name is Jacob," I said. "And I'm terribly sorry about the inconvenience, but my associates and I need the black box you are holding."

"Just over a minute 'til broadcast time," announced Thomas through the earbud.

The woman looked down at the box in her hands and back up to us. I noticed the quiver in her chin that indicated her fear, but she seemed to push it back. "And if I refuse to give it to you?"

I applauded her bravery, however misguided it was. It occurred to me how threatening we were, and the impression that might leave. Even though they were the enemy, I couldn't bring myself to leave that sort of lasting impression on these women. Better to muddy up their perceptions with politeness.

"Miss, I cannot accept your refusal, but I promise you, my associates and I would never hurt you and your friends, unless it's in self-defense."

She swallowed and then looked around the room.

"Sixty seconds," Thomas barked at me.

I moved closer to her, and she flinched back a bit, but managed to keep her feet planted on the ground.

"The case, please, miss," I said, holding out my hand.

Eying my hand nervously, she seemed to struggle with her indecision, when Amber's voice piped up from behind the guards.

"Jacob doesn't kill women," she said. "And he's not good at threatening them, either. But as a woman myself, I don't have his moral inhibitions."

The tech stiffened, and I frowned at Amber over her shoulder, but then the blond girl held out the case to me. I passed it over to Cad just as Thomas announced there were thirty seconds left to go. I heard Cad kneel down, but my eyes were focused on the three women in front of me.

"Over there," I said, pointing with the gun.

The women filed over and sat down next to Cruz and the other two guards. Ms. Dale stepped farther into the room, her gun trained on them all while I pulled out the zip ties.

"Fifteen seconds."

I glanced over to where Cad was quickly connecting leads into the box, Jeff watching him closely. "Jeff!" I breathed. I yanked the box containing our video clip from my pants pocket and held it out to him. He grabbed it and moved over to Cad.

"Five, four, three, two... one."

The stadium went dark, and in the dim red light of the control room, I froze, wondering if, after everything, we had screwed it all up.

CHAPTER 36

Violet

"So, Violet, not to be rude, but the whole boy look you have going on is a bit much."

I heard Dr. Tierney's appalled gasp, but I couldn't help but crack a smile at Henrik's quip. Turning from my work, I made my mouth into an 'o' of surprise.

"Oh, darn—here I was hoping it would help me blend in with the locals."

"Well, now that you mention it, you do make a very fetching boy," said Henrik, a merry twinkle in his eye.

"Well, at least that makes one of us," I shot back with a wink.

Henrik chuckled, and then began to cough, a wet, racking thing, and I immediately took a step closer. Dr. Tierney was already there, the scanner in her hand, her eyes on the screen. "Fluid is still building up in your lungs," she tsked at him. "I'm going to have to up that medication after all."

Wheezing, Henrik fell back on his pillow and nodded weakly, his energy seeming to desert him. "You said if you did, I would also have to start using a blood thinner," he replied in a hoarse voice after catching his breath. Dr. Tierney frowned, looking at him.

"You will," she said. "But it's a risk we have to take. It's been some time since the surgery, plenty of time for the holes Dr. Arlan patched to start to heal up. We'll keep monitoring it."

Henrik nodded, and Dr. Tierney reached out to touch his shoulder. He smiled at her, his white-speckled beard breaking apart like the clouds after a storm. I watched the exchange, worry gnawing a hole in my stomach. Even though Henrik was doing better—sitting up, eating, making jokes—it was clear he was still struggling on his road to recovery.

One lousy bullet. One lousy bullet that had somehow ricocheted in him, causing severe organ damage. Not to mention his age was working against him. Still, I had hope the man would pull through. Not just because he was a good strategic thinker and a gentle, wise leader, but because I liked him. He was a good man who followed his heart rather than the social norms that dominated our two societies.

Sighing, I turned back to Quinn and stepped back up to the bed. I felt a slight twinge in my ribs, but they still felt okay; they had been getting better every day. I was so glad I hadn't broken any of them on top of all the other injuries.

Reaching out with my left hand, I worked my thumb under the bandage covering the remains of Quinn's ear, slowly peeling the cotton back. I winced as some of it caught on the stitches there, but, with a degree of patience that surprised even me, I carefully untangled it and pulled it back.

"When will his stitches come out?" I asked as I tossed the cotton into a bucket next to the bed.

"Soon," replied Dr. Tierney from behind me. "Probably today or tomorrow."

I reached up and smoothed some hair from the young man's forehead. The people assisting Dr. Tierney, including me, had tried to keep his hair tidy over the days of his convalescence.

"Why is he still asleep?"

"Well, he originally must have gone into shock from the blood loss, but to be honest, it's probably a mental response to the trauma he experienced. It's not that surprising. Sometimes people just... break."

Frowning, I dipped a gauze pad into the salve Dr. Tierney had given me and smeared it carefully around the stitches, trying not to snag any of them. "Do you think he'll ever wake up?"

I heard Dr. Tierney's footsteps approach, and I cast a look over my shoulder, watching as she approached the foot of the bed. She leaned on the bedframe using both hands and shook her head, not as a simple no, but in an expression of uncertainty.

"I honestly don't know, Violet. I've got him hooked up to everything I can think of to help him. Physically, his wounds were mostly superficial, except his eye. But the experience? For him?" She turned her gaze to me, her eyes dark. "Would *you* want to wake up after that?"

I thought about it. I knew what it was like to be under Tabitha's knife—but only to a minimal extent. My eyes traced the lines of Quinn's stitches, the way they cut through the natural lines of his body. I thought of the nightmarish hallucinations

I'd had of Tabitha, the flashbacks to that one stab, the flash of the knife…

"Maybe not," I admitted softly.

"Don't worry, Violet. He's a young man, a vibrant one. I want nothing more than for him to come back to us, and I have hopes that he will. He just needs some time."

"Or some water," came a soft rasp. I danced back from the bed, my reflexes kicking in.

Dr. Tierney, on the other hand, moved forward, her eyes studying Quinn breathlessly. He coughed slightly, and then peeled open his single visible eye, shuddering slightly.

"Dry," he coughed, smacking his lips.

Looking around, I spotted a pitcher of water and a cup on Dr. Tierney's desk in the corner of this room, and I moved over to it, quickly pouring the liquid into the cup. Crossing the room, I returned to him. Dr. Tierney helped me by lifting his head up slightly, and I pressed the cup against his lips.

"Just a sip," Dr. Tierney ordered with a nod. I nodded and carefully tilted the glass up, letting some water splash over the boy's mouth. He smacked his lips together as I pulled the glass away.

"That's a little better," he rasped, his eye blinking slowly. He stared at my face, the corners of his lips tugging up just slightly. "Hey, Violet."

"Hey, Quinn," I replied with a smile, clutching the cup to my chest. "How are you feeling?"

"Pretty dry. And… something's wrong with my eye. I'm… having a hard time seeing you."

I frowned, but it was Dr. Tierney who replied. "One of your

eyes is damaged, Quinn. There's a bandage on it."

His mouth worked open slightly, and then he expelled a shaky breath. "Gone?" he asked, his voice tremulous.

Dr. Tierney's mouth dipped in sympathy, but she met his gaze and nodded. "I'm afraid so."

Quinn's face fell. I reached out, pressing a hand to his shoulder, and he looked at me silently, just one brown eye glistening with tears. My heart clenched. Quinn had been a full-fledged member of the Liberators, and I'd gone on more than one mission with him—but at times like these, it was easier to see the teenager he still was. Younger than me, even.

"It's going to be okay, Quinn," I said.

He sniffled, and then nodded halfheartedly. "Yeah. Maybe this means I can try out the pirate life." I wanted to smile encouragingly at him, but I could see the haunted look in his eye, could hear the forced quality of his voice, brittle and raw. "Can I have more water?" he asked.

"Not yet, but soon," Dr. Tierney replied. "Just take it easy, okay?"

He started to nod, and then paused. "Oh God, Amber! Is she okay?"

"She's fine," I said. "She came and got me, and, well, we mounted a rescue."

"We?"

"Amber, Jay, Thomas, me… and Tim." I hesitated around Tim's name, my throat constricting as I thought of my brother.

"Everyone's okay?"

I hesitated again, and then shook my head, unable to stop my face from contorting, just a bit. "Tim's missing," I said hoarsely. Quinn's mangled face twisted more, and I shook my head at him. "It's not your fault," I said, leaning over him. "It's nobody's fault. It just... it just happened. Besides, we will find him. Just focus on getting better."

Quinn managed a half nod, his eyes drifting closed, whether from physical pain or the weight of reality, I couldn't tell. I shifted from leg to leg, and then accepted he wasn't going to talk anymore. In fact, his breathing was already beginning to slow into the deep, even inhalations of sleep.

It was good he'd woken up, if only for a few minutes, but still. His loss was horrific. He would need all the help we could offer him on his road to recovery.

I moved over to the desk, returning the glass of water to it. "I'm going to go work on the bedding," I mumbled to Dr. Tierney, turning toward the door. I was opening it when Quinn's voice pulled me up short once more.

"You look good with no hair."

Turning back to him, I saw his one eye staring at me from where he lay on the pillow, a crooked smile on his lips.

"Thank you," I replied, feeling a smile touch my own face. He nodded again, and then, seemingly satisfied, closed his eye and turned his head on the pillow. I watched him for a moment more, and then stepped across the threshold, closing the door behind me.

Even though Quinn's situation was grim, it was nice to see the sweet side of him was in there, still coming up to the surface. It helped make the stone in my gut feel less heavy.

I moved into the kitchen, heading for the fire on the hearth, where a large cauldron of water hung over the flames. One of the men had helped me fill it, since buckets of water were a difficult thing for me to carry—much like everything else, really. A pile of bedding sat a few feet away on the floor, waiting to be cleaned.

Checking on the water, I was pleased to see it steaming up nicely. I grabbed a tin filled with soap flakes and held it under my right arm. Using my left hand, I carefully pried off the lid and reached in to find the spoon inside, scooping several generous portions into the steaming water. Once the water had turned a milky color, I replaced the spoon and lid, returning the canister to the shelf.

Doing the laundry was hard work without any form of machine to assist, but right now I enjoyed the labor. I was starting to realize why Viggo had spent so much of his time working in the days after Ian's death: it had been a great distraction. For me, the work kept my mind off what was going on in the city without me. Helped me to cope with the fact that my brother was still missing after twelve days. If I didn't keep busy, I'd probably just go crazy.

I started transferring the cloth into the water. The bedding billowed, and I used a stick one of the refugee women had fashioned to push it beneath the surface before adding more to the pot. I had to be careful not to let the water get too high, or it would splash out and douse the fire.

The task held me completely absorbed, so much so that I didn't notice when someone came into the kitchen. Not until I accidently bumped into them. My confidence in my solitude had been so concrete that, when confronted with another body, I jumped back in alarm.

Owen raised an eyebrow at me, crossing his arms over his chest. "I didn't mean to surprise you," he said.

I recovered almost instantly. A smile broke out on my face, and I took a few steps forward and threw my arms around the blond man's neck in a hug, ignoring my ribs' protest.

"Thomas said you'd be back, but I didn't realize it would be so soon," I said against his chest. His hand came up, patting me gently on the middle of my back. I pulled back, beaming up at him. "What happened? What made you change your mind?"

"Oh, well—"

"Was King Maxen driving you crazy?"

Owen paused and then rolled his eyes. "He's pretty demanding, that's for sure. It takes a lot of patience not to deck him."

"Well, I don't envy you that. But I'm happy to see you." I took a step back, bending over to pick up a few more pieces of laundry.

"Violet…"

"Yes?" I said as I eased them into the pot.

"I… Well, this is hard to say, but the reason I'm here is because… because we found your brother."

The sheets slipped from my hand, water slopping up around them and hissing in the fire. I blinked and turned around.

"What? How? Where is he? Is he alive?"

Owen held up his hands, and I fell silent. I was asking too much, too fast. Still, I chafed at the delay, at even that slight interruption, even as I knew he needed me to stop so he could answer me.

"Thomas apparently stumbled over the information while

they were in the city. He sent it to me. It's not much, but there have been reports about a boy matching Tim's description wandering the countryside. He disappears whenever anyone tries to draw near, but the locations have been pretty localized to a specific area."

"Really? Oh my God. We have to go and look for him!"

Owen frowned, and I could see the indecision on his face. I knew what he was thinking—I wasn't well, and he was worried for my health.

"Look," I told him, "I promise, if we run into any Matrian patrols, we will run. I won't try to keep looking for him and risk us as well. I just… I need to see him. Need to make sure he's okay, and get him home, where I know he'll be safe."

"Well, I have a vehicle. Thomas warned me not to let you go off half-cocked, but I'll be damned if I see another boy get hurt if I can avoid it. Especially not Tim."

I was already moving, heading upstairs to grab my bag. I opened the door to our makeshift hospital, and Dr. Tierney looked up at me in surprise.

"We just got word about Tim," I explained quickly. "Owen is here, and he's going to take me out to go look for him. Can you handle things until I get back? Any problems, you can just get a hold of me on Owen's handheld. No, better—I'll bring an extra one just in case."

"All right," Dr. Tierney said, standing up. "But, Violet, are you sure you're feeling well enough to—"

"It's Tim, Doc," I said. "I have to try."

Her mouth hardened as though she were holding in some comment, but she nodded. "Be careful, all right?"

"I will be," I promised, straightening up and closing the door. I moved down the hall toward the room Viggo and I had been sleeping in, where I grabbed my bag before heading back to the kitchen, where Owen was waiting.

"I'm ready," I said.

He looked me over, nodding. "Good. Let's go."

CHAPTER 37

Viggo

The darkness in the stadium held for five seconds, and then ten, and I shot a glance at Cad, who shrugged and began checking the wiring leading to the box the tech had brought. Little glittering lights from the console glowed against his face, so at least there was power moving through parts of the room… I turned, prepared to have Jeff get on the subvocalizer to Thomas, when the massive screens over the seats lit up, throwing a blue glow over the crowds below, and lighting up the faces of those who stood in the room with me.

I moved over to the windows, watching as the symbol of the Matrian flag—a curved grain of wheat—flashed across the screen. The image held, and then faded. Then words, blocky and white, appeared:

Citizens of Patrus—you have been lied to.

Tabitha's face filled the screen, her face smug. "What's done is done—Patrus had no idea what was happening, and now they'll see us as their saviors."

It faded, followed by the words, *King Maxen lives.*

King Maxen's image filled the screen, his expression imperious. "Citizens of Patrus! I am alive and well, but hidden away from Elena's forces. To prove this was not previously recorded, I should tell you what only the darkest rumors have alluded to: I was there when the palace fell."

Even I had a visceral reaction to his face on the screen, and I could tell, even from up here, the crowd below felt the same way. It had been a smart idea on Thomas' part to include video of the king; his death was one of the biggest lies Elena had fed to the populace. No doubt she would try to spin it—but this would be hard to spin.

"The king can be dealt with," Tabitha sneered on the screen. "Perhaps he'll go insane after being kidnapped by terrorists and have to spend the rest of his life taking his own drugs… Perhaps he'll get in a fight with the Chancellor and fall down some stairs…"

"In spite of the late Princess Tabitha's claims, I have not been taken by terrorists," said the king, his face returning to the screen. "But rather, patriots of humanity." I smirked, knowing that last bit had been Violet's idea. According to Ms. Dale, it had taken Maxen several takes before he could say it without a sneer. "They sheltered me, kept me safe… and many of them originally hail from Matrus. But they saw their government's corruption, and chose to take a stand, to help us. While the ideological differences of the past have kept us apart, these individuals have chosen to overlook them in order to help free us from this tyranny."

The screen switched back to Tabitha. "As soon as our scientists crack the code, we'll be on our way to creating a new race of humans, far superior to what your kind has churned out for the last few generations."

"As you can see," the king continued, "Princess Tabitha and her sister, Queen Elena, have been working on a plan to supplant us all with a new race of humans, capable of extraordinary feats of strength, speed, invulnerability. You see…"

I turned my gaze away from the screen and looked out at the crowd as King Maxen began to explain the genetic experiments performed on Elena and her sisters, and later performed on the boys collected by the Matrian screening process. He didn't touch on that for very long—Thomas had said this was, statistically, the least believable part of the situation—before he began discussing the Matrian bombing of the city, the slaughter at Ashabee manor, and the horrific death camps.

"I myself saw," his voice told the crowd, "Matrian wardens open fire on a room full of innocent women and children. I was there." I felt a spike of fury at the sadness he affected, remembering the day he was referring to—how he had hidden like a shameless coward. I tried to set it aside.

The crowd's faces were too far away for me to make out their expressions, but all were locked on the screen, on King Maxen. A few were standing up, their shock propelling them into motion. It was a good sign. I imagined the crowds of Patrians gathered to watch the streaming in every other stadium right at this moment, having the same reaction.

"All right," I said, dragging my attention away from the

presentation. "Jeff, tell Thomas to bring the ambulance around to the southern entrance."

Jeff nodded and began mouthing the orders, while I went over to Cruz. Pulling a knife from my boot, I cut the bonds securing him to the pipe, then removed the tape from his mouth. His gaze, too, was focused on the screen, his lips parted and his brows drawn tight.

"Is this for real?" he gasped as I untied his shoelaces and helped him up from the ground.

"As real as it gets," I replied. Jeff rushed over to us, unclipping the subvocalizer from around his throat.

"Here," he said, thrusting it out to me and taking his handgun out of the holster cinched under his jacket. I wrapped the black swatch around my throat, the icy tingle freezing my vocal cords in place, while he moved to the door, pulling it open and joining Amber and Ms. Dale in the hall. We had no idea if or when the guards would be coming—in fact, we had planned for there to be guards pouring into the room about now—but we knew there was going to be a massive response to this, so we needed to get going.

I tapped Cad on the shoulder. *Let's go*, I subvocalized, knowing he'd hear me through his earbud.

He was standing, staring out at the screen, his eyes drinking in the images. "All those images of Tabitha… they're from the video Violet made?" He turned, looking at me, and I nodded. His mouth flattened, his grip on his pistol tightening. "Right. Let's go."

Towing Cruz behind me with a firm grip under his arm, I followed Cad to the door. He pulled it open for me, and I cleared it out of habit before stepping out into the dimly lit hallway—apparently it was only dark inside the actual stadium. The security checkpoint nearest us was still eerily empty, although there was an ominous buzzing coming from a left-behind handheld, no doubt someone frantically trying to get a hold of the guards.

Ms. Dale and Amber were waiting, waving me forward. Jeff stood on the opposite side of the hall, his handgun sighted down it. I pulled Cruz farther into the hall, glancing back over my shoulder just in time to see Amber and Cad following us. When the room's door was closed, Ms. Dale stepped forward, slamming the butt of her gun into the black security clearance lock until it popped off the wall. Then she grabbed the box, jerking it away from the wires with an electric pop.

"That'll slow 'em down," she said with a satisfied little smirk, tucking the box into her pocket. She looked over at where Cruz stood, still stunned, but now staring at her as though he'd never seen a woman in his life.

"Mr. Cruz?" I asked, disabling the subvocalizer. A part of me wanted to take a moment to bask in his shock, but we didn't have time.

"Y-Yes?"

"Here's what's going to happen: you're going to walk us out with our armed escort here." I pointed to Ms. Dale and Amber. "If we run into security, you'll do your best to convince them we are running behind schedule, hence why we are being escorted out. Once we get to our vehicle, you will be free to go. Do you understand?"

His eyes sought out mine, and I raised an eyebrow at him. He nodded. "I understand."

I let him go, taking a step back. Popping the collar of my shirt up to try to disguise the subvocalizer, I slid my gun back into the hidden holster and tugged my jacket down, straightening it. Within moments, we were moving back toward the last checkpoint we'd passed. I could no longer hear King Maxen's voice through the concrete that separated us from the main part of the stadium, but a quick glance at my watch told me it had been playing for over a minute. That left another two minutes before the message repeated. Why hadn't anyone thought to check the projector box yet?

We were moving quickly, but within moments, I heard the distinctive sound of footsteps coming up behind us at an alarming speed, probably guards coming to find out what had happened at the checkpoint we had gone through only minutes before. I pressed everyone forward, knowing they would be distracted by the control box for a minute or two.

"Are there any checkpoints between here and the next set of stairs?" demanded Ms. Dale, her eyes narrowed at Cruz.

The man gave her a confused look and then nodded. "One more," he replied.

"New plan," she announced, pulling her gun. "Vivian and I are taking you downstairs after discovering you tied up."

We're on our way, Thomas, I subvocalized. *Meet us at the access road that goes around the back of the stadium, off the main road. Be prepared to drive around looking for us—I don't know which exit we'll be coming out of yet, but it will be one of the farther ones.*

Ms. Dale took point, Cad, Cruz, Jeff, and I holding down the middle of the party, with Amber bringing up the rear. The checkpoint was clear as we approached it, only a cursory guard standing there. She drew down on us as we approached, but Ms. Dale held up a hand and quietly explained the situation.

"We have to get them downstairs and out of the building to question," she said in a hushed and urgent tone. "We have no idea their role in all this."

"Our role is that we were taken by surprise!" Jeff cried primly, and Ms. Dale shot him a withering glance, disgust on her face.

"Shut your mouth, you Patrian pig!" she snapped, before turning back to the warden. "Whoever is responsible is still in the control room. Radio the captain and inform her I will be taking these suspects downstairs."

Without waiting for the flummoxed woman to respond, she raised her hand and waved us forward. The woman's mouth worked up and down a few times, as though part of her wanted to object, but she didn't stop us as we moved past her, heading past the main stairs that would get us to the second level.

As we reached the landing, I pulled off the subvocalizer. "How many checkpoints are between here and the stairs leading to exit C?"

"Three," Cruz replied. "But wouldn't it be easier to keep heading down these stairs, and then—?"

I shook my head. "Once the Patrians finish the video, this place is going to explode into mayhem. They're all on the lower levels, so it'll be better to move on this one to avoid the panic."

He nodded, his forehead crinkled, and then pointed down the hall. "This way," he urged. "We've got about eighty feet to the next checkpoint."

We started moving, silence stretching between us. After a

moment, I leaned in toward him. "Start talking. Like you have no idea what's going on and you're angry about this."

Cruz hesitated, and then began speaking. I didn't hear a word of it; my heart was beating so hard against my ribcage that it seemed to drown out his voice. I shot a glance over my shoulder, just to make sure we were all still together, and then turned my focus on the approaching checkpoint.

A guard was waiting at the narrow gap in the sandbags, her rifle held loosely in her hands. Others rose to their feet, watching us approach, but the one at the sandbags was clearly in charge. As we approached, she held up her hand, and we drew to a stop. "Mr. Cruz, what are you doing here right now?" She flashed a curious gaze to Ms. Dale.

"No need to talk to him," Ms. Dale announced, her mouth set in a grim line. "We found them unconscious just outside the control room. Has the captain breeched the door yet?"

The warden frowned, her eyes gazing at us with suspicion. "No, ma'am. The mechanism has been damaged."

"I see. Well, allow us to pass, so I can escort these potential traitors downstairs as I was ordered."

I had to give it to Ms. Dale: she exuded authority. By the time she was finished, the other woman had no reservations, and she stepped aside to allow us past her.

"Take them down the next staircase," the woman said with a nod as we moved by her. "The contingency plan is being authorized on this level."

"Now, really, madam! I must protest!" said Cruz, imbuing his tone with indignation. Ms. Dale's eyes were hard as ice as she ignored him, her mask secure.

We hurried away from the checkpoint, and I was hyper-aware of the eyes watching us all, not just the main warden's, but everyone who worked there. Sweat was collecting on my chest right now, making my shirt cling to my skin. I was grateful for the coat I was wearing, in spite of its constricting nature, as it hid the stains no doubt growing on my shirt.

As soon as we were out of earshot, I grabbed Cruz, hauling him over to the doors leading to one of the VIP boxes. "What's going on? What contingency plan?"

"I have no idea," he replied, his voice reflecting his confusion. "Clearly something is going on, some sort of response to your video. But beyond that, I don't know."

Frowning, I looked at Ms. Dale, who shrugged her shoulders. "We have to keep going," she said softly. "We can't stop to question it now."

I took a deep breath, sticking my head out slightly to check the halls. "How far to the next checkpoint?"

Cruz looked down the hall over my shoulder. "Maybe a hundred, a hundred and twenty feet."

"All right, then. Abigail, you and Kurtis take point, Vivian and Jeff, you're in the rear. Get ready with some more security babble, and Cruz—get ready to be more and more irate about this whole situation."

We were halfway to the next checkpoint when we passed by another set of doors leading to a VIP booth, and the sound coming through it stopped me cold. I dropped from formation and dashed over to the door, my heart skipping a beat as I heard the screams of rising panic tearing through the walls—punctuated by the definitive sound of automatic gunfire.

CHAPTER 38

Viggo

"**W**hat's happening?" Cad asked me. "What are we—?"

"We gotta get as many people as we can out alive!" I said, my eyes meeting his.

I snatched my gun from its holster, looking over my shoulder at Ms. Dale and Amber as the sounds of gunfire and shrill screaming ripped through the corridor. Ms. Dale's face was grim, her mouth an angry slash across her face.

"Do what you can here," she barked. "Vivian, on me. Mr. Cruz, you're still coming with us!" Then she turned back down the corridor the way we'd been going, breaking into a run.

Amber nodded, taking off down the hall after Ms. Dale, her weapon at the ready. Cruz stared from them, to me, to them again, as if questioning.

"I don't have a weapon!" he began, but I overrode him, shouting, "Just go!"

He went, and I paused at the door handle for just a moment. "Are you two ready?"

"I've got your back," said Jeff, dropping to a knee behind a metal trashcan, his gun coming out of the holster.

"Good. Cad, with me."

The young man nodded, and I tore open the door, not wanting to waste any more time. The panic that had been muffled by the door exploded into our ears, and I moved down the carpeted steps into the VIP box we'd entered, my eyes scanning the second level before falling toward the ground. Wardens had encircled the crowd, blocking the exits, standing there and firing mercilessly into the crowd. It was a brutal scene, one that made my vision go red: the thousands of people trapped inside, diving this way and that, crawling around behind the seats for cover, using their neighbors as shields or trying to shield them… I had no way of knowing whether the same thing was happening in the other stadiums yet. Right now, all we could do was save as many witnesses as we could from this one.

I moved quickly down the stairs, hardening myself, becoming mechanical and precise. I raised my handgun, sighting the wardens I had a good angle on and squeezing the trigger once, and then again. The woman on the left dropped immediately, but the second one grabbed her shoulder and sagged back against the door. I squeezed the trigger again, not letting in any emotion, save a grim sense of satisfaction.

Amber had lied when she'd said I didn't kill women. I would kill any human who had stooped to something like this.

Cad rushed up to the wall next to me and began firing at the wardens covering another set of doors. I cursed and grabbed his shirt, hauling him back as someone looked up at him and began firing at us. Bullets whined as they flew by, and I pulled Cad down onto the ground as they impacted the walls overhead.

Meeting my gaze, Cad's eyes were tight and furious. As soon as the first round of bullets lulled, he rose to his knees and squeezed off a few more rounds. I followed suit, dropping two more wardens and losing four bullets in the process. Seven rounds down, four more to go.

I ducked as another spattering of automatic gunfire hailed up at us, the bullets hitting the concrete wall and making shards and powder rain down. I gritted my teeth, then burst up, training my gun on our attacker. I squeezed the trigger, satisfied to see her drop.

Movement on my left caught my eye, and I turned my head in time to see two wardens burst through the doors of a VIP box two doors away. "Left side," I shouted to Cad, turning my gun toward them.

Cad sat up, his eyes wide in alarm, and then ducked back down as one of the women swung her aim toward us. I compressed the trigger—two left—and then ducked, cursing when she didn't go down. More bullets streaked overhead, and I had an intense, momentary debate with myself about whether I should change the clip before it was spent, when I heard the gunfire stop suddenly.

I risked a glance and saw the woman fiddling with her rifle. Without hesitating, I pulled the trigger twice, and was up and moving the second she fell, racing past Cad and angling for the next box, hanging ten feet away.

I planted my foot on the railing around the box and pushed off it hard. There wasn't even enough time to feel like I was falling before I had breached the gap, my feet just missing the railing of the other box. I hit the ground, my ankles and knees absorbing an impact that made me grunt in pain, but I didn't stop moving.

Ejecting the clip while running took practice and experience, but it wasn't a problem for me, not after all these years. It fell to the floor with a clatter, and I reached into my holster pocket and pulled out the first of my spare clips, slapping it into the gun just as I reached the second railing.

The second guard's gun was on me at this point, but I ignored it, my heart thudding hard as I raced toward the box where she stood, my breath coming in pants. I planted a foot on the railing, just like before, and leapt. My thumb released the slide, slipping it back in place, as I flew through the air.

Everything felt like it was going in slow motion. The warden, standing next to the body of her dead comrade, pointed up at me as I came down, but I stretched out my arm, an angry yell tearing from my lungs. It was going to be one of us, possibly both. I squeezed the trigger again and again as I fell, certain she would get a shot off even then.

I landed hard in the VIP box, my breath hitching. The woman had fallen on her back, blood already beginning to pour from the three bullets I had put in her chest. I ran my hands over my body, certain she had struck me somewhere, and then exhaled when I realized I hadn't been hit at all.

There was no time for relief, however, as I heard Jeff's shout ringing in from the hall, where the two women had left the door open. Scrambling up toward the doors of the VIP booth I was in, I heard the sound of gunfire coming from both sides. Figuring Amber and Ms. Dale would be okay, I headed for Jeff, racing down the curved hall.

A volley of bullets ricocheted throughout it, and I was forced to slow, pressing my back against the wall. I heard Jeff shout, this time in alarm, and slid myself carefully forward, praying I would have enough time…

I came around the curved edge, keeping myself low, and saw that Jeff was still kneeling behind the trashcan, his face red and his breathing ragged. More gunfire sounded, and then he was up, squeezing the trigger.

"So sorry!" he shouted, before ducking back in.

Creeping up behind him, I raised my gun and dropped the first warden kneeling in the middle of the hall farther down, her gun trained on Jeff's position. Jeff looked back at me, alarmed by my sudden appearance, but I ignored him and moved forward.

Another guard stood off to one side, busy changing her clip, and I leveled my gun at her just as she looked up. She barely had a chance to register what was happening when my shot caught her in the shoulder. Her gun fell loudly, clattering on the floor, and she screamed in pain as she fell back. I shot her in the other shoulder for good measure, but didn't go for the kill shot.

Jeff stood up, a bewildered expression on his face. "Are you okay?" I asked, and he nodded, blinking.

I moved back through the doors of the first VIP box, relieved to see Cad still firing down at the wardens below. I could already see the remains of the crowd surging toward the openings we had given them, streaming in shouting, horrified disarray for the doors. As much as I hated it, we needed to go if we wanted to get out of here alive. Now the people could see to themselves.

"Cad, let's go!" I shouted, and he turned back to me, nodding. He kept himself low as he raced up the stairs toward me. I waited until he was through and then slammed the door closed. The gunfire from farther down the hall had stopped, and I found myself suddenly worried about the fate of Ms. Dale and Amber.

I moved toward the next checkpoint, taking a moment to eject the clip and double check how many bullets were inside. Our plan was becoming a wild mess, thanks to the Matrians. The sounds of panic continued through the doors, and I exhaled sharply, angry that I had to leave them all behind, that I couldn't stay and help them more. Angry that once again I had to be in the position of watching innocents die. But I wouldn't think about that now. I couldn't. My team's lives were depending on me and my decision, and it was my responsibility to make sure we all got out alive.

Still, a part of me feverishly hoped one of the citizens below would at least go for one of the weapons that had been dropped by the dead Matrian soldiers. Better to die fighting than running.

As the checkpoint came into view, I felt a supreme sense of satisfaction to see Amber and Ms. Dale on their feet, waiting for us. There were several bodies on the floor around them, but it seemed their battle had left them unscathed.

"You okay?" I asked, noticing Cruz standing off to the side, now with a rifle in his hands.

"Peachy," Amber answered for all of them. "Can we get the

hell out of here, please?"

I nodded, looking around for the signs guiding us to the various exits. We had come around the backside of the stadium, and the signs read that we were close to exit F. I spent an instant debating the pros and cons of staying on this level.

"We need to get to the ground level," Ms. Dale announced, her mind grappling with the same problem. "There's the stairs. Let's head down them and get lost in the crowd."

Opening my mouth to reply in agreement, I looked over her shoulder and froze as I saw a pair of wardens leveling their weapons at us. My right hand shot up, finger on the trigger, but a spray of fire tore across them before I could pull it, their bodies jerking as the bullets impacted.

They fell bonelessly to the floor, and behind me, I saw Cruz lower the rifle, smoke trailing from its muzzle. He met my gaze with a shrug, and then nodded toward the exit.

"Let's get out of here," he called, heading forward.

Jeff and Cad were already moving. I let out a breath, shook my head, and then hightailed it after them, urging Ms. Dale and Amber forward. We headed toward the gap in the wall where the stairs were waiting, moving at a flat run.

Cruz reached the stairs first and positioned himself right behind the wall at the top, covering us. I peered over my shoulder, well aware that wardens could be coming up behind us. Jeff and Cad made the stairs, and I grimaced as Cad practically leapt down to the first landing, hearing the sound of his shoes sliding on the floor as he hit. Amber and Ms. Dale were more practical as they raced down, their feet flying down the steps. I tapped Cruz, and he followed them.

I waited, wanting to give them a few seconds to head downstairs in safety, my eyes flicking from one end of the hallway to the other. I could still hear the sound of gunfire through the doors just past me, but it was growing more sporadic, the screams inside lost in the sound of nearer screams tearing through the halls as, hopefully, people got out.

My heart hammered in my chest as I waited for Cruz to clear the next landing. As soon as he was down, I moved. The back of my neck tingled in anticipation of a gunshot as I raced down the stairs, but none came. Clearing the landing, I saw Cad and Jeff waiting for me, waving me forward and left. I ran past them just as gunfire exploded overhead, the crack of it echoing loudly in the enclosed, concrete stairwell.

I didn't stop. Ms. Dale and Amber had reached the bottom floor, which opened onto a small foyer for a back exit—thankfully, we'd reached one of the main stairwells that ran all the way down to the ground floor. The two women stopped at the sight of two wardens guarding this entrance, currently facing sideways from us to pour bullets into the encroaching crowd.

I raised my gun, but Amber and Ms. Dale were already on it, mowing them down—hopefully making room for more panicked people to escape. If there were any left, that was.

Apparently there were. People began clamoring into the foyer from the wide doors that led to the stadium, surging toward us as we raced from the stairs to the door, our paths intersecting in a rush like an old cavalry battle. I pressed my shoulder against the wall, steadying myself in the crowd that swirled around me, and followed Ms. Dale and Amber as they raced for a small lobby door twenty feet ahead. Ms. Dale kicked it open as she reached it and pushed Amber through, pressing out behind her. The late afternoon sunlight beamed through the opening into the dim room like a ray of hope. Cruz was seconds behind them, seeming to appear from nowhere as he leapt through.

I raced for it as well, grunting as a woman slammed into me, her face splattered with blood. She took a look at the gun in my hand and then screamed, jerking away. I reached out, trying to catch her, to steady her, but she disappeared into the crowd as it raced by. I cursed, my anger souring in my stomach, but didn't stop moving, even as the crowd jostled me.

We were at the doors now. "Come on," I shouted to Jeff and Cad over my shoulder as I made it to the door, but I wasn't sure where they were in the crowd.

A group of civilians pushed me through it, and I snagged the doorframe, using it to swing myself around and off to the side. Jeff tumbled through a moment later, his gun flying from his hand and getting lost under the crowd's pounding feet. I reached out and grabbed him under his arm, pulling him to his feet before the rush of fleeing people plowed him under as well.

Cad was there seconds later, pushing us forward. I raced ahead, pulling Jeff with me for a few feet, and saw Cruz standing fifty feet away on the pavement. He was waving his arm frantically in the narrow access road that curved around the stadium, leading to the main street. Beyond him, a few exits down, I saw the ambulance. Ms. Dale and Amber were already sprinting toward it, their faces red from exertion. I poured on the speed, Jeff and Cad sprinting toward the car in my wake. When we finally made it there, Ms. Dale had yanked open the doors, and the group of us simply leapt into the back. Everyone stayed there, except for me: I pushed forward to the front.

Thomas gunned the engine as I sat down hard in the passenger seat, sucking in air to try to calm the frantic beating of my heart. I heard the doors slam just as I was buckling up.

"Go!" yelled Ms. Dale, and Thomas pressed his foot to the gas, the vehicle surging forward.

We were all silent as we sped away from Starkrum Stadium, turning sharply onto the road leading out of the city. My gut twisted as my mind went to the other stadiums, and the countless more deaths that might take place within them, or had already. Deaths we had no way of preventing. Elena would have her mass of troops scrambling. We were outmanned and outgunned by a fantastic amount, without enough weaponry to supply even the people we'd managed to help escape. It was a harrowing feeling, knowing all the death that was taking place today was thanks to our plan.

I just had to believe that we'd dealt a death blow of our own.

That today would be the beginning of the end.

CHAPTER 39

Violet

The sun rode low on the horizon as Owen drove his vehicle, probably one from Ashabee's stash, off the road and up a hill. I chewed my lower lip nervously, squinting against the brightness. This was our third stop today, following the last bit of Thomas' information. The engine roared loudly as Owen pressed the gas, but the pace was painfully slow as we crept up the steep, rough-and-tumble terrain.

At the top, he killed the engine, and I reached across my lap with my left hand to open the door and step out. "Tim!" I shouted. "Tim!"

I sucked in a deep breath, my ears straining to hear even the faintest of responses. But the only sounds were the whispering of the trees moving in the breeze, and the evening birds singing to each other. On the other side of the car, Owen got out and unfolded the map he'd brought with us, placing it on the hood.

Moving to the front of the vehicle, I watched as he compared the information he had received from Thomas with our current position, and drew a small 'x' at the corresponding location on the map.

"Are there any houses or farms nearby?" I asked.

Owen shook his head. "No. This place is pretty undeveloped. Looks like it's just forest and…" He trailed off, his frown deepening.

"What? What is it?"

He met my gaze, running a hand over the back of his neck. "Well, we're only three or four miles from Ashabee's manor."

"Really?" I looked around, as if expecting to see the manor sitting off in the distance, but even from our vantage point, all I saw were fields, hills, and trees. I shot Owen a questioning look.

"The backside of his compound is on the other side of these woods," he supplied. "It runs right up against the forest."

I considered this, and then looked at the map. "Where is it on this map?"

Owen leaned over it, and I pressed closer, peering over his shoulder as he carefully marked out a small area. The other two points we had already explored were farther away than our current location, but still close enough. I felt a surge of excitement.

"You don't think he's at Ashabee's, do you?"

Leaning on an elbow, Owen gave the map a thoughtful look. "It's possible. I mean, he didn't know about our new location—none of us at the palace did. Ms. Dale had just discovered it."

"Why didn't we think of that?!" I whispered. "Of course he

would go back to the mansion."

Owen's face was dubious. "Well, I don't want to get your hopes up too high. Tim's a smart boy: if he had come back here and found us gone, he wouldn't stick around, would he?"

"He would if he thought it was the best chance of finding us," I said, thinking of the occasions I had taken Tim out in public when he was a child. I'd always told him, if we got separated, to go back to the last place he'd seen me. "Owen, we're this close. It's risky, but we have to check it out. It's only four miles away." Glancing at my watch, I tried to recall the projected schedule for Viggo's mission in the city and smiled. "The city is going to be crazy right now—maybe any surveillance will be distracted by the chaos. The leadership will probably be trying to run damage control."

Owen was still frowning. "Hmm. You can't bank on that, though. We have no idea whether the mission was even a success."

"I mean, the odds are against them, but between Viggo, Ms. Dale, Amber, and Thomas…" I took a deep breath. "Even if it isn't technically a success, even if someone… gets hurt, I trust our team has been able to get the message to people through the stadium."

"They were already in the control room when Thomas messaged me," Owen said cautiously. "But somebody could have shut off the video."

I rubbed my forehead restlessly, my anxiety spiking. "Look—what if Tim *is* here and we don't check?"

A span of silence followed my words. Owen wetted his lips, but didn't offer any argument.

"We can also be smart about it," I continued, beginning to formulate a plan in my head. "If there are cameras at the mansion, we'll be able to see them. If there are guards visible, Tim is probably either not there, or held prisoner. We probably won't be able to rescue him with just the two of us, so in that scenario, we'll just leave without being seen and go consult the others. How does that sound?"

Owen turned away from me, moving a few steps off. I stood, knowing he didn't have much reason to follow me, but hoping he might—because I definitely couldn't do this alone.

Finally, he turned around, his face grim but determined.

"Okay, Violet. We'll check there."

The smile that grew on my face was wide and hurt a little on one side, but no amount of pain could stop it. "Owen, you have no idea how much this means to me. Thank you so, so much."

The look he gave me was one of melancholy, but he seemed to push it aside, offering me a wan smile. "Of course. Let's just get this done, okay?"

I realized, in my hurry to thank him, my response had been an insensitive one. *Of course he knows what this means to me. He'd do anything to get his brother back.* My first instinct was to apologize, but that would have only rubbed in the painful subject, so I cleared my throat and nodded silently, before sliding back into the passenger's seat.

Owen started the car and backed us down the hill, heading toward the road. I stared out the window as we drove, trying to contain my hope and fear. We navigated the slow, small dirt roads, a car or two passing us, but there didn't seem to be any sign of Matrian forces on patrol, raising my hopes just a little further. Then, as Owen made a turn, I saw the familiar lines of the mansion's outer walls begin.

He slowed as we approached the gate. It was still there, closed, with the wooden slats on one side, from where Tim and Jay had fixed it.

"See any new cameras on the inside?" I asked Owen. I knew where the cameras were on the gate, but they couldn't see us yet through the vehicle's tinted windows.

"Not yet," he replied tersely.

"Okay. Why don't you pull up past that spot over there?" I indicated a place on the wall that looked familiar to me, and Owen did as I asked. Swiveling in my seat, I grabbed a gun with a silencer from the backseat and raised it with my left hand. I rolled the window down just a crack and stuck out the muzzle. Aiming carefully, I fired several times.

"What are you doing?" Owen whispered.

"I'm destroying the camera by the gate," I replied, "so it won't see you when you try to open the gate."

Owen exhaled. "Okay." He pulled up to the terminal, rolling down the tinted window and quickly entering Amber's code while I looked nervously down the drive. I checked my side, but the road was clear. No vehicles were in sight.

The gate rattled as the unbroken half slid out of the way. It moved too loudly and too slowly for my taste, but I used the time to rummage through the car, gathering supplies we might need. As soon as there was enough space, Owen nudged the car up the drive, the two of us scanning for danger while we headed for the massive steps that led up to the house.

"Clear here," Owen admitted. "Still no guards."

"Can you pull up as close to the porch steps as possible?" I asked.

I did the same as before, taking aim at the other camera I knew was somewhere outside, with its own microphone, waiting to capture whomever was coming in the front door. The window held my gun steady, but it still took me more rounds than I would have liked to clip the small electronic eye, damaging it and obscuring the lens with chips of stucco and dust.

After that we waited—for what seemed like hours, but must have only been fifteen minutes. I figured if nobody came to the door to check on who had blown the camera out, either they weren't checking the security system, they were huge cowards, or there was just nobody there at all.

Finally, after glancing at my watch over and over again, I looked at Owen. "You still think somebody might be here?"

"We can't be too cautious," was his reply. "But I'm willing to risk it. I'll take the ground floor and the secret basement. You head upstairs."

"Thank you." I grasped his right forearm and squeezed it, then began moving.

Reaching the doors of the house, I pushed them open and stepped in. Nothing had really changed, but there were signs of our evacuation everywhere—dirty footprints, abandoned pieces of equipment. Still, the furniture was intact, everything where we had left it.

A shiver ran down my spine as my footsteps broke through the clinging silence. "This place is kind of creepy now, huh?" I said softly, wincing at how loud my voice was in the quiet.

"Yeah," Owen murmured. "Let's just get this over with."

"Tim?" I called cautiously, as I headed up the stairs. "Tim, are you here?"

I pushed open the door to the bedroom Viggo and I had shared, finding it empty. *C'mon, Tim, please be here.* I moved through the hallways, opening doors and checking each one for any sign of my brother, but each room was empty. I moved past the damaged walls, still stained with blood from where Henrik had been shot.

It took nearly thirty minutes to check each room, but to be honest, after ten, I had already begun to doubt. There was no sign that anyone had been here since our group had abandoned the place. Everything looked the same on these levels, some of it unchanged since I had left. Beds were unmade, and every-thing wore a dark layer of dust.

After checking the last room in the servants' quarters, I felt my heart sink even lower. Given the fact that Owen hadn't called up to me, he hadn't found Tim either.

A swollen knot formed in my throat. He wasn't here. It had been a long shot, but that didn't change the crushing disap-pointment I felt as my last lead vanished. The only thing that kept me standing was the fact that I knew, without a shadow of a doubt, Tim was alive. I didn't have any evidence to support my theory, but I could *feel* it, deep in my bones. My instincts had served me well before, and I had to put faith in them—and in Tim.

He was a smart boy with enhanced reflexes. If I could sur-vive the fight at the palace, so could he.

Bolstered by the thought, I took a breath and moved down

the carpeted halls toward the stairs heading down, guessing Owen was waiting for me.

The silence of the house seemed even more noticeable now that I wasn't tearing open doors and calling for Tim. Was that what gave the whole manor an ominous feel? The sun was beginning to set behind the mountains, creating long shadows that cut through the house, bathing parts of it in darkness. I regretted leaving my bag in the car. My flashlight would have come in handy for some of the darker places.

I made for the massive staircase and began descending it. Nearing the foyer, I could see the front door hung open, some forty feet away, light pouring through it.

"Hey, Owen," I said, when my eyes didn't immediately spot him. "I don't think Tim's here. Did you find anything?"

Taking the last step off the staircase, I paused, my ears straining. Maybe Owen hadn't heard me—he might be in the basement. That was a thought… While we were here, maybe we should go down there and secure any equipment we'd left behind in our initial exodus.

I turned toward the shadowy interior that was the ground floor, but then hesitated. It was really dark in that part of the house. A chill ran through me in warning, and I rolled my lips between my teeth. "Owen?" I called again.

A floorboard creaked behind me, and I whirled. A figure stood in the doorway, features obscured by the light of the sun pouring in behind them. I took a step forward, raising my left hand to block out the light. "Owen?"

"No, Ms. Bates. It's not."

I froze as the distinctly familiar, clipped, refined voice filled the room. The figure took several long, slow steps forward, and, purely out of instinct, I took a step back, my eyes growing wide as Desmond's features became visible. My breath hitched, my blood pounding in my ears.

"How are you here?" I asked, my voice hoarse with barely repressed shock. I was already looking around, searching for the guards she was sure to have brought with her.

Desmond's smile was a facsimile of kindness. "You should come out now," she called over her shoulder—her eyes never leaving mine.

As someone stepped out of the room leading to the study, I almost choked on my tongue.

Owen's eyes flicked to mine and then away, his shoulders and face slumped in defeat.

"Owen?" I gasped.

"I'm sorry, Violet," he said, meeting my gaze again, his blue eyes swimming with guilt. "But I couldn't let any more of the boys get hurt."

"Yes, it seems Mr. Barns here has at last come to his senses," said Desmond. "Which means you, my precious Violet, are in an interesting predicament."

And then she smiled, her lips curling in feline satisfaction.

My mind worked too slowly, unable to process the presence of Desmond and Owen's role in it. But my body reacted, propelled by desperate fear, and anger that tasted bitter and hot on my tongue. I turned and began to run up the stairs, panic lending adrenaline to help me ignore my injuries as I put one foot in front of another.

On reaching the third step, an escape route flashed across

my mind, and I angled myself toward it. By the time I hit the fifth step, Desmond seemed to get over her initial shock. Maybe she hadn't expected me to simply try to escape from her.

"Grab her," she shouted, annoyance and anger rife in her voice.

"I've got her," replied Owen.

I couldn't help but throw him a look over my shoulder as he spoke, disbelief still coursing through me. A small, hopeful voice in my mind reminded me Owen was my *friend.* Yet the churning anger and terror in the pit of my stomach reached up and engulfed my heart with a grip of violence, reminding me of his betrayal.

Torn in two, I kept running, hooking a left into the dark recesses of Ashabee's home. I tore through the house, dodging furniture and walls left and right. My breath was coming in sharp bursts, my ribs already starting to ache. Only the sounds of Owen's footsteps behind me kept me moving forward.

I headed for the stairs with the secret entrance to Ashabee's vault. The door was partially closed as I approached, and I felt myself shudder with fright as I leapt over an overturned chair. I needed more time. Turning, I kicked the chair at Owen. It didn't slide far, but it was far enough for him to catch a knee on. He went down hard with a loud *oof,* but I'd already whirled and moved to the door, throwing it open.

"Violet!" he shouted insistently behind me.

I ignored him as I pulled back the heavy bit of door disguised as a wall, making my way down the small stairs, not bothering to close it behind me.

The room was dark, but I didn't have time to hit the

lights—I dove forward, using my memory of the place to guide me. I was so frantic, so desperate to get away, that I was moving too fast. My foot caught on something, and the next thing I knew, I was falling forward.

My head! I thought as I began to fall, my arms raising up over my face. I had seconds before I impacted, but even then, I knew my head was going to collide with my cast, shattering my skull. My second thought was, *I can't go through this again.*

Something grabbed me from behind, hooked low around my hips, arresting my fall somewhat. Bracing myself, my hands shot out, the cast slipping across the floor. Waves of agony rolled up my right arm. I stayed in that position for five seconds, not trusting the sudden return of gravity.

And then I lashed out with my elbow, twisting and trying to get a good angle on Owen's head. "Get off me," I shouted, panic giving my tone a brittle, frantic edge. Ducking, he missed my jab and let me go. I scrambled away from him on the floor as he stood over me, his features hidden by the room's darkness.

"Violet, please! I'm not going to hurt you!" Owen's voice had its own panicked tone to it, something that gave me pause, egging the voice in my brain to continue its reminders that I had always been able to trust Owen.

The bitter seed in my heart formed words that I spat out as I awkwardly flipped over to my backside and sat up. "You… You brought Desmond here!" I eyed the distance between us, gauging how much I needed to kick out his knee.

"I did," he said, running a hand through his hair. "And I'm sorry for not telling you, but this is our chance, Violet. This is our chance to kill her!"

I froze. "You're setting me up so you can kill her," I breathed, horrified.

"I'm setting her up so *we* can kill her. Please, Violet—I'm your friend. I would never betray you. Not really."

"Do you have her?" came a muffled shout from somewhere above, and my heart palpitated in response to Desmond's voice.

Owen turned back to me and knelt down, his hands reaching through the darkness to seize my shoulders. "Please," he whispered, his voice thick with desperation. "Please help me kill her. I promise I will get you out of this alive."

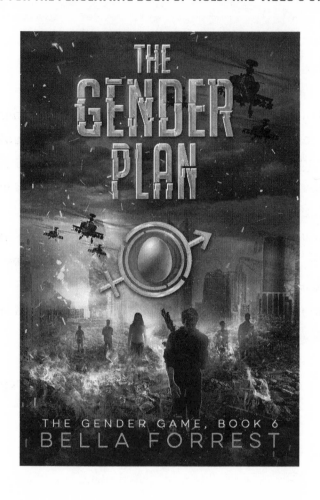

Dear Reader,

Thank you for reading! I hope you enjoyed The Gender Fall.

The next book in Violet and Viggo's journey, Book 6, The Gender Plan, releases May 10th, 2017, and it is the explosive **penultimate** book in The Gender Game series—as we move toward the grand finale in Book 7 (The Gender End)!

If you visit www.morebellaforrest.com and join my email list, I will send you an email reminder as soon as The Gender Plan is live.

You can also visit my website for the most updated information about my books: www.bellaforrest.net

Until we meet again between the pages,
—Bella Forrest x

ALSO BY BELLA FORREST

THE GENDER GAME
The Gender Game (Book 1)
The Gender Secret (Book 2)
The Gender Lie (Book 3)
The Gender War (Book 4)
The Gender Fall (Book 5)
The Gender Plan (Book 6)

THE SECRET OF SPELLSHADOW MANOR
The Secret of Spellshadow Manor (Book 1)
The Breaker (Book 2)

A SHADE OF VAMPIRE SERIES

SERIES 1: DEREK & SOFIA'S STORY
A Shade of Vampire (Book 1)
A Shade of Blood (Book 2)
A Castle of Sand (Book 3)
A Shadow of Light (Book 4)
A Blaze of Sun (Book 5)
A Gate of Night (Book 6)
A Break of Day (Book 7)

Series 2: Rose & Caleb's story

A Shade of Novak (Book 8)

A Bond of Blood (Book 9)

A Spell of Time (Book 10)

A Chase of Prey (Book 11)

A Shade of Doubt (Book 12)

A Turn of Tides (Book 13)

A Dawn of Strength (Book 14)

A Fall of Secrets (Book 15)

An End of Night (Book 16)

Series 3: The Shade continues with a new hero...

A Wind of Change (Book 17)

A Trail of Echoes (Book 18)

A Soldier of Shadows (Book 19)

A Hero of Realms (Book 20)

A Vial of Life (Book 21)

A Fork of Paths (Book 22)

A Flight of Souls (Book 23)

A Bridge of Stars (Book 24)

A SHADE OF DRAGON TRILOGY
A Shade of Dragon 1
A Shade of Dragon 2
A Shade of Dragon 3

A SHADE OF KIEV TRILOGY
A Shade of Kiev 1
A Shade of Kiev 2
A Shade of Kiev 3

BEAUTIFUL MONSTER DUOLOGY
Beautiful Monster 1
Beautiful Monster 2

DETECTIVE ERIN BOND (Adult thriller/mystery)
Lights, Camera, GONE
Write, Edit, KILL

FOR AN UPDATED LIST OF BELLA'S BOOKS,

please visit her website: www.bellaforrest.net

Join Bella's VIP email list and she'll personally send you an
email reminder as soon as her next book is out!
Visit to sign up: www.MoreBellaForrest.com

Made in the USA
Middletown, DE
20 January 2018